P9-DVY-241

THE ACE PERFORMER COLLECTION
will be a series of books
by and about Dashiell Hammett

VOLUME 1:
Lost Stories
by Dashiell Hammett

VOLUME 2:
Discovering The Maltese Falcon *and Sam Spade*
edited by Richard Layman

VOLUME 3:
Hammett's Moral Vision
by George J. Thompson

FORTHCOMING:
The Crime Wave: Collected Nonfiction
by Dashiell Hammett

ADDITIONAL VOLUMES
TO BE ANNOUNCED

DASHIELL HAMMETT

LOST STORIES

21 long-lost stories
from the bestselling creator of
Sam Spade, The Maltese Falcon,
and The Thin Man

Introduction by
3-time Edgar Award winner
JOE GORES

Edited by
Vince Emery

Vince Emery
PRODUCTIONS®
SAN FRANCISCO

Lost Stories by Dashiell Hammett
Introduction by Joe Gores
Edited by Vince Emery

Book design and composition by Desktop Miracles
Del LeMond, Designer
Printed and bound in the United States of America

Published by Vince Emery Productions
P.O. Box 460279
San Francisco, California 94146

ISBN 0-9725898-1-3

FOR JO

CON T

ENTS

Background

By Vince Emery

DASHIELL HAMMETT, the bestselling creator of Sam Spade, *The Maltese Falcon*, and *The Thin Man*, was one of the twentieth century's most entertaining authors, and one of its most influential.

Even so, many of Hammett's stories—including some of his best—have been out of the reach of anyone but a handful of scholars and collectors—until now.

Lost Stories rescues twenty-one Hammett stories otherwise never published in a book, or unavailable for decades. Stories range from the first fiction Hammett ever wrote to his last. All stories have been restored to their initial texts, replacing often heavily-cut revisions with the original versions for the first time.

I have added a running commentary on Hammett's life and works to place the writing of each story in a setting and time. The commentary tells what was going on in Hammett's life when each story was written, and how the story affected his life.

Researching, collecting, restoring, writing, and publishing the contents of the book in your hands has taken more than three years. Why take on so much work? I confess, I did it because I got annoyed.

Annoyed because some Hammett stories that I wanted to read I could not find anywhere.

Annoyed because other stories I wanted to read were available only in hard-to-find books in cut and changed versions.

Annoyed because I wanted more background about the stories than I could find—I wanted to understand the author's life, and the place and the time when the stories were created.

Nobody was going to give me the book I wanted to read. So I made my own. I gathered the tough-to-find Hammett tales and added the kind of background I wanted to read myself, with enough context to help you, my reader, share my sense of discovery.

To round off this celebration of Hammett, three-time Edgar Award-winner Joe Gores wrote an introduction. He describes how Hammett influenced literature, movies, television, and his own life.

Why these particular twenty-one pieces? First, I wanted to make available stories that most readers cannot find. So I omitted all thirty-eight stories in the four Hammett anthologies available today (*The Big Knockover*, edited by Lillian Hellman; *The Continental Op*, edited by Steven Marcus; *Nightmare Town*, edited by Kirby McCauley, Martin H. Greenberg, and

Ed Gorman; and the authoritative *Crime Stories and Other Writings*, edited by Stephen Marcus).

Second, I wanted stories that could shape this book into something richer than just another disconnected anthology, because stories can be more than mere recitations of events.

As Samuel Butler observes in his book *The Way of All Flesh:* "Every man's work, whether it be literature or music or pictures or architecture or anything else, is always a portrait of himself, and the more he tries to conceal himself the more clearly will his character appear in spite of him."

Butler was right. When people tell stories, they reveal themselves. Hammett's stories expose points that provided direction in his life; what forces he fought, which choices he felt were important, what he was proud of, what he was ashamed of, what things gave meaning to his life, what things destroyed meaning.

The only way to understand Hammett's writings and Hammett's life, and to fully appreciate each, is to see his stories and his life together. His life illuminates his writings. His writings help tell the story of his life.

I selected stories that would show Hammett's development as a writer from the first glimmering of his career to its apparent sunset, stories that could illustrate how Hammett did not want to imitate what had gone before, how he was an explorer into uncharted territory.

But my decision to intertwine Hammett's life with his stories made the creation of *Lost Stories* a bigger mountain than I anticipated. Most readers have a hard time finding *any* version of these rare stories. To fulfill my aims, I needed *original* versions.

Each of the stories in this volume first appeared in a magazine between 1922 and 1941. Some have never been reprinted anywhere. Ten stories were reprinted in magazines and books edited by Frederic Dannay, who wrote and edited under the pen name of Ellery Queen. Compared to their original printings, the ten Dannay versions have changes large and small: titles were replaced, texts were changed, sentences and entire paragraphs were deleted. Some original versions were ten percent longer.

There is no evidence that any of these changes were made by Hammett. Remarks in Hammett's letters indicate that Lillian Hellman made revisions, and Dannay almost certainly had a hand in them. As author Bill Pronzini observed in an email to me, "Fred Dannay was notorious for editing published stories even by writers of the quality of Hammett." To get back to the original texts, I had to dig up the earliest printings in rare, often obscure magazines, many of them not available in libraries.

For two stories, I got lucky. The Harry Ransom Humanities Research Center at the University of Texas at Austin holds Hammett's original typescripts for "Itchy" and "This Little Pig." Helpful HRC librarians provided access.

To find other stories' earliest versions sent me on quite a hunt. I dug through research libraries. I put searches out to Abebooks.com, eBay, and rare book dealers. I pestered collectors. I asked other researchers for aid, and they provided immense help, especially Richard Layman, Victor Berch, Bill Pronzini, and William F. Nolan. Without their kind assistance, this book would be much shorter. I was also able to include original illustrations for three stories.

After I unearthed the originals, I needed permission to reprint them. The trustees of the Literary Property Trust of Dashiell Hammett cheerfully granted my requests, and I am grateful. I enjoyed working with Alexia Paul of the Joy Harris Literary Agency, who arranged the permissions.

To build the connecting narrative of Hammett's life, I started with *Selected Letters of Dashiell Hammett, 1921-1960*, edited by Richard Layman with Julie M. Rivett, and I returned to that book again and again. It is the most important resource on Hammett's life, and contains some of the most revealing and most moving prose Hammett wrote.

In my library of books about Hammett, the most well-thumbed are those by Richard Layman, Joan Mellen, Jo Hammett, William F. Nolan, Don Herron, and Diane Johnson. Those authors' works and Hammett's letters provided most of the facts in my account of Hammett's life.

The remainder required digging through bookshelves, archives, and microfilms in more than a dozen libraries. The three that contributed most to this book were the already-mentioned HRC, the University of California's Northern Regional Library Facility, and the San Francisco Public Library. (Thank you, Susan Goldstein!)

On a hunch that Hammett used a real Burlingame mansion as the locale for his story "Laughing Masks," I gave a copy of the restored story to Diane Condon-Wirgler of the Burlingame Historical Society. She put together a team of researchers who not only determined which Burlingame house in 1923 most closely fit Hammett's descriptions, but also found photographs of it. The photos show Hammett's descriptions to be accurate even about a rainspout that the hero climbs. I am grateful to Ms. Condon-Wirgler and the Burlingame Historical Society for their contributions to Hammettology. You will find one never-before-seen photo of the "Laughing Masks" house in this book.

The book came together slowly, one story at a time, one fact at a time, one element at a time. Sometimes the obstacles and drudgery seemed unending. Julie Rivett, Joe Gores, and Joe's delightful wife Dori gave help that kept me moving forward, and provided encouragement when I needed it most. They earned my eternal appreciation—especially Joe, for his big contribution in writing this book's introduction.

Historian and biographer Don Herron, who led me down the Hammett rabbit hole in the first place, was kind enough to act as a gruff reality check, shooting down my wilder ideas and trying to talk some sense into me.

My aunt, mystery lover Rosemary Auer, made my life in San Francisco sunnier, as she has done since I first moved to this "cool, grey city of love" years ago. My love Rita Sinclair brought her warm heart and zest for living into my life; words are not enough to express my joy for her.

Rita helped big time on *Lost Stories*, but I save my final thanks for two exceptional people. Without them, I would never have gathered the courage to start this climb, let alone finish it. The good qualities you enjoy in *Lost Stories* are due to their friendship, their encouragement, their knowledge, their advice.

The first exceptional person is Rick Layman. Anyone serious about Hammett starts with Rick's six-and-a-half books on Hammett. His work is the foundation for anything worthwhile about Hammett that I may have contributed, but that is just the start. Rick has been a friend, inviting me to take part in his projects, supporting mine, celebrating when I reported good news, helping me around obstacles, digging up obscure information I needed, correcting my errors, sharing advice from his own rich experience. All this while writing books at a fierce pace, running a company, and raising a family. I don't know *how* he does it, but I know *the way* he does it: with passion, intelligence, elegance, and grace. Joe Gores calls Rick "a prince," and I concur. Thank you, Rick.

If Rick is a prince, the second exceptional person is a queen. Jo Marshall somehow manages to be regal and down-to-earth at the same time. Her encouragement has meant a lot to me. Even without it, I would still enjoy Jo's company. How could I not? She is charming, kind-hearted, and wise. She has a love of literature, a smart sense of humor, and a fondness for peoples' absurdities that I somehow find inspirational. I treasure the time we've spent together, and her willingness to answer my questions, even the silly ones. *Gratias!*

Many more people contributed than I have mentioned. So if you like *Lost Stories*, you can light a perfumed candle for a small army of people, including, of course, "the ace performer" himself, Dashiell Hammett.

Lost Stories brings you some of his stories surrounded by the bigger story of Hammett's life. I'm not sure if these stories will change your life. Maybe you'll just forget your taxes and troubles for a few hours. Either way, if you want stories you have not seen before, you've come to the right place. Turn the page, and join our celebration.

INTRODUCTION

"It Was a Diamond, All Right"

BY JOE GORES

THE HOUSE where I grew up in Rochester, Minnesota had a study with a wall of built-in bookshelves. When I was six, my Mom told me I could read any book I could reach. Since a three-foot-high flat-topped wooden cabinet was built out from under the shelves, this restricted my reading to the books on the bottom shelf. *The Lives of the Saints*. The *Holy Bible*. *Pilgrim's Progress*. You get the picture.

But if I scrambled up on top of the cabinet I could reach all the shelves. There I found a bonanza: *The Sun Also Rises. Captain Blood. Cannery Row. The Moon and Sixpence. Appointment in Samarra. Before Adam.* Most of them I couldn't understand.

With the *Tarzan* novels, I didn't have to try: I had the Big Little Book abridgements up in my room on my own bookshelf. My Mom's bigger, longer versions were a whole lot more exciting.

My folks never said a word to me about climbing up on the cabinet, even though they knew I was doing it. Dusty shoe-prints, right? I remember only two of the many mysteries on those more lofty shelves. *The Mysterious Mr. Quinn*—the best book Dame Agatha ever wrote—with its train's smoke forming a hand of doom on the dustjacket. And *The Dain Curse* with that absolutely compelling opening line: "It was a diamond, all right . . . "

After high school, I went to the University of Notre Dame intending to become what today is called a graphic novelist. I soon realized I was a better story-teller than an artist, and so became an English major. From there, just a short step to wanting to become a writer.

To most wanna-be writers of my generation, only "serious" novelists were worthy of our attention: Hemingway, Dos Passos, Faulkner, maybe Steinbeck, this new cat Salinger, and of course the Europeans. But even then I found myself gravitating more toward Dumas and de Maupassant and Joyce Cary than Proust and Mann and Tolstoy. Raskolnikov was cool, however.

I went on to grad school at Stanford, planning to get a creative writing master's degree because I didn't have the confidence to strike out on my own as a writer. I was sending out stories to the magazines, but nobody wanted them. I needed more instruction, more of the warm safe womb of Academe.

That's when the wheels came off. The sample stories I submitted so the Stanford English Department could judge my suitability for the creative writing degree were rejected. They *"read as if they had been written to be sold."*

Wasn't that the idea of writing stories? So you could sell them and people would read them? But I couldn't write like the literary giants I had read as an undergrad, and I didn't

know how to write about what I wanted to write about. So I was
going to have to do the reading for a standard research M.A. in
English, and somehow, someway, eventually find a subject I'd
want to write a thesis about. Most of the required reading was
dry as dust. And *long*. But I kept trying. And kept stumbling
through, laboriously translating *Beowulf* from the Old English:
it was a lot more fun than Victorian novels. *Beowulf*, after all,
had Grendel tearing arms off people.

One evening, while trolling the bookrack at a Palo Alto
drugstore, sunk in the classic slough of despond, I spotted a
25-cent Bantam paperback called *The Name Is Archer*. On the
cover was a grey-faced gentleman with a gun. I opened it at
random to a story titled "Gone Girl." I read the first paragraph.

> "It was a Friday night. I was tooling home from the
> Mexican border in a light blue convertible and a dark
> blue mood. I had followed a man from Fresno to San
> Diego and lost him in the maze of streets in Old Town.
> When I picked up his trail again, it was cold. He had
> crossed the border, and my instructions went no further
> than the United States."

I was thunderstruck.

"I was tooling home from the Mexican border in a light
blue convertible and a dark blue mood" was haunting and
evocative—and tough. All at the same time. It also had *authority*. "He had crossed the border, and my instructions went no
further than the United States." Period, the end. He cuts out.

But then he goes on: "Halfway home, just above Emerald
Bay, I overtook the worst driver in the world" and immediately
we are immersed in the real story of the "Gone Girl."

I stood there in the drugstore and finished the story, then
laid out my 25 cents for the book. *This was the way I was trying
to write!* Who the hell was this John Ross Macdonald and who

else was writing like this? I soon found out there was a whole exciting world of "hard-boiled" writing out there that I in my quest for "literature" had dismissed.

I continued to attend classes at Stanford—damned if I was going to have done all that work and not come out with *some* kind of graduate degree—but mostly I read, mostly the *Black Mask* boys and beyond. For me, Hammett was the best. His stuff felt *real*. The penny dropped from my bookshelf-climbing days of 16 years before: *"It was a diamond, all right . . ."*

Hey! Since Stanford wouldn't let me do a creative thesis for my Master's, I would do a standard critical thesis on who I now knew were The Big Three of the hard-boiled world: Hammett, Chandler, and Macdonald.

Ohhh no, said Stanford. You can't write a thesis about them, since obviously what these men write isn't literature.

I drew solace from the fact that in March, 1602, Sir Thomas Bodley had instructed the librarian of Oxford University's Bodleian Library to refuse "riffe raffe bookes," denying shelf space to the plays of Shakespeare for the same reason Stanford subsequently rejected the works of Hammett: they were not literature.

My course work at Stanford was finished. I still had to get *some* Masters thesis subject approved. (Years later I did one on writers of South Seas adventure tales my advisors had never heard of, so they couldn't reject them out of hand.)

But right now, I was living in a tiny room with a table and a chair and a bed above Floyd Page's gym in Palo Alto. Typewriter on the table, butt on the chair. Keep typing. Teach bodybuilding for the rent, devour up to five paperbacks a day, mostly hard-boiled mysteries. Hammett and his ilk had sunk their fangs into me.

One of the men who worked out at the gym, Gene Matthews, was a private eye specializing in the repossession of delinquent automobiles. In between sets on the free weights, Gene told tall tales of his adventures as a repo man. Exciting yarns. They sounded just like oral versions of Hammett's Continental Op detective stories. Only right now.

I asked Gene if I could ride around with him at night. I could. A month later, I drove up to San Francisco and proudly told his boss, Dave Kikkert, manager of the L.A. Walker Company at 1610 Bush Street, that I had just finished my course work at Stanford for a Master's degree in English Lit and had decided I wanted to be a repo man.

Dave, a stocky, tough-faced guy right out of the Op stories, said, "Na. College kids don't work out."

I persisted. Dave resisted. I finally offered to work for two weeks without pay. How could he refuse?

He couldn't.

For 12 years, off and on, I was a private eye. In 1960, Dave and I founded our own repo/skip-tracing/investigation firm, David Kikkert and Associates, in a former cathouse at 760 Golden Gate Avenue. Dave in the office, me and the other guys in the field. I was a Hammett op in Hammett's city. Working the fog-cloaked streets at night, I often imagined Sydney Greenstreet or Peter Lorre scuttling down an alley with a suspicious football-shaped package under one arm.

Meanwhile, I wrote. And sold. To the men's and the mystery magazines. Almost everything I did owed a great deal to Hammett's work. My DKA File stories for *Ellery Queen Mystery Magazine* that eventually segued into a series of DKA File novels were about my kind of private-eying, the way Hammett's Op stories were about his. One of my yarns, "Beyond the Shadow," is a "challenge to the reader" glancing off Hammett's masterful Op tale "The Scorched Face."

In 1966, I searched my soul and quit full-time repo work to write. My first novel, *A Time of Predators*, was published in 1969.

During thirteen weeks of 1972 I wrote a novel called *Interface*. I wanted it to be a hard-boiled thriller that was also a sort of love story—without getting into *anyone*'s mind. I deliberately followed Hammett's template of *The Glass Key*.

The next year my book agent, Henry Morrison, visited from New York. We were driving across the Golden Gate Bridge at night to the wail of the foghorns, and I said, "It's a Hammett kind of night."

Henry mused, "I wonder what would happen if someone wrote a novel with Hammett as the detective?"

No more was said, but I couldn't get the thought out of my head. I was writing a novel called *Rejoice, Young Man* that nobody ever bought. Nevertheless, the next week I called Henry and said, "I want to try that Hammett novel idea."

He said, "Forget about it. Hellman would raise legal hell." So I forgot about it.

A month later, Henry called and said, "I've got a contract for you on that Hammett-novel idea of yours. Just figure out a way to get around Hellman." Henry does stuff like that.

I researched Hammett and 1920s San Francisco for two years, then wrote *Hammett*. I set it in 1928: since Hammett hadn't met Hellman yet, legally there was nothing she could do to stop the book. She tried. She tried to stop Coppola's movie version but couldn't do that, either.

In the novel I forced Hammett the writer back into being Hammett the detective, because an old friend had been murdered. Thus I could explore the knife-edge between the two professions: both Hammett and I had to stop being real private eyes (which we both loved) to create fictional private eyes we loved even more.

Recently scholar and publisher Matt Bruccoli told me, "You did a Hammett while writing a book called *Hammett*."

I have received no higher praise.

Who Followed Hammett?

I never knew Hammett the man, but as a writer I sure know his work. As does just about anyone else who writes fiction—even, and this is interesting—if they have never actually read *him*. Hammett's fiction has affected almost all subsequent American writers' work, whether they know it or not. I am sure most don't know it.

It goes without saying that mystery/suspense writers such as Donald E. Westlake before he got funny (*The Mercenaries, Killing Time, 361, Killy*) and most especially when he is writing about a thief called Parker under his Richard Stark *nom de plume*, are direct Hammett descendants. Look at Larry Block—*Deadly Honeymoon*, all of the Matt Scudders, his pseudonymous novels as Paul Kavanagh (*Such Men Are Dangerous, The Triumph of Evil*). Frederic Brown in such novels as *The Fabulous Clipjoint* and *The Screaming Mimi*. Almost the entire John D. MacDonald *ouvre*—especially his Travis McGee books.

Loren Estleman (although he, like Michael Connelly, is arguably closer to the Chandler than the Hammett style), Ross Thomas and Robert Crais and Thomas Perry and Elmore Leonard, James Ellroy (king of the paranoid, psycho hero), Tony Hillerman (his Leaphorn and Chee exhibit Hammett-hero characteristics in a vastly different milieu), Dennis Lehane and Lee Child and Harlan Coben and Bill Pronzini and David Dodge . . . The list of debtors is literally endless.

The most successful women mystery writers must acknowledge the same debt (although, again, some of them have never read Hammett). But try to think of the novels of Sara Paretsky, Marcia Muller, or Sue Grafton with the Hammett influence removed. Even such a solid "literary" novelist as P. D. James had her stab at the private eye novel in *An Unsuitable Job for a Woman*, with its unmistakable Hammett overtones—suitably

Britishized, of course. All of Minette Walters' hard-minded books draw much of their strength from Hammett's work.

It is of course more difficult to show direct Hammett influences on the work of our so-called mainstream or literary novelists.

But let's go for the throat and start with Ernest Hemingway. A chicken-or-egg argument about Hemingway influencing Hammett or vice versa has simmered for years (until it is hard-boiled?), and this is the perfect place to crack the shell.

That they knew each other's work is not in dispute. Hemingway's library in his house in Cuba still contains his copy of Hammett's novel *$106,000 Blood Money*. In *Death in the Afternoon,* Hemingway remarks that his wife is reading *The Dain Curse* and adds, "Hammett's bloodiest yet." In Hammett's "The Main Death," the Op goes to interview a witness and says, "Mrs. Gungen put down a copy of *The Sun Also Rises* . . ."

One of Hemingway's four best short stories, "The Killers," is set squarely in Hammett country. A diner at night. Hitmen. An ex-boxer. I find no corresponding Hemingwayesque writing in Hammett's work. The late Lee Wright of Random House, the doyen of mystery editors, knew both men well and always believed that Hemingway learned his clipped, precise style from Hammett.[1]

---

1. An interesting footnote on the taut Hammett style. In 1972, Vintage brought out a paperback *The Maltese Falcon* in which some rocket scientist of an editor moved all of the dates up by twenty years. Maybe seeking relevance or a tie-in with Huston's 1941 *The Maltese Falcon* movie. Nobody noticed. Hammett's dialogue is so free of slangy catchphrases, his descriptions of people, places, cars, and buildings so spare, that they are timeless. I caught it only because Spade's Flitcraft story to Brigid O'Shaugnessy (Flitcraft's name is taken from insurance company actuarial tables, something any private eye of Hammett's day would be familiar with), was set in 1922. In this paperback, Spade's era has become 1942. It makes no difference at all to the story.

The dates bear this out. Hammett's first Op story ("Arson Plus") was published in *The Black Mask* issue that hit the newsstands on October 1, 1923. In the years immediately following, the Op appeared frequently.

Hemingway's first collection of short stories, *In Our Time*, was published in Paris in a limited edition in 1924, and was not printed in the United States until 1,335 copies were issued in October, 1925. By that time, Hammett was already a well-established writer with his own style firmly in place. If influence there was, it flowed from Hammett to Hemingway, not in the other direction.

We have only to think of Hammett's objective approach, style, vocabulary, spare, lean dialogue, plotting, characters, and superb sense of irony to know that murder in the night need not be the theme of a work for it to show Hammett influences. John O'Hara and William Saroyan and John Steinbeck and J. D. Salinger and Margaret Atwood spring immediately to mind.

Joseph Heller's *Catch 22* could never have been written without Hammett's work. William Gibson, who has spoken of Hammett's influence on his work, is an easy read, as are Henry Miller and William Burroughs. A little more surprising is Jack Kerouac's *On the Road* (which mentions Sam Spade), but Kerouac himself called his writing "hopped-up Hammett." Kenneth Rexroth, nobody's idea of a fawning mystery critic, remarked that "It is from Chandler and Hammett and Hemingway that the best modern fiction derives."

To me, it is readily apparent that Hammett was one of the most influential writers of the twentieth century, period. Not just among mystery writers. Most mainstream critics would not agree with me: too many have only scorn for mystery/suspense writing. What, they demand, could Hammett have as a writer that could possibly affect literature outside his own little tiny incestuous hard-boiled mystery field?

Well, *in* his own field, he was the first. He didn't have anyone to follow, so he had to break new ground. That is the first great point, perhaps the greatest point. Hammett broke new ground, and writers read other writers' stuff. I read about a hundred novels a year, not all of them mystery/suspense. Literary influences cut across time and space and language all the time. Each writer works within his own society, his own era. But he does not work alone. He uses what has come before, he influences what comes after.

Without Homer writing as he did, Shakespeare wouldn't have written as he did. Without Shakespeare, Poe would not have written as he did. Without Poe inventing all of the basic mystery plots, Doyle wouldn't have written Sherlock Holmes as he did and Hammett wouldn't have written as he did. Without Hammett writing as he did, crime fiction writers of today—and I believe mainstream writers, too—would not write as they do.

Yeah, Sure, But What Makes Hammett So Different?

What was it that Hammett did that no one else had done before, that those who followed could only expand upon? Let's start with Raymond Chandler's essay, "The Simple Art of Murder." Chandler observes that Hammett was:

> "spare, frugal, hard-boiled, but he did over and over again what only the best writers can ever do at all. He wrote scenes that seemed never to have been written before."

This by itself is not enough to explain why Hammett's writing had such a singular and lasting impact not only on the mystery story, but on literature in general. In his 1941 book *Murder for Pleasure: The Life and Times of the Detective Story*, critic Howard Haycraft almost gets one of the main reasons, but doesn't understand the point he himself is making:

> "Because of their startling originality, the Hammett novels virtually defy exegesis even today . . . As straightaway detective stories they can hold their own with the best. They are also character studies of close to top rank in their own right, and are penetrating if shocking novels of manners as well . . . "

Merely in passing, Haycraft notes that for eight years Hammett was an operative with the Pinkerton's National Detective Agency, and adds as an afterthought:

> "It was this last experience . . . which . . . gave him his backgrounds and many of the characters for his stories . . . "

Haycraft doesn't realize that Hammett's experiences as a Pink were the heart, the soul, the guts of his stories. He had been a manhunter. No other writer of his day had been, and damned few are, even in our day. Hammett's novels stand or fall by the quality of their manhunters *as manhunters*. Manhunting is always volatile, unpredictable. Men do not like to be hunted. They often turn back and try to make the hunter into the hunted. As a result, in fact and in fiction, true manhunters are a rare breed. Tough, brave, resourceful, dogged, and above all sure of themselves and their abilities, sure they can outwit anyone, sure they can get the job done.

And Hammett knew it. In his intro to the Modern Library edition of *The Maltese Falcon*, he wrote:

"Spade . . . is what most private detectives I worked with would like to have been and what quite a few of them in their cockier moments thought they approached. A hard, shifty fellow, able to take care of himself in any situation, able to get the best of anybody . . . whether criminal, innocent bystander, or client."

Two more quotes. In 1925 a short, dumpy, fortyish man tells a Russian princess who is seducing him:

"You think I'm a man and you're a woman. That's wrong. I'm a manhunter and you're something that has been running in front of me. There's nothing human about it."

In 1956, a tall, solid, fortyish man says to himself after interviewing a teen-age hooker who is mainlining heroin:

"The problem was to love people, try to serve them, without wanting anything from them. I was a long way from solving that one."

The first man is of course Hammett's Op. The second is Ross Macdonald's Lew Archer, who's come a long way from the cold, hard, tight days of *The Name Is Archer.* Not surprising: the highly-educated Macdonald was always a man with a deep social consciousness, and it was inevitable that he would pass this on to his creation, Lew Archer. In his later years he told me that he wanted Archer to be little more than an observer, a character so thin that if he turned sideways he would be nearly invisible.

What is it in Hammett's work that creates such a huge difference between his philosophy and Macdonald's? After all, both men are characterized as hard-boiled detective writers.

When he started, Hammett was not a writer learning about private detection. He was a private detective learning about writing. As he wrote, he retained the detective's subconscious attitudes toward life. It is this subconscious state of mind that separates his work from that of his followers Chandler and Macdonald.

When I started getting published, the late Anthony Boucher said I was "one of the very few authentic private eyes to enter the field of fiction since Dashiell Hammett." True, until relatively recent years. But we all had someone to follow: Chandler, Macdonald, me, all of us. Hammett did not.

Despite the genre demands, Hammett's novels have all the hallmarks of fine literature: economy of expression, creation of character with a few bold strokes, realistic depiction of milieu, sentiment without sentimentality. But the stories he told were about *real* private eyes in their world because real private eyes in their world were who he knew.

Spade and the Op are not somber men who dislike themselves and their work. They not only put the job first, they like the job. They have fun at it. Like real private detectives, they derive much of their enjoyment from it, take a lot of pride in it, even define themselves by it. When you're a manhunter, your goal is to seek out other human beings and take from them something they treasure: their pelf, their illusions, their gold, their freedom, perhaps their greatest treasure of all, life itself. As Spade tells Brigid in the closing moments of *The Maltese Falcon*:

> "Don't be too sure I'm as crooked as I'm supposed
> to be. That kind of reputation might be good busi-
> ness—bringing in high-priced jobs and making it easier
> to deal with the enemy."

The Enemy. The man he is tracking down is *The Enemy*. Hammett's detective has a pitiless knowledge that when he faces *The Enemy*, it is going to come down to *him* or *me*. This is Hammett's hero. This hero is what makes his novels different from those that came before and those that came after. The reading public instantly recognized this starkly *real* element in Hammett's stories, and responded.

The *real*, not the *realistic*. *Realism*. Realism in its best sense equals truth, and it is *truth* that makes Hammett's work so successful and so seminal to American literature. Fiction takes what is there and refines it until it is more true than fact itself. It is the writer's job *as writer* to chronicle life as he sees it, rather than to directly comment on it. Or to make a point with it.

Are Hammett's detective novels "real"? Can any hard-boiled detective novel be "real"? After all, the mystery—especially the hard-boiled mystery coming out of the rock-em-sock-em pulps with blood spilled over every page—presents the writer with specialized problems.

First, the mystery demands a *plot*. A real plot. A plot that often is as intricate as rhyming patterns in sonnets: 400 pages of navel-gazing does not cut it. The stern logic of the mystery plot demands a tightly-knit series of causes and effects leading to a logical resolution. Or at least a solution.

But the mystery—especially the hard-boiled mystery—simultaneously demands a serious compression of some essential dimensions of the story. Something has to be happening all the time. Often a whole lot of somethings at the same time.

Again, that masterful practitioner Raymond Chandler says it best, in his "Casual Notes on the Mystery Novel":

"[The mystery novel] deliberately outrages probability by telescoping time and space."

Without getting too literary here, I feel that Hammett's work is not only *real* in the sense we have been talking about, but is also in the literary traditions of realism and naturalism. That said, Hammett's work must ultimately stand or fall with the reader's reaction to it. Is it plausible? Credible? Believable? Is it *authentic?* In his last published interview, Hammett said, "People thought my stuff was authentic."

Authentic. Hammett's genius was that he made his people not only real but also authentic, even when his plot was full of twists and turns, even when he was "outrageously telescoping" the time and space in which these events occurred. Hammett's characters and the backgrounds against which they move are meticulously true to life. *Real* and *authentic.*

The reader feels that these things *could* happen to Sam Spade or the Op or those like them, maybe even are *likely* to happen to them. Hammett cheats not in what happens, but in making it happen within days rather than weeks or months. And in making it happen here and now in a single case, rather than on a dozen different investigations at a dozen different times.

His stubborn hewing to the *reality* of the private detective, based on his own Pinkerton's experiences, is what sets Hammett's central character apart from all who went before and sets the stage for all who were to come after. No matter how exotic and fanciful his plots, he never abandoned that central reality. This is the true art and accomplishment of Hammett's hard-boiled writing.

Fred Dannay, writing under the Ellery Queen pseudonym he shared with his cousin Manny Lee, makes us understand why Hammett could construct a seminal realistic novel around the figure of a falcon from the time of the Crusades—a black-enameled solid gold falcon studded with precious gems, no less, that everyone in San Francisco is chasing.

"We would not label Hammett a 'realist' and merely let it go at that . . . we would call him a 'romantic realist'

. . . The secret is in Hammett's method. Hammett tells
his modern fables in *terms* of realism . . . His stories are
the stuff of dreams while his *characters are the flesh and
blood of reality.*"

The Hammett Hero

What are the characteristics of this Hammett Hero that changed
the course of world literature?

He is usually a private investigator, of course. (The most
important exception is Ned Beaumont in *The Glass Key,* who is
a political fixer. But he *operates* as a private detective.) Whatever
the Hammett hero does, first, last, and always he is a man who
gets the job done, and he is a man who is both mentally and
physically competent to do that job.

Many of today's fictional private eyes don't seem to like
themselves; they seem more motivated by empathy and a desire
to better society than to solve the case. The Hammett hero
doesn't make that mistake. He doesn't believe in empathy. He
doesn't give the other fellow—or woman—an even break. Spade
and the Op know that the person to whom you show compas-
sion will often be the one who does you in.

It was the more poetic Chandler who introduced the idea
of the private eye as knight errant:

> "But down these mean streets a man must go who
> is not himself mean, who is neither tarnished nor afraid
> . . . He must be a complete man and a common man
> and yet an unusual man . . . the best man in his world,
> and a good enough man for any world . . . The story is
> this man's adventure in search of a hidden truth, and it
> would be no adventure if it did not happen to a man fit
> for adventure."

The picture begins to emerge. Hammett saw the private detective as a manhunter. Chandler saw him as a knight errant. And Macdonald saw him as a social worker.

The Hammett hero is on the side of the law but not particularly law-abiding. He has a job to do. Both the Op and Spade are masters at bending the rules to attain their ends. When I was a repoman, one of our favorite sayings was, "A felony a week whether we want it or not." We didn't *want* to break-and-enter—you could go to jail, for God's sake! But occasionally we had to if we wanted to get the job done.

The Hammett hero goes by his gut feelings. Spade knows Wilmer Cook is murderous and corrupt, and deals with him accordingly. As the Op deals with a corrupt Continental operative in "$106,000 Blood Money." As a corollary, both Spade and the Op are ruthless in pursuit of their objectives. If opponents must die, so be it. Him or me.

The Hammett hero is not concerned with truth in the abstract, or justice in the abstract, but only with truth and justice in the here and now. Enough to get the job done. When that becomes too much—or too little—for the detective hero to live with, he quits. As Hammett himself did, as Nick Charles has done in *The Thin Man* before the novel even begins.

Finally, the Hammett hero goes his own way and operates by his own moral code. If that code comes into contention with society's moral code, if the detective's mores are at odds with society's mores, then he does it his way, depends on his intelligence guided by experience (as Rex Stout so often has Nero Wolfe tell Archie Goodwin to do) and sleeps just fine at night.

Hammett did all of this with his short stories and just five novels. Call it a dozen years of writing. Then to all intents and purposes he quit. Came the great silence that no one has ever adequately explained (I have my own theory, of course). But the end of his output didn't mark the end of his influence. In many ways, it was beginning of his influence.

And of the influence of the Hammett Hero. Sam Spade and the Op have accepted the world in which they find themselves. Now they are to trying to do something about it, with a wisecrack and a pitiless masculinity that helped define what it means to be a man. They are trying to create order in the chaos. It is why their stories work so well. In times of utter confusion and despair, they tell us there is a beginning, a middle, and an end to misery. Murder will out. There are order and structure under the chaos. They do this while entertaining the hell out of us at the same time.

How Hammett's Hero Influenced Movies and TV

The Hammett hero—not Hammett, but his hero—virtually created *film noir*. It is tempting to say that this is a result of the societal changes taking place in the 1920s and 1930s caused by Prohibition and the Great Depression. Tempting to embrace the conspiracy theory of history, rather than the effect a single person can have on events: to say that Nazi Germany would have happened without Hitler, Communism would have destroyed Tsarist Russia even without Karl Marx, Lenin, Trotsky and Stalin.

Apparently supporting this interpretation is the *Library Journal*'s review of Mick LaSalle's 2002 book *Dangerous Men: Pre-Code Hollywood and the Birth of Modern Man*. The *Journal* says, in part:

> "LaSalle, a film critic at the *San Francisco Chronicle*, believes that the leading men of Hollywood's pre-Code era (1929-1934) represent a distinct break from their wimpy or exaggeratedly heroic predecessors in the silent era. They could truly be called 'dangerous,' both

to others and to themselves, because they lived (and frequently died) by their own rules. Whether good guys or villains—they were sometimes an intriguing combination of both—they reflected the social chaos going on around them, caused largely by the Depression and Prohibition. Even the slimiest of gangsters, often played by Warner Bros. stalwarts Edward G. Robinson and James Cagney, could be admired because they were their own men."

Well, sure, okay. But hey, I don't buy it.

Prohibition and the Depression were real, and of course they had a tremendous impact on American society. In American fiction (especially hard-boiled pulp fiction) and films, the heroes soon reflected what the *Journal*'s review calls "the social chaos going on around them." But the gangster heroes are an *exploitation of* the status quo rather than an *action against* it.

In film, the real start of *film noir* is John Huston's 1941 *The Maltese Falcon* movie. (There had been two *Falcon* movies before, during the 1930s, but they didn't work well because they tampered with the nature of Hammett's Spade.) In this day of the *auteur*, we are tempted to say that it is director Huston's vision up there on the screen. It isn't. Hammett's work reads like fleshed-out screenplays anyway; Huston had a secretary make a precis of the *Falcon* from which he wrote his script. Huston's genius lies in the cinematic way he shows the story. The story, the characters, are pure Hammett.

After World War II that sort of film story—the lone man who operates outside the bounds society dictates, yet works on behalf of society's survival—became the norm. Returning war vets couldn't get enough of him, because that is what they felt they had done, they had faced split-second life-and-death decisions outside the usual societal norms, and many of them could not settle back into the life they had led before the war. *Film noir* grew out of and fed upon their almost unacknowledged—even unrecognized—discontent.

This new American style of filmmaking is quite different from the gangster films of the 1930s mentioned above, with their heroes who always must go down in defeat. (Robinson: "is this the end of Rico?" Indeed it is. Cagney: "Top of the world, Ma!" just before the gas storage tank blows with him on top of it.) But the detective heroes are *acting*, not *reacting*.

Film noir eventually migrated to France where it got its name, and where it shaped the work of the young, brash, New Wave directors who created the *auteur* theory of film-making. Francois Truffaut is an obvious example. He said he kept a Hammett book by his bedside. Later, Wim Wenders of Germany strengthened Hammett's influence on his career by directing the film version of my novel *Hammett*.

Back home *film noir* dominated what were often called "programmers"—the dark, hard, taut B-pictures like *The Devil Thumbs a Ride* that filled out a double-feature and were shot in days for a few thousand dollars. Today many of these *noir* B-movies are recognized as some of the most compelling films ever made. Hammett was not consciously responsible for all of this, but the hero he created was.[2]

The difference between the gangster films of the 1930s and the private eye films of the 1940s and beyond reflects other factors that go far beyond genre films and spill over into mainstream filmmaking. The detective story is essentially a moral

---

2. Hammett actually did quite a lot of script work himself, and new research not yet published suggests that he did even more uncredited script-doctoring on other writers' work. That Chandler followed in his footsteps is well-known, writing at least one classic *noir* epic, *Double Indemnity*. William Faulkner did a lot of film work also, much of it in the mystery/suspense field. (He co-wrote the screenplay for Chandler's *The Big Sleep*.)

tale, at time almost a morality play. Our hero, however flawed, is on the side of righteousness and social order. Evil (which may be masquerading as good) is defeated. Right triumphs. This sort of morality is often missing in films of the 1930s, but fills the screen in post-World War II detective tales and even mainstream films. Men returning from the horrors of war literally ached to come home to the honest, the honorable, the moral.

I don't believe it is too much of a stretch to say that without *The Maltese Falcon* and *The Thin Man* movies there probably would have been no *Roman Holiday* with its world-weary newsman and brash, wisecracking photographer who are nevertheless honorable men. No *Best Years of Our Lives*, no *Laura*, no *Gentleman's Agreement*, especially no *To Kill A Mockingbird* with its hero Atticus Finch, who stands up to a whole town's beliefs.

Television? Start as far back as *77 Sunset Strip* and you merely have the Hammett hero with long hair and a sassy manner.

Who is Magnum except the Hammett hero softened down?

Cannon? He almost could be the Continental Op.

Mannix started out at an agency like the Continental, soon went private to operate like Sam Spade.

Mike Hammer on film is just a psychotic version of the Hammett hero. On TV, Stacey Keach as Hammer, toned down for the strictures of television, is Hammett's man to a T.

Remington Steele is the Hammett hero as P.I./conman—even his name is a lie—but like the Op he gets the job done.

Banacek—though he rows on the Charles and has a chauffeur-driven limo, dresses up like Nick Charles, and wisecracks like Philip Marlowe—is just Sam Spade gone uptown.

Jim Rockford traces his Hammett roots through Chandler and is my favorite TV private eye because he makes it up as he goes along—just as Spade did, just as real private eyes do.

One of the most direct lines from Hammett to film and TV starts with the *Thin Man* movies of the 1930s starring William Powell and Myrna Loy. There have been literally dozens of cinematic and television clones of this couple (think *Hart to Hart*, think *McMillan and Wife*).

The direct line to police dramas is not so strong, because cops are by definition company men with a chief whose wrath they fear, and a pension at the end of their career they don't want to lose. *Dragnet* for example took the terseness, the dedication to the job, but did not use a central tenet of the Hammett hero: operating outside the system.

Other cop dramas rely more on the Hammett hero. Kojak is a man within the system, but because of his strong sense of justice he often goes outside it, bending the rules whenever he has to. I wrote scripts for *Kojak*, and there was an unspoken acknowledgement that he could be a cowboy and get away with it.

We see the shadow of Hammett's hero even in such unlikely venues as *NYPD Blue* and its followers, even *Cagney and Lacey*. Police officers with rules they don't always follow. This is at the core of many of these shows' most dramatic episodes.

There would be no hard-boiled school of writing without the influence of the Hammett hero. No *film noir*, not as we know it. No spate of idiosyncratic private eyes on TV.

About This Book

The book you hold in your hands does not contain Hammett's most famous stories. The very title of the collection, *Lost Stories*, tells us that almost no one has seen them in the forty to eighty years since their original publication. Some of them are in the tradition of Hammett's hard-boiled tales. Some of them,

I am sure, are destined for "classic" status. "Ber-Bulu," "Night Shade," and "Holiday" are shining examples.

Others are wonderful journeyman tales. They show Hammett's beginnings as a writer, show him feeling his way, finding his rhythm, hitting his stride.

Mixed in with the longer fiction are short pieces, the offhand scribbles that all writers find themselves doing, the pieces that they fit into the larger projects of their creative years. Some of Hammett's pieces are poignant because they came near the end of his writing career.

Hammett couldn't learn by imitating someone else. There wasn't anyone else. He was the first. This collection shows us the gradual emergence of the hard-boiled writer who would change the face of American letters forever by stubbornly writing his own way.

Not bad for a kid with an eighth-grade education.

Dashiell Hammett bequeathed us a proud, independent, crafty, tough, hard-minded protagonist who closely mirrors the ideal real-life investigator. Whether on paper or on film, he mesmerizes us. Whether he is seen as a scoundrel or a hero or a role model mostly depends on who hired him to do what, the context within which history places his work, and who is reading the story.

So read. Enjoy.

PART ONE

A Rough Start

THE MOST SURPRISING THING about Samuel Dashiell Hammett is *not* that he became one of the world's most influential writers.

The most surprising thing is that he ever became any sort of writer at all.

His early life would have choked off most literary careers. He was born not in a cultural center but on a farm in a remote backwoods corner of Maryland. His dad was not a creative role model but an alcoholic would-be politician and failed salesman—such a failure that when Dashiell was seven, his father had to move the family into his mother-in-law's house in Baltimore. His father became ill. Young Dashiell quit school after barely half a year of high school to help support his family.

He took whatever menial jobs he could get: paperboy, railroad office boy, clerk, nail machine operator, dockworker. "Usually, I was fired," he remembered.

At age twenty-one, he later wrote, "A firm of stock-brokers had fired me because I not only could seldom get the same approximate total out of any column of figures twice in succession, but still seldomer managed to get down early enough in the day to make any of my mistakes before noon. A week or so later, hunting for a job, I answered an enigmatic want-ad, and thus became a Pinkerton operative," or "op" for short—what we laypeople call a detective.

Operative Hammett loved to read. He read the detective stories of the day and found them silly. Fictional detectives were rich and famous, but for a seven-day work week Hammett was paid $21. The glamorous detectives in novels wore tuxedos and hobnobbed with high-society swells, but as a real-life op Hammett worked with criminals, lowlifes, and laborers. When he met rich people, they treated him like the hired help he was. Fictional investigators never did paperwork. Hammett spent hours filling out hundreds of case reports and expense reports. Fictional detectives solved headline-making murders and saved countries, but Pinkerton's ops often worked as strikebreakers and labor spies.

His job was not the stuff that novels were made of, but it was work he was good at, and he liked it.

A year and a half after the United States entered the World War, Hammett (at age twenty-four, still living in his parents' home in Baltimore) left the "Pinks" and joined the Army. He was sent to nearby Fort Meade and became an Army ambulance driver.

He later claimed that he overturned his ambulance and dumped wounded soldiers out on a road, although the accident does not appear in his service record. In any case, he was frightened enough to add driving to his list of phobias. After he left the Army, he rarely drove again.

Scarier yet was the twentieth century's most disastrous epidemic. To put it in perspective, think back to 2003 and the worldwide panic caused by a more recent disease, severe acute respiratory syndrome (better known as SARS). In one year, SARS killed 774 people. The epidemic of Hammett's time in one year wiped out more than *twenty million*. Misnamed "Spanish Flu" (it did not come from Spain), it burned itself out the next year and vanished. But while the disease raged during 1918, it killed more U.S. soldiers than the World War, and as an Army ambulance driver, Hammett worked in the thick of it. At some Army bases, men died faster than coffins could be built, so ambulance drivers piled the bodies of hundreds of soldiers in stacks like cordwood. Hammett caught the new disease and was hospitalized. For eight days he was so near death that he was too weak to sit up in bed.

Luckily, he recovered. Unluckily, in his weakened state he came down with something just as bad.

Death Sentence

Hammett developed tuberculosis, the greatest killer in history. More people have died from it than from all wars put together. In the last two centuries TB killed over one billion people.

Tuberculosis is called "a family disease." It spreads when one infected family member coughs or sneezes near others or their food, and when pregnant mothers infect their unborn babies. Hammett's mother had TB. He likely caught it from her and carried it for years, his symptoms showing only after Spanish Flu had ravaged his immune system.

He was a prime candidate for TB. People who are ten percent or more below normal body weight are more likely to develop the disease, and Hammett had always been a thin man. Smokers are four times as likely to die from TB as nonsmokers, and Hammett smoked. Most victims are men.

Psychological influences probably played a part. Since ancient times, people have recognized that the onset of tuberculosis is often preceded by emotional factors. A Hindu text of 1500 B.C. mentions grief as one influence. The great Greek physician Galen discusses "fury and grief."

Modern researchers have found that TB occurs more often in people stressed by social marginality, performance problems at school or work, personal unhappiness, or conflict. In all countries at war, tuberculosis increases. Children who move from a farm to a city—as Hammett did—are more likely to develop TB as an adult.

Sufferers from pulmonary tuberculosis usually first notice that they cough a lot—a cough that will not go away. Their muscles grow weak from lack of oxygen. They feel tired all the time. They feel hot and feverish and dizzy. They lose their appetite. That leads to severe weight loss and the emaciated physique that gives the disease its most popular nickname, *consumption*. Tuberculosis sufferers look as if they are consumed, as if their disease is eating them alive.

As the disease tears up their lungs and surrounding blood vessels, breathing becomes difficult and painful. Night sweats drench their sheets and disrupt their sleep. They cough up bright red blood.

As TB destroys a victim's lungs, it creates pockets that are breeding grounds for pneumonia. The pneumonia kills many TB victims. Others drown in their own blood when their ripped arteries fill their lungs with blood faster than they can cough it up. Some bleed to death.

Even the lucky ones who survive and apparently regain their health find that their disease is not really gone: it is arrested, not cured. A relapse can occur forty years later.

In Hammett's time, more than two-thirds of advanced-stage TB patients died. No medicine was effective. The only treatment was enforced bed rest to give the lungs a chance to heal, and isolation to keep a patient from infecting others. This was before TV or radio, so a patient's only companions were books, magazines, maybe a deck of cards for solitaire. Isolation and confinement to bed would last for months, perhaps years. It is understandable that one study found alcoholism forty times more common among TB patients than in the general population.

Many people believed that tuberculosis provided benefits as well. Alexandre Dumas explains in his memoirs: "In 1823 and 1824, it was the fashion to suffer from the lungs; everybody was consumptive, poets especially; it was all good form to spit blood after each emotion that was at all sensational, and to die before reaching the age of thirty." Tuberculosis was taken as a sign that a person was more sensitive and more creative. As examples, people named Frederic Chopin, the Brontës, and Robert Louis Stevenson. Another alleged benefit was an increased sex drive. This supposed side effect had been discussed for thousands of years; a poem by the Chanter of Theos (563-478 BC) called tuberculosis "the lover's mark." TB sufferers were rumored to have a greater-than-normal appetite for love and sex.

When told that he had tuberculosis, a patient usually had predictable reactions. Shock, fear, anger, worry, and depression were the most common—he knew he was going to die. During treatment, a typical patient would grow to resent his long confinement, his isolation, his lack of liberty, his ostracism by people afraid of infection, and the restrictions on his physical activity. Ostracism and isolation would lead a patient to see himself as an outsider. It was common for a TB patient to describe himself as "an outcast" or "a leper." He became dependent on others, dependencies he would either accept or resent.

If the disease was arrested, then the tubercular patient's biggest fear would not be death. It would be a relapse.

Hammett found that he had TB one day in the Army infirmary. The doctors said he had untreatable tuberculosis, and the Army discharged him the same day. He lost twenty pounds through illness, so in spite of standing over six feet tall, he weighed only 140 pounds.

The skinny twenty-five-year-old invalid came home to his parents in Baltimore. He healed enough to return to work as a Pinkerton's operative. But tuberculosis is a yo-yo disease: a patient seems to recover, then sickness comes back just as bad or worse. Typically in Hammett's time the cycle stopped only when the patient died. Hammett worked as an op for six months when TB hit hard and pushed him back into a hospital bed.

He returned to work in January, 1920, when enforcement of the Volstead Act went into effect. This marked the effective start of Prohibition, which dramatically changed the nature of crime in America. The poorly-written law made Americans criminals when they made, sold, or transported alcoholic beverages, but it was perfectly legal for them to own alcohol and drink it. This built-in conflict led ordinary citizens to openly break laws. Organized crime surged to unprecedented levels. Criminal organizations became big business. Some had hundreds of members. Some took over entire American towns.

In May, Hammett moved to Spokane, Washington, still working as a Pinkerton's op. The Pinks sent him to Montana, where he worked for mining companies against the Industrial Workers of the World (IWW) union. He later said this was his most exciting work as an op.

People who move long distances have a three to ten times greater incidence of tuberculosis. Six months after Hammett's move, his TB returned with a vengeance. He broke down completely. He was declared one hundred percent disabled and sent to a veterans' hospital between Tacoma and Seattle.

Young Lovers

In the hospital, he improved. When his health permitted, he left the hospital to visit Seattle. He rented an apartment in the city, his own place where he could read and entertain between hospital stays.

At the hospital, he fell in love with a petite twenty-three-year-old brunette who, like the mother he loved, was a nurse. She had trained in Butte, Montana, during some of the worst of the labor violence there. She outranked him. Lieutenant Josephine Dolan noticed the tall, brown-eyed, hawk-nosed ex-Sergeant Hammett, who dressed neatly even when all he wore was pajamas. He followed her around the hospital and helped her as if he was her orderly. She found he was intelligent, a good storyteller with a sense of humor so funny she couldn't help but laugh. She was so attracted to him that she ignored the diagnosis of his deadly communicable disease. The nurse and her patient began a passionate romance.

Doctors interrupted the lovers. It was a cold, wet winter, and the doctors decided Hammett would do better where the climate was warm and dry. They transferred him to a hospital near far-off San Diego.

He wrote teasing love letters in green ink to Lt. Josephine, whom he addressed as "Dear Little Fellow," "Dear Dear," "Dear Little Handful," "Dear Boss," "Dearest woman," frequently "Lady" (his beloved mother was nicknamed Lady), and sometimes just "Dear Josephine," but not by the nickname most people called her, Jose (pronounced "Joe's").

In San Diego, he was judged 100 percent disabled from tuberculosis. Once again, he got better. He was granted one-day passes to leave the camp. He visited nearby Tijuana to escape Prohibition, get drunk, and gamble. He wrote to her about it, and how much he loved her and missed her.

Jose was transferred to another hospital in Helena, Montana. She had not caught Hammett's communicable disease, but he did leave her with something else. She was pregnant.

Eager to rejoin Jose, he requested release from the San Diego hospital. He convinced his doctors to grant his request, although he had not been in their hospital for even three months.

The Army would give him a train ticket only to Spokane, where he stopped briefly and then returned to his Seattle apartment. He was still sick. He tried to tough it out, but during his first three weeks in Seattle, he had to go back to the hospital twice. He was too sick to work as a Pinkerton's op, so he pathetically told the hospital his occupation was "former detective."

He and Jose made plans. They had no medical insurance to cover delivering a baby. She was pregnant and could not work. He was in bad shape, but they needed money. Even though he was sick, he had to return to work.

Hammett went to San Francisco. Working for Pinkerton's, he helped a character called Blackjack Jerome bust a dockworkers' strike.

Hammett found a fresh city. Thanks to the recent earthquake and fire, almost everything in San Francisco was new. Most buildings were less than fifteen years old. Stores and apartments were new and clean. Bus, trolley, and cable car lines everywhere meant he had no need to drive. Prohibition was on, but liquor was easily available. So were gambling, prostitution, and cops on the take. He found plenty of the boxing matches and horse races he loved to watch. It was a lively place, and the city's setting on hills by a blue bay was beautiful. Hammett liked it.

Hammett asked Jose to join him in San Francisco and marry him. She did. He was twenty-seven. She was twenty-four and six months pregnant.

Sick in San Francisco

They needed to leave their hotel rooms for an apartment of their own, but some landlords did not rent to people with TB.

At that time, tuberculosis killed more people by far than any other disease in California. The alarmed San Francisco government tried to reduce TB infections by passing a law that in San Francisco: " ... it shall be unlawful for any person suffering from tuberculosis to change his or her residence or to be removed therefrom until the Department of Public Health has been notified so that the vacated apartment or premises may be disinfected ... Such articles that cannot be disinfected or renovated to the satisfaction of the Health Officer shall be destroyed."

When a TB sufferer moved out of an apartment, the landlord could not rent it out. He had to wait until a health officer visited and directed its cleaning and disinfection—which the landlord had to pay for. If the apartment was furnished, the health officer could order the burning of the landlord's carpets, mattresses, couches, whatever—all at the landlord's expense. The penalty for not following the law was steep: half a year in jail, a stiff fine, or both. Some landlords simply refused to rent to tuberculars. This was especially true for landlords of furnished apartments, because their furniture might be destroyed. The newlywed Hammetts had no money to buy furniture. They needed a furnished place.

They found a landlord who would rent to them. The place was a studio apartment on Eddy Street; perhaps the furniture was so shabby that the landlord didn't care what happened to it. The apartment cost $45 a month, which was covered by the $80 check the new United States Veterans' Bureau sent Hammett each month for being 100 percent disabled.

Then the Veterans' Bureau evaluated his medical condition and found him better. His disability was reduced from one hundred percent to fifty percent. That reduced his monthly check amount. The smaller check might not even pay the Hammetts' rent.

Desperate for money, Hammett continued with Pinkerton's. On days when he had enough strength, he worked.

One sunny, breezy Sunday in October, Jose Hammett gave birth to a baby. They named her Mary Jane Hammett. Her husband was amazed by the tiny girl. Usually, the infant of a tubercular parent was sent to a foster home to avoid the deadly infection. Instead, Hammett, Jose, and the baby stayed in the same apartment, but Hammett kept his distance. At night he slept in the hall of their apartment while his wife and baby slept in the bedroom.

He was not well. That fall, he weighed only 135 pounds, suffered from dizziness, and was short of breath. When he exerted any physical effort, his chest hurt. Still, on good days he worked as an op for $6 a day.

He grew sicker. By December, his weight had dropped to 126 pounds—shockingly thin for a man nearly six feet two inches tall. He had only enough energy to leave bed for three or four hours a day. Sometimes he was so weak he could not walk from his bed to the bathroom by himself. Jose nursed both her baby and her husband. She got credit from neighboring shopkeepers for food. At the end of December, his disability was revised back up to 100 percent, so his check went back up to $80 a month.

In February, 1922, he quit the Pinks for good. He was too sick to work as an op. He was probably dying. The new year of 1922 had begun with a bleak start.

Desperation

The Hammetts had seen income from his disability checks vary undependably; the Veterans' Bureau policy was to reduce or halt disability payments whenever possible. Its neglect of ill veterans was an open scandal. (So much so that the director of California's Bureau of Tuberculosis, Edythe Tate Thompson, wrote in her 1922 annual report: "The bureau has continued its cooperation with the U.S. Veterans' Bureau, but the director is greatly humiliated as any citizen must be, at the delay in giving the tuberculous ex-service man the care he is entitled to.")

Early in 1922, Hammett's father refused to send money to help Sam—the name the younger Hammett used at that time—get by. Jose's parents were dead, so she could not ask them for help. She couldn't work; she needed to stay at home to care for the baby. The Veterans' Bureau checks were not reliable. Sam and Jose had no alternative. To feed their family, he needed to do some kind of work.

He was not healthy enough to work as an op. He needed a job that required no physical exertion. His first effort in this direction was to convince the Veterans' Bureau to pay for vocational training, and to continue his disability checks while he attended classes.

That February, Hammett began classes at the Munson School for Private Secretaries. Established fifteen years earlier, the San Francisco school taught secretarial skills and a popular method of shorthand created by James E. Munson, a New York shorthand reporter. Hammett stated "newspaper reporting objective" as his reason for attending classes at the Munson School, but the school offered no courses to train reporters, only training for secretaries. If he completed the year-and-a-half course, he could look for work as a shorthand stenographer, and take verbatim notes of meetings and dictation from executives. He attended the Munson School long enough to learn to touch type, then dropped out.

He thought of another way to earn money. He decided to create advertisements: come up with ideas, write the copy, and draw the art. (Hammett was a good cartoonist.) This was work he could do, if necessary, while lying in bed. He talked his way into freelance advertising projects. His first advertisement was for a shoe store. His payment: a pair of shoes.

When he was strong enough, he spent afternoons in the San Francisco Main Library, four blocks from the Hammetts' apartment. There he sat in the spacious reading room, reading books and magazines while sunlight streamed through large arched windows. He once called the building his university. To make up for his lost education, he wanted to read as many of its books as he could.

At the age of twenty-seven, seemingly out of nowhere, this thin, unemployed invalid came up with another idea to make money.

The Mystery of Dashiell Hammett

Near the end of some Ellery Queen mystery stories, the author makes an announcement to the effect of, *All right, at this point in the story you have all the clues. Can you solve the mystery?*

At this point in the story of Dashiell Hammett, you have all the clues. Can you solve his mystery? Where did this man get the crazy idea he could write fiction for money?

Writers' lives commonly include an appropriate education (Hammett had almost no high school and no college), or experiments in writing in their childhood or adolescence (none known for Hammett), a family history in writing or a related field (none), a job in a related field (none), or friends or a mentor who write (none). Most writers have at least one of these five ingredients in their pockets. Hammett had zero.

Even with qualifications, many would-be writers fail utterly. In fact, on Halloween 1921, twenty-four-year-old Aline Maxwell killed herself just six blocks from Hammett's apartment for that very reason, drinking poison because she had failed as a short story writer.

At first glance, Hammett's only related background seems to have been writing hundreds (maybe thousands) of case reports as an op and writing a handful of ads.

If we look closer, however, we find that he did have skills that could help a writer.

As an op, he learned to observe the details of how a person looked and dressed and to remember those details so he could write a report enabling an op in another city to identify the same person. He learned to remember conversations so he could relate them accurately in his reports.

He had devoured how-to books to learn ad writing techniques: know your outcome before you start, make each sentence work towards that outcome, use the right tone of voice for your target reader, use simple words, write clear sentences, reread your work when done to find and delete any unneeded words.

He had a ferocious intelligence, and a near-photographic memory. For instance, he could read a book about botany once, and many years later recall technical details almost verbatim. And he read quickly, finishing a book in a few hours, often a few books in one day. Thanks to months of enforced rest, he was a well-read, self-educated man.

He was a good oral story-teller, with an understated but wickedly funny sense of humor.

He probably read books in the San Francisco Main Library on how to write and sell fiction. But he would have read them after having his idea to write for money. It was on the surface an unreasonable, unlikely, preposterous choice, but he had enough confidence to try; confidence in his own intelligence, his creativity, and his sense of what worked and what did not.

In the spring of 1922, Samuel Dashiell Hammett set out to write short stories to earn money. Soon he told a nurse that he was writing four hours a day. When he was well, he wrote at the kitchen table. When he was sick, he wrote in bed.

And he finished his first-ever story.

PART TWO

1922,
New Writer

IT WAS NEITHER the first story he sold, nor his first story to see print. However, Hammett later recalled that when "I installed my first typewriter and picked out my first story" at age twenty-eight, his virgin effort was this story, "The Barber and His Wife."

At first glance, this may not be the sort of story you associate with Hammett. But look closer and you will see many characteristics of his mature writing, already present in this, his first literary experiment.

First, his style is tight and controlled. Hammett's prose never slips into looseness, even though conversations are informal. Each word is deliberately chosen.

Second, there is a complete lack of sentimentality.

Third, Hammett seems to reflect on a question that critics point out in his later work: What is a real man? In other words, how can a man be both masculine and authentic?

Fourth, this first story provides the first instances of many recurring elements that Hammett would use repeatedly throughout his stories, novels, and movie writings, elements I call "Hammettisms." It is remarkable to find so many elements of an author's mature fiction packed into the very first piece he wrote.

Hammettisms in Hammett's First Story

"The Barber and His Wife" provides the first instances of "Hammettisms"—recurring elements that Hammett used repeatedly throughout his work. Some Hammettisms are unique to Hammett. Others are techniques, themes, or motifs that are common in many good works of fiction, but that are especially prominent in Hammett's writing. In this first story, look for these Hammettisms:

♠ **Vivid characters**. In any medium, the key to successful storytelling is to provide memorable characters who have vivid and distinct personalities. Hammett's ability to populate stories with striking characters is perhaps his greatest strength. In this story, note how Hammett gives the barber, his wife, and his brother very distinct personalities. They dress differently, move differently, speak differently, even breathe differently.

♠ **Flavorful, naturalistic dialog**. Hammett keeps his dialog crisp, makes it sound like real people talking and not written prose, and makes each conversation move his plot forward. In most fiction, characters all speak alike. That's because most writers write in only one voice. Hammett gives each character a different way of speaking—each with his or her own vocabulary, rhythm, and sentence structure. Hammett's ability to sustain many distinct voices— one for his narration, others for his characters—is rare and a source of pleasure for readers.

♠ **Biting humor**. The dry, understated wit that Hammett used in everyday conversation is here harnessed for fiction for the first time.

♠ **Struggles for dominance**. Hammett makes some of his characters attempt to psychologically dominate others. He shapes the resulting struggles in ways that add character revelation, conflict, and color.

♠ **Corruption and breakdown of social institutions**. In this case, the institution is marriage.

♠ **Main character is working class**. In Hammett's time, much fiction focused on upper-class and middle-class people. Almost all of Hammett's central characters are working class or poor.

♠ **Main character takes pride in competence in his job**. Most of Hammett's main characters—whether they are detectives, criminals, or, in this case, a barber— pride themselves on doing their jobs well.

♠ **Main character does not drive**. Hammett had many phobias. One was his fear of driving. Few of Hammett's central characters drive. It is entertaining to note the alternatives Hammett employs to avoid having his main characters drive.

♠ **A fat man**. Hammett was extremely thin all his life. Fat men must have fascinated him, because he featured many in his stories. Hammett uses fat in this story to make a character pathetic. The physical contrasts between round Ben Stemler and his proudly well-conditioned brother Louis intensifies the personalities of both.

♠ **A stenographer**. If Hammett had not dropped out of the Munson School for Secretaries, he could have become a stenographic reporter. He puts a stenographer in most of his novels and some of his short stories. One makes a brief appearance here.

♠ **A movie theater or a movie theater owner.** Hammett peppers his stories and novels with characters who go to movie theaters and others who own movie theaters.

♠ **No children.** Surprisingly for a man who had two daughters and who loved kids all his life, almost all Hammett stories take place in a world without children.

♠ **Meticulous descriptions of clothing.** Terms such as "cerise stripes" are not often found in stories written by men, but Hammett is famous for describing clothes in precise detail. He paid careful attention to clothing all his life. He was a fastidious dresser, and in his detective work he not only had to notice the details of a person's appearance, but also to remember those details and describe them clearly in written reports. His descriptions of men's outfits are usually more meticulous than his descriptions of women's clothing.

♠ **Superspecificity.** Author William Gibson invented this term. It refers to passages in which Hammett describes objects or events using extreme detail to draw us deeper into a scene. In an interview, Gibson described his feelings when he realized what Hammett was doing with superspecificity: "I remember being very excited about how he had pushed all this ordinary stuff until it was different—like American naturalism but cranked up very intense, almost surreal." The beginnings of this technique are in this story in the descriptions of Louis' morning routine and of his barbershop as he enters it.

♠ **The phrase "all right".** Hammett included this phrase in most of his stories and uses it twice here.

♠ **Asyndetons, lists without a connective before the final item**. For example, the list of things Becker hadn't done. Most writers would have put an *and* before the final *hadn't*. Hammett often skips the *and*.

♠ **Set in a place where Hammett lived**. The second paragraph mentions an unnamed "coast city" as the story's setting. That could be either Seattle or San Francisco—both places where Hammett lived—or other cities on the West Coast. Later in his tale, Hammett gives us further clues—the city's hills and the name of a boxer—that locate this story in San Francisco, the city where Hammett wrote it.

You can spot all these Hammettisms in "The Barber and His Wife" and in many of Hammett's other works as well. As Hammett wrote he continued to use these recurring elements and added others, such as his frequent use of the double entendre *dingus*. As he introduces them in his stories they will be pointed out in this book.

Whether you hunt for "Hammettisms," or you ignore them and read this story for sheer pleasure, I'm sure you'll enjoy Hammett's first.

The Barber and His Wife

EACH MORNING AT SEVEN-THIRTY the alarm clock on the table beside their bed awakened the Stemlers to perform their daily comedy; a comedy that varied from week to week in degree only. This morning was about the mean.

Louis Stemler, disregarding the still ringing clock, leaped out of bed and went to the open window, where he stood inhaling and exhaling with a great show of enjoyment—throwing out his chest and stretching his arms voluptuously. He enjoyed this most in the winter, and would prolong his stay before the open window until his body was icy under his pajamas. In the coast city where the Stemlers lived the morning breezes were chill enough, whatever the season, to make his display of ruggedness sufficiently irritating to Pearl.

Meanwhile, Pearl had turned off the alarm and closed her eyes again in semblance of sleep. Louis was reasonably confident that his wife was still awake; but he could not be certain. So when he ran into the bath-room to turn on the water in the tub, he was none too quiet.

He then re-entered the bed-room to go through an elaborate and complicated set of exercises, after which he returned to the bath-room, got into the tub and splashed merrily—long enough to assure any listener that to him a cold bath was a thing of pleasure. Rubbing himself with a coarse towel, he began whistling; and always it was a tune reminiscent of the war. Just now "Keep the Home Fires Burning" was his choice. This was his favorite, rivaled only by "Till We Meet Again," though occasionally he rendered "Katy," "What Are You Going to Do to Help the Boys?" or "How're You Going to Keep Them Down on the Farm?" He whistled low and flatly, keeping time with the brisk movements of the towel. At this point Pearl would usually give way to her irritation to the extent of turning over in bed, and the rustling of the sheets would come pleasantly from the bed-room to her husband's ears. This morning as she turned she sighed faintly, and Louis, his eager ears catching the sound, felt a glow of satisfaction.

Dry and ruddy, he came back to the bed-room and began dressing, whistling under his breath and paying as little apparent attention to Pearl as she to him, though each was on the alert for any chance opening through which the other might be vexed. Long practice in this sort of warfare had schooled them to such a degree, however, that an opening seldom presented itself. Pearl was at a decided disadvantage in these morning encounters, inasmuch as she was on the defensive, and her only weapon was a pretense of sleep in the face of her husband's posturing. Louis, even aside from his wife's vexation, enjoyed every bit of his part in the silent wrangle; the possibility that perhaps after all she was really asleep and not witnessing his display of manliness was the only damper on his enjoyment.

When Louis had one foot in his trousers, Pearl got out of bed and into her kimono and slippers, dabbed a little warm water on her face, and went into the kitchen to prepare breakfast. In the ensuing race she forgot her slight headache. It was a point of honor with her never to rise until her husband had his trousers in his hand, and then to have his breakfast on the table in the kitchen—where they ate it—by the time he was dressed. Thanks to the care with which he knotted his necktie, she usually succeeded. Louis's aim, of course, was to arrive in the kitchen fully dressed and with the morning paper in his hand before the meal was ready, and to be extremely affable over the delay. This morning, as a concession to a new shirt—a white silk one with broad cerise stripes—he went in to breakfast without his coat and vest, surprising Pearl in the act of pouring the coffee.

"Breakfast ready, pet?" he asked.

"It will be by the time you're dressed," his wife called attention to his departure from the accepted code.

And so this morning honors were about even.

L OUIS READ THE SPORTS PAGES while he ate, with occasional glances at his cerise-striped sleeves. He was stimulated by the clash between the stripe and his crimson sleeve-garters. He had a passion for red, and it testified to the strength of the taboos of his ilk that he did not wear red neckties.

"How do you feel this morning, pet?" he asked after he had read what a reporter had to say about the champion's next fight, and before he started on the account of the previous day's ball games.

"All right."

Pearl knew that to mention the headache would be to invite a display of superiority masked as sympathy, and perhaps an admonition to eat more beef, and certainly one to take more exercise; for Louis, never having experienced any of the ills to which the flesh is heir, was, naturally enough, of the opinion that even where such disorders were really as painful as their possessors' manners would indicate, they could have been avoided by proper care.

Breakfast consumed, Louis lighted a cigar and addressed himself to another cup of coffee. With the lighting of the cigar Pearl brightened a little. Louis, out of consideration for his lungs, smoked without inhaling; and to Pearl this taking of smoke into the mouth and blowing it forth seemed silly and childish. Without putting it into words she had made this opinion known to her husband, and whenever he smoked at home she watched him with a quiet interest which, of all her contrivances, was the most annoying to him. But that it would have been so signal an admission of defeat, he would have given up smoking at home.

The sports sheets read—with the exceptions of the columns devoted to golf and tennis—Louis left the table, put on his vest, coat, and hat, kissed his wife, and, with his consciously buoyant step, set out for his shop. He always walked downtown in the morning, covering the twenty blocks in twenty minutes—a feat to which he would allude whenever the opportunity arose.

L OUIS ENTERED HIS SHOP with a feeling of pride in no wise lessened by six years of familiarity. To him the shop was as wonderful, as beautiful, as it had been when first opened. The row of green and white automatic chairs, with white-coated barbers bending over the shrouded occupants; the curtained alcoves in the rear with white-gowned manicurists in attendance; the table laden with magazines and newspapers; the clothes-trees; the row of white enameled chairs, at this hour holding no waiting customers; the two Negro boot-blacks in their white jackets; the clusters of colored bottles; the smell of tonics and soaps and steam; and around all, the sheen of spotless tiling, porcelain and paint and polished mirrors. Louis stood just within the door and basked in all this while he acknowledged his employees' greetings. All had been with him for more than a year now, and they called him "Lou" in just the correct tone of respectful familiarity—a tribute both to his position in their world and his geniality.

He walked the length of the shop, trading jests with his barbers—pausing for a moment to speak to George Fielding, real estate, who was having his pink face steamed preparatory to his bi-weekly massage—and then gave his coat and hat to Percy, one of the bootblacks, and dropped into Fred's chair for his shave. Around him the odor of lotions and the hum of mechanical devices rose soothingly. Health and this . . . where did those pessimists get their stuff?

The telephone in the front of the shop rang, and Emil, the head-barber, called out, "Your brother wants to talk to you, Lou."

"Tell him I'm shaving. What does he want?"

Emil spoke into the instrument; then, "He wants to know if you can come over to his office some time this morning."

"Tell him 'all right!'"

"Another shipment of bootleg?" Fielding asked.

"You'd be surprised," Louis replied, in accordance with the traditional wit of barbers.

Fred gave a final pat to Louis's face with a talcumed towel, Percy a final pat to his glowing shoes, and the proprietor stepped from the chair to hide the cerise stripes within his coat again.

"I'm going over to see Ben," he told Emil. "I'll be back in an hour or so."

BEN STEMLER, THE ELDEST of four brothers, of which Louis was the third, was a round, pallid man, always out of breath—as if he had just climbed a long flight of steps. He was district sales-manager for a New York manufacturer, and attributed his moderate success, after years of struggling, to his doggedness in refusing to accept defeat. Chronic nephritis, with which he had been afflicted of late years, was more truly responsible for his increased prosperity, however. It had puffed out his face around his protuberant, fishy eyes, subduing their prominence, throwing kindly shadows over their fishiness, and so giving to him a more trustworthy appearance.

Ben was dictating pantingly to his stenographer when Louis entered the office. "Your favor of the . . . would say . . . regret our inability to comply . . . your earliest convenience." He nodded to his brother and went on gasping. "Letter to Schneider . . . are at a loss to understand . . . our Mr. Rose . . . thirteenth instant . . . if consistent with your policy . . . would say . . . in view of the shortage of materials."

The dictation brought to a wheezing end, he sent the stenographer on an errand, and turned to Louis.

"How's everything?" Louis asked.

"Could be worse, Lou, but I don't feel so good."

"Trouble is you don't get enough exercise. Get out and walk; let me take you down to the gym; take cold baths."

"I know, I know," Ben said wearily. "Maybe you're right. But I got something to tell you—something you ought to know—but I don't know how to go about telling you. I—that is—"

"Spit it out!" Louis was smiling. Ben probably had got into trouble of some sort.

"It's about Pearl!" Ben was gasping now, as if he had come from an unusually steep flight of steps.

"Well?" Louis had stiffened in his chair, but the smile was still on his face. He wasn't a man to be knocked over by the first blow he met. He had never thought of Pearl's being unfaithful before, but as soon as Ben mentioned her name he knew that that was it. He knew it without another word from Ben; it seemed so much the inevitable thing that he wondered at his never having suspected it.

"Well?" he asked again.

Unable to hit upon a way of breaking the news gently, Ben panted it out hurriedly, anxious to have the job off his hands. "I saw her night before last! At the movies! With a man! Norman Becker! Sells for Litz & Aulitz! They left together! In his car! Bertha was with me! She saw 'em too!"

He closed with a gasp of relief and relapsed into wheezes.

"Night before last," Louis mused. "I was down to the fights—Kid Breen knocked out O'Toole in the second round—and I didn't get home until after one."

F ROM BEN'S OFFICE to Louis's home was a distance of twenty-four blocks. Mechanically timing himself, he found it had taken him thirty-one minutes—much of the way lay uphill—pretty good time at that. Louis had elected to walk home, he told himself, because he had plenty of time, not because he needed time to think the situation over, or anything of that sort. There was nothing to think over. This was a crystal-clear, tangible condition. He had a wife. Another man had encroached, or perhaps only attempted to, on his proprietorship. To a red-blooded he-man the solution was obvious. For these situations men had fists and muscles and courage. For these emergencies men ate beef, breathed at open windows, held memberships in athletic clubs, and kept tobacco smoke out of their lungs. The extent of the encroachment determined, the rest would be simple.

Pearl looked up in surprise from the laundering of some silk things at Louis' entrance.

"Where were you night before last?" His voice was calm and steady.

"At the movies." Pearl's voice was too casual. The casual was not the note she should have selected—but she knew what was coming anyway.

"Who with?"

Recognizing the futility of any attempt at deception, Pearl fell back upon the desire to score upon the other at any cost—the motive underlying all their relations since the early glamour of mating had worn off.

"With a man! I went there to meet him. I've met him places before. He wants me to go away with him. He reads things besides the sporting-page. He doesn't go to prizefights. He likes the movies. He doesn't like burlesque shows. He inhales cigarette smoke. He doesn't think muscle's everything a man ought to have." Her voice rose high and shrill, with a hysterical note.

Louis cut into her tirade with a question. He was surprised by her outburst, but he was not a man to be unduly excited by his wife's display of nerves.

"No, not yet, but if I want to I will," Pearl answered the question with scarcely a break in her high-pitched chant. "And if I want to, I'll go away with him. He doesn't want beef for every meal. He doesn't take cold baths. He can appreciate things that aren't just brutal. He doesn't worship his body. He—"

As Louis closed the door behind him he heard his wife's shrill voice still singing her wooer's qualities.

"Is Mr. Becker in?" Louis asked the undersized boy behind a railing in the sales-office of Litz & Aulitz.

"That's him at the desk back in the corner."

Louis opened the gate and walked down the long office between two rows of mathematically arranged desks—two flat desks, a typist, two flat desks, a typist. A rattle of typewriters, a rustling of papers, a drone of voices dictating: "Your favor of . . . our Mr. Hassis . . . would say . . . " Walking with his consciously buoyant step, Louis studied the man in the corner. Built well enough, but probably flabby and unable to stand up against body blows.

He stopped before Becker's desk and the younger man looked up at Louis through pale, harassed eyes.

"Is this Mr. Becker?"

"Yes, sir. Won't you have a seat?"

"No," Louis said evenly, "what I'm going to say ought to be said standing up." He appreciated the bewilderment in the salesman's eyes. "I'm Louis Stemler!"

"Oh! yes," said Becker. Obviously he could think of nothing else to say. He reached for an order blank, but with it in his hand he was still at sea.

"I'm going to teach you," Louis said, "not to fool around with other men's wives."

Becker's look of habitual harassment deepened. Something foolish was going to happen. One could see he had a great dread of being made ridiculous, and yet knew that was what this would amount to.

"Oh! I say!" he ventured.

"Will you get up?" Louis was unbuttoning his coat.

In the absence of an excuse for remaining seated, Becker got vaguely to his feet. Louis stepped around the corner of the desk and faced the salesman.

"I'm giving you an even break," Louis said, shoulders stiffened, left foot advanced, eyes steady on the embarrassed ones before him.

Becker nodded politely.

The barber shifted his weight from right to left leg and struck the younger man on the mouth, knocking him back against the wall. The confusion in Becker's face changed to anger. So this was what it was to be! He rushed at Louis, to be met by blows that shook him, forced him back, battered him down. Blindly he tried to hold the barber's arms, but the arms writhed free and the fists crashed into his face and body again and again. Becker hadn't walked twenty blocks in twenty minutes, hadn't breathed deeply at open windows, hadn't twisted and lowered and raised and bent his body morning after morning, hadn't spent hours in gymnasiums building up sinew. Such an emergency found him wanting.

Men crowded around the combatants, separating them, holding them apart, supporting Becker, whose legs were sagging.

Louis was breathing easily. He regarded the salesman's bloody face with calm eyes, and said: "After this I guess you won't bother my wife any. If I ever hear of you even saying 'how do' to her again I'll come back and finish the job. Get me?"

Becker nodded dumbly.

L OUIS ADJUSTED HIS NECKTIE and left the office. The matter was cleanly and effectually disposed of. No losing his wife, no running into divorce courts, no shooting or similar cheap melodrama, and above all, no getting into the newspapers as a deceived husband—but a sensible, manly solution of the problem.

He would eat downtown tonight and go to a burlesque show afterward, and Pearl's attack of nerves would have subsided by the time he got home. He would never mention the events of this day, unless some extraordinary emergency made it advisable, but his wife would know that it was always in his mind, and that he had demonstrated his ability to protect what was his.

He telephoned Pearl. Her voice came quietly over the wire. The hysteria had run its course, then. She asked no questions and made no comment upon his intention of remaining down-town for the evening meal.

It was long after midnight when he arrived home. After the show he had met "Dutch" Spreel, the manager of "Oakland Kid McCoy, the most promising lightweight since the days of Young Terry Sullivan," and had spent several hours in a lunch-room listening to Spreel's condemnation of the guile whereby the Kid had been robbed of victory in his last battle—a victory to which the honest world unanimously conceded his right.

Louis let himself into the apartment quietly and switched on the light in the vestibule. Through the open bed-room door he saw that the bed was unoccupied and its surface unruffled. Where was Pearl, then? he thought; surely she wasn't sitting up in the dark. He went through the rooms, switching on the lights.

On the dining-room table he found a note.

> I never want to see you again, you brute! It was just like you—as if beating Norman would do any good. I have gone away with him.

Louis leaned against the table while his calm certitude ran out of him. So this was the world! He had given Becker his chance; hadn't taken the advantage of him to which he had been entitled; had beaten him severely—and this was the way it turned out. Why, a man might just as well be a weakling!

———

OF COURSE, A WEAKLING is exactly what the author was him-self. Is this first story a weakling's revenge on muscular men? The situation Hammett constructs is not that clear-cut. He takes care not to make Louis Stemler completely unsympathetic—mostly by showing his wife, Pearl, pelt him with her hostility—and he bases some of Louis' traits on his own: Hammett was a boxing fan; he loved to eat beef; like Louis, he had little respect for the movies. He is careful not to make Louis a cardboard villain.

(Note how Hammett copies his own shortness of breath for Louis' pathetic brother, Ben.)

He also avoids making Norman Becker a too-obvious good guy, providing no details about Becker that would let us identify with him. Instead, he makes Becker vague, so we neither sympathize with him nor dislike him. Is Becker a better man for Pearl? We cannot know.

We do know that Louis sees his problem as a threat to his marriage from the *outside*. He does not try to solve the problem by improving his relations with Pearl. He tries to remove what he sees as an external threat with violence—but, as in other Hammett stories, violence leads to unintended consequences.

Read Me after "The Barber and His Wife"

"The Barber and His Wife" introduces four more Hammett-isms that I held until after the story so as not to reveal plot points:

♠ **A troubled or unconventional romantic relationship**. Hammett portrays many sexual relationships as distorted and manipulative. On his website "A Guide to Classic Mystery and Detection," Michael E. Grost points out that Hammett's writings provide "bizarre relationships that subvert all our notions of romantic bliss." You do not find a stereotypical romance in "The Barber and His Wife." Nothing like the word *love* is ever used.

♠ **A lack of feeling and its consequences.** Several Hammett stories portray a loss caused by characters' lack of feeling.

♠ **An untrustworthy woman.** Louis finds that Pearl is not to be trusted, a lesson he shares with many men who trust women in Hammett's fiction, from Paulette Key in the next story to Brigid O'Shaughnessy, Eva Archer, and Rhea Gutman in *The Maltese Falcon.*

♠ **A conspiracy.** Hammett put many conspiracies in his stories. In his mysteries especially, the main characters often find other characters colluding to hatch secret schemes—a change from Hammett's mystery-writing counterparts, who usually wrote stories in which crimes were committed by one lone criminal. We have the simplest form of conspiracy in this story: two people conspire to keep their illicit relationship secret from the main character.

"The Barber and His Wife" is an accomplished first story, especially for a man untrained in writing fiction.

Note the assurance in the author's tone of voice. Instead of the inconsistency and hesitancy of a typical first-time writer, Hammett has a smooth, confident tone. Supporting details (such as Becker automatically reaching for an order blank) are handled well.

A fashion note: When Hammett writes "... it testified to the strength of the taboos of his ilk that he did not wear red neckties," he refers to the then-popular view that a man wears a red necktie to show he is a socialist, anarchist, or communist. Five years later, a red necktie again appears in a Hammett work, this time in his novel *Red Harvest.*

Hammett submitted "The Barber and His Wife" to magazines. He wrote other stories and sent them out as well. By return mail, his manuscripts came back to him.

Rejected.

W HILE "THE BARBER AND HIS WIFE" was being rejected, another Hammett piece had better luck.

Sometime in June or July 1922, Hammett received his first letter of acceptance from a magazine. His excitement was so great that his wife could remember it decades later. To celebrate, the Hammetts had dinner sent in from a restaurant to their little apartment.

The accepted story was minor, only a humorous anecdote. But the magazine that published it was anything but minor, and one of the magazine's editors was one of the most remarkable literary men of the century—one whose influence on Hammett would be great.

The magazine was *The Smart Set*, one of the most irreverent and influential literary magazines of its time. It nurtured Sinclair Lewis, F. Scott Fitzgerald, James Joyce, Eugene O'Neill, Theodore Dreiser, Willa Cather, Ezra Pound, Edgar Lee Masters, and many other new writers.

The Smart Set was also one of the most snobbish and opinionated magazines of its time, thanks to its two editors, H. L. Mencken and George Jean Nathan.

Mencken was the more important of the two. He wrote about literature, politics, and culture in *The Smart Set*; in his witty, opinionated books; and in his columns for newspapers in major cities. During the early 1920s he was the American intellectual most often quoted and widely discussed in the United States and Europe. In fact, *The English Review* wrote, "He and he alone has put America on the literary map." Walter Lippmann called him "the most powerful personal influence on this whole generation of educated people."

On the other hand, the *Palm Beach News* called Mencken "the most universally hated man in the United States" for his outrageous opinions. Many people agreed—so many people that Mencken was able to collect insults about himself and publish an entire book of them!

Also important, from Hammett's point of view: Mencken lived in Hammett's hometown of Baltimore, where he was by far the most famous Baltimorean. Hammett wrote to his father, bragging that he had swapped letters with the celebrated publisher.

That an unpublished writer could correspond with a famous publisher happened because *The Smart Set* employed no readers for incoming manuscripts. Mencken read almost all of them himself. "Whenever a volunteer showed the slightest sign of talent, I wrote to him encouragingly," Mencken later wrote, "and kept on blowing his spark so long as the faintest hope remained of fanning it into flame." Fortunately for Hammett, Mencken saw a spark in "The Parthian Shot" and a new literary career received its tiny launch.

What is a "Parthian shot"?

Mentioned in the Bible (Acts 1:9), Parthia was the only major rival power that the classical Romans were never able to conquer. The Persian-speaking Parthian empire flourished where Iran sits today. A Parthian warrior was a skilled archer and horseman, renowned for being able to fire an arrow *backward* over his shoulder with deadly accuracy while he galloped away from his enemy. A "Parthian shot" became a common term for a final insult hurled with deadly accuracy as the insulter departs, wounding the victim and leaving no time for a response. Arthur Conan Doyle used the term in *A Study in Scarlet*, the first Sherlock Holmes novel, when Holmes delivers a zinger to Scotland Yard inspectors Gregson and Lestrade: "With which Parthian shot he walked away, leaving the two rivals open-mouthed before him."

It is a bit of literary irony for a parting remark to be transformed into an introduction as this tiny story, "The Parthian Shot," introduced a new writer to the world.

This issue of The Smart Set *presented Hammett's first published story. Its logo features a devil wearing a black mask.*

The Parthian Shot

WHEN THE BOY WAS six months old Paulette Key acknowledged that her hopes and efforts had been futile, that the baby was indubitably and irremediably a replica of its father. She could have endured the physical resemblance, but the duplication of Harold Key's stupid obstinacy—unmistakable in the fixity of the child's inarticulate demands for its food, its toys—was too much for Paulette. She knew she could not go on living with *two* such natures! A year and a half of Harold's domination had not subdued her entirely. She took the little boy to church, had him christened Don, sent him home by his nurse, and boarded a train for the West.

WHEN H. L. MENCKEN received a manuscript, he usually decided yes or no on it within a week, and *The Smart Set* paid for a manuscript immediately when he accepted it. This earned gratitude from writers. They often waited long times for payment from magazines that paid only *after* a story was published, months or even years after it was received. So when Hammett received his letter of acceptance from Mencken, with it came his first check for writing fiction.

How much did Hammett get paid for "The Parthian Shot"? *The Smart Set* paid about one penny per word for prose, so with his acceptance letter he received a check for about $1.13.

That amount isn't much, but in 1922 the Hammetts could buy more with $1.13 than we can today.

If you lived then, you could buy lunch at a good French restaurant in San Francisco for 75¢, or dinner for $1.50 (plus a few cents for a tip, of course). At the grocery store, you could buy a pound of bacon for 19¢. You could see a movie for a nickel. Need clothes? In 1922 you could buy fine neckties for $1 to $4, a pair of new socks for 15¢. If you wanted to travel, you could take a steamship cruise from San Francisco to Los Angeles for a $25 round trip. If you wanted to stay put, you could buy a brand new five-room San Francisco house with a three-car garage for $6,200. Your mortgage payment would be about $60 per month. The same apartment the Hammetts rented for $45 per month including furniture now costs $750 per month without, and today's rent is artificially low, thanks to rent control laws.

Of course, your paycheck would have been smaller then. Average earnings of workers were never more than $1,500 per year during the 1920s and 1930s. Many people earned less. Unskilled laborers earned an average of $795 per year. Nurses were paid an average of $1,310. Newspaper reporters averaged $2,120. Attorneys made around $4,730; doctors $4,850. Those earnings rarely included medical insurance or other benefits that are common today.

When you read an amount in 1920s or 1930s dollars, you can get a rough equivalent in today's prices by multiplying it by twenty or thirty. So Hammett's first writing paycheck was worth $22 to $33 when he received it in June or July 1922, not as bad as it first sounded. It was probably all spent long before Hammett received his copy of the magazine that contained his first story two or three months later.

Then, as now, monthly magazines arrived on newsstands and in mailboxes the month before their cover dates, so even though "The Parthian Shot" appeared in the issue of *The Smart Set* for October, Hammett would have received his copy in mid-September.

Seeing the magazine—checking to see that, yes, they did spell his name right—must have given him a thrill. But the thrill would have been bittersweet. His mother, Annie Dashiell Hammett, whom Hammett loved and whom her family called Lady, had died on August 3. She did not live to see her son's first appearance in print.

Hammett saw his second and third appearances in print the next month. One of them was another humorous piece accepted by H. L. Mencken for *The Smart Set*.

Doubtlessly compiled from Hammett's reading at the San Francisco Public Library, this piece is nonfiction, but is included here to present together all five of Hammett's pieces published in 1922, the first year that he wrote. This is the first time "The Great Lovers" has appeared in a book.

The Great Lovers

Now that the meek and the humble have inherited the earth and it were arrogance to look down upon any man—the apologetic being the mode in lives—I should like to go monthly to some hidden gallery and, behind drawn curtains, burn perfumed candles before the images of:

Joachim Murat, King of Naples, who mourned, "Ah, the poor people! They are ignorant of the misfortune they are about to suffer. They do not know that I am going away."

The Earl of Chatham, who said, "My lord, I am sure I can save the country and no one else can."

Louis XIV of France, who perhaps said, "*L'etat c'est moi*," and who, upon receiving news of the battle of Ramillies, cried, "God has then forgotten all that I have done for Him!"

William Rufus, who held that if he had duties toward God, God also had duties toward him.

Prince Metternich, who wrote in his diary, "Fain's memoirs of the year 1813 are worth reading—they contain my history as well as Napoleon's"; and who said of his daughter, "She is very like my mother; therefore possesses some of my charm."

Joseph II of Austria, who said, "If I wish to walk with my equals, then I must go to the Capuchin crypt."

Charles IV of Spain, who, playing in a quartet, ignored a three-bar pause which occurred in his part; and upon being told of his mistake by Olivieri, laid down his bow in amazement, protesting, "The king never waits for anyone!"

The Prince of Kaunitz Rietberg, whose highest praise was, "Even I could not have done it better"; and who said, "Heaven takes a hundred years to form a great genius for the generation of an empire, after which it rests a hundred years. This makes me tremble for the Austrian monarchy after my death."

Virginicchia Oldoni, Countess of Castiglione, who kissed the baby, saying, "When he is grown up you will tell him that the first kiss he ever received was given him by the most beautiful woman of the century."

The Lord Brougham, who paid for his dinner with a cheque, explaining to his companions, "I have plenty of money, but, don't you see, the host may prefer my signature to the money."

Paul of Russia, who had his horse given fifty strokes, exclaiming, "There, that is for having stumbled with the emperor!"

And Thomas Hart Benton, who, when his publishers consulted him concerning the number of copies of his book, *Thirty Years' View*, to be printed, replied, "Sir, you can ascertain from the last census how many persons there are in the United States who can read, sir"; and who refused to speak against Calhoun when he was ill, saying, "When God Almighty lays His hands on a man, Benton takes his off!" . . .

IN THE SAME MONTH that "The Great Lovers" appeared, another humorous anecdote of Hammett's was published. It gets my vote for the most inconsequential story by Hammett ever printed. Like the previous two pieces, it is short and ironic.

This is the first time this little piece has been published in a book.

Immortality

I KNOW LITTLE OF SCIENCE or art or finance or adventure. I
have never written anything except brief and infrequent letters to my sister in Sacramento. My name, were it not painted on
the windows of my shop, would be unknown to even the Polish
family that lives and has many children across the street. Yet I
shall live in the memories of men when those names that are
on every one's lips now are forgotten, and when the events of
today are dim. I do not know whether I shall be remembered
as a great wit, a dreamer of strange dreams, a great thinker, or a
philosopher; but I do know that I, Oscar Blichy, the grocer, shall
be an immortal. I have saved nearly seventeen thousand dollars
from the profits of my shop during the last twenty years. I shall
add to this amount as much as I can until the day of my death,
and then it is to go to the writer of the best biography of me!

HAMMETT HAD TO ENDURE publishers' rejections of his first story, "The Barber and His Wife," until *Brief Stories*, a pulp fiction magazine, accepted the tale for its December 1922 issue.

That same month, a more groundbreaking piece by Hammett was published, although it seemed so trivial at the time—perhaps even an embarrassment—that it was printed under a pseudonym, Peter Collinson, instead of under Hammett's own name. The story is called "The Road Home," and it breaks ground in four ways:

1. It is Hammett's first detective story. Although "The Road Home" is not a mystery story in the classical sense—it is, in fact, an anti-mystery—the main character is Hammett's first try at creating a fictional detective, and the plot is his first reaction to the predictable and nonsensical storylines used by mystery writers.
2. It is his first story using another country as its locale, and one of only four and a half stories he set outside the United States during his entire career.[1]
3. It is Hammett's first appearance in *The Black Mask*, the magazine that introduced more than half of his short stories and all of his novels but one. It provided most of his paychecks for the next seven years.
4. In turn, it marks the first appearance in *The Black Mask* of the man who became the magazine's most important author. The innovations of Hammett and his followers made *The Black Mask* a huge financial success, and—much to everyone's surprise—an influential literary force.

These developments were all H. L. Mencken's fault.

---

1. The four and a half stories and their settings are: "The Road Home," Burma; "Holiday," Tijuana, Mexico; "Ber-Bulu," Malay Archipelago; "This King Business," fictional European kingdom of Muravia; half of "The Golden Horseshoe," Tijuana, Mexico.

Two years earlier, Mencken had written to San Francisco poet George Sterling: "*The Smart Set* is a pleasant recreation. It barely pays for itself. Both Nathan and I have to live by other devices. The chief fun consists in giving promising youngsters a chance. We dig up a good many of them and exhibit them to the nobility and gentry. Then they are offered five cents a word by Lorimer, or Hearst, or *McCall's Magazine*—and go away denouncing us for not paying them ten cents."

Because Mencken and his co-editor George Jean Nathan could not support themselves with *The Smart Set*, they came up with another scheme to make money: They would start new pulp fiction magazines and sell them to publishers for a quick profit. In 1920 they started a magazine of mystery, western, and romance stories and named it *The Black Mask*. After six months, they sold it to a publisher for $6,125 apiece (worth $150,000 or more apiece today), and continued to help the publisher on a consulting basis.

At first, *The Black Mask* published the cheapest hack writers that Mencken and Nathan could find. Mencken later recalled, "In a little while we began to recruit authors of more skill, including S. Dashiell Hammett, a strange Marylander who had been a Pinkerton detective and was to develop into one of the most successful manufacturers of homicidal fiction ever heard of."

A reasonable assumption is that Hammett submitted "The Road Home" to Mencken for *The Smart Set*, but Mencken decided it lacked the sophisticated, ironic touch of that publication and accepted it instead for *The Black Mask*, which paid about the same stingy penny-per-word rate, or perhaps less.

So sometime in the summer of 1922 (before Mencken went abroad in August and September), Hammett received a letter of acceptance from Mencken and a check for about $12. He needed the money, but must have felt disappointed; instead of running in the prestigious *Smart Set*, his story would run in a pulp fiction magazine that educated people dismissed as trash. He surely did not brag about being published in *The Black Mask*. He may have felt ashamed of it.

Regardless of which magazine published it, Hammett's story was an innovation. Instead of following the rules used for detective fiction in his time, he shattered them. To properly understand what a transformation this was, we must shed our modern expectations and read this tale as readers would have in 1922, anticipating what they would expect.

What kind of *character* would we expect a detective to be?

The detective tradition established by Edgar Allan Poe and refined by Arthur Conan Doyle dictated that a fictional detective would be upper class. He (rarely a she) would be European, or if American, would imitate European habits and culture. (Yes, Poe was American, but he made his detective French.) The detective would be an eccentric, brilliant, and preposterous outsider with an artificial style of speech. He would possibly work with a dense sidekick. He would often be well known by the public, famous for his or her feats of deduction. (A moment's thought will convince you that this is absurd. How many real-life detectives have you seen in the news over the past year? Probably zero. Real detectives are anonymous.) The detective would be incorruptible: always on the side of good, never tempted to sway. That would be the detective *character*.

What would we expect for a detective *plot*? The solving of a puzzle, without any bothersome character development or moral struggle.

In 1922, plots in detective fiction were fixed into a six-step ritual as predictable and comforting as a Catholic Mass:

1. The detective is called as an outsider into a setting populated by upper-class people,
2. where a murder or robbery is committed in a clever, complicated way

3. by one of a closed circle of suspects.
4. The police are benevolent but incompetent, and focus on the most obvious suspect.
5. The detective investigates the crime without being threatened by physical danger,
6. and determines that an intelligent upper-class villain (who is not the obvious suspect) worked alone to plan and commit the crime.

By correcting the police and identifying the culprit, the detective restores peacefulness to the elegant setting, bringing the reader a sense of resolution: all is right with the world. (Hammett knew that in real life identifying the guilty party could be the easy part. But if the culprit fled, the hard part would often be what detectives call skip tracing: finding the fugitive.)

That was the detective fiction plot formula. Hammett's writing, however, is anti-formulaic. Hammett knew the rules and wrote counter to them. Throughout his life, his writing reflected a man who knew what his readers expected—whether from literary conventions, character creation, or plotting—and took care to give them something they did *not* expect.

Keep those clichés in mind and see whether Hammett's first detective story meets your expectations or subverts them.

The Road Home

"You're a fool to pass it up! You'll get just as much credit and reward for taking back proof of my death as you will for taking me back. And I got papers and stuff buried back near the Yunnan border that you can have to back up your story; and you needn't be afraid that I'll ever show up to spoil your play."

The gaunt man in faded khaki frowned with patient annoyance and looked away from the blood-shot brown eyes in front of him, over the teak side of the *jahaz* to where the wrinkled snout of a *muggar* broke the surface of the river. When the small crocodile submerged again, Hagedorn's grey eyes came back to the pleading ones before him, and he spoke wearily, as one who has been answering the same arguments again and again.

"I can't do it, Barnes. I left New York two years ago to get you, and for two years I've been in this damned country—here and in Yunnan—hunting you. I promised my people I'd stay until I found you, and I kept my word. Lord! man," with a touch of exasperation, "after all I've gone through you don't expect me to throw them down now—now that the job's as good as done!"

The dark man in the garb of a native smiled an oily, ingratiating smile and brushed away his captor's words with a wave of his hand.

"I ain't offering you a dinky coupla thousand dollars; I'm offering you your pick out of one of the richest gem beds in Asia—a bed that was hidden by *Mran-ma* when the British jumped the country. Come back up there with me and I'll show you rubies and sapphires and topazes that'll knock your eye out. All I'm asking you is to go back up there with me and take a look at 'em. If you don't like 'em you'll still have me to take back to New York."

Hagedorn shook his head slowly.

"You're going back to New York with me. Maybe man-hunting isn't the nicest trade in the world but it's all the trade I've got, and this jewel bed of yours sounds phoney to me. I can't blame you for not wanting to go back—but just the same I'm taking you."

Barnes glared at the detective disgustedly.

"You're a fine chump! And it's costing me and you thousands of dollars! Hell!"

He spat over the side insultingly—native-like—and settled himself back on the corner of the split-bamboo mat.

Hagedorn was looking past the lateen sail, down the river—the beginning of the route to New York—along which a miasmal breeze was carrying the fifty-foot boat with surprising speed. Four more days and they would be aboard a steamer for Rangoon; then another steamer for Calcutta, and in the end, one to New York—home, after two years!

Two years through unknown country, pursuing what until the very day of capture had been no more than a vague shadow. Through Yunnan and Burma, combing wildernesses with microscopic thoroughness—a game of hide-and-seek up the rivers, over the hills and through the jungles—sometimes a year, sometimes two months and then six behind his quarry. And now successfully home! Betty would be fifteen—quite a lady.

Barnes edged forward and resumed his pleading, with a whine creeping into his voice.

"Say, Hagedorn, why don't you listen to reason? There ain't no sense in us losing all that money just for something that happened over two years ago. I didn't mean to kill that guy, anyway. You know how it is; I was a kid and wild and foolish—but I wasn't mean—and I got in with a bad bunch. Why, I thought of that hold-up as a lark when we planned it! And then that messenger yelled and I guess I was excited, and my gun went off the first thing I knew. I didn't go to kill him; and it won't do him no good to take me back and hang me for it. The express company didn't lose no money. What do they want to hound me like this for? I been trying to live it down."

The gaunt detective answered quietly enough, but what kindness there had been in his dry voice before was gone now.

"I know—the old story! And the bruises on the Burmese woman you were living with sure show that there's nothing mean about you. Cut it, Barnes, and make up your mind to face it—you and I are going back to New York."

"The hell we are!"

Barnes got slowly to his feet and backed away a step.

"I'd just as leave—"

Hagedorn's automatic came out a split second too late; his prisoner was over the side and swimming toward the bank. The detective caught up his rifle from the deck behind him and sprang to the rail. Barnes' head showed for a moment and then went down again, to appear again twenty feet nearer shore. Upstream the man in the boat saw the blunt, wrinkled noses of three *muggars*, moving toward the shore at a tangent that would intercept the fugitive. He leaned against the teak rail and summed up the situation.

"Looks like I'm not going to take him back alive after all—but my job's done. I can shoot him when he shows again, or I can let him alone and the *muggars* will get him."

Then the sudden but logical instinct to side with the member of his own species against enemies from another wiped out all other considerations, and sent his rifle to his shoulder to throw a shower of bullets into the *muggars*.

Barnes clambered up the bank of the river, waved his hand over his head without looking back, and plunged into the jungle.

Hagedorn turned to the bearded owner of the *jahaz*, who had come to his side, and addressed him in his broken Burmese.

"Put me ashore—*yu nga apau mye*—and wait—*thaing*—until I bring him back—*thu yughe*."

The captain wagged his black beard protestingly.

"*Mahok!* In the jungle here, *sahib*, a man is as a leaf. Twenty men might find him in a week, or a month. It may take five years. I cannot wait that long."

The gaunt white man gnawed at his lower lip and looked down the river—the road to New York.

"Two years," he said aloud to himself, "it took to find him when he didn't know I was hunting for him. Now—Oh hell! It may take five years. I wonder about them jewels of his."

He turned to the boatman.

"I go after him. You wait three hours," pointing overhead, "until noon—*ne apomha*. If I am not back then do not wait—*malotu thaing, thwa, Thi?*"

The captain nodded.

"*Hokhe!*"

For five hours the captain kept the *jahaz* at anchor, and then, when the shadows of the trees on the west bank were creeping out into the river, he ordered the lateen sail hoisted, and the teak craft vanished around a bend in the river.

THIS NEW STORY SLAPS down our expectations one after the other. The traditional whodunit plot structure has been thrown away. The detective is not an upper-class intellectual, but a tough professional who works for a living and uses bad grammar. He is definitely not European, but American. The criminal is not an upper-class, grammatically correct genius, but a lower-class thug. Instead of restoring order, the detective chooses disorder, returning to the jungle. Instead of ending with a feeling of closure, the story ends unresolved: Is Barnes as innocent as he claims? Will Hagedorn catch him? Is the detective motivated by a desire to bring the criminal to justice, to get rich ("I wonder about them jewels of his"), to meet his commitment to others, or just to do his job? We don't know. This story is as open-ended as the classic "The Lady or the Tiger?"—but who'd ever heard of an open-ended detective story?

"The Road Home" is an attempt to break away from unrealistic detective conventions. In its own way it marks a milepost in the evolution of contemporary fiction.

Innovations in Fiction

In "The Road Home," you can spot these eight elements that Hammett introduced or popularized, none of which were commonplace in early twentieth-century fiction:

1. **The detective is placed in an adventure story.** When Hammett wrote "The Road Home," crossword puzzles showed more action than many detective stories. Hammett and his followers put the thrill back in detective fiction. The focus of the story is not just sterile puzzle-solving, but heroic action. The detective is required to show courage. Writer Erle Stanley Gardner described the innovation as "the new

action type of detective story" and followed suit. So did other writers.

2. **The hero moves in a dangerous world**, not a safe world. To solve the crime, the hero makes his way through a world where he is threatened with physical danger, where violence and corruption happen every day.

3. **The detective is a manhunter.** Hagedorn explains "Maybe man-hunting isn't the nicest trade in the world but it's all the trade I've got ... " His pride in being a competent manhunter is new in detective fiction.

4. **The hero is tough**. Main characters in much early twentieth-century literature are wimps like the mama's boy protagonist of D. H. Lawrence's *Sons and Lovers*, or optimists incapable of hurting others. Our heroes today are tough, dangerous men, and Hammett was one of the writers who made them that way, not just in detective stories, but in all types of fiction, television, and films.

5. **The hero is a working stiff**. Hagedorn is no rich blueblood. He works for a living, unlike many early twentieth-century fictional protagonists.

6. **The detective hero is distinctly American**. Hammett leaves no doubt that Hagedorn thinks and talks as an American, not a would-be European.

7. **Criminals act and talk like criminals**. Barnes is not an educated genius. He is a working crook, an ungrammatical lowlife from the streets.

8. **The hero's moral sense is offended**. The detective is affronted when the fugitive tries to con him that the criminal's actions were not his own fault, and by "the bruises on the Burmese woman you were living with ... " Note that the detective is not offended by Hagedorn's attempt to bribe him.

William F. Nolan calls "The Road Home" the first hardboiled detective story. Literary historians will armwrestle over whether Nolan is right or wrong. There is no doubt, however, that the changes that Hammett planted with this seed still sprout today throughout literature, television, and film, where working-class heroes, fallible but strongly masculine characters who are also strongly American, realistic dialog, crisp writing, and a lack of sentimentality are commonplace—as they were not when this story was written.

New Hammettisms in "The Road Home"

"The Road Home" introduces six new Hammettisms that reappear in future Hammett stories:

♠ **The protagonist makes his own moral rules**—The main character in "The Road Home" and the main characters in Hammett's strongest subsequent fiction share an awareness that was observed by author James Sallis: " ... much of their power derived from a recognition that there is no moral order save that which a man creates for himself." This individualistic ethic clashes with Hammett's upbringing in the Roman Catholic Church, which promotes institutionalized morality by claiming that valid moral principles can come only from the teachings of its hierarchy. Hammett's most powerful works show a man dealing with the troubles of life by making his own definitions of what is right and wrong, by adhering—no matter how much pain it costs—to a moral code that he defines for himself. He renders his own judgment. There is no other.

♠ **The detective is tempted**—Traditional detectives were morally one-dimensional, so obviously incorruptible that an offer like Barnes' would be silly. Hammett was very interested in the temptation of the detective by money, power, physical threats, and sex. Temptation starts in this story in the first paragraph with Barnes berating the detective for not taking his bribe. Even the title "The Road Home" is ironic, because the road home is not taken. It is another temptation to which the detective does not succumb. He rejects the feminine attractions of wife, daughter, and home to continue the single-minded hunt for his quarry in the jungle.

♠ **Spicy slang**—Hammett loved colorful slang. This is his first published story spiced with extensive slang. Almost all his subsequent fiction followed suit. His use of slang is so masterful that today the editors of the *Oxford English Dictionary* study Hammett as an authority on American slang.

♠ **The detective gets surprised**—Sherlock Holmes is famous for being omniscient and rarely surprised. Most fictional detectives of the 1920s are similarly unflappable. Hammett counters this convention by ensuring that in every one of his stories that feature a detective, the detective is surprised or wrong at least once. His detectives are vulnerable.

♠ **A thin man**—Hammett populates several of his stories with men who share his slim physique. In this case, he describes his detective as "gaunt."

♠ **A circular fable**—Hammett wrote some stories in which a character moves through dramatic events only to return to circumstances similar to those at the beginning of his tale. This is the first of them, as the detective concludes by chasing the fugitive, just as he was doing before the story began.

As 1922 drew to a close, Hammett could look back on the completed year with some satisfaction. He had five pieces published in three magazines—two in Mencken's prestigious *Smart*

Set—plus he had written more stories, some of which had sold and would appear in print in the first months of the next year. Against all odds, he had established a toehold for scaling a new career.

Even more importantly, his tuberculosis had not killed him yet. Most people as sick as he was could not have said the same. In fact, most could not have said anything. During 1922, 71.2 percent—nearly three-quarters—of the tuberculosis patients in California died.

Hammett was alive. Years later, he claimed that what saved his life was writing.

PART THREE

1923,
The Sixteen-Story Year

THE YEAR 1923 began a burst of productivity by Hammett. Sixteen pieces by the fledgling writer were published that year.

He began the year as an unknown with little experience. He closed the year as an established writer with a popular series character, a bread-and-butter relationship with the magazine that would publish most of his fiction, a growing recognition among readers, and the beginnings of writing that would influence story-telling worldwide.

The first Hammett story of 1923 was his second detective story, "The Master Mind," another sale to *The Smart Set* magazine. Like "The Road Home," it is not a mystery.

The Master Mind

WHEREVER CRIME OR CRIMINALS were discussed by enlightened folk, the name of Waldron Honeywell could be heard. It was a symbol—to the citizens of Punta Arenas no less than to those of Tammerfors—for the ultimate in the prevention and detection of crime. A native of the United States, Honeywell's work had overflowed the national boundaries. Thirty years of warfare upon crime had taken him into every quarter of the globe, and his fame into every nook where the printed word penetrated.

Bringing to his work a singularly perspicacious intellect, and combining an exhaustive knowledge of both the scientific and more practical phases of his profession, he had reduced it to as nearly exact a science as possible; and his supremacy in his field had never been questioned.

He had punctured Lombroso's theories at a time when the scientific world regarded the Italian as a Messiah. The treatise with which he exploded the belief—fostered by no less an authority than the great W. J. Burns—that Sir Arthur Conan Doyle would have made a successful detective, and showed that the mysteries confronting Sherlock Holmes would have been susceptible to the routine methods of the ordinary policeman, was familiar to the readers of eight languages. The mastery with which he unearthed and frustrated the Versailles bomb plot before it was well on its feet; the dispatch with which he recovered the aircraft program memoranda; his success in finding the assassin of the emperor of Abyssinia, the details of which were suppressed for some obscure political reason; the effectual manner in which he coped with the epidemic of postal robberies—these were matters of history, but in no way more remarkable than a thousand-odd other exploits in which he had figured.

Honors and decorations were showered upon him, governments sought his advice, scientists deferred to him, criminals shuddered at the sound of his name (one, who had avoided arrest for seventeen years, surrendered to the nearest policeman upon learning that Honeywell had been engaged to hunt him down), and his monetary rewards were enormous.

Early in 1922 Waldron Honeywell died, and left an estate consisting of $182.65 in cash, 37,500 shares of International Solar Power Corporation common, 42,555 shares of Cousin Tilly Gold, Platinum & Diamond Mining Company common, 6,430 shares of Universal Petroleum Corporation of Uruguay, S. A. preferred, and 75,000 shares of New Era Fuelless Motor Company common.

THE JOKE, OF COURSE, is that this seemingly brilliant detective was stupid in financial matters, investing in companies that were laughably worthless. (Solar power is big business now, but in 1923 it was a silly pipedream.)

In this brief satire Hammett outlines the reasons for his contempt of contemporary detective fiction. His comment that "the mysteries confronting Sherlock Holmes would have been susceptible to the routine methods of the ordinary policeman" points out a genre stupidity that irked Hammett enough for him to repeat it later about other fictional detectives. Waldron Honeywell embodies the clichés that Hammett's own private eye experience proved inauthentic: the detective is famous, he hobnobs with the upper class, he is paid "enormous" fees, and, of course, he knows everything and is infallible.

Detecting won't make you rich; detectives are working-class guys; detectives get their hands dirty; detectives are only human are recurring underlying premises of Hammett's. The observations are commonplace now, but they were novel thoughts in the days when writers created detective characters not too different from Waldron Honeywell and expected their readers to take them seriously.

Brief Stories, the same pulp magazine that bought "The Barber and His Wife," purchased its second Hammett story to run in its February 1923 issue. Among other Hammettisms in "The Sardonic Star of Tom Doody," look for "all right" five times and a fat man.

This story was later reprinted in *Ellery Queen's Mystery Magazine* but renamed "The Wages of Crime," a better title.

The Sardonic Star
of Tom Doody

"COME ALONG without any fuss and there won't be no trouble," said the tall man with the protruding lower lip and the black bow tie.

"And remember, anything you say will—" the fat man under the stiff straw hat warned, the rest of the prescribed caution dying somewhere within the folds of his burly neck.

A frown of perplexed interrogation reduced the none too ample area between Tom Doody's eyebrows and the roots of his hair. He cleared his throat uneasily and asked, "But what's it for?"

The protruding lower lip overlapped the upper in a smile that tempered derision with indulgence. "You ought to be able to guess—but it ain't a secret. You're arrested for stealing sixty-five thousand dollars from the National Marine Bank. We found the dough where you hid it, and now we got you."

"That's what," the fat man corroborated. . . .

TOM DOODY leaned across the plain table in the visitors' room and bent his beady eyes on the tired, middle-aged eyes of the woman from the *Morning Bulletin*.

"Miss Envers, I have served three and a half years here and I've got nearly ten more to do, taking in account what I expect to get off for good behavior. A long time, I guess you think; but I'm telling you that I don't regret a minute of it." He paused to let this startling assertion sink in, and then leaned forward again over hands that lay flat, palms down, fingers spread, on the top of the table.

"I came in here, Miss Envers, a safe-burglar that had been caught for the first and only time in fifteen years of crime. I am going out of here completely reformed, and with only one aim in my life; and that's to do all I can to keep other people from following in my footsteps. I'm studying, and the chaplain is helping me, so that when I get out I can talk and write so as to get my message across. I used to be pretty good at reciting and making speeches when I was a kid in school, and I guess it'll come back to me all right. I'm going from one end of the country to the other, if I have to ride freights, telling of my experiences as a criminal, and the light that busted—burst on me here in prison. I know what it is, and lots of people that maybe wouldn't listen to a preacher or anybody else will pay attention to me. They'll know that I know what I am talking about, that I've been through it, that I'm the man who robbed the National Marine Bank and lots of others."

"You were very nearly acquitted, at that; weren't you?" Evelyn Envers asked.

"Yes, nearly," the convict said, "and as truly as I'm sitting here, Miss Envers, I thank God that I was convicted!"

He stopped and tried to read surprise in the faded gray eyes across the table. Then he went on. "But for that—the chance for self-knowledge and thought that this place has gave—has given me—I might have gone on and on, might never have come to an understanding of what it means to be a Christian and know the difference between right and wrong. Here in prison I found for the first time in my life, liberty—yes, liberty!—freedom from the bonds of vice and crime and self-destruction!" With this paradox he rested.

"Have you made any other plans for your career after leaving here?" the woman asked.

"No. That's too far ahead. But I am going to spend the rest of my life spreading the truth about crime as I know it, if I have to sleep in gutters and live on stale bread!"

"He's a fraud, of course," Evelyn Envers told her typewriter as she threaded a sheet of paper into it, "but he'll make as good a story as anything else."

So she wrote a column about Tom Doody and his high resolves and because the thought behind his reformation was so evident to her she took especial pains with the story, gilding the shabbier of his mouthings and garnishing him with no inconsiderable appeal.

For several days after the story's appearance letters came to the *Morning Bulletin* Readers' Forum, commenting on Tom Doody and tendering suggestions of various sorts.

The Rev. Randall Gordon Rand made Tom Doody the subject of one of his informal Sunday evening talks.

And then John J. Kelleher, 1322 Britton street, was crushed to death by a furniture van after pushing little Fern Bier, five-year-old daughter of Louis Bier, 1304 Britton street, to safety; and it transpired that Kelleher had been convicted of burglary several years before, and was out on parole at the time of the accident.

Evelyn Envers wrote a column about Kelleher and his dark-eyed little wife, and with doubtful relevance brought Tom Doody into the last paragraph. The *Chronicle* and the *Intelligencer* printed editorials in which Kelleher's death was adduced as demonstrative of the parole system's merit.

On the afternoon before the next regular meeting of the State Parole Board the football team of the state university— three members of the board were ardent alumni—turned a defeat into a victory in the last quarter.

Tom Doody was paroled.

FROM HIS ROOM on the third floor of the Chapham hotel, Tom Doody could see one of the posters. Red and black letters across a fifteen-by-thirty field of virginal white gave notice that Tom Doody, a reformed safe-burglar of considerable renown, would talk at the Lyric Theater each night for one week on the wages of sin.

Tom Doody tilted his chair forward, rested his elbows on the sill, and studied the poster with fond eyes. That bill-board was all right—though he had thought perhaps his picture would be on it. But Fincher had displayed no enthusiasm when a suggestion to that effect had been made, and whatever Fincher said went. Fincher was all right. There was the contract Fincher had given him—a good hundred dollars more a week than he had really expected. And then there was that young fellow Fincher had hired to put Tom Doody's lecture in shape. There was no doubt that the lecture was all right now.

The lecture began with his childhood in the bosom of a loving family, carried him through the usual dance-hall and pool-room introductions to gay society, and then rose in a crescendo of vague but nevertheless increasingly vicious crime to a smashing climax with the burglary of the National Marine Bank's sixty-five thousand dollars, the resultant arrest and conviction, and the new life that had dawned as he bent one day over his machine in the prison jute-mill. Then a tapering off with a picture of the criminal's inherent misery and the glory of standing four-square with the world. But the red meat of it was the thousand and one nights of crime—that was what the audience would come to hear.

The young fellow who had been hired to mold and polish the Doody epic had wanted concrete facts—names and dates and amounts—about the earlier crimes; but Tom Doody had drawn the line there, protesting that such a course would lay him open to arrest for felonies with which the police had heretofore been unable to connect him, and Fincher had agreed with him. The truth of it was that there were no crimes prior to the National Marine Bank burglary—that conviction was the only picturesque spot in Tom Doody's life. But he knew too much to tell Fincher that. At the time of his arrest the newspapers and the police—who, for quite perceptible reasons, pretend to see in every apprehended criminal an enormously adept and industrious fellow—had brought to light hundreds of burglaries, and even a murder or two, in which this Tom Doody might have been implicated. He felt that these fanciful accusations had helped expedite his conviction, but now the fanfare was to be of value to him—as witness the figure on his contract. As a burglar with but a single crime to his credit he would have been a poor attraction on the platform, but with the sable and crimson laurels the police and the press had hung upon him, that was another matter.

For at least a year these black and red and white posters would accompany him wherever he went. His contract covered that period, and perhaps he could renew it for many years. Why not? The lecture was all right, and he knew he could deliver it creditably. He had rehearsed assiduously and Fincher had seemed pleased with his address. Of course he'd probably be a little nervous tomorrow night, when he faced an audience for the first time, but that would pass and he would soon feel at home in this new game. There was money in it—the ticket sales had been large, so Fincher said. Perhaps after a while—

The door opened violently and Fincher came into the room—an apoplectic Fincher, altogether unlike the usual smiling, mellow manager of Fincher's International Lecture Bureau.

"What's up?" Tom Doody asked, consciously keeping his eyes from darting furtively toward the door.

"What's up?" Fincher repeated the words, but his voice was a bellow. "What's up?" He brandished a rolled newspaper shillalah-wise in Tom Doody's face. "I'll show you what's up!" He seemed to be lashing himself into more vehement fury with reiterations of the ex-convict's query, as lions were once said to do with their tails.

He straightened out the newspaper, smoothed a few square inches of its surface, and thrust it at Tom Doody's nose, with one lusty forefinger laid like an indicator on the centre of the sheet. Tom Doody leaned back until his eyes were far enough away to focus upon the print around his manager's finger.

> . . . by the police, Tom Doody, who was paroled
> several days ago after serving nearly four years for
> the theft of sixty-five thousand dollars from the
> National Marine Bank, has been completely exon-
> erated of that crime by the deathbed confession of
> Walter Beadle, who . . .

"That's what's up!" Fincher shouted, when Tom Doody had shifted his abject eyes from the paper to the floor. "Now I want that five hundred dollars I advanced to you!"

Tom Doody went through his pockets with alacrity that poorly masked his despair, and brought out some bills and a handful of silver. Fincher grabbed the money from the ex-convict's hands and counted it rapidly.

"Two hundred and thirty-one dollars and forty cents," he announced. "Where's the rest?"

Tom Doody tried to say something but only muttered.

"Mumbling won't do any good," Fincher snarled. "I want my five hundred dollars. Where is it?"

"That's all I've got," Tom Doody whined. "I spent the rest, but I'll pay every cent of it back if you'll only give me time."

"I'll give you time, you dirty crook, I'll give you time!" Fincher stamped to the telephone. "I'll give you till the police get here, and if you don't come across I'm going to swear out a warrant for obtaining money under false pretenses!"

IN JANUARY OR FEBRUARY, Hammett sold another story to *The Black Mask*, a short piece about blackmail. About the same time he sold another tale to the pulp *Brief Stories*.

He had already made his fourth sale to *The Smart Set*, a non-fiction piece called "From the Memoirs of a Private Detective." H. L. Mencken had become Hammett's steadiest customer.

That May, Sam and Jose Hammett celebrated his twenty-ninth birthday. That month they received a copy of the June issue of *The Black Mask* with his blackmail story and the June *Brief Stories*, which included this story, "The Joke on Eloise Morey."

Critics of the time were atwitter over stream-of-consciousness, which James Joyce had used in his novel *Ulysses*, published the year before. Hammett must have read about *Ulysses*, and he was familiar with the character introspection of Henry James. It was only natural for him to experiment in that direction, which he does here. This story features Hammett's third fictional detective, and it was one of only five stories (including "The Parthian Shot") by Hammett ever published with a woman as its lead character. Hammett bibliographer Mark Sutcliffe points out that this story provides early examples of Hammett's frequent descriptions of eyes to reveal character and mood. Look for an untrustworthy woman, the phrase "all right" three times, a fat man, the absence of children, and other Hammettisms as well.

The Joke on Eloise Morey

"Bᴜᴛ, ɢᴏᴏᴅ Gᴏᴅ, Eʟᴏɪsᴇ, I love you!"

"But, good God, Dudley, I hate you!"

The cold malevolence of her mimicry brought a quiver to his sensitive lips, as she had known it would, and his pale, tortured face went altogether bloodless. These not unfamiliar, and in this case anticipated, indications of pain infuriated her even as they pleased her. From her advantage of perhaps two inches in height she let her hard gray eyes—twin points of steel in a beautiful, selfish face—range with studied insult from the wave of chestnut brown hair that swept over his forehead to the toes of his small shoes, and then up again to his suffering red-brown eyes.

"What are you?" she asked with frigid bitterness. "You're not a man; are you a child? or an insect? or what? You know I don't want you—you'll never be anything. I've certainly made that clear enough. And yet you won't give me my liberty. I wish I never had seen you—that I'd never married you—that you were dead!"

Her voice—she usually took pains to keep it carefully modulated—rose high and shrill under the pressure of her wrath.

Her husband blenched, cringed under the lash of each acrid word, but said nothing. He could not say anything. His was far too sensitive, too delicate, a mechanism to permit of any of the answers he might have made. Where a cruder nature would have met the woman on her own ground, and hammered its way to victory, or at least an even distribution of the honors, he was helpless. As always, his silence, his helplessness, the evident fact that he did not know what to do or say, spurred her on to greater cruelties.

"An artist!" she derided, making the phrase heavy with contempt. "You were a genius; you were going to be famous and wealthy and God knows what all! And I fell for it and married you: a milk-and-water nincompoop who'll never be anything. An artist! An artist who paints pictures that nobody will look at, much less buy. Pictures that are supposed to be delicate. Delicate! Weak and wishy-washy daubs of color that are like the fool who paints them. A silly fool smearing paint on canvas—too fine for commercial art—too fine for anything! Twelve years you've spent learning to paint and can't turn out a picture anybody will look at twice! Great! You're great now: a great big fool!"

She paused to consider the effect of her tirade. It was indeed worthy of her oratory. Dudley Morey's knees shook, his head hung, his abject eyes were on the floor, and tears coursed down his pale cheeks.

"Get out!" she cried. "Get out of my room, before I kill you!"

He turned and stumbled blindly through the doorway.

A LONE, SHE RAGED up and down the room with the lethal, cushioned step of some great forest cat. Her lips were drawn back, revealing small, even teeth; her fists were clenched; her eyes burned with an intensity more eloquent than the tears that never came to them could have been. For fifteen minutes she paced the room. Then she flung open a closet door, caught up the first coat that came to her hand, a hat, and left the room, the confines of which seemed too small to hold her anger.

The maid was in the hall, dusting the balustrade; she looked at her mistress' passionate face with stupid surprise. Eloise passed her without a word, hardly seeing her, and descended the stairs. At the front door Eloise stopped suddenly. She remembered that when she had passed the library door she had seen a desk drawer standing open; and it had been the drawer in which Dudley's revolver was kept. She went back to the library. The revolver was gone.

She bit her lip thoughtfully. Dudley *must* have taken the revolver. Would he really kill himself? He always had been morbidly sensitive, and he had courage enough, if it came down to that, even if he was such a failure—such a fool at puddling with his paints. His inability to encompass success of one sort or another was the result of inordinate sensitiveness rather than anything else; and, taunted sufficiently, that sensitiveness could easily drive him to self-destruction. Suppose he did? What then? Wouldn't she— But, no! As likely as not he would bungle it somehow, as he had bungled everything else, and there would be a lot of unpleasant publicity, with her name displayed in not too flattering a light. Then, too, it would be hard upon her to think that she had driven him to it; though, of course, his failure with his work was more directly responsible. Still— She decided to go to his studio at once. That was the only thing to do. She couldn't telephone; he had no telephone in the studio. If she arrived in time she would stop him; and perhaps his attempt, or the bare intent, could be made to win the divorce he had refused her. Lawyers were clever at twisting things like that around to their clients' advantage. And if she arrived too late—well, she would have done her part. She knew her husband too well to doubt that she would find him in his studio.

She left the house and boarded a street car. The line ran past the building in which he had his studio, and she would get there sooner than if she called a taxicab.

She left the car at the corner above the studio and found herself running toward the building. The studio was on the fourth floor and there was not an elevator. She became excited as she climbed and her breath came with difficulty. The stairs seemed interminable. Finally she reached the top floor and turned down the corridor that led to Dudley's room. She was trembling now, and moisture stood out on her face and in the palms of her hands. She tried not to think of what she might see when she opened her husband's door. She came to the door and stopped, listening. No sound. Then she pushed the door open.

Her husband stood in the middle of the room, under the skylight with his back to the door. His right arm was raised in an awkward position: the elbow level with his shoulder, his forearm bent stiffly toward his head. Even as she divined the import of the pose, and screamed, "Dudley!" the air vibrated with the force of the explosion. Dudley Morey rocked slowly, once forward, once backward, and then crumpled face down upon the bare floor.

E LOISE CROSSED THE ROOM slowly; she felt surprisingly calm now that it was all over. Beside her husband she stopped; but she did not bend to touch the body; it was too repulsive in death for that. A hole gaped in one temple—ringed by a dark, burnt area. The revolver had fallen over against the wall, under a window.

She turned away with a feeling of disgust: the sight sickened her. She went to a chair and sat down. It was all over now.

On the table before her she saw an envelope addressed to her in Dudley's tiny handwriting. She tore it open and read the inclosed letter.

> *Dear Eloise—*
> *You are right, I suppose, about my being a failure.*
> *I can't give you up while I live—so I am doing the best*
> *I can for you. Between losing you and never succeeding*
> *in finding what I want in my painting I can't think of*
> *anything to live for anyway. Don't think that I am bitter,*
> *or that I blame you for anything, dear.*
> *I love you,*
>
> *Dudley.*

She read it through twice, her face flushing with chagrin. How like Dudley to leave this note to brand her as the cause of his death! Why could he not have shown some thought, some consideration of her position? It was fortunate that she had found it: what an idea it would have given anyone else! And then it would have got into the newspapers. As if she were responsible for his death!

She went to the little iron stove in the corner, in which a feeble coal fire burned, and thrust the letter in. Then she remembered the envelope and consigned it to the flames, too.

Several men and an old woman—apparently a char-woman—were at the door, turning curious glances from the man on the floor to the woman beyond. They edged into the room, grew bolder, and crowded around Dudley's body. Some of them mentioned his name as if recognizing him. A man whom Eloise knew—Harker, an illustrator and a friend of her husband's—came in, savagely routed the group around the dead man, and knelt beside him. Harker looked up and saw

Eloise for the first time. He got to his feet, took her by the arm with gentle force, and led her to his studio, on the floor below. He made her lie on the couch, spread a blanket over her, and left her. He returned in a few minutes and sat silently in a chair across the room, sucking at a great calabash pipe, and staring at the floor. She sat up, but he would not let her talk about her husband, for which she was grateful. She sat on the edge of the couch looking with cold, inscrutable eyes at her hands clasped about a handkerchief in her lap.

Some one knocked on the door and Harker called, "Come in."

A heavy, middle-aged man with a florid face and a bellicose black mustache came in. He did not seem to think it necessary to remove his hat, but his manner was polite enough, in a stolid way. He introduced himself as detective-sergeant Murray, and questioned Eloise.

She told him that her husband had been worrying over his lack of success with his painting; that he had seemed especially distraught that morning; that after he had gone she found his revolver was missing; that, fearing the worst, she had come to his studio, arriving just as he shot himself.

The detective asked further questions in his callous, albeit not unkindly, tone. She answered truthfully on the whole, though she told rather less than the complete truth here and there. Murray made no comment, and then turned his attention to Harker.

Harker had heard the shot, but was too engrossed with his work to pay immediate attention to it. Then the thought had intruded that the noise, which might have been made by something falling, had come from the vicinity of Morey's studio, and he had gone up to investigate. He said that Morey had seemed increasingly worried of late, but had never talked of himself or his affairs.

Murray left the room and returned after a few minutes accompanied by a man whom he introduced as "Byerly of the bureau."

"You'll have to go down to headquarters, Mrs. Morey," Murray said with a deprecatory gesture. "Byerly'll show you what to do. Just red tape. Only take a few minutes."

ELOISE LEFT THE BUILDING with Byerly. As he turned toward the corner past which the street-car line ran she suggested a taxicab. He telephoned from the corner drug store; and a few minutes later they were climbing the gray steps of the City Hall. Byerly led her through a door marked "Pawn-Shop Detail" and gave her a chair.

"Just wait a couple minutes here," he said. "I'll see if I can hurry things up."

Time dragged past. Half an hour. An hour. Two hours.

The door opened and Murray came in, followed by Byerly and a little fat man with a sparse handful of white hair spread over a broad pink scalp. Byerly called the fat man "Chief" when he pulled up a chair for him. The fat man and Byerly sat on chairs facing Eloise. Murray sat on a desk.

"Have you got anything to say?" Murray asked carelessly.

Her eyebrows went up. "I beg your pardon?"

"All right," Murray said without emotion. "Eloise Morey, you're arrested for the murder of your husband, and anything you say may be used against you."

"Murder!" she exclaimed, startled out of her poise.

"Exactly," Murray said.

Some measure of her assurance came back to her. She wanted to laugh, but instead she said haughtily, "Why, that's ridiculous!"

Murray leaned forward. "Is it?" he asked imperturbably. "Now listen. You and your husband ain't been on good terms for some time. This morning you had a peach of a battle. You said you wished he was dead, and you threatened him. Your servant girl heard you. Then after he left she saw you rush out, all worked up, and she saw you go to the drawer where the gun was kept. And she looked in the drawer after you was gone and the gun was gone, too. Two people saw you going up toward your husband's studio looking pretty wild, and they heard a woman's voice—an angry voice—just before the shot. And you admit yourself that you were in the room when your husband died. How is that? Still ridiculous?"

She had the sensation of a heavy net, sinuous, clammy, inescapable, closing about her.

"But people don't kill each other every time they have a little family quarrel—even if all you say were true. Murder is supposed to require a stronger urge than that, isn't it? And I told you about finding the revolver gone, and trying to get to his studio in time to save him, didn't I?"

Murray shook his head.

"Oh, I've got the 'strong urge' all right, Mrs. Eloise Morey. I found a batch of hot love letters, signed Joe, in your room, and some of 'em are dated as recent as yesterday. And I find that your husband was a Catholic, the same as I am, and I guess maybe just as set against divorces. And I also find that he's got a tidy bit of life insurance and an income of three or four thousand a year that you'd come into. I got enough motive all right."

Eloise struggled to keep her face composed—everything appeared to hinge upon that—but the threatening net seemed closer, and now it was not so much a net as a great smothering blanket. She closed her eyes for an instant, but it was not to be escaped that way. Rage burned within her. She stood up and her eyes glared into the three alert, impassionately complacent faces before her.

"You fools!" she cried, "You—"

She remembered the letter Dudley had left behind; the letter that would have told the truth unmistakably; the letter that would have cleared her in a twinkling, the letter she had burned in the little iron stove.

She swayed, tears of despair came to the hard grey eyes. Detective-sergeant Murray left his seat and caught her as she fell.

————————

WITH THIS STORY, Hammett once again struggles against the rituals of the traditional mystery story. This time he turns the mystery formula inside out:

1. The story structure is not that a crime happens and is unraveled, but that events happen and are misinterpreted as a crime.
2. Hammett retains the mystery cliché of the most obvious suspect (Eloise Morey) being legally innocent, but twists it so she is *morally* guilty, having purposely driven her husband Dudley to suicide.
3. Hammett shapes Mrs. Morey's feelings and behavior to distance our sympathy from her, inverting the mystery tradition of making the reader feel sympathy for an innocent accused person.
4. Hammett's third detective character, Detective-Sergeant Murray, sniffs out the clues just like detectives in formulaic mysteries, but unlike them, he interprets their significance all wrong.
5. The big surprise in this story comes from the accusation of murder, not from the traditional unmasking of the murderer.

The story also contains autobiographical echoes. Hammett's own wife "was a Catholic ... set against divorces," and Hammett wanted his own studio to work in like Dudley Morey's. He later rented one on San Francisco's Turk Street.

The next month's *Brief Stories* printed a letter from attorney Paul I. Mackey, of Vinita, Oklahoma: "The writer of 'The Joke on Eloise Morey' made out a perfect case of circumstantial evidence. In fact, it was the cleanest, clearest cut case of circumstantial evidence I can recall in story form. I want to congratulate the author of it."

That author must have felt grateful. As far as I can tell, Mackey's congratulation was the first comment printed anywhere about Hammett's writing.

Hammett had less gratitude for the Veterans' Bureau. It decided his health was nearly normal and stopped his monthly disability checks. Hammett was dismayed. His family needed that money. He wrote to the bureau protesting its new evaluation of his health. The bureau forwarded his file to the Board of Appeals, where it sat ignored. "The Joke on Eloise Morey" had earned about $26; without his disability checks, even writing and selling two such stories a month would not pay the Hammetts' bills.

He needed to increase his writing income. In the first half of 1923, he came up with a plan: he would develop and sell a series of stories about one detective. A detective series would be easier to write—he would not have to create everything from scratch for each new story—and because a successful detective series could build a loyal following, magazines might pay more per word for stories starring his series character. History was on Hammett's side. Sherlock Holmes had taken off only after Arthur Conan Doyle had written several stories about him. The same was true of other fictional detectives: from Martin Hewitt to Father Brown, they had built a following through a series of stories.

To create his new series character, Hammett drew from two sources. First, from his own former life working for a national detective agency. Second, from his contempt for what he found predictable and nonsensical about detective stories. He wrote that he deliberately made his character "neither the derby-hatted and broad-toed blockhead of one school of fiction, nor the all-knowing infallible genius of the other."

His new detective character was neither stupid nor brilliant, but a competent working man who liked his work and was proud of his competence. Hammett wrote what he knew, so he made his fictional detective a San Francisco op as he had been himself, working for Pinkerton's National Detective Agency, which he renamed the Continental Detective Agency. He even set Continental's San Francisco office in the same building where he had worked as a Pink. Hammett's new stories would be the first ever to take readers *inside* a detective agency, to show how an op worked as part of a nationwide firm.

Hammett's new creation is his reaction against other writers' clichés. The stereotypical detective was young, tall, and handsome. Instead, Hammett gives us a middle-aged man, short (five and a half feet), fat (more than 180 pounds), balding, and not handsome. As the character sarcastically describes himself, "My face doesn't scare children, but it's a more or less truthful witness to a life that hasn't been overburdened with refinement and gentility."

By the middle of 1923, Hammett had completed three or four stories featuring his wisecracking, energetic op. He seems to have sent them together to *The Black Mask*, then waited for a response. Would his new op character be bought or would he be rejected?

In the meantime, stories he had written earlier appeared. He remembered his days in San Diego and had put them to use by writing "Holiday," a story about a tuberculosis patient confined in a San Diego hospital who receives a day of freedom in Tijuana, Mexico.

The story appeared in a respectable literary magazine, *The New Pearsons*, in its July issue. One of his most autobiographical stories, it is his first to feature a *lunger*, a man afflicted with Hammett's own lung disease. He would later include lungers in short stories and nearly all of his novels. He even gives this lunger an $80 disability "cheque," the same amount that he was paid.

It is also his first to feature a hard-drinking character. (Later, Hammett introduced his hard-drinking detectives.) And it is his first to feature gambling, another recurrent feature in his writing, and, unfortunately, in his life. Drunkenness and compulsive gambling caused problems for Hammett throughout most of his life.

Richard Layman in *Shadow Man: The Life of Dashiell Hammett* observes that "'Holiday' is sensitive, yet unsentimental. It is perhaps the finest story of Hammett's first year as a writer."

Holiday

P AUL LEFT THE POST-OFFICE carrying his monthly compen-
sation cheque in its unmistakable narrow manila envelope
with the mocking bold-faced instructions to postmasters should
the addressee have died meanwhile, and hurried back along the
wooden walk to his ward, intent upon catching the physician
in charge before he left for the morning. The ward surgeon,
a delicately plump man in khaki, with a mouth permanently
puckered, perhaps by its habit of framing a mild, prolonged
"oh" whenever, as not infrequently happened, he could not find
the exactly adequate words, was just leaving his office.

"I'd like to go to town this afternoon," Paul said.

The doctor went back to his desk and reached for a pad of
pass blanks. This was a matter of routine; suitable words came
easily. "Have you been out this week?"

"No, sir."

The physician's pen scratched across paper and Paul turned
away waving in the air—to dry the ink, there never was a blotter
at hand—the slip which permitted Hetherwick, Paul, to be absent
from the United States Public Health Service Hospital No. 64
from 11 a.m. to 11 p.m. for the purpose of going to San Diego.

In the city he went first to a bank and exchanged the cheque for eight ten-dollar bills; then he filled his pockets with cigarettes and cigars and bought a racing program, studying it carefully, together with some figures in a memorandum book, while he ate luncheon.

He rode to Tijuana on the rear seat of an automobile stage, tightly wedged between a hatchet-faced tout who chewed gum unrestingly all the way and a large, perspiring, too-pink-and-yellow woman under a wide, limp hat. For a brief moment just beyond National City the savory fragrance of citrous fruits came into the car; for the rest of the trip his nostrils were busy with the unblending odors of spearmint, a heavy strawberry-like perfume from the woman beside him, burning oil, and the hot dust that scorched his throat and lungs and kept him coughing his sharp, barking cough.

He hurried through the gate at the race track and reached the betting ring just in time to place his bets on the first race: five dollars on "Step At a Time" to win and five to place. He watched the race from the rail in front of the paddock, leaning forward to peer nearsightedly at the horses. "Step At a Time" won easily and at the paying booths Paul received thirty-six dollars and some silver for his two colored tickets. He had not been especially stirred by either the race or the result: he had thought the horse would win without difficulty.

At the grandstand bar he drank a glass of whisky, then, consulting the penciled notes on his program, he bet ten dollars on Beauvis to win the second race. Beauvis finished second. Paul was not disappointed; that had been pretty close. His selection in the third race finished far in the rear; he won twenty-some dollars on the fourth, won again on the fifth, plunged a little on the sixth and lost. Between races he drank whisky at the grandstand bar, being served liquor of the same quality that was procurable north of the border and paying the same prices.

He had fourteen dollars in his pockets when he left the race track. The Casino was closed; he got into a dusty jitney and was driven to the Old Town.

He walked the length of the dingy street—a street that no mood of esthetic yea-saying could ever gild—and entered a saloon far down on the left-hand side, one that he had never visited before. A large, heavily muscled woman—she could easily, he thought, have been a blood relative of the woman in the automobile—broke off the song she was shouting to the nearly empty bar, linked a powerful arm through one of his, and said, "Come on over and sit down with me, honey; I want to talk to you."

He let her lead him to a booth—feeling a perverse delight in her utter coarseness—where she sat leaning heavily against him, one hand on his knee. He wondered what it would be like to lie in the arms of such a monster: middle-aged, bull-throated, grotesquely masked even under her tawdry garniture, manifestly without sex.

"You stick with me, dearie," she was saying, the words rolling out with a mechanical volubility and an absence of any attempt at glibness that testified to their too-frequent employment, "and I'll treat you right. You'll be a lot better off than you'd be fooling around with some of them sluts up the road."

He smiled and nodded politely. A sub-harlot, he decided, holding out false promises of her monstrous body to bring about that stimulation of traffic in liquor for which she was employed: a paradox, a sort of burlesque perhaps on a more familiar feminine attitude. The liquor he had drunk had fuddled him pleasantly, had clouded his never keen sight—though his eyes glowed brighter than usual—and had softened his speech. He bought several more drinks, amused by the keenness with which she watched the waiter, making sure that she received her metal tokens—upon which her commission was computed—for each order of drinks, and the naked greed with which she seized whatever change the waiter laid on the table.

He wondered after a while how much money he had left; it couldn't be much, and he must save from this enormity sufficient to buy a drink or two for the girl with the amazing red hair at the Palace. He motioned the waiter away.

"I'm flat," he told the woman. "They took me down the line at the track."

"Tough luck," she said, with facial sympathy, and began to grow restless.

"Run along and let me finish my drink," he suggested.

She grew confidential. "I'd like to, but once we girls start drinking with a man the boss makes us stay with him until he leaves."

He chuckled with joyful appreciation—he called that a neat arrangement—and got just a little unsteadily to his feet. She went to the door with him. "Be sure and come see me next time." He chuckled again at that, and then he felt an obscure shame: not at having squandered his few remaining dollars upon her, but at letting her think him so easily taken in.

"You've got me all wrong," he assured her, seriously. "I don't mind letting you take me for a ten or so when it's all I've got. Ten isn't much money one way or the other. But don't think I'm coming down here with a roll to let you—" Suddenly he saw himself standing in the doorway trying to justify himself to this monstrosity. He broke off with a clear, ringing laugh and walked away.

The girl with the red hair was dancing with a fat youth in tweeds to the achievements of a ferocious three-man orchestra when Paul entered the Palace. He waited, buying a drink for himself and one for a girl in soiled brown silk who had come over to his side and who kept saying over and over: "This is too good to be true! I been here a week and I can't believe it yet. Think of all this!" Her arm took in all the bottles behind which one wall was hidden.

The fat youth in tweeds disappeared presently and the girl with the red hair saw Paul, waited for his beckoning nod, and joined him.

"Hello."

"Hello."

They drank and he motioned toward the change the bartender had put before him. She took it with a casual thanks.

"How's the game go?" he asked.

"Pretty soft! And with you?"

"Not so good," he cheerfully complained. "The track knocked me over for most of what I had this afternoon."

She smiled sympathetically and they stood drinking slowly, close together but not touching, not talking very much, but smiling now and then with a certain definite delight each into the other's face. The clamor of the place, its garishness, were softened, nearly shut off from him by the pinkish alcoholic haze through which he regarded the world. But the girl's face, hair, figure, were clear enough to him.

He was filled with a strange affection for her: an affection that, though it was personal enough, had nothing of desire in it. Drunk as he undoubtedly was he did not want her physically. For all her beauty and pull upon his heart she was a girl who "hustled drinks" in a border town. That she might be a virgin— there wasn't anything impossible about that unlikely hypothesis: her profession didn't preclude it, even compelled continence during working hours—made no difference. It wasn't even so much that she was tainted by the pawing of strange hands—she had a freshness that had withstood that—as that in some obscure way the desires of too many men had rendered her no longer quite desirable. If he ever turned to a woman of this particularly sordid world it would be to some such monster as the one down the street. Given a certain turn of temper, there would be a savage, ghoulish joy in her.

He signalled the bartender again. They emptied their glasses, and he told her, "Well, I'm going to run along. I've got just about the price of a meal left."

"Won't you dance with me before you go?"

"No," he said, a warm feeling of renunciation flooding him, "you run along and get a live one."

"I don't care whether you've got any money or not," she said gravely. And then, resting one hand lightly on his sleeve, "Let me lend—"

He backed away shaking his head. "So long!" He turned toward the door.

The girl in soiled brown silk called out to him as he passed the end of the bar where she stood drinking with two men, "It's too good to be true!" He smiled courteous agreement and went out into the street.

He stood for a moment beside the door, leaning against the wall, looking at the hazy figures around him—servicemen from San Diego in the uniforms of three branches, tourists, thieves, people who defied classification, the Mexicans (special policemen, all of them, rumor said) standing along the curb, the dogs—tasting a melancholy disgust at the tawdriness of this place which he thought could so easily be a gay play-spot.

From the doorway of the saloon he had just left, a pale girl spoke listlessly: "Come on in and get happy."

He raised an arm in a doubtful gesture. "Look at 'em," he ordered sadly, "a flock of—" He thrust his hands into his trouser pockets and walked down the street grinning. He'd make a damned fool of himself yet!

A rack of picture post cards in the window of a curio shop caught his eye. He went in and bought half a dozen. Five of them he sent to friends in Philadelphia and New York. Over the sixth he pondered for some time: he could think of lots of people to send it to but he couldn't remember their addresses. Finally he sent it to a former casual acquaintance whom he hadn't seen since before the war but whose address he remembered because it was 444 Fourth Avenue. He penciled the same message on all six cards. "They tell me the States have gone dry."

In the street again he searched his pockets and counted his resources: eighty-five cents in silver and two return tickets: one from Tijuana to San Diego and the other from there to the hospital.

A husky voice whined at his elbow: "Say, buddy, can you give me the price of a cup of coffee?"

Paul laughed. "Fifty-fifty," he cried. "I got eighty-five cents. You get forty and we match for the odd nickel." He spun a coin in the air and was elated to find he had won. In an alley entrance across the street a San Diego stage was loading; he went over to it and sat beside the driver. He slumped down in the seat, half dozing through the ride back to the city, while behind him a girl with an undeveloped body and too-finely-drawn features sang a popular song in a thin, plaintive voice, and her companions—two sailors from the Pacific fleet—argued loudly some question having to do with gun-pointing.

Leaving the stage at its terminus, Paul walked up the side of the plaza to Broadway and turned toward a lunchroom where his forty-five cents would buy him a meal of sorts. Passing the entrance of the Grant Hotel he found himself in the center of a cluster of people and looking into the most beautiful face he had ever seen. He did not know he was staring until the beautiful face's escort in the uniform of a petty officer whispered to him, with peculiar, threatening emphasis: "Like her looks?"

Paul went on down the street slowly, turning the query over in his mind, wondering just what would be the mental processes of a man who under those conditions would ask that question in just that tone. He thought of turning around, finding the couple, and staring at the woman again to see what the petty officer would say then. But, looking back, he could not see them, so he went on to the lunch-room.

He found a cigar in his pocket after he had eaten, and smoked it during the ride back to the hospital. The fog-laden air rushing into the automobile chilled him and kept him coughing almost continuously. He wished he had brought an overcoat.

THE YEAR 1923 had begun with a burst of headlines about the Ku Klux Klan. The uproar had kicked off in January with articles in Hammett's hometown newspaper, *The Baltimore Sun*, exposing the reign of the Klan in Louisiana by terror, torture, and murder. In spite of overwhelming evidence, a Louisiana grand jury refused to indict Klan leaders. At the same time, the *New York World* exposed Klan activities in the North, where charges were filed, and a Klan grand dragon was convicted of murder.

The KKK was then at its peak size of five million members. It supported Prohibition. It opposed immigrants, pacifism, birth control, internationalism, Darwin's theory of evolution, Negroes, Catholics, Jews, and other religious and racial minorities—all views that made the Klan a frequent target of H. L. Mencken's satire.

So a KKK tale was an easy sale to Mencken. Hammett wrote this short-short story in the first half of 1923. It ran in the August issue of *The Smart Set*. Its author was listed as Mary Jane Hammett, Sam and Jose's not-quite-two-year-old daughter.

Except for one printing in a miniature book published only in a collector's edition limited to eighty-five copies, this is the story's first inclusion in a book.

It is a rare instance of a Hammett story featuring a child.

The Crusader

BERT PIRTLE FIDGETED IMPATIENTLY with his newspaper until the last loose thread had been severed by his wife's little sharp teeth, and with a gesture of finality she had taken off her thimble; then he bore the robe off to the bedroom.

Drawing it down over his head and shoulders before the bureau glass, he perceived that a miracle had taken place: suddenly, as the folds of the garment had settled, Bert Pirtle had been whisked away, was gone from this room wherein every night for seven years he had slept with his wife. In the place where he had been stood a stranger, though perhaps not a strange man, for the newcomer seemed rather a spirit, a symbol, than a thing of frail bone and flesh. The figure within the white robe—if figure it really was—loomed larger and taller than the vanished Bert Pirtle had ever been, and was for all its shapelessness more pronouncedly existent. Out of twin holes—neatly finished with button-hole stitching—in the peaked hood eyes burned with an almost ineffable glow of holy purpose. It was not a man that stood before the mirror now, but a spirit: the spirit of a nation, even a race.

As he stood there, not moving, Bert Pirtle saw a vision. In one of his old school-books had been a picture of a Crusader, a white surcoat bearing a large cross worn over his armor. He remembered the picture now, not only remembered it but faced it across the oak top of the bureau. For the first time he visualized that Crusader, realized the wonderful pageantry of the Crusades, really saw the flower of Christendom—separate identities lost within iron helms even as his own selfness was lost behind white sheeting—moving in a strangely clear white light toward Jerusalem.

Beyond the lone figure in the foreground the glass held long marching columns, massive phalanxes of men who were iron under their snowy robes with emblazoned scarlet crosses going out to meet the Saracen; sunlight glinting on weapons and trappings of gold and silver and on plumes and banners of green and crimson and purple; dust swirling behind and over-head. And somewhere in one of those sacred regiments was he who had once been Bert Pirtle but who now was simply—with an almost divine simplicity—a knight.

He was unused to dreams of such intensity—the Bert Pirtle who stood in front of the bureau mirror—his body quivered, he breathed gulpingly, perspiration started from his pores. Never had he known such exaltation, not even at the initiation the night before, when he had stood on Nigger Hill among a white-shrouded throng, grotesque in the light of a gigantic bonfire, listening to and repeating a long, strange, inspiring, and not easily comprehensible oath.

Presently the swirling dust blotted out the files of men in the mirror and then out of the saffron cloud came a single rider all in white upon a white charger—another who rode in a Cause. A second school-day memory came to the man who dreamed; under the white hood his mouth muttered a name. "Galahad!"

The bedroom door opened. A baby tripped over the sill, thudded in a heap on the floor, rolled into the room, and bounced to its feet with awkward lightness. The child's eyes widened at the sight of the figure before the bureau, two pink palms beat the air, a shriek of pure ecstasy came from its mouth. It tottered across the floor toward the man, gurgling joyously: "Peekaboo! Papa play peekaboo!"

———————

I LIKE HAMMETT'S HUMOROUS, homey touch of "buttonhole stitching" around the eyeholes.

Any ripples that his story might have made were dwarfed that August by the biggest news story of the year, set in San Francisco's Palace Hotel: On August second, President Warren G. Harding suddenly died. In the middle of the night, Vice President Calvin Coolidge was sworn in as president. Harding's notoriously corrupt administration and his active sex life gave rise to conspiracy and murder theories.

Harding's death indirectly pushed Mencken out of his editorship of The Smart Set. Mencken was already thinking of quitting; the publisher paid Hammett and its other authors, but he owed Mencken several months of back salary. The editors and the publisher of The Smart Set had tried to find a buyer for the money-losing magazine but failed. When Mencken and Nathan wrote a piece lampooning the dead president only a few days after he died, the publisher found it disrespectful and refused to print it. That was the last straw for Mencken, who had been talking with another publisher, Alfred A. Knopf, about starting a new magazine.

The next month, September, while Hammett was prodding the Veterans' Bureau Board of Appeals about his disability check—still without result—he would have found pleasant distractions in his mailbox: magazines with October cover dates, containing a total of five appearances by Hammett, more in one month than he ever achieved at any other time: three in *The Black Mask*, one in *Saucy Stories* (another pulp Mencken and Nathan had started and sold to raise cash), and one in *The Smart Set*.

The story in *The Smart Set* was, in fact, his last sale to that magazine. Called "The Green Elephant," it is set in Spokane and Seattle, where Hammett had lived three years before. The story's title is a variation on "white elephant," an object that is of little use to its owner, requiring much care, and difficult to dispose of.

When the story appeared, Hammett probably did not know he was about to lose his most frequent customer.

The Green Elephant

I

JOE SHUPE stood in the doorway of the square-faced office building—his body tilted slantwise so that one thin shoulder, lodged against the gray stone, helped his crossed legs hold him up—looking without interest into the street.

He had stepped into the vestibule to roll a cigarette out of reach of the boisterous wind that romped along Riverside avenue, and he had remained there because he had nothing better to do. In fact, he had nothing else to do just now. Tomorrow he would revisit the employment offices—a matter of a few blocks' walk along Main and Trent avenues, with brief digressions into one or two of the intersecting streets—for the fifth consecutive day; perhaps to be rewarded by a job, perhaps to hear reiterations of the now familiar "nothing in your line today." But the time for that next pilgrimage to the shrines of Industry, through which he might reach the comparative paradise of employment, was still some twenty hours away; so Joe Shupe loitered in the doorway, and dull thoughts began to crawl around in his little round head.

He thought of the Swede first, with distaste. The Swede—he was a Dane, but the distinction was too subtle for Joe—had come down to the city from a Lost Creek lumber camp with money in his pockets and faith in his fellows. When the men came together and formed their brief friendship only fifty dollars remained of the Swede's tangible wealth. Joe got that by a crude and hoary subterfuge with which even a timber-beast from Lost Creek should have been familiar. What became of the swindled Swede's faith is not a matter of record. Joe had not given *that* a thought; and had his attention been called to it he probably would have been unable to see in it anything but further evidence of the Swede's unfitness for the possession of money.

But what was vital to Joe Shupe was that, inspired by the ease with which he had gained the fifty dollars, he had deserted the polished counter over which for eight hours each day he had shoved pies and sandwiches and coffee, and had set out to live by his wits. But the fifty dollars had soon dribbled away, the Swede had had no successors; and now Joe Shupe was beset with the necessity of finding employment again.

Joe's fault, as Doc Haire had once pointed out, was that he was an unskilled laborer in the world of crime, and therefore had to content himself with stealing whatever came to hand—a slipshod and generally unsatisfactory method. As the same authority had often declared: "Making a living on the mace ain't duck soup! Take half these guys you hear telling the world what wonders they are at puffing boxes, knocking over joints, and the rest of the lays—not a half of 'em makes three meals a day at it! Then what chance has a guy that ain't got no regular racket, but's got to trust to luck, got? Huh?"

But Joe Shupe had disregarded this advice, and even the oracle's own example. For Doc Haire, although priding himself upon being the most altogether efficient house-burglar in the Northwest, was not above shipping out into the Coeur d'Alenes now and then to repair his finances by a few weeks' work in the mines. Joe realized that Doc had been right; that he himself was not equipped to dig through the protecting surfaces with which mankind armored its wealth; that the Swede's advent had been a fortuitous episode, and a recurrence could not be expected. He blamed the Swede now . . .

A commotion in the street interrupted Joe Shupe's unaccustomed introspection.

Across the street two automobiles were twisting and turning, backing and halting, in clumsy dance figures. Men began to run back and forth between them. A tall man in a black overcoat stood up in one of the cars and began shooting with a small-caliber pistol at indeterminate targets. Weapons appeared in the other automobiles, and in the hands of men in the street between the two machines. Spectators scrambled into doorways. From down the street a policeman was running heavily, tugging at his hip, and trying to free his wrist from an entangling coat-tail. A man was running across the street toward Joe's doorway, a black gladstone bag swinging at his side. As the man's foot touched the curb he fell forward, sprawling half in the gutter half on the sidewalk. The bag left his hand and slid across the pavement—balancing itself as nicely as a boy on skates—to Joe's feet.

The wisdom of Doc Haire went for nothing. With no thought for the economics of thievery, the amenities of specialization, Joe Shupe followed his bent. He picked up the bag, passed through the revolving door into the lobby of the building, turned a corner, followed a corridor, and at length came to a smaller door, through which he reached an alley. The alley gave to another street and a street-car that had paused to avoid a truck. Joe climbed into the car and found a seat.

Thus far Joe Shupe had been guided by pure instinct, and—granting that to touch the bag at all were judicious—had acted deftly and with beautiful precision. But now his conscious brain caught up with him as it were, and resumed its dominion over him. He began to wonder what he had let himself in for, whether his prize were worth the risk its possession had entailed, just how great that risk might be. He became excited, his pulse throbbed, singing in his temples, and his mouth went dry. He had a vision of innumerable policemen, packed in taxicabs like pullets in crates, racing dizzily to intercept him.

He got to the street four blocks from where he had boarded the street car, and only a suspicion that the conductor was watching him persuaded him to cling to the bag. He would have preferred leaving it inconspicuously between the seats, to be found in the car barn. He walked rapidly away from the car line, turning thankfully each corner the city put in his path, until he came to another row of car tracks. He stayed on the second car for six blocks, and then wound circuitously through the streets again, finally coming to the hotel in which he had his room.

A towel covering the keyhole, the blind down over the one narrow window, Joe Shupe put the bag on his bed and set about opening it. It was securely locked, but with his knife he attacked a leather side, making a ragged slit through which he looked into depths of green paper.

"Holy hell!" his gasping mouth exclaimed. "All the money in the world!"

II

HE STRAIGHTENED ABRUPTLY, listening, while his small brown eyes looked suspiciously around the room. Tiptoeing to the door, he listened again; unlocked the door quickly and flung it open; searched the dark hall. Then he returned to the black bag. Enlarging the opening, he dumped and raked his spoils out on the bed: a mound of gray-green paper—a bushel of it—neatly divided into little soft, paper-gartered bricks. Thousands, hundreds, tens, twenties, fifties! For a long minute he stood open-mouthed, spellbound, panting; then he hastily covered the pile of currency with one of the shabby gray blankets on the bed, and dropped weakly down beside it.

Presently the desire to know the amount of his loot penetrated Joe's stupefaction and he set about counting the money. He counted slowly and with difficulty, taking one package of bills out of its hiding place at a time and stowing it under another blanket when he had finished with it. He counted each package he handled, bill by bill, ignoring the figures printed on the manilla wrappers. At fifty thousand he stopped, estimating that he had handled one-third of the pile. The emotional seething within him, together with the effort the unaccustomed addition required of his brain, had by then driven his curiosity away.

His mind, freed of its mathematical burden, was attacked by an alarming thought. The manager of the hotel, who was his own clerk, had seen Joe come in with the bag; and while the bag was not unusual in appearance, nevertheless, any black bag would attract both eyes and speculation after the evening papers were read. Joe decided that he would have to get out of the hotel, after which the bag would have to be disposed of.

Laboriously, and at the cost of two large blisters, he hacked at the bag with his dull knife and bent it until, wrapped in an old newspaper, it made a small and unassuming bundle. Then he distributed the money about his person, stuffing his pockets and even putting some of the bills inside his shirt. He looked at his reflection in the mirror when he had finished, and the result was very unsatisfactory: he presented a decidedly and humorously padded appearance.

That would not do. He dragged his battered valise from under the bed and put the money into it, under his few clothes.

There was no delay about his departure from the hotel: it was of the type where all bills are payable in advance. He passed four rubbish cans before he could summon the courage to get rid of the fragments of the bag, but he boldly dropped them into the fifth; after which he walked—almost scuttled—for ten minutes, turning corners and slipping through alleys, until he was positive he was not being watched.

At a hotel across the city from his last home he secured a room and went up to it immediately. Behind drawn blinds, masked keyhole, and closed transom, he took the money out again. He had intended finishing his counting—the flight across the city having rekindled his desire to know the extent of his wealth—but when he found that he had bunched it, had put already counted with uncounted, and thought of the immensity of the task, he gave it up. Counting was a "tough job," and the afternoon papers would tell him how much he had.

He wanted to look at the money, to feast his eyes upon it, to caress his fingers with it, but its abundance made him uneasy, frightened him even, notwithstanding that it was safe here from prying eyes. There was too much of it. It unnerved him. A thousand dollars, or perhaps even ten thousand, would have filled him with wild joy, but this bale. . . . Furtively, he put it back in the valise.

For the first time now he thought of it not as money, —a thing in itself,—but as money—potential women, cards, liquor, idleness, everything! It took his breath for the instant—the thought of the things the world held for him now! And he realized that he was wasting time, that these things were abroad, beckoning, while he stood in his room dreaming of them. He opened the valise and took out a double handful of the bills, cramming them into his pockets.

On the steps descending from the office to the street he halted abruptly. A hotel of this sort—or any other—was certainly no place to leave a hundred and fifty thousand dollars unguarded. A fine chump he would be to leave it behind and have it stolen!

He hurried back to his room and, scarcely pausing to renew his former precautions, sprang to the valise. The money was still there. Then he sat down and tried to think of some way by which the money could be protected during his absence. He was hungry—he had not eaten since morning—but he could not leave the money. He found a piece of heavy paper, wrapped the money in it and lashed it securely, making a large but inconspicuous bundle—laundry, perhaps.

On the street newsboys were shouting extras. Joe bought a paper, folded it carefully so that its headlines were out of sight, and went to a restaurant on First avenue. He sat at a table back in one corner, with his bundle on the floor and his feet on the bundle. Then with elaborate nonchalance he spread the paper before him and read of the daylight holdup in which $250,000 had been taken from an automobile belonging to the Fourth National Bank. $250,000! He grabbed the bundle from the floor, knocking his forehead noisily against the table in his haste, and put it in his lap. Then he reddened with swift self-consciousness, paled apprehensively, and yawned exaggeratedly. After assuring himself that none of the other men in the restaurant had noted his peculiar behavior, he turned his attention to the newspaper again and read the story of the robbery.

Five of the bandits had been caught in the very act, the paper said, and two of them were seriously wounded. The bandits, who, according to the paper, must have had information concerning the unusually large shipment from some friend on the inside, had bungled their approach, bringing their own automobile to rest too far from their victim's for the greatest efficiency. Nevertheless, the sixth bandit had made away with the money. As was to be expected, the bandits denied that there was a sixth, but the disappearance of the money testified irrefragably to his existence.

From the restaurant Joe went to a saloon on Howard Street, bought two bottles of white liquor, and took them to his room. He had decided that he would have to remain indoors that night: he couldn't walk around with $250,000 under his arm. Suppose some flaw in the paper should suddenly succumb to the strain upon it? Or he should drop the bundle? Or someone should bump heavily into it?

He fidgeted about the room for hours, pondering his problem with all the concentration of which his dull mind was capable. He opened one of the bottles that he had brought, but he set it aside untasted: he could not risk drinking until he had safeguarded the money. It was too great a responsibility to be mixed with alcohol. The temptations of women and cards and the rest did not bother him now; time enough for them when the money was safe. He couldn't leave the money in his room, and he couldn't carry it to any of the places he knew, or to any place at all, for that matter.

III

H E SLEPT LITTLE that night, and by morning had made no headway against his problem. He thought of banking the money, but dismissed the thought as absurd: he couldn't walk into a bank a day or so after a widely advertised robbery and open an account with a bale of currency. He even thought of finding some secluded spot where he could bury it; but that seemed still more ridiculous. A few shovels of dirt was not sufficient protection. He might buy or rent a house and conceal the money on his own premises; but there were fires to consider, and what might serve as a hiding place for a few hundred dollars wouldn't do for many thousands. He must have an absolutely safe plan, one that would be safe in every respect and would admit of no possible loophole through which the money could vanish. He knew half a dozen men who could have told him what to do; but which of them could he trust where $250,000 was concerned?

When he was giddy from too much smoking on an empty stomach, he packed his valise again and left the hotel. A day of uneasiness and restlessness, with the valise ever in his hand or under his foot, brought no counsel. The gray-green incubus that his battered bag housed benumbed him, handicapped by his never-agile imagination. His nerves began to send little fluttering messages—forerunners of panic—to his brain.

Leaving a restaurant that evening he encountered Doc Haire himself.

"Hello, Joe! Going away?"

Joe looked down at the valise in his hand.

"Yes," he said.

That was it! Why hadn't he thought of it before! In another city, at some distance from the scene of the robbery, none of the restrictions that oppressed him in Spokane would be present. Seattle, Portland, San Francisco, Los Angeles, the East!

Although he had paid for a berth, Joe Shupe did not occupy it; but sat all night in a day coach. At the last moment he had realized that the ways of sleeping-cars were unknown to him—perhaps one was required to surrender one's hand baggage. Joe did not know, but he did know that the money in his valise was not going to leave his hands until he had found a securer place for it. So he dozed uncomfortably through the ride over the Cascades, sprawled over two seats in the smoking-car, leaning against the valise.

In Seattle he gained no more liberty than he had had in Spokane. He had purposed to open an account with each bank in the city, distributing his wealth widely in cautious amounts; and for two days he tried to carry out his plan. But his nervous legs simply would not carry him through the door of a bank. There was something too austere, too official, too all-knowing, about the very architecture of these financial institutions, and there was no telling what complications, what questioning, awaited a man inside.

A fear of being bereft of his wealth by more cunning thieves—and he admitted frankly now that there might be many such—began to obsess him, and kept him out of dance-hall, pool-room, gambling-house, and saloon. From anyone who addressed even the most casual of sentences to him he fled headlong. On his first day in Seattle he bought a complete equipment of bright and gaudy clothes, but he wore them for only half an hour. He felt that they gave him an altogether too affluent appearance, and would certainly attract the attention of thieves in droves; so he put them away in his valise, and thereafter wore his old clothes.

At night now he slept with the valise in bed beside him, one of his arms bent over it in a protecting embrace that was not unlike a bridegroom's, waking now and then with the fear that someone was tugging at it. And every night it was a different hotel. He changed his lodgings each day, afraid of the curiosity his habit of always carrying the valise might arouse if he stayed too long in any one hotel.

Such intelligence as he was ordinarily in possession of was by this time completely submerged beneath the panic in which he lived. He went aimlessly about the city, a shabby man with the look of a harried rabbit in his furtive eyes, destinationless, without purpose, filled with forebodings that were now powerless except to deepen the torpor in his head.

A senseless routine filled his days. At eight or eight-thirty in the morning he would leave the hotel where he had slept, eat his breakfast at a nearby lunch-room, and then walk—down Second to Yessler Way, to Fourth, to Pike—or perhaps as far as Stewart—to Second, to Yessler Way, to Fourth. . . . Sometimes he would desert his beat to sit for an hour or more on one of the green iron benches around the totem in Pioneer Square, staring vacantly at the street, his valise either at his side or beneath his feet. Presently, goaded by an obscure disquietude, he would get up abruptly and go back to his promenade along Yessler Way to Fourth, to Pike, to Second, to Yessler Way, to . . . When he thought of food he ate meagerly at the nearest restaurant, but often he forgot to eat all day.

His nights were more vivid; with darkness his brain shook off some of its numbness and became sensitive to pain. Lying in the dark, always in a strange room, he would be filled with wild fears whose anarchic chaos amounted to delirium. Only in his dreams did he see things clearly. His brief and widely spaced naps brought him distinct, sharply etched pictures in which invariably he was robbed of his money, usually to the accompaniment of physical violence in its most unlovely forms.

The end was inevitable. In a larger city Joe Shupe might have gone on until his mentality had wasted away entirely and he collapsed. But Seattle is not large enough to smother the identities of its inhabitants: strangers' faces become familiar: one becomes accustomed to meeting the man in the brown derby somewhere in the vicinity of the post office, and the red-haired girl with the grapes on her hat somewhere along Pine Street between noon and one o'clock; and looks for the slim youth with the remarkable mustache, expecting to pass him on the street at least twice during the course of the day. And so it was that two Prohibition enforcement officers came to recognize Joe Shupe and his battered valise and his air of dazed fear.

They didn't take him very seriously at first, until, quite by accident, they grew aware of his custom of changing his address each night. Then one day, when they had nothing special on hand and when the memory of reprimands they had received from their superiors for not frequently enough "showing results" was fresh, they met Joe on the street. For two hours they shadowed him—up Fourth to Pike, to Second, to Yessler Way . . . On the third round-trip, confusion and chagrin sent the officers to accost Joe.

"I ain't done nothing!" Joe told them, hugging the valise to his body with both arms. "You leave me be!"

One of the officers said something that Joe did not understand—he was beyond comprehending anything by now—but tears came from his red-rimmed eyes and ran down the hollows of his cheeks.

"You leave me be!" he repeated.

Then, still clasping the valise to his bosom, he turned and ran down the street. The officers easily overtook him.

Joe Shupe's story of how he had come into possession of the stolen quarter-million was received by everyone—police, press and public—with a great deal of merriment. But, now that the responsibility for the money's safety rested with the Seattle police, he slept soundly that night, as well as those that followed; and when he appeared in the courtroom in Spokane two weeks later, to plead futilely that he was not one of the men who held up the Fourth National Bank's automobile, he was his normal self again, both physically and mentally.

H. L. MENCKEN and George Jean Nathan decided they had had enough of their troubles with *The Smart Set.* On October 10, they issued a statement that they were resigning. New editors replaced them and quickly changed the magazine's style; Hammett made no more sales to it. His most frequent buyer was lost.

Fortunately, he landed a new frequent customer. *The Black Mask* said yes to his series of stories about an op who worked for the Continental Detective Agency. Three op stories ran in the October issues of the magazine. They were fast-paced, witty, and a joy to read. These Continental Op stories—together with poorly written but exciting detective stories that appeared earlier that year, written by ex-stenographer and former movie theater owner Carroll John Daly—ushered detective fiction into a new era.

Here is how Dennis Dooley describes the innovation in his 1984 book *Dashiell Hammett*:

"For it was in the work of Dashiell Hammett that the fictional detective reached self-consciousness. Before Hammett, the emphasis—for all the eccentricities of character indulged for the amusement of the reader—was on the solving of the crime. With Hammett, the detective himself—his aches and pains, his motives, values, feelings, and needs, his fears of growing old—has become the real subject."

David Geherin observes in his 1985 book *The American Private Eye: The Image in Fiction*,

"The cultured mannerisms of the Great Detective and the graceful style of the formal whodunit gave way to the tough-talking vernacular of the new hard-boiled mystery. In a significant departure from the past, these new mystery tales were narrated by the detective himself, and in his own words. No longer was there required a Boswell-like intermediary to record and deify the exploits of the master crime-solver. There was a new immediacy to these first-person narratives as the reader shared with the detective his successes and failures, doubts and determination. ... Prior to Daly and Hammett, mystery readers were invited to admire from afar the lofty accomplishments of the Great Detective, whose success was always a reminder to the reader of his own intellectual shortcomings. Now, thanks to Race Williams [Carroll John Daly's detective character] and the Op, readers could *identify* with rather than merely admire the accomplishments of the hero. ... For the first time since his creation by Poe, the detective was portrayed as a hero for the common man, and he has remained so ever since."

But all that critical adulation was years in the future. For right now, the important thing was that the combination of his Continental Op character and *The Black Mask* magazine gave Hammett's family a steady meal ticket.

The same month that the first Continental Op stories and "The Green Elephant" appeared, the following tale ran in *Saucy Stories*, a Mencken-Nathan pulp magazine that specialized in fiction that was considered risqué.

The Dimple

WALTER DOWE took the last sheet of the manuscript from his typewriter, with a satisfied sigh, and leaned back in his chair, turning his face to the ceiling to ease the stiffened muscles of his neck. Then he looked at the clock: three-fifteen. He yawned, got to his feet, switched off the lights, and went down the hall to his bedroom.

In the doorway of the bedroom, he halted abruptly. The moonlight came through the wide windows to illuminate an empty bed. He turned on the lights, and looked around the room. None of the things his wife had worn that night were there. She had not undressed, then; perhaps she had heard the rattle of his typewriter and had decided to wait downstairs until he had finished. She never interrupted him when he was at work, and he was usually too engrossed by his labors to hear her footsteps when she passed his study door.

He went to the head of the stairs and called:

"Althea!"

No answer.

He went downstairs, into all the rooms, turning on the lights; he returned to the second story and did the same. His wife was not in the house. He was perplexed, and a little helpless. Then he remembered that she had gone to the theater with the Schuylers. His hands trembled as he picked up the telephone.

The Schuylers' maid answered his call. . . . There had been a fire at the Majestic theater; neither Mr. nor Mrs. Schuyler had come home. Mr. Schuyler's father had gone out to look for them, but had not returned yet. The maid understood that the fire had been pretty bad. . . . Lots of folks hurt. . . .

Dowe was waiting on the sidewalk when the taxicab for which he had telephoned arrived. Fifteen minutes later he was struggling to get through the fire lines, which were still drawn about the theater. A perspiring, red-faced policeman thrust him back.

"You'll find nothing here! The building's been cleared. Everybody's been taken to the hospitals."

Dowe found his cab again and was driven to the City Hospital. He forced his way through the clamoring group on the grey stone steps. A policeman blocked the door. Presently a pasty-faced man, in solid white, spoke over the policeman's shoulder:

"There's no use waiting. We're too busy treating them now to either take their names, or let anybody in to see them. We'll try to have a list in the late morning edition; but we can't let anybody in until later in the day."

Dowe turned away. Then he thought: Murray Bornis, of course! He went back to the cab and gave the driver Bornis' address.

Bornis came to the door of his apartment in pajamas. Dowe clung to him.

"Althea went to the Majestic tonight, and hasn't come home. They wouldn't let me in at the hospital. Told me to wait; and I can't! You're a police commissioner; you can get me in!"

While Bornis dressed, Dowe paced the floor, talking, bab-
bling. Then he caught a glimpse of himself in a mirror, and
stood suddenly still. The sight of his distorted face and wild eyes
shocked him back into sanity. He was on the verge of hysterics.
He must take hold of himself. He must not collapse before he
found Althea. Deliberately, he made himself sit down; made
himself stop visualizing Althea's soft, white body charred and
crushed. He must think about something else: Bornis, for
instance. . . . But that brought him back to his wife in the end.
She had never liked Bornis. His frank sensuality, and his unsa-
vory reputation for numerous affairs with numerous women,
had offended her strict conception of morality. To be sure, she
had always given him all the courtesy due her husband's friend;
but it was generally a frigid giving. And Bornis, understanding
her attitude, and perhaps a little contemptuous of her narrow
views, had been as coolly polite as she. And now she was lying
somewhere, moaning in agony, perhaps already cold. . . .

Bornis caught up the rest of his clothes and they went down
to the street. He finished dressing in the taxicab.

They went to the City Hospital first, where the police
commissioner and his companion were readily admitted. They
walked down long rooms, between rows of groaning and writh-
ing bodies; looking into bruised and burned faces, seeing no one
they knew. Then to Mercy Hospital, where they found Sylvia
Schuyler. She told them that the crush in the theater had sepa-
rated her from her husband and Althea, and she had not seen
them afterward. Then she lapsed into unconsciousness again.

When they got back to the taxicab, Bornis gave directions
to the driver in an undertone, but Dowe did not have to hear
them to know what they were: "To the morgue." There was no
place else to go.

Now they walked between rows of bodies that were mangled horribly; denuded, discolored, and none the less terrible

because they could not scream. Dowe had exhausted his feelings: he felt no pity, no loathing now. He looked into a face; it was not Althea's; then it was nothing; he passed on to the next.

Bornis' fingers closed convulsively around Dowe's arm.

"There! Althea!"

Dowe turned. A face that stampeding leather heels had robbed of features; a torso that was battered and blackened and cut, and from which the clothing had been torn. All that was human of it were the legs; they had somehow escaped disfigurement.

"No! No!" Dowe cried.

He would not have this begrimed, mangled thing his exquisite white Althea!

Through the horror that for the moment shut Dowe off from the world, Bornis's vibrant, anguished voice penetrated—a shriek:

"I tell you it is!" Flinging out a hand to point at one smooth knee. "See! The dimple!"

HAMMETT WAS STILL NOT HEALTHY. His weight dropped to 131 pounds, and in October he returned to the hospital, where he was diagnosed with active pulmonary tuberculosis. His disability was set at fifty percent, and his disability pension was restored. He did not let his illness stop his writing. He and Jose did not go out and had few friends. His life was simple: his disease, his family, and his writing.

In its November issue, the pulp *Action Stories* ran Hammett's longest piece of fiction yet. Set in San Francisco and the town of Burlingame south of the City, it is an adventure story. It drops a small-fry working-class gambler into a fairy-tale struggle against an upper-class villain. The *Action Stories* editor introduced "Laughing Masks" as "a breath-taking tale of adventure and mystery that will whisk you out of a humdrum world of taxes and troubles!"

"Laughing Masks" features a standoff between people trapped in a confined space, a situation the claustrophobic Hammett uses in several stories. It is the first story to show Hammett's fascination with Russians, who appear often in his later fiction. It is also notable as a precursor of elements that Hammett develops further in his novels *The Maltese Falcon* and *The Glass Key*, and for its insights into the mindset of a compulsive gambler.

The Burlingame mansion in which much of the story is set seems to be based on a real house in Burlingame, in 1923 the headquarters of a well-known bootlegger. A photo of the house is included on pages 158-159.

This story was reprinted only once, in a heavily edited form in a 1962 paperback, which replaces Hammett's title "Laughing Masks" with the gambler's mantra: "When Luck's Running Good."

Laughing Masks

A SHRIEK, UNMISTAKABLY FEMININE, and throbbing with terror, pierced the fog. Phil Truax, hurrying up Washington street, halted in the middle of a stride, and became as motionless as the stone apartment buildings that flanked the street. The shriek swelled, with something violin-like in it, and ended with a rising inflection. Half a block away the headlights of two automobiles, stationary and oddly huddled together, glowed in the mist. Silence, a guttural grunt, and the shriek again! But now it held more anger than fear, and broke off suddenly.

Phil remained motionless. Whatever was happening ahead was none of his business, and he was a meddler in other people's affairs only when assured of profit therefrom. And, too, he was not armed. Then he thought of the four hundred dollars in his pocket: his winnings in the poker game he had just left. He had been lucky thus far tonight; mightn't his luck carry him a little further if he gave it the opportunity? He pulled his hat down firmly on his head and ran towards the lights.

The fog aided the headlights in concealing from him whatever was happening in the machines as he approached them, but he noticed that the engine of at least one was running. Then he skirted one of them, a roadster, checking his momentum by catching hold of a mudguard. For a fraction of a second he hung there, while dark eyes burned into his from a white face half hidden under a brawny hand.

Phil hurled himself on the back of the man to whom the hand belonged; his fingers closed around a sinewy throat. A white flame seared his eyeballs; the ground went soft and billowy under his feet, as if it were part of the fog. Everything—the burning eyes, the brawny hand, the curtains of the automobile—rushed toward him—

Phil sat up on the wet paving and felt his head. His fingers found a sore, swelling area running from above the left ear nearly to the crown. Both automobiles were gone. No pedestrians were in sight. Lights were shining through a few windows; forms were at many windows; and curious voices were calling questions into the fog. Mastering his nausea, he got unsteadily to his feet, though his desire was to lie down again on the cool, damp street. Hunting for his hat, he found a small handbag and thrust it into his pocket. He recovered his hat from the gutter, tilted it to spare the bruise, and set out for home, ignoring the queries of the pajamaed spectators.

Dressed for bed, and satisfied that the injury to his head was superficial, Phil turned his attention to the souvenir of his adventure. It was a small bag of black silk, trimmed with silver beads, and still damp from its contact with the street. He dumped its contents out on the bed, and a bundle of paper money caught his eye. He counted the bills and found they aggregated three hundred and fifty-five dollars. Pushing the bills into the pocket of his bath-robe, he grinned. "Four hundred I win and three hundred and fifty I get for a tap on the head—a pretty good night!"

He picked up the other articles, looked at them, and returned them to the bag. A gold pencil, a gold ring with an opal set in it, a woman's handkerchief with a gray border and an unrecognizable design in one corner, a powder-box, a small mirror, a lip-stick, some hairpins, and a rumpled sheet of note-paper covered with strange, exotic characters. He smoothed out the paper and examined it closely, but could make nothing out of it. Some Asiatic language, perhaps. He took the ring from the bag again and tried to estimate its value. His knowledge of gems was small, but he decided that the ring could not be worth much—not more than fifty dollars at the most. Still, fifty dollars is fifty dollars. He put the ring with the money, lit a cigarette, and went to bed.

CHAPTER II
The Mysterious Advertisement

PHIL AWOKE AT NOON. His head was still tender to the touch, but the swelling had gone. He walked downtown, bought early editions of the afternoon papers, and read them while he ate breakfast. He found no mention of the struggle on Washington street, and the Lost and Found columns held nothing pertaining to the bag. That night he played poker until daylight and won two hundred and forty-some dollars. In an all-night lunch-room he read the morning papers. Still nothing of the struggle, but in the classified section of the *Chronicle*:

> LOST—Early Tuesday morning, Lady's black silk
> bag trimmed with silver, containing money, ring,
> gold pencil, letter, etc. Finder may keep money
> if other articles are retuned to CHRONICLE
> OFFICE.

He grinned, then frowned, and stared speculatively at the advertisement. It had a queer look to it, this offer! The ring couldn't be worth three hundred dollars. He took it from his pocket, shielding it with his hand from the chance look of anyone in the lunch-room. No; fifty dollars would be a big price. The pencil, powder-box, and lip-stick case were of gold; but a hundred and fifty dollars, say, would more than replace everything in the bag. The undecipherable letter remained— that must be some important item! A struggle between a woman and some men at four in the morning, nothing about it in the newspapers, a lost bag containing a paper covered with foreign characters, and then this generous offer—it might mean almost anything! Of course, the wisest plan would be either to disregard the advertisement and keep what he had found, or to accept this offer and send everything but the money to the *Chronicle*. Either way would be playing it safe; but when a man's luck is running good he should crowd it to the limit. Times come, as every gambler knows, when a man gets into a streak of luck, when everything he touches proves fruitful; and his play then is to push his luck to a fare-you-well—make a killing while the fickle goddess is smiling. He thought of the men he had known who had paid for their timidity in the face of Chance's favor—men who had won dollars where they might have won thousands, men who were condemned to be pikers all their lives through lack of courage to force their luck when it ran strong, an inability to rise with their stars. "And my luck's running good," he whispered to the ring in his hand. "A thousand smacks in two days, after the long dry spell I've been through."

He returned the ring to his pocket and reviewed the chain of incidents leading up to the advertisement. Two facts that had lurked in his subconsciousness came out to face him: the shrieking voice had been musical even in its terror, and the eyes that had burned into his had been very beautiful, though he did not know what their owner's other features might be like. Two influencing elements; but the question at hand was whether the monetary reward in keeping with any danger that might ensue could be expected. He made up his mind as he finished his coffee.

"I'll sit in this racket, whatever it is, for a little while, anyway; and see what I can get myself."

CHAPTER III
Matching Wits

A T TEN O'CLOCK that morning Phil telephoned the office of the *Chronicle*, told the girl to whom he talked that he had found the bag but would return it to no one but its owner, and went back to bed. At two o'clock he got up and dressed. He returned the ring to the bag, with everything except the money, and went into the kitchen to prepare breakfast. He usually went out for his meals, but today he wanted to be sure that he would not miss whoever might telephone or call. He had scarcely finished his meal then the door-bell rang.

"Mr. Truax?"

Phil nodded and invited the caller in. The man who entered the flat was about forty years old, nearly as tall as Phil, and perhaps twenty-five pounds heavier. He was fastidiously groomed in clothes of a European cut, and a walking-stick was crooked over one arm.

He accepted a chair with a polite smile, and said, "I shall take but a moment of your time. It is about the bag that I have come. The newspaper informed me you had found it." He betrayed his foreignness more by the precision of his enunciation than by any accent.

"It is your bag?"

The caller's red lips parted in a smile, baring twin rows of even white teeth.

"It is my niece's, but I can describe it. A black silk bag of about this size"—indicating with his small, shapely hands—"trimmed with silver, and holding between three and four hundred dollars, a gold pencil, a ring—an opal ring—a letter written in Russian, and the powder and rouge accessories that one would expect to find in a young woman's bag. Perhaps a handkerchief with her initial in Russian on it. That is the one you found?"

"It might be, Mr. —"

"Pardon me, sir!" The visitor extended a card. "Kapaloff, Boris Kapaloff."

Phil took the card and pretended to scrutinize it while he marshaled his thoughts. He was far from certain that he cared to force himself into this man's affairs. The man's whole appearance—the broad forehead slanting down from the roots of the crisp black hair to bulge a little just above the brows; the narrow, widely spaced eyes of cold hazel; the aquiline nose with a pronounced flare to the nostrils; the firm, too-red lips; the hard line of chin and jaw—evidenced a nature both able and willing to hold its own in any field. And while Phil considered himself second to no man in guile, he knew that his intrigues had heretofore been confined to the world of tin-horn gamblers, ward-heelers, and such small fry. Small schooling for a game with this man whose voice, appearance and poise proclaimed a denizen of a greater, more subtle world. Of course, if some decided advantage could be gained at the very outset. . . .

"Where was the bag lost?" Phil asked.

The Russian's poise remained undisturbed.

"That would be most difficult to say," he replied in his cultured, musical voice. "My niece had been to a dance, and she carried several friends to their homes before returning to hers. The bag may have dropped from the car anywhere along the way." A temptation to speak of the struggle on Washington street came to Phil but he put it aside. Kapaloff might have been present that morning but it was obvious that he did not recognize Phil. The bag could have been found by someone who passed the spot later. Phil decided to leave Kapaloff in doubt on that point for as long as possible, in hope that some advantage would come out of it; and he was further urged to postpone the clash that might ensure by a faint fear of coming to a show-down with this suave Russian. Nothing would be lost by waiting. . . .

Kapaloff allowed a gentle impatience to tinge his manner. "Now about the bag?"

"The three hundred and fifty-five dollars is reward?" Phil asked.

Kapaloff sighed ruefully.

"I am sorry to say it is. Ridiculous, of course, but perhaps you know something of young women. My niece was very fond of the opal ring—a trinket, worth but little. Yet no sooner did she discover her loss than she telephoned the newspaper office and offered the money as reward. Ridiculous! A hundred dollars would be an exaggerated value to place upon everything in the bag. But having made the offer, we shall have to abide by it."

Phil nodded dumbly. Kapaloff was lying—no doubt of that—but he wasn't the sort that one baldly denounces. Phil fidgeted and found himself avoiding his visitor's eyes. Then a wave of self-disgust flooded him. "Here I am," he thought, "letting this guy bluff me in my own flat, just because he has a classy front." He looked into Kapaloff's hazel eyes and asked with perfect casualness, keeping every sign of what was going on in his brain out of his poker-player's face: "And how did the scrap in the automobiles come out? I didn't see the end of it."

"I am so glad you said that!" Kapaloff cried, his face alight with joyous relief. "So very glad! Now I can offer my apologies for my childish attempts at deception. You see, I wasn't sure that you had seen the unfortunate occurrence—you could have found the bag later—although I was told that someone had tried to interfere. You were not injured seriously?" His voice was weighted with solicitude.

None of the bewilderment, chagrin, recognition of defeat that raged in Phil's brain showed in his face. He tried to match the other's blandness. "Not at all. A slight headache next morning, a sore spot for a few hours. Nothing to speak of!"

"Splendid!" Kapaloff exclaimed. "Splendid! And I want to thank you for your attempt to assist my niece, even though I must assure you it was most fortunate you were unsuccessful. We certainly owe you an explanation—my niece and I—and if you will bear with me I shall try not to take up too much of your time with it. We are Russians—my niece and I—and when the tsar's government collapsed our place in our native land was gone. Kapaloff was not our name then; but what is a title after the dynasty upon which it depends and the holdings accruing to it are gone? What we endured between the beginning of the revolution and our escape from Russia I pray may never come to another!" A cloud touched his face with anguish, but he brushed it away with a gesture of one delicate hand. "My niece saw her father and her fiancé struck down within ten minutes. For months after that the real world did not exist for her. She lived in a nightmare. We watched her night and day for fear that she would succeed in her constant efforts to destroy herself. Then, gradually, she came back to us. For six months she has been, we thought, well. The alienists assured us that she was permanently cured. And then, late Monday night, she found between the pages of an old book a photograph of Kondra—he was her betrothed—and the poor child's mind snapped again. She fled from the house, crying that she must go back to Petrograd, to Kondra. I was out, but my valet and my secretary followed her, caught her somewhere in the city, and returned with her. The roughness with which your gallantry was met—for that I must beg your forgiveness. Serge and Mikhail have not yet learned to temper their zeal. To them I am still 'His Excellency,' in whose service anything may be done."

Kapaloff stopped, as if waiting for Phil's comment, but Phil was silent. His brain was telling him, over and over, "This bird has got you licked! The generosity of the reward isn't accounted for by this tale, but it will be before he's through. This bird has got you licked!"

His genial eyes still on Phil's, Kapaloff fulfilled the prophesy. "After my niece was safely home and I heard what had happened, I had the advertisement put in the paper. It seemed the most promising way of learning the extent of the injury to the man who had tried to aid my niece. If he were unhurt and had found the bag, he would turn it over to the *Chronicle*, and the three hundred and fifty dollars would be little enough reward for his trouble. On the other hand, if he were seriously injured he would use the advertisement to get in touch with me and I could take further steps to provide for him. If the bag were found by someone else I would remain in ignorance; but you will readily understand that I had no desire to have my niece's distressing plight paraded before the public in the newspapers."

He paused, waiting again.

When the pause had become awkward Phil shifted in his chair and asked, "And your niece—how is she now?"

"Apparently well again. I called a physician as soon as she returned, she was given an opiate and awoke that afternoon as if nothing unusual had happened. It may be that she will never be troubled again."

Phil started to get up from his chair to get the bag. There seemed to be no tangible reason for doubting the Russian's story—except that he did not want to believe it. But was the story flawless? He relaxed in the chair again. If the tale were true, would Kapaloff have dictated the advertisement so that the bag would be delivered to the *Chronicle*? Wouldn't he have wanted to interview the finder? The Russian was waiting for Phil to speak, and Phil had nothing to say. He wanted time to think this affair over carefully, away from the glances of the hazel eyes that were lancet-keen for all their blandness.

"Mr. Kapaloff," he said, hesitantly, "here is how all this stands with me: I saw the bag's owner and found it under—well—funny circumstances. Not," he interjected quickly, as Kapaloff's eyebrows rose coldly, "that your explanation is hard to believe; but I want to be sure I'm doing the right thing. So I'll have to ask you either to let me deliver the bag to your niece, or to go to the police, tell our stories, and let them straighten it out."

Kapaloff appeared to turn the offers over in his mind. Then he objected: "Neither alternative is inviting. The first would subject my niece to an embarrassing interview, and so soon after her trouble. The second—you should appreciate my distaste for the publicity that would follow the police's entry into the affair."

"I'm sorry, but—" Phil began, but Kapaloff cut him short by rising to his feet, smiling genially, with out-stretched hand.

"Not at all, Mr. Truax. You are a man of judgment. In your position I should probably act in like manner. Can you accompany to call upon my niece now?"

Phil stood up and grasped the dainty hand extended to him, and though the Russian's grip was light enough Phil could feel the swell of powerful muscles under the soft skin.

"I'm sorry," Phil lied, "but I have an engagement within half an hour. Perhaps you and your niece will be in the neighborhood within a few days and will find it convenient to call for it?" He did not intend dealing with this man on alien ground.

"That will do nicely. Shall we say, at three tomorrow?"

Phil repeated, "At three tomorrow," and Kapaloff bowed himself out.

Alone, Phil sat down and tried to torture his brain into giving him the solution of this puzzle; but he made little headway. Except in two minor instances the Russian's story had been impregnable. And those two details—the fact that he did not want the police dragged into the affair, and that he had worded the advertisement so as to retain his anonymity behind the screen of the newspaper—were not, upon close examination, very conclusive. On the other hand, insanity was notorious as a mask for villainy. How many crimes had been committed by use of the pretext that the victim, or the witnesses, were insane! Kapaloff's manner had been candid enough; and his poise had survived every twist of the situation, but . . . It was upon this last that Phil hung his doubts. "If that bird had contradicted me just once I'd believe him, maybe; but he was too damned agreeable!"

CHAPTER IV

Unwelcomed Visitors

PHIL RETURNED HOME early that night. The cards had failed to hold him, now that his mind was occupied with what threatened to be a larger, more intricate game. He puzzled over the letter in Russian, but its characters meant nothing to his eyes. He tried to think of someone who could translate it for him; but the only Russian he knew was not a man to be trusted under any circumstances. He tried to read a magazine, but soon gave it up and crawled into bed, to toss about, smoke numerous cigarettes, and finally drop off to sleep.

The least expert of burglars would have laughed at the difficulty and resultant noise with which the two men opened the door of Phil's flat; but not the most desperate of criminals would have found anything laughable in their obvious determination. They were bent upon getting into the flat, and the racket incidental to their bungling attacks on the lock disconcerted them not at all. It was evident they would force an entrance even if it were necessary to batter the door down. Finally the lock succumbed, but by that time Phil was flattened behind his bath-room door, with a pistol in his hand and a confident grin on his face. The crudeness of the work on the lock precluded whatever doubts of his ability to take care of himself he might ordinarily have had.

The outer door swung open but no light came through. The hall light had been extinguished. The hinges creaked a little, but Phil, peering through the slit between the bath-room door and the jamb, could see nothing. A whisper and an answer told him that there were at least two burglars. However noisy the men had been with the door, they were silent enough now. A slight rustling and then silence. Not knowing where the men were, Phil did not move. A faint click sounded in the bedroom, and a weak, brief reflection from a flash-light showed an empty passage-way. Phil moved soundlessly toward the bedroom. As he reached the door the flash-light went on again and stayed on, its beam fixed upon the empty bed. Phil snapped on the lights.

The two men standing beside the bed, one on either side, wheeled in unison and took a step forward, to halt before the menace of the weapon in Phil's hand. The men were very similar in appearance; the same bullet heads, the same green eyes under tangled brows, the same sullen mouths and high, broad cheek-bones. But the one who held a blackjack in a still uplifted hand was heavier and broader than the other, and the bridge of his nose was dented by a dark scar that ran from cheek to cheek, just under his eyes. For perhaps two seconds the men stood thus. Then the larger man shrugged his enormous shoulders and grunted a syllable to his companion. The momentary confusion left their faces, to be replaced by mated looks of resolve as they advanced toward Phil.

His brain was racing. Kapaloff's "secretary and valet," of course; and as their indifference to the noises they had made at the door testified to their determination to do what they had come to do at any cost, so now did their indifference to the pistol in Phil's hand. Close upon him as they were, he could hardly expect to drop both of them; but even if he did—the whole story would be bound to come out in the police investigation that must follow, and his chance of getting greater profit out of the affair would be blasted.

As the two men, working together like twin parts of a machine, contracted their muscles to spring, Phil hit on a way out. He leaped backward through the bedroom door, whirled, and jumped into the hall, shouting: "Help! Police!"

There was a snarling at the door, a scuffling, and the noise of two men running through the dark hall toward the front door. The laughter that welled up in Phil's throat silenced his shouts; he fired his pistol into the floor and returned to his bedroom. He laid a chair gently on its side and swept some books and papers from the table to the floor. Then he turned with a wide-eyed semblance of excitement to welcome the callers in various degrees of negligée who came in answer to his bellowing. After a while a policeman came and Phil told his story.

"A noise woke me up and I saw a man in the room. I grabbed my gun and yelled at him, but I forgot to take the safety catch off the gun." With sham sheepishness: "I guess I was kind of scared. He ran out in the hall with me after him. I remembered the safety, then, and took a shot at him, but it was too dark to see whether I hit him. I looked through my stuff and don't think he got anything, so I guess no harm's done."

After the last question had been answered and the last caller had gone, Phil bolted the door and shook hands with himself. "Well, that fixes Mr. Kapaloff's story. And you've got him faded to date, my boy, so don't let me catch you letting him run a bluff on you again."

CHAPTER V
Forcing His Luck

A T FIVE MINUTES PAST THREE Thursday afternoon the Kapaloffs arrived. Romaine Kapaloff acknowledged her uncle's introduction in easy and faultless English, and thanked Phil warmly for his efforts in her behalf Tuesday morning. Phil found himself holding her hand and straining his self-possession to the utmost to keep from gaping and stammering. The girl—she couldn't have been more than nineteen—was looking up through brown eyes that glowed now with friendliness and gratitude into Phil's grey ones, and asking: "And you really weren't hurt?"

To Phil she seemed the loveliest creature he had ever seen. His attempts at extortion seemed mean and sordid. Because he was bitterly ashamed of his attempt to wring profits from her uncle, and was badly rattled, he answered almost gruffly; and in his effort to keep the chaos within him from his face he made it a mask of stupidity.

"Not at all. Really! It was nothing."

Kapaloff stood watching them with the smile of one who sees his difficulties dissipated. Finally their hands fell apart and they sought chairs. There was an awkward pause. Phil knew that though they sat there until nightfall he could not bring up the question of the girl's sanity, demand the corroboration of her uncle's story, which was the excuse for the meeting.

Kapaloff said nothing, sat smiling benignly upon girl and boy. The girl glanced at her uncle, as if expecting him to open the conversation, but when he ignored her silent appeal she turned impulsively to Phil, putting out her hand.

"Uncle Boris told you about my—about the trouble?"

Phil nodded, started to reach for the extended hand, thought better of it, and twined his fingers together between his knees.

"Then you know how fortunate it was that your gallantry wasn't successful. I can't understand why you didn't laugh at Uncle Boris' story—it must have sounded fantastic to you. But— Oh, it is horrible! I can never trust myself again, no matter what the doctors say!"

Phil found that he was holding her hand, after all. He looked at Kapaloff, who was smiling sympathetically. Phil and the girl stood up, and for an instant her eyes held a baffling undertone of pleading. Then it was gone, and she was turning to her uncle. Phil had but one idea in his mind now: to hand over the bag, get rid of these people, and be alone with his shame and disgust. He moved toward the door. "I'll get the bag," he said in a tired, weak voice.

A silver purse that dangled from the girl's wrist clattered to the floor. As Phil turned his head at the sound, Kapaloff bent to pick up the purse, and Romaine Kapaloff's eyes met Phil's. For an infinitesimal part of a second her eyes burned into his as they had Tuesday morning, and stark terror wiped out the smooth young beauty of her face. Then her uncle was holding out the purse, her face was composed again, and Phil was walking toward his bedroom door with blood pounding in his temples. He sat on the top of his trunk, gnawed a thumb-nail, and thought desperately. Then he took the bag from the trunk and thrust it under his coat and returned to his guests.

"It is gone."

Kapaloff's urbanity seemed about to desert him. His face darkened and he took a swift step forward. Then he was master of himself again, and was asking pleasantly, "Are you positive?"

"You may look if you like."

Phil went to the telephone and a few seconds later was talking to the desk sergeant at the district police station.

"A burglar got in here last night. One of your men was in afterward, and I told him I hadn't missed anything. Now I find that a lady's handbag is gone. All right."

He turned from the telephone to the Kapaloffs.

"I woke up some time this morning and found two burglars in the room. They escaped, and I thought everything was safe. I forgot about the bag, and didn't look to see if it was still here. I am sorry."

Neither of the Kapaloffs gave any indication of previous knowledge of the burglary. Boris Kapaloff said evenly, "Very unfortunate, but the bag and its contents were not so valuable that we should worry unduly over the loss."

"I am going to the police station this afternoon to give a description of the bag. Shall I tell them that it is your property and have them turn it over to you?"

"If you will be so kind. Our address is, La Jolla Avenue, Burlingame."

Conversation lagged. Several times Kapaloff seemed about to speak, but each time he restrained himself. The girl's eyes, when Phil met them, held a question which he made no attempt to answer. The Kapaloffs departed. Phil shook hands with both of them, answering the girl's unspoken question with a quick pressure.

When they were gone, he withdrew the bag from under his vest, counted three hundred and fifty-five dollars from the bills in his pocket, and put the money in the bag. Then he drew a deep breath. That was the end of three years of searching for an "easy living." Since his discharge from the army he had been drifting, finding himself at odds with the world, gambling, doing chores for political factors—never doing anything very vicious, perhaps, but steadily becoming more and more enmeshed in the underworld. As he looked back now, with the memory of his shame and self-disgust of a few minutes ago still fresh, he thought that he would not feel quite so worthless if there had been some outstanding crime in his past, instead of a legion of petty deeds. Well, that was past! After this tangle came to an end he would get a job and go back to the ways he had known before the war interrupted his aspirations.

He wrapped the bag in heavy paper, tied it, and sealed it securely. Then he took it downtown and turned it over to the friendly proprietor of a poolroom to be put in the safe.

For two days Phil kept to his rooms—days in which he sprang to the telephone at the first tingling of the bell. He tried to reach Romaine Kapaloff by telephone, got her house, and was told by a harsh voice in broken English that she was not at home. Three times he tried it, but the results were the same. Then he tried to talk to her uncle, and got the same answer. On the second night he slept hardly at all. He would doze and then spring into wakefulness, imagining that the bell had sounded, race to the telephone, to be asked, "What number are you calling?"

Then he decided to wait no longer. When a man's luck is running good he should force the issue—not wait in idleness until his fortunes turn.

CHAPTER VI
"Flashing, Dripping Jaws"

I N Burlingame Phil easily found the Kapaloffs' house. At the first garage where he inquired, the name was unknown, but they knew where "the Russians" lived. Even in the dark he had no difficulty in recognizing the house from the garage-man's description. He drove past it, left his borrowed car in the darkest shadow he could find, and returned afoot. The building loomed immense in the night, a great gray structure set in a park, ringed about by a tall iron fence overgrown with hedging. The nearest house was at least half a mile away.

No light came from the house, and Phil found the front gate locked. He crossed the road and squatted under a tree some two hundred feet away. His plan involved nothing further than waiting in the vicinity until he saw Romaine, found some means of communicating with her, or found an avenue through which his luck could carry him toward a solution of whatever mystery existed in the house across the road. The chances were that Romaine was a prisoner; otherwise she would have got word to him before this. His watch registered 10:15.

He waited.

When his watch said 1:30 his youth and his faith in his luck overcame his patience. A man might as well be home in bed as sitting out here waiting for something to turn up. When a man's luck is running good . . . He skirted the hedge-grown fence until he found a tree with a branch that grew over the barrier. He climbed the tree, crawled out on the overhanging limb, swung for a minute, and dropped. He landed on hands and knees in

"The nearest house was at least half a mile away."
Photo by Gabriel Moulin courtesy Burlingame Historical Society.
Copyright © 2005 Moulin Archives

soft, moist loam. Carefully he moved forward, keeping a cluster of bushes between himself and the house. When he reached the bushes he halted. Nothing that might serve to conceal him was between the bushes and the building, and he was afraid to trust himself out in the pale starlight. He sat on his heels and waited.

Three-quarters of an hour passed, and then he heard the sound of metal scraping against wood. He could see nothing. The sound came again and he identified it: someone was opening a shutter, cautiously, stopping at each sound the bolt made. A babel of dogs' voices broke out at the rear of the house, and around the corner swept a pack of great hounds, to throw themselves frenziedly against one of the lower windows.

Phil heard the shutter slam sharply. In the wake of the dogs a man stumbled. The shutter opened and Kapaloff leaned out to speak to the man in the yard. Above the men's words Phil heard Romaine Kapaloff's voice, raised in anger. In the rectangle of light shining from the window six wolfhounds were twisting and leaping—not the sedate, finely bred borzois of my lady's promenade; but great, shaggy wolf-killers of the steppes, over half a man's height from ground to shoulder, and more than a hundred pounds each of fighting machinery. Phil held his breath, shrunk behind his screen, and prayed that what he had heard somewhere of these wolfhounds hunting by sight and not by scent be true, that his presence escape their noses. Kapaloff withdrew his head and closed the shutter. The man in the yard shouted at the dogs. They followed him to the rear of the house. A door closed, shutting off the dogs' voices. Phil was damp with perspiration, but he knew that the dogs were kept indoors.

From an upper story came a muffled scream and a sound of something falling against a shutter. Then silence. The sound had come from the front of the house, Phil decided; the corner room on the third floor, at a guess.

For a moment Phil was tempted to leave the place and enlist the services of the police; but he was not used to allying himself with the police—on the few occasions when he had had dealings with the law he had found it on the other side. Then, too, would not the glib Kapaloff have the advantage of his aristocratic manner, his standing as a property holder, and his seemingly secure position in the world? Against all this Phil would have but his bare word and a vague story, backed by three years of living without what the police call "visible means of support." He could imagine what the outcome would be. He would have to play this hand out alone. Well, then . . .

He left the protecting bush and crept to the front of the house. Around the corner he paused to scan the building. So far as he could determine in the dark every window was fitted with a shutter. He was afraid to try the shutters on the first floor; but it was unlikely that one of them would have been left unbolted, anyway. The upper windows held out the best promise of an entrance. He crept up on the porch, removed his shoes, and stuck them in his hip pockets. Mounting the porch-rail, he encircled a pillar with arms and legs and pulled himself up until his fingers caught the edge of the porch-roof. Silently he drew himself up and lay face down on the shingles. No sound came from house or grounds. On hands and knees he went to each of the four windows and tried the shutters. All were securely fastened.

He sat up and studied the third-story windows. The window on the extreme left should open into the room from which the last noises had come—Romaine Kapaloff's room, if his reasoning was correct. A rainspout ran up the corner of the house, within arm's length of the window. If the spout would support him, he could reach the window and risk a signal to the girl. He crawled over and inspected the spout, testing it with his hands. It shook a little but he decided to risk it.

He found a niche for the stockinged toes of one foot, drew himself up, reached for a higher hold on the spout with his hands, and felt for a support for the other foot. There was a tearing noise, a rattle of tin, and Phil thumped to the roof of the porch with a length of pipe in his hands. He rolled over, let go the spout, and caught at the roof in time to keep from going over the edge. The released piece of tin hit the roof with a clang and rolled over the edge to clatter madly on the paved walk.

The night was suddenly filled with the snarling of hounds. The pack careened around the corner, flung themselves against the porch, tore up and down the yard—lithe, evil shapes in the starlight, with flashing, dripping jaws. Peeping over the edge of the roof, Phil saw a man following the dogs, a gleam of metal in his hands.

A sound came from behind Phil. A second-story shutter was being opened. He wormed his way to it and lay on his back under it, close to the wall. The shutter swung open and a man leaned out—the man with the scarred face. Phil lay motionless, not breathing, his body tense, a forefinger tight around the trigger of his pistol, the pistol's muzzle not six inches from the body slanting over him. The man called a question to the one in the yard. The front door opened, and Kapaloff's easy voice sounded. The man at the window and the man in the yard called to Kapaloff in Russian; he answered. Then the man at the window withdrew, his footsteps receded, and a door closed within the room. The window remained open. Phil was over the sill in an instant, and in the dark room. As his feet touched the floor he sensed something amiss, heard a grunt, and lunged blindly forward. The room filled with dancing lights, and there was a roaring in his ears. . . .

CHAPTER VII

The Third Degree

PHIL AWOKE with his nostrils stinging from ammonia administered by the man with the scarred face. Phil tried to push the bottle away, but his hands were lashed. His feet, too, were tied. He looked around, turning his head from side to side. He was lying on a bed in a luxuriously furnished chamber, fully clothed except for coat and shoes. Kapaloff stood across the room, looking on with a smile of mild mockery. On one side of the bed stood the man with the scar; on the opposite side, the other man who had entered Phil's flat. At a word from Kapaloff this man assisted Phil to a sitting position.

Phil's head ached cruelly and his stomach felt queerly empty, but taking his cue from Kapaloff, he tried to keep his face composed, as if he found nothing disconcerting in his position. Kapaloff came over to the bed and asked solicitously: "You are not seriously injured this time either, I trust?"

"I don't think so. But if these hired men of yours keep it up they'll wear my head away," Phil said lightly.

Kapaloff exhibited his teeth in an affable smile. "You are the fortunate possessor of a tough head. But I hope it will not prove as little amenable to persuasion as it has been to force."

Phil said nothing. Every iota of his will was needed to keep his face calm. The pain in his head was unbearable. Kapaloff went on talking, his voice a mixture of friendliness and banter.

"Your tenacity in clinging to the bag would, under other circumstances, be admirable; but really it must be terminated. I must insist that you tell me where it is."

"Suppose my head stays tough on the inside, too?" Phil suggested.

"That would be most unfortunate. But you are going to be reasonable, aren't you? When you stumbled into this affair you saw, or suspected, much that did not appear on the surface—being an extremely perspicacious young man—and thought you could unearth whatever was hidden and exact a little—well—not blackmail, perhaps, though a crude intellect might call it that. Now, you must see that I have the advantage; and assuredly you are enough the sportsman to acknowledge defeat, and make what terms you can."

"And what are the terms?"

"Turn the bag over to me and sign a few papers."

"Papers for what?"

"Oh! the papers are unimportant. Merely a precaution. You will not know what they contain exactly—just a few statements supposedly made by you: confessions to certain crimes, perhaps—to insure me that you will not trouble the police afterward. I am frank. I do not know where you have put the bag. After you so obligingly entered the window that Mikhail left open for you, Mikhail and Serge visited your rooms again. They found nothing. So I offer terms. The bag, your signature, and you receive five hundred dollars, exclusive of the money that was in the bag."

"Suppose I don't like the terms?"

"That would be *most* unfortunate," Kapaloff protested. "Serge"—motioning toward the man who had helped Phil sit up—"is remarkably adept with a heated knife; and remembering the ludicrous manner in which you put him and Mikhail to rout, I fancy he would relish having you as a subject for his play."

Phil turned his head and pretended to look at Serge, but he scarcely saw the man. He was trying to convince himself that this threat was a bluff, that Kapaloff would not dare resort to torture; but his success was slight. If his ability to read men was of any value at all then this Russian was one who would stop at nothing to attain his ends. Phil decided he would not submit to any excruciating pain to save the bag. In the first place, he did not know how valuable the paper might be; secondly, he seemed to be the girl's only ally, and he flattered himself that he was more valuable an aid than a letter could be. However, he would fight to the last inch—bluff until the final moment.

"I can't make terms until I talk with your niece."

Kapaloff expostulated gently but firmly. "That is not possible. I am sorry, but you must understand that my position is very delicate, and I cannot permit it to become more complicated."

"No talk, no terms," Phil said flatly.

Kapaloff let his distress furrow his brow. "Think it over. You must know that I shall not be pleased by the necessity of making you suffer. In fact"—with a whimsical smile—"Serge will be the only participant who enjoys it."

"Bring on the knife," Phil said coolly. "No talk, no terms."

Kapaloff nodded to Serge, who left the room.

"There is no hurry—a few minutes' delay doesn't matter," Kapaloff urged. "Consider your position. Think! Under Serge's skilled hands you will tell—do not doubt it—but then you lose the extra five hundred dollars, besides causing me no little anguish—to say nothing of your own plight."

Phil's smile matched Kapaloff's for affability. "It would be just wasting time. If I can't see Miss Kapaloff I'll stand pat."

Serge returned with an alcohol-lamp and a small poniard. He set the lamp on the table, lit it, and held the blade in the flame. Phil watched the preparations with a face that was tranquil. He noticed, suddenly, that the hand holding the poniard trembled, and, raising his eyes, he saw tiny globules of moisture glistening on Serge's forehead. His face was haggard, with white lines around the mouth. Mikhail put Phil down on the bed again, gripping his ankles firmly. Phil said nothing. He was beginning to enjoy himself—knowing that he could stop the whole thing with a word. Serge's knees were trembling noticeably now; and Mikhail's fingers around Phil's ankles jerked and were moist with perspiration.

Phil grinned and spoke banteringly to Kapaloff: "You should rehearse these men of yours. I bet their torturing is not better than their burglary."

Kapaloff chuckled good-naturedly. "But you must consider that a bungling torturer may obtain effects that are beyond a skilled one."

Then Serge came to the bed, the poniard glowing in his shaking hand.

Phil spoke casually: "If you don't mind, I'd like to sit up and watch this."

"Certainly!" Kapaloff assisted him to a sitting position. "Is there anything else I can do to make it more bearable?"

"Thanks, no. I can manage nicely now."

Serge was extending the heated dagger toward the soles of Phil's feet, from which Mikhail had removed the stockings. The blade was wavering in the man's nervous hands; his eyes were bulging, and his face was wet with perspiration. Mikhail's fingers were pressing into Phil's ankles, grinding the flesh painfully; both of Kapaloff's assistants were breathing hoarsely. Phil forced himself to disregard the pain of Mikhail's grip, and smiled derisively. The point of the poniard was within an inch of his feet. Then Serge let it fall to the floor, and shrank back from the bed. Kapaloff spoke to him. Slowly Serge stooped for the poniard, and went to the lamp to reheat it, his body quivering as with ague.

He came to the bed again, his teeth clenched behind taut, bloodless lips. He bent over the bed, and Phil felt the heat of the approaching blade. Lazily he glanced at Kapaloff, carrying his acting to its pinnacle just before surrendering. Then, with a choking cry, Serge flung the poniard from him and dropped on his knees before Kapaloff, pleading pitifully. Kapaloff answered with exaggerated gentleness, as one would speak to an infant. Serge got to his feet slowly, and backed away, his head hanging. One of Kapaloff's hands came out of his pocket, holding a pistol. The pistol spat flame. Serge caught both hands to his body, and crumpled to the floor.

Kapaloff walked unhurriedly to where the man had fallen, put the toe of one trim shoe under Serge's shoulder, and turned him over on his back. Then, the pistol hanging loosely at his side, he sent four bullets into Serge's face, wiping out the features in a red smear.

Kapaloff turned and looked, with eyes that held nothing but polite expectation, at Mikhail. Mikhail had released Phil's ankles at the first shot, and now stood erect, his hands at his sides. His chest was moving jerkily and the scar across his face was crimson; but his eyes were fixed upon the wall and his face was wooden. For a full minute Kapaloff looked at Mikhail, and then turned back to the figure at his feet. A drop of blood glistened on the toe of the shoe with which he had turned the man over. Carefully he rubbed the foot against the dead man's side until the blood was gone. Then he spoke to Mikhail, who lifted the lifeless form in his powerful arms and left the room.

Kapaloff pocketed his pistol, and a courteously apologetic smile appeared on his face; as if he were a housewife who had been compelled to rebuke a maid in the presence of a guest. Phil was sick and giddy with horror, but he forced himself to accept the challenge of the smile, and said with a fair semblance of amusement: "You shouldn't have misinformed me about Serge's love for the hot knife."

Kapaloff chuckled. "The persuasion is postponed until tomorrow. I am afraid I shall have to leave you bound. Ordinarily I should simply leave Mikhail to guard you; but I am not sure that I can trust him now. Serge was his brother."

He picked up the lamp and the poniard.

"The distressing scene you have just seen should at least convince you of my earnestness." Then he left the room and the key turned in the lock.

CHAPTER VIII
Double-Crossed

PHIL ROLLED OVER and buried his face in the bed; giving away to the sickness he had fought down in Kapaloff's presence. He lay there and sobbed, not thinking, weak and miserable. But he was too young for this to last long; and his first thought was a buoying one: the torturing had been interrupted at the last moment, almost miraculously! His luck held!

He worked himself into a sitting position and attempted to loosen the cords around his wrists and ankles. But he only drove them deeper into the flesh, so he gave it up. He wormed his way to the floor and slowly, laboriously went over the room in the dark, hunting for something that would serve to free him, but he found nothing. The shutters were bolted and padlocked; the door was massive. He returned to the bed.

Time passed—hours he had no means of counting—and then the door opened and Mikhail came in, with a tray of food in his hands, followed by Kapaloff who went to a window and stood with his back to it while Mikhail set the tray on the table and untied Phil.

Kapaloff gestured toward the table. "I am sorry I cannot offer you greater hospitality, but my household is disorganized. I trust you will find my humble best not too uninviting."

Phil drew a chair to the table and ate. His appetite was poor, but he forced himself to eat with every appearance of enjoyment. When the food was disposed of he lighted one of the cigarettes on the tray and smiled his thanks.

"Unless you have reconsidered," the Russian said, "I regret that you will have to sleep tied. I am sorry, but I find myself in a position where I must not let my regard for you and my sense of what is due a guest outweigh the necessity of protecting my interests."

Phil shrugged. The food had heartened him, and he was too young not to meet the challenge of his captor's manner.

"I'm tough. Mind if I stretch my legs first?"

"No, no! I want you to be as comfortable as may be. Walk about the room and smoke. You will sleep the better for it."

Phil left the table and slowly paced up and down the room, turning over in his mind the latest development in this game. Kapaloff had entered the room behind Mikhail, had kept his right hand in his jacket pocket, and had not allowed his servant to get out of the range of his vision for an instant. If Kapaloff couldn't trust Mikhail, perhaps Phil could. The man was standing across the room from Kapaloff. His face showed nothing.

Kapaloff was asking: "You are still obdurate, then; and will not make terms?"

"I'm willing to make terms; but not to accept the ones you have made."

Passing the table, Phil's glance fell on the knife with which he had cut his meat. It was silver, and of little value as a weapon, but it would serve to cut the cords with which he had been bound. He reached the wall and turned. The cigarette between his lips was but a stub now. He went to the table and selected a fresh cigarette. Reaching for a match, he placed his body between Kapaloff and the tray. Mikhail, on the other side of the room, could see every movement of Phil's hands. Fumbling with the matches, he picked up the knife with his left hand and slid it up his sleeve. Mikhail's face was expressionless. Phil turned with the lighted cigarette in his mouth and resumed his pacing, thrusting his hands in his trouser pockets and allowing the knife to slide down into one of them. He reached the end of the room and started to turn. His elbows were seized, and he looked over his shoulder into Mikhail's stolid face. Mikhail drew the knife from the pocket, returned it to the tray, and went back to his post by the wall.

Kapaloff spoke approvingly to Mikhail in Russian, and then said to Phil: "I did not see you get it. But, behold, you cannot put faith even in the disloyalty of my servitors!"

Phil felt tired and spent—he had counted on the scarred man's help. He went to the bed and Mikhail bound him. Then the lights were turned off and he was left alone.

CHAPTER IX
A Break for Freedom

THE SOUND OF A KEY being turned slowly, cautiously, in the door awakened Phil from the fitful sleep into which he had fallen. The noise stopped. He could see nothing. Something touched the sole of one bare foot and he jumped convulsively, shaking the bed.

"Sh-h-h!"

A cool, soft hand touched his cheek, and he whispered: "Romaine?"

"Yes. Be still while I cut the cords."

Her hands passed down his arms, and his hands were freed. A little more fumbling in the dark and his feet were loose. He sat up suddenly and their faces bumped in the dark, and quite without thought he kissed her. For an instant she clung to him. Then she retreated a few inches, and said: "But first we must hurry."

"Sure," he agreed. "What do we do next?"

"Go downstairs to the front of the house, and wait until we hear the dogs in the rear. Mikhail will call them back there under some pretext, and hold them until we get out of the yard."

She pressed a heavy revolver into Phil's hand.

"But aren't the dogs kept locked up?"

"No."

"They were last night," Phil insisted, "or I never would have made it."

"Oh, yes! Uncle Boris expected you, and kept them in the garage until after you arrived."

"Oh!" So he had done what was expected of him! "Well, if Mikhail's with us, why not slip down and grab your uncle and wind this thing up?"

"No! Mikhail wouldn't help us do that. Even when his brother was killed before his eyes he would do nothing. For generations his people have been serfs, slaves, of uncle's—and he hasn't the courage to defy him. If he's to help at all it must be secretly. If it comes to a point where he must choose, he will be with uncle."

"All right, let's go!" His bare feet touched the floor and he laughed. "I haven't seen my shoes since I came through the window. I'm going to have a lot of fun running around on my naked tootsies!"

She took his hand and led him to the door. They listened but heard nothing. They crept out into the hall and toward the stairs. An electric light over the stairs gave a dim glow. They halted while Phil mounted the balustrade and unscrewed the bulb, shrouding the steps into darkness. At the foot of the flight they halted again, and Phil darkened the light there. Then she guided him toward the front door.

Somewhere in the night behind them a door opened. A noise of something sliding across the floor. Kapaloff's mellow tones:

"Children, you had best return to your rooms. There really is nothing else to do. If you move toward the door, you will show up in the moonlight that is shining through there. On the other hand, I have thoughtfully pushed a chair a little way down the hall from where I am, so that even if you could creep silently upon me you must inevitably collide with the chair and give me an inkling of where to send my bullets. So there is really nothing else to do but return to your rooms."

Huddled against the wall, Phil and Romaine said nothing, but in the hearts of each a desperate hope was born. Kapaloff chuckled and he killed their hopes.

"You need expect nothing from Mikhail. Your escape meant nothing to him, but he trusted you to exact the vengeance that he is too much the serf to take himself. So he supplied you with a weapon, I suppose, and sent you down into the hall. Then he pretended to hear a noise—thinking that I would rush out here to fall before your bullets. Happily, I know something of the peasant mind. So when he started and pretended to hear something that my keener ears missed I knocked him down with my pistol, and came out here knowing about what to expect. Now I must ask that you return to your rooms."

Phil pressed the girl down until she lay flat on the floor, close to the wall. He stretched out in front of her, his eyes trying to dissolve the darkness. Kapaloff was lying on the floor somewhere ahead; but which wall was he clinging to? In a room something of his position could have been learned from his voice, but in this narrow passage all sense of direction was lost. The sounds simply came out of the night.

The Russian's cultured voice reached them again. "You know, we are on the verge of making ourselves ridiculous. This reclining in the dark would be well enough except that I fancy we are both exceptionally patient beings. Hence, it is likely to be prolonged to an absurd length."

With the hand that was not occupied with the revolver Phil felt in his pockets. In a vest pocket he found several coins. He tossed one of them down the hall; it hit a wall and fell to the floor.

Kapaloff laughed. "I was thinking of that, too; but it isn't easy to imitate the sound of a person in motion."

Phil cursed under his breath. "There must be some way out of this hole!" Toward the front the hall was too light, as Kapaloff had said; and there seemed to be no other exits except by the stairs, or past the Russian. He might chance a volley—but there was the girl to consider. He never questioned that Kapaloff would shoot. Romaine crawled to his side.

"If we go upstairs," she whispered, "we are trapped."

"Can you think of anything?"

"No!" And then she added naively: "But here with you I am not afraid." She clutched his arm. "I believe he has gone. It feels as if no one else was here."

"What would that mean?"

"The dogs, maybe!"

He thought of the sinewy bodies and dripping jaws he had seen in the yard, and shuddered.

"You wait here," he ordered, and started crawling silently toward the rear of the hall. After it seemed that he must have gone a hundred feet his hand touched the chair of which Kapaloff had spoken. He moved it aside carefully, and went on. His fingers touched a door-frame—the end of the hall.

He whispered to the girl, "He's gone," and she joined him.

"Shall we make a break for it?" he asked.

"Yes. Better try the back."

She pushed past him, took his hand, and led him through the room beyond.

CHAPTER X
"My Hands Will Be Steady"

THREE STEPS THEY TOOK into the darkness, and then the lights clicked on and Phil found himself helpless, his arms pinned in Mikhail's powerful embrace. Kapaloff plucked the revolver from Phil's hand and smiled into his face.

"The variable Mikhail—whom you see allied with me again—has a tough head, and I feared that my blow would not quiet him for long. You can imagine in what an unenviable position I found myself out in the hall: with you ahead and my erratic compatriot behind. When I could stand it no longer I came back and resuscitated him, enlisting him on my side again."

Mikhail released Phil and stepped back. Kapaloff went on, with a gay mockery of plaintiveness:

"You will readily understand, Mr. Truax, that I cannot go on this way. A few more days of this and I shall be a wreck. I am a simple soul and cannot bear this distraction. You have seen Romaine. Do you accept my terms?"

Phil shook off the feeling of disgust with himself for having been so easily recaptured; and decided to play the same game he had played before: bluff until the actual pain came. He smiled and shook his head. "I'm afraid we'll never agree."

Kapaloff sighed. "I shall attend to the rites myself this time; so do not expect an outburst of tenderness to halt them. Though my heart bleeds for you my hands will be steady."

Then the girl spoke. Her voice was tense, vibrant. Both men turned toward her. She was speaking to Mikhail, in Russian. Her voice gradually sank lower and lower until it was but a murmur, and took on an urgent, pleading tone. Mikhail's lips were pressing together with increasing tension, and his carriage became rigid. His eyes fixed on a spot on the opposite wall. Phil shot a puzzled look at Kapaloff and saw that he was watching his niece and servant with dancing eyes. The girl's voice crooned on, and the moisture came out on Mikhail's face. His mouth was a thin, straight line, now, and the skin over the knuckles of his clenched hands seemed about to split from the strain. Still Romaine talked and, as she mentioned Serge's name, suddenly it came to Phil what was happening. She was making an open appeal to Mikhail, reminding him of his brother's death, goading him into desperation! The man's eyes were distended and the scar across his nose was a vivid gash—it might have been made yesterday. The muscles of his forehead, jaws, and neck stood out like welts; his breath hissed through quivering nostrils. Still the girl's voice went on. Phil looked at Kapaloff again. A sardonic smile of amused expectancy was on his face. He spoke softly, mockingly, a few words, but neither the girl nor Mikhail heeded him. Her voice droned on: a monotonous chant now. Mikhail's great fists opened and drops of blood ran down his fingers from where his nails had bitten into the palms. Slowly he turned and met his master's eyes. For a second the eyes held, but Mikhail's heritage of servility was too strong within him. His eyes dropped and he shifted uneasily from one foot to the other.

The girl gave him no rest. The syllables came from her lips in a torrent, and her voice went abruptly high and sharp. Despite his unfamiliarity with the language, Phil felt his pulse drumming under the beat of her tone. Mikhail's shoulders swayed slowly and a white froth appeared in the corners of his mouth. Then his face lost every human quality. A metallic snarl rasped from deep in his chest. Without turning, without looking, he sprang upon the man who had killed his brother. There was no interval the eye could discern. He was standing, swaying, looking at the floor with bulging, bloodshot eyes. Then he was upon Kapaloff and they were rolling on the floor. There was no appreciable passage!

Kapaloff discharged his pistol once, but Phil could not see where the bullet hit. Over and over they rolled—Mikhail a brute gone mad, blindly fumbling for a grip on his enemy's throat; Kapaloff fighting with every trick in his cool head, and as little disturbed as if it were a game. His eyes met Phil's over Mikhail's shoulder, and he made a grimace of distaste. Then Kapaloff twisted free, whirled to his feet, dashed a foot into the face of his rising assailant, and vanished into the dark of the hall. The kick carried Mikhail over backward, but he was up immediately, bellowing and plunging after Kapaloff.

Phil picked up the weapon Kapaloff had dropped—the revolver he had taken from Phil—and turned to the girl. Her hands were over her face and she was trembling violently. He shook her.

"Where's the phone?"

She tried twice, and finally spoke: "In the next room."

He patted her cheek. "You phone the police and wait for me here."

She clung to him protestingly for a moment, then pulled herself together, smiled with a great show of courage, and went into the next room.

Phil moved to the hall door and listened. A scuffling sound and Kapaloff's mocking chuckle came from somewhere on the stairs. A shot thundered. Mikhail bellowed. Phil felt his way to the foot of the stairs and started up. From above came the noise of a struggle, and Mikhail's rasping breath. Two shots. A body fell, sliding down the steps. Phil had gained the second floor and was climbing toward the third. The sliding body came toward him. He recognized it as Mikhail by the gibbering snarls it emitted. Kapaloff's laugh came from the head of the stairs. As he braced his legs to halt Mikhail's descent, Phil raised his revolver and fired into the darkness above. Streaks of orange flame darted down at him; a bullet burned his cheek; others hit around him. Then the man at his feet was dragging him down with grim fingers that felt for his throat. He screamed into Mikhail's ear, trying to bring comprehension to the man that his enemy was above, that he was attacking an ally. But the crushing fingers felt their way higher and higher up Phil's chest, closed about his throat. He felt his breath going. With a desperate summoning of his failing strength he drove his pistol into the face he could not see in the dark, and wrenched himself away. The fingers slipped, clutched at him, missed, and Phil was stumbling up the steps ahead of something that had been a man, but was now a rabid thing clambering through the night, with death in its heart and no understanding of the difference between friend and enemy.

Phil reached the top of the stairs and, not knowing it in the dark, reached for the next step, stumbled, and fell forward in the hall. As he fell Kapaloff's pistol spat, bringing down a shower of plaster. At the head of the stairs Mikhail was snarling. Phil rolled, jerking himself to one side, and pressed against the wainscoting, just in time to let the madman charge past. Two more shots rang out, but Mikhail's broad body held all but a feeble reflection of the flashes from Phil. Then a bestial voice rose in a bellow of insane triumph, a scuffle, a groan so faint that it might have been a sigh, heavy bodies falling . . . silence.

Phil got to his feet and advanced warily up the hall. His legs touched a body. Something liquid, warm and sticky, was under his bare feet. He stumbled on and opened the first door he reached. He found the light button and pressed it. Then he turned and looked down the hall in the light that came through the open doorway. . . .

He closed his eyes and groped his way to the stairs, down to the room where he had left the girl.

CHAPTER XI
The Death Letter

THE GIRL RAN to him. "Your face! You are hurt!"
"Just a scratch. I had forgotten it."
She drew his head down and dabbed at this torn cheek with a handkerchief.
"The others?" she asked.

"Dead! Did you get the police?"

She said, "Yes," and then could no longer withstand the weakness that tugged at her. She drooped into his arms, sobbing. He carried her to a couch and knelt beside her, stroking her hands and soothing her.

When she had mastered her weakness sufficiently to sit up, he asked her, more to take her mind from the gruesome termination of the affair than because his curiosity was so pressing, "Now, what's this all about?"

As she talked she gradually regained her composure, and the dread that the night's events had stirred within her subsided. Her voice grew steadier, her words more coherent, and some measure of color returned to her cheeks.

Her father had been a Russian nobleman, her mother an American woman. Her mother had died when she was still a child. Later the little girl had been sent to a convent in the United States, in accordance with her mother's desire. When the war broke out in Europe she had returned to Russia, despite her father's orders, with the childish thought that she would be near him. She had seen him twice before his death. He was reported "killed in action" shortly before the revolution. His brother Boris had been appointed her guardian and administrator of the estate. Then the revolution came. Her uncle had foreseen the uprising and had converted much of the girl's wealth—he had no personal means—into money, which he had deposited in English and French banks. When they were forced to leave their native land they had considerable wealth at their disposal. For the next few years they had moved from place to place. Her uncle had seemed filled with a strange uneasiness, and would seldom stay long in one city or country. He had taken the name of Kapaloff and had persuaded the girl to do likewise, though he had given no reason for the change. Finally they came to the United States, lived in various cities, and then came to

Burlingame. Since their departure from Russia her uncle had been withdrawing more and more from society, and frowning upon Romaine's desire for friends. In the United States she had made no new acquaintances. He had selected the most isolated house he could find in Burlingame and had had the windows fitted with heavy shutters, and massive doors and bolts installed. She had wondered at the change in him but had never questioned him. His manner toward her was, as always, affectionate, protecting and generous. Except in the matter of making new acquaintances—and he was not crudely insistent there—he allowed her to indulge every whim.

Then, late the preceding Monday night, she had found the letter that was in the bag. She had found it on the library floor, had picked it up carelessly to lay it on the table, from which she supposed it had blown. Her eyes had fallen upon the word *murder*, in Russian, heavily underscored. She had read the next few words, and then feverishly read the letter from beginning to end. It had been written to her uncle by someone who apparently had been very intimate with him in Russia, and boldly threatened that unless Boris paid the money he had promised the truth about his brother's *murder* would be published.

She could not miss the import of the letter. It could mean but one thing: that Boris, whose own means had been dissipated, had had his brother killed that he might gain control of the estate until the child became of age. Dazed and bewildered, she went to her room, carrying the letter with her, and threw herself across the bed. But she had something to do. She knew of but one person to whom she could turn: a prominent Los Angeles attorney, the father of one of her schoolmates. She took what money she had, left the house, got in her roadster, and started for the city, intending to take the first train to Los Angeles. But she had wasted too much time. Her uncle had missed the letter and, fearing the worst, had gone to her room.

Not finding her there, he had come downstairs just as she drove away. He had sent Mikhail and Serge in another machine to bring her back. They had done so, but the bag had been lost in the scuffle on Washington Street.

She had been imprisoned in her room until the afternoon, when she was taken to call on Phil. Her uncle had coached her carefully and she feared him too much to risk open defiance, but she had mastered her fright sufficiently to drop her purse and signal Phil. Then she had been brought back to the house and locked in. She had made one attempt to escape but had been caught at the window.

Phil tried to keep his mind on her story but he missed great stretches of it, watching her face, which, with youthful resilience, was regaining its bloom. The shadows that lingered under the eyes enhanced their beauty.

When she had finished they were silent for a moment. Phil wondered how much of the story he had missed. He cleared his throat and said, "You'll probably have to stay in Burlingame for a day or two until the police get through with their investigating. But if you'll give me that fellow's address—the Los Angeles lawyer—I'll wire him to come up if he can and take you back with him when it's all over."

She looked puzzled. "But everything is all right now. I won't have to bother him."

"You'll need him. There'll be lots of trouble straightening out your affairs and your uncle's; and you'll have to have somebody to take care of you."

"But you are—" She stopped and the blood flooded her face.

Phil shook his head emphatically. "Listen! I would—" He stopped, cleared his throat, and tried again. "We are going to do this different. You are going to have this lawyer made your legal guardian. If you don't, the courts will probably appoint some old bum who happens to be a friend of the judge's. Then I'm going to convince him that I'm—that I'm not too tough an egg. And then we'll see."

A strange speech for one whose creed was: When your luck runs good, force it!

The girl frowned. "But—"

"Now don't argue! I haven't got what you might call a spotless record. Nothing so terrible, maybe, but plenty that's bad enough. And another thing: you've got money, and I—well, when the cards run right I have enough to eat regular; when they run wrong . . . Anyway, we'll see. I'll do my talking to this lawyer fellow after he's made your guardian."

The doorbell forestalled the girl's answer. Phil went to the door, where four uniformed policemen stood, using their nightsticks to keep the hounds at bay. Phil led them back to the room where the girl was waiting and told his story briefly. The grizzled sergeant in charge stared with round eyes from the girl to the youth with bloodstained bare feet, but he made no comment. Leaving one man with Phil and Romaine, he led the others upstairs.

Fifteen minutes later he returned.

"I thought you said the dead men were in the hall?"

"That's right," Phil said.

The sergeant shook his head. "They're both dead, all right; and one of 'em is in the hall with half a dozen bullets in him. But we found the other one in one of the rooms—all mangled up—leaning over a sort of desk, with this under his arm."

He held out a sheet of notepaper to Phil. In a small, firm, regular handwriting, but thickly besmeared with blood, was written:

> My dear Romaine—
> Leaving you, I want to extend to both you and your new-found champion my heartiest wish that joy and happiness attend you.

My only regret is that so little of your heritage remains—but I was always careless with money! I advise you to cling to Mr. Truax—never have I seen a more promising young man. And he has at least three hundred and fifty dollars!

There is much that I would write, but my strength is going and I fear that my pen will waver. And I who have never shown a sign of weakness in my life am vain enough to desire that I leave this gentle world with that record intact.

Affectionately,
UNCLE BORIS.

––––––––––––––

HAMMETT MUST HAVE LIKED THIS STORY, because he returned to it twice later in his career.

At the close of the year, he could look back and tally a total of sixteen articles and stories published in six magazines in 1923. He had sold eight more pieces that would appear January through March of the following year. He was still poor, but he had showed he could make his living as a writer, with the annoyingly irregular assistance of the Veterans' Bureau.

Hammett was not the only person angry about the Veterans' Bureau's sins. An investigation was launched. At the end of the year, the bureau's general counsel, Charles Cramer, committed suicide by shooting himself. The head of the bureau, Charles R. Forbes, fled to France. Two years later Forbes was caught; convicted of fraud, conspiracy, and bribery; then fined and thrown in prison.

PART FOUR

1924,
Fiction Factory
Slowdown

IN JANUARY 1924 H. L. Mencken launched his new magazine, *The American Mercury*. Backed by publisher Alfred A. Knopf, the new monthly was an instant financial and critical success. It made Mencken the most famous writer in America. He saw *The American Mercury* as a "more serious and mature" magazine than *The Smart Set*. It featured established, well-known writers; editor Mencken rejected stories sent by an aspiring young writer, Ernest Hemingway. No Hammett stories ever appeared in *The American Mercury*.

Hammett turned to less prestigious buyers. This story, written in 1923, appeared in the January 1924 issue of the pulp *Brief*

Stories. It includes a stenographer, a movie theater, the phrase "all right," and other Hammettisms. Note the two-paragraph miniature essay on crookhood at the beginning of section III.

Itchy

DEBONAIR BANDIT ROBS OAKLAND BANK
LOCKS OFFICIALS IN VAULT
ESCAPES WITH $2500

Shortly after the Bay City State Bank of Oakland
opened its doors for business this morning, an
unmasked bandit, locking officials and employees
in the vault, fled with the contents of the money
drawer.

No depositors were in the bank at the time, the
front door having been unlocked but a few minutes before. The robber came in quietly from the
street, whipped out a revolver, and drove Milton
Beecroft, president, James K. Kirkbride, cashier,
and Miss Marcella Redgray, stenographer, into
the vault, politely assuring them that they would
not be harmed if they did as they were told. After
locking the door upon them the bandit walked out
of the bank with about $2500 in bills of various
denominations. $300 in silver in the same drawer
was not taken, and a large amount of money in the
vault at the time was overlooked.

Half an hour later Beecroft released himself
and his employees by removing the inside combination plate with a screwdriver kept in the vault for
that purpose, and notified the police. It is believed
that the bandit left in an automobile seen standing in the neighborhood at the time of the robbery.
He is described as about 30 years of age, short and
muscular, and dressed in a dark rough suit, dark
cap, and khaki shirt. Police inspectors assigned to

the case are of the opinion that this clothing may
have been worn to lead suspicion astray, as the
bandit's manner was that of a man of culture and
refinement.

"WHAT THE HELL, ITCHY?" Pete Judge demanded. "You
must of put on the high hat for them guys! What's a
debonair?"

"That's a lot of bunk!" Itchy protested with warmth. "I
didn't make no cracks that that kind of stuff could be got out
of. I went in there and flashed the rod, and said, 'Get in there,
all of you,' pointing to the box. The stenog—one of them goofy
kids—has me worried for a minute. I'm afraid she's going to try
to be funny, or let out a squawk, or something: she's got that kind
of look in her eye. So I tell her, sharp, 'Now you run along with
'em, sister, I don't want to have to hurt you.' She goes, I slam
the door on them, make the till, and duck out to you. That's all
there was to it. It's these newspapers! Like making it twenty-five
centuries, when eighteen hundred was all we got."

Pete's mouth widened in a grin at the earnestness of this
defense, a grin which, for all its breadth, did not tighten his lips
appreciably, or give them the least semblance of resilience.

"You ought to get yourself some spats and one of these here
monocles. Ain't no use of doing things half-way. Funny I never
rapped to it that I was throwing in with a dude!"

Itchy scowled at his partner and picked up another paper.
In this one also the robbery held a place of honor on an outside sheet that was a shade paler pink than the one he had just
read aloud, but nothing was said here of the bandit's comity.
So Itchy read it to Pete, and then the third version,—against a
background of green, this one,—likewise devoid of objectionable adjectives.

But Pete was not to be denied his humor.

"I guess I better shake up the scoffings, Mister Maker," he said as he carried the packages he had brought in with the afternoon papers over to the gas stove in a corner of the room. "You oughtn't to spoil your lily-white hands with cooking. It ain't debonair."

Itchy returned his stockinged feet to the window sill, leaning back in his chair and lighting a cigarette with a pretense of vast indifference to the witticisms that came over his partner's shoulder between the rattling of pans. He was sorry he hadn't laughed with Pete at first. No use giving Pete a chance to ride him: Pete would make a song of it. But it was too late now.

Those damn reporters, twisting things around, trying to be funny! "Debonair," whatever that was, "politely," "culture," "refinement." He'd show them! Next time he'd dent somebody's skull, and let them see what they could make out of that. And as for Pete,—who had by now discarded "Mister" Maker in favor of "Debonair" Maker,—if Pete kept this up he was going to get smacked. That was all!

II

IN A TOURING CAR stolen that morning, Itchy and Pete caught up with the automobile they had trailed from broom factory, to bank, and now half-way back to factory. They drew abreast of it, slackened their own to its pace, and edged over toward it, forcing it against the curb. There was a moment of hesitancy on the part of the three men in the factory car, then obedience, and a bag of money, meant until now to cover a payroll, changed cars. Nothing remained to the robbery except the escape.

Itchy, however, did not immediately give the word for Pete to drive on. He remembered his self-given promise to slug somebody next time, that his reputation might be redeemed from the calumny of gentility. He could easily swing the weapon in his left hand into the scared fat face of the nearest factory employee—maybe knock some of his teeth out.

He screwed around in his seat a little, for better leverage, and Pete's breath rasped in his ear. Pete was a partner to be trusted without stint: no matter how badly frightened Pete might be he would hold up his end, wouldn't dog it in a pinch. But Pete was always scared. He was without joy in his vocation. He knew nothing of exaltation in the power of a crooked forefinger to take what it wanted from the world. Robbery was to him—exclusive of the money involved, and even that was powerless to stimulate him during the actual operation—no more pleasant than to his prey. And to Pete this lingering to no purpose when the work was done was agony.

Itchy, in the pride of his own imperturbable subnormality, found inspiration in the hoarse panting beside him. Pete had ridden him ragged about the Oakland job, had he? Had called him a dude, had he? Called him "Itchy the debonair"? He'd give Pete a bellyful this time!

"I regret exceedingly," Itchy told the factory employees, "the necessity of having to do this"—hazy remembrance of a letter he had once received from a collecting agency carried him this far—"and I hope—I trust you boys won't do nothing you'll be sorry for."

Pete had enough. He bent over the wheel, and they shot up Mission Street, Itchy leaning out to call back: "I bid you good-day!"

How did Pete like that?

But Pete didn't say whether he liked it or no. He said nothing about it, even when they were safely at home again. Toward evening he went out for groceries, and did not come back. He had his share of the loot. He and Itchy had been together for nearly a year: seven or eight months on the road, and the last few "jungling up" in this housekeeping room on Ellis Street. Pete liked Itchy, and in association with him had prospered as never before. But Pete had had experience with partners who became swollen with success, and he did not intend being involved in the ensuing wreckage this time.

Itchy waited an hour, and then went down to the corner for food and the afternoon papers. He understood now why Pete hadn't raised a row over the hold-up. Well, if Pete didn't like his style, all right. He could find another partner, or perhaps he'd be better off working alone. He had done all the real work anyway,—the actual going up against the gun,—though Pete had been handy with a car.

Itchy read the afternoon papers before he cooked his meal. They were unanimous now: the paler pink and the green anxious to make up for their oversight of the previous month, and the deeper pink secure in the confirmation of its original stand. The bandit, they agreed, was the same who had robbed the Oakland bank, and he was a gentleman crook, a brother to those suave dandies of fiction who so easily confound the best policing brains of the several continents.

Fiction, Itchy knew, meant stories, books. He had never thought of stories having any connection with actuality, any relation with life; but it seemed that they did, and not only with life but with him personally. Books had been written about men like him; that was what the newspapers were getting at.

III

THERE IS A STRATUM of American criminal society whose constituents—almost without exception either bandits or burglars; the latter, once predominant, now a dwindling minority—are primarily hoboes. They have all the caste consciousness of those wanderers, all their contempt for the niceties of gentler modes of life. You will find them in the cities often, but they bring with them all their pride in their hardness, in their independence, in their ability to do for themselves whatever needs to be done.

The tawdry resort of the town criminal seldom sees them: even before Prohibition came they preferred to buy their liquor in the form of pure alcohol, which they could dilute to their taste; they affect a fine disesteem for women, and their contacts with them are infrequent and brief. Their ideal abode in a city is a house in some shoddy suburban quarter, or, if that is not practicable, a flat, or a room with a stove, where they may live free of traffic with cooks and other devices of civilisation. In short, they are outcasts and that is their pride. And they like to treat a city as if it were not a city at all, but merely another sort of countryside.

Itchy—idling now most of the days in his room, reread-ing the three coloured clippings and mulling over the phrase, "gentlemen crooks of fiction"—was of this tribe. And his place among them, he boasted, was second to none. He was as tough as any, as independent of the comforts of less hardy existences, as able to take care of himself.

But it wasn't as if he had been born to that life. If you came right down to it, his people were as good as the best. Hadn't his old man been a letter carrier for twenty-five years? No, his people weren't riff-raff by any means. And he had been given a good education before he slipped away on his own account: he had gone through the seventh grade of grammar school. So if he was a "stiff" it was from choice, not because—like Pete, for instance—he wasn't fit for anything else. He could do other things if he wanted to. And maybe he would want to. There might be something in this gentleman crook stuff. People had written books about them. . . .

In a downtown bookstore a saleswoman told Itchy that she did have gentleman crook stories, and she sold him five of them.

At the outset he found them disappointing, meaningless. They hadn't anything to do with life after all. Four of them he put aside with their initial chapters only partly read, but on the fifth he got the swing of the thing, read it through, went back to the others, read them, and returned to the bookstore for more.

The books weren't on the whole satisfactory. In the first place, most of them had to do with house-burglars. And, although these fellows were undoubtedly a very superior breed, with their elegant clothes and manners, their brilliant repartee, and their daring audacity, Itchy couldn't spare them a large measure of the contempt he felt for house-burglars. Then, in many of the stories, the thief was revealed, toward the end, as a detective going deviously, foolishly, and with much trouble to himself, about his hunt for the missing jewels, or one thing or another. And, if really a crook, he was more than likely to reform in the last few chapters; but as he usually bettered his financial condition by this "going queer," he wasn't to be blamed so much for that.

The girls with whom these fellows soon or late became involved Itchy found to his liking. Their very difference from anything he had ever known made them more plausible to him. The women with whom he had come in contact from time to time certainly hadn't been very wonderful, even discounting his tribal pose of misogyny. But these were different. More like—the girl in the bookstore was something on their order. . . .

Still, say what you would about these men in the books,— neglecting the most simple precautions, always being surprised at work, showing themselves unnecessarily gullible, and only succeeding through the miraculous favors of chance,—they

did have something. They made big hauls, they enjoyed themselves, people wrote stories about them. . . . Take, for example,
that one who told the detective: "I'm tired of you. You bore me.
You weary me. You exasperate me. Now get out." That wasn't a
bad line at all. Imagine the look on an "elbow's" face if you told
him that! Naturally, though, you'd want to be sure you were
sitting pretty before you made a crack like that.

Of course, you couldn't go around pulling jobs as these
fellows did: they were no good in a practical way. But a man
who knew his business through and through might, by copying
their manners, their dress, and their talk, not only increase his
profits by being able to get into places from which less polish
would bar him, but have a lot of fun in the bargain. The newspapers liked that kind of stuff, too. Look what a fuss they raised
over those two jobs of his, and he hadn't even tried to make
them fancy.

Another visit to the bookstore exhausted its stock of gentleman crook fiction, but he learned that what he wanted could be
found on the screen now and then and in the magazines often.

He was in earnest now. His hair was carefully parted and
weighted down with a thick gummy substance that he bought
in large jars; he spent time in the barber's chair, and even submitted his hands to a manicure. Nor had he neglected tailor,
haberdasher, hatter, and booter.

He read aloud to himself in his room at night, and felt that
his language was being improved thereby. Every day or two he
visited the bookstore, ostensibly to enquire for new books, but
actually for the sake of the saleswoman's conversation. The
books could give him the right words and the correct combi-
nations, but they didn't give him the right pronunciations. The
saleswoman could, however, and not only the pronunciations
but the right sort of accent. She formed her words high in the
roof of her mouth, and they came out roundly and clearly in

what he knew instinctively for the correct form. After he had returned to his room he would repeat everything she had said, painstakingly aping each trick of enunciation.

He was going to stick up the bookstore some day, he decided. There wouldn't be much money in the damper (he must remember to say cash register if he spoke of it), and, in the center of the shopping district, the store was unfavorably located for a quick get-away. But the saleswoman was the only person he knew whom he thought capable of unerringly judging the false from the true, and by her attitude he would know the degree of his success. But he wouldn't do it for a while yet; he wasn't quite ready for so severe a testing, and, besides, she would be getting new books in from time to time, and there was no use closing that source of supply.

Another month passed before Itchy ordered evening clothes. But all the books had insisted upon them,—dinner jackets were indicated also,—so he finally came to it. He didn't, however, buy a dinner suit. He felt that since he was taking this step forward he might as well make it a decisive one, and waste nothing on the compromise between formality and informality which the dinner suit offered.

He wore the new dress suit every night from the first, which necessitated his remaining indoors for a while, until he became accustomed to the new garments. But he usually kept to his room in the evenings, anyway. He had no desire for the society of his familiars. He knew how they would greet this new Itchy, with his silk shirts and hose, his carefully tended face and hands, his glossy hair, his natty clothes. For those who dressed as he did now—the gaudy city breed—he had lost none of his old contempt. Thus he spent much time by himself.

He became, at about this time, unpleasantly aware of his nickname. He had grown accustomed to it, had come to think of it more natural a part of him than the baptismal Floyd; but now, considering it in terms of his new development, he found it distasteful. He had acquired it five or six years before, sitting with a group of his fellows around a fire in the "jungles" outside of Fresno one night. He had been digging savagely at the flea-bites with which he was covered at the time, and some old "stiff" had flung the name across the flames at him. He had laughed with the others, and the name had stuck. Itchy Maker. What difference did it make? One name was as good as another. But now one name was not necessarily so good as another. And while the chances were that he would never mingle again with those who knew him by it, still the name might crop up at the most unexpected times to embarrass him. If he found new associates now—as he undoubtedly would before long—he meant to see to it that they knew him as "Debonair" Maker. That was a lot better than Itchy—had a fine sound, in fact.

Another fortnight, and Itchy was wearing his correct evening clothes on the streets and into the lobbies of the better hotels, where he would loiter for hours, gazing condescendingly on those whose more common garb did night and day duty. And, as his familiarity with them increased, the new clothes began to tempt him to wear them on a robbery. But he resisted that, for a while.

Within the next two months he held up a small jewelry store and the office of a laundry company. He was sure of himself in his new role now, and he enlivened both banditries with copious quotations from the books he had read, and even extemporized a trifle. In the laundry office he was fortunate enough to encounter two girls who were addicted to the same sort of literature, and their appreciation of his manner was gratifying. And even more gratifying was the warmth with which the press accepted the girls' stories, polishing them, gilding them, and setting them out at great length for the world to see. Itchy had column after column of type devoted to him now—even editorials.

IV

THE LOBBY OF A THEATER just before the box office closed one night was the scene of the dress suit's baptism. The top hat he had, of course, finally left at home; there was no use overdoing the thing. His grammar had improved by now until the double negative was rare, though tenses still puzzled him, and his accents were worth all the imitative labors they had cost him.

His light overcoat drooping to each side, exposing the full chiaroscuro of his immaculate costuming, he smiled at the girl behind the grille and wrought beautifully with what he knew of the graces of speech. And the girl, once she had become relatively accustomed to the sight of the pistol in his hand, enjoyed the robbery perhaps as much as he.

Nevertheless she gave the alarm as soon as he left.

It happened there were only two other men in dress clothes on the streets of San Francisco that night, and one of them was very old and the other was very tall. And thus, though the police went astray once at the corner of Powell and Geary Streets, and again, momentarily, at Mason and Sutter, they still arrived at Itchy's quarters—he had an apartment now, on California Street—only a few minutes behind him.

There was a broken door, a bullet that went wild, a blow or two, and Itchy was taken.

V

IN A BARELY FURNISHED ROOM in the Hall of Justice Itchy sat ringed by detectives.

"So, my pretty boy," one of them grinned down at the slightly rumpled black and white of the prisoner's clothes, "we got you."

Itchy's glance ran coolly along the circling line of faces until it rested upon the speaker's, and there was utter nonchalance in the crossing of Itchy's legs.

"I'm tired of you," he said. "You weary me. You bore me. You exasperate me. You—you're a big slob!"

THUS HAMMETT SHOWS what might happen if a real criminal tried to conform to the literary stereotype of a gentleman thief such as Raffles or Arsne Lupin. In a way, "Itchy" is Hammett's criticism of the preposterousness of popular crime fiction. It makes a fitting companion to the classic crime story about clothing and criminals, "Clothes Make the Man" by Henri Duvernois.

AFTER HIS SUCCESS telling "The Joke on Eloise Morey" partially in stream-of-consciousness mode, Hammett tried his hand at a story told completely in that style. In his book *A Dashiell Hammett Companion* (2000), Robert L. Gale writes of this story: "This internal monologue is a tour de force, a veritable verbal *Bolero*, anticipating Maurice Ravel's by four years." In other words, he likes it.

The story appeared in the February 1924 issue of *Brief Stories* and has never been reprinted until now. After being hidden for eighty years, "Esther Entertains" is finally making its first appearance in a book. You can decide for yourself if it reminds you of *Bolero*.

Hammett was raised as a Southerner and a Roman Catholic. You'll find references to both roots in this story.

Esther Entertains

H E SHOULDN'T (HE THOUGHT) have come. These four hours, if so applied, would have disposed all the incidentals to his departure tomorrow, sending him away with no loose ends to be taken care of later. But her voice had come over the wire so alluringly; and no doubt she really had missed him, not seeing him for two weeks. And to have excused himself tonight would have been to prolong that fortnight to nearly two months, since his trip would cover six weeks at the least. Perhaps he could leave an hour early, get away at eleven-thirty or forty-five without seeming anxious to go.

"You know I did, dear. If you had waited another ten minutes, or fifteen at the outside, I'd have been calling you up."

He had almost called her "honey": an endearment for which she professed aversion, finding it reminiscent, possibly, of some former lover who had been disappointing. Southerners, he believed, were addicted to the word; and she came from somewhere in the Carolinas.

"Not a thing except work."

She didn't look so well tonight. Her gown was less than becoming; and her hair, dressed in this new manner, was also at fault, accentuating the slenderness of her throat: a slenderness that was on the point of aging into scrawniness. She must be getting along in years. Even in this light, diluted and tinted to friendliness, she failed to appear quite young. Her figure, too, was less youthfully slim now than merely thin. Her eyes were good, though, and they saved her: she would never be unattractive while they held their beauty. If only she wouldn't maneuver them with so little subtlety, with so obvious a consciousness: pulling them around like fat blue puppets beneath the heavy dark fringe of her lashes: lashes edging lids that slid down and up on occasion with all the smooth precision of well-handled drop-curtains.

"Sit still, baby, I'll get them."

If he didn't light his cigarette, she would, and pass it to him limp and hot from the excessive draught she had applied, its end sodden with saliva, and he would have to smoke it with a pretense of extra enjoyment. Of course, that would happen once or twice before the evening was over; but by exercising a reasonable amount of alertness, and keeping the cigarettes near him, he could prevent its too frequent occurrence.

"I did. You know, or you should, without my telling you."

It was peculiar, how he was invariably disappointed in her. It wasn't, either, that he had any illusions. He would leave tonight—as he had left the last time and the several times before that—to hardly think of her again until he had an evening whose emptiness promised to be irksome, or until he heard from her. Such vagrant thoughts as came to him meanwhile would not draw him toward her. Yet, between the time when his engagements were made and the time for their keeping, he was somehow filled with inflated notions of her charm and appeal—an anticipation of vague ecstacies. Not consciously; but that he always experienced this disappointment testified to the existence of some such process of delusion.

"*Yes, much nicer.*"

It was nicer. The light at their feet, a mellow glow, tilted upward the shadows on her face, softened the texture of her skin, lent her an appearance of girlishness—almost. She was, for that matter, girlish, in a way. Arrested development you could call it if you liked, but it went well with her smallness; and, now that the only illumination came slanting up from the gas log, you could believe in her youngness, or very nearly.

"*Utterly.*"

He would be utterly comfortable if only she wouldn't fidget so much, tickling his face with her hair; and if she wouldn't call him "dearest" or that ridiculous "most beloved boy." Superlatives were weak, almost cheap. Furthermore, superlatives carried with them the postulant that there were others in the speaker's mind. To call him dearest was to think of one who was dear and another who was dearer; though it was unlikely that it worked out that way—that she had anyone else in her mind at the time. But the inference, the suggestion, was there. Not that he cared, really, how many others there might be; but it was nevertheless faulty technic. The pleasurableness of these evenings depended upon the maintenance of certain illusions whose very high artificiality made them delicate and all the more vulnerable to the least discordance.

"*I wasn't thinking at all. I don't when I am with you. There's nothing to think about. It's all here. This afternoon there may have been a world—I'm not quite sure. Tomorrow there may be another, or even a continuation of the same one; with business and things in it, and scheming and conniving to be done. But now there's nothing anywhere but you and me, and the aim of existence is to sit still, like this, close to you, doing nothing, neither remembering nor imagining—just sitting still with you.*"

More than a bit silly, but it would at least keep her from jumping up and turning on that damned talking machine for

a while. She needn't, however, have received it with so much
rapture. The Lord knew he had made the same speech, or one
of its variants, often enough before. She would know by now
that it didn't have any particular meaning, that it was just one
of the things you say. She did know it, of course, but she should
also know that he was aware of her knowledge. Her antics threw
a spotlight on the speech, gave it a prominence that was never
meant for it and that made it seem sillier than ever. And why
did women always want to know what you were thinking about?
And if, as was probable, they didn't, why did they ask? The sort
of answers they got would become monotonous after a while.

. . . It was easier to kiss than to talk, and more satisfying. She
did kiss well. Even the solemnity, with its insistence upon an
equal seriousness on his part, which she brought to the business
failed to mar it; though it would have been more thoroughly
enjoyable without this alien reverence. She surely didn't expect
him to believe that she held these kisses, embraces, caresses, so
sacred as she pretended. That was the worst side of her: she not
only invested her amours with all the trappings of the theater,
but she went to the amateur theater for her properties.

. . . There it was again. It was as if there were hidden and
not very sophisticated spectators to be satisfied. A kiss wasn't,
properly, a sacrament; nor was she any more deeply stirred than
he, for instance, himself. It could all have been done just as
neatly and a whole lot more enjoyably without the burning
glances, the shivers and sighs, the devout emotion with which
she embellished it—sometimes caricatured it. He must be careful not to smile, though, not even when she reached her highest
histrionic altitude; or she would sulk, and that was a nuisance.
True enough, her sulkiness seldom endured for longer than
it took him to light a cigarette, but even that was sufficient to
irritate him and make him feel rather sullen himself. Now and
then, when a smile wouldn't be repressed, he could hit upon

the right thing to say—something without flippancy but at the same time whimsical—and pass it off; but she didn't as a rule like trivialities of any sort when her emotions were rampant.

. . . That was safer: a smile before it had twisted itself into view could be buried beneath another kiss. And she did kiss well; she was undeniably delectable in spite of her gestures, her dramatics, and her italicized fervors. After all, the difference between her acting and his was only one of degree. But that made the flaw a matter of crudity, which was bad. Still—

. . . Funny—the similarity of women's faces remembered in dim lights on nights like this: the same leanness of cheek, the same shininess of eye, the same deepened lines spreading from between the eyes down and out around the mouth. It was as if something—some same thing behind all of them—was looking out through their faces: some aboriginal—but that was fantastic!

. . . If only for a little while she would put away that posturing. This wasn't a mass. If only— But it was possible that he was being hypercritical; it was possible that she wasn't exaggerating so much as he thought. She was an impulsive, high-keyed little thing: she might be nearly in earnest—or even quite. Sincere or affected, she was devilishly fascinating, nevertheless.

. . . If only she—

. . . By Jove, she was glorious!

MY GUESS is that Hammett was pleased with this story, because he planned to use the technique again in a more ambitious work. Four years later he wrote his publisher that he wanted to write a stream-of-consciousness novel, "carrying the reader along with the detective, showing him everything as it is found, giving him the detective's conclusions as they are reached, letting the solution break on both of them together."

He never wrote it. Instead, he abandoned the stream-of-consciousness technique, and with an eye on Hollywood money, he decided to write novels "sticking to the more objective and filmable forms."

SINCE SUBMITTING his first Continental Op stories to *The Black Mask* the previous year, nearly every issue of the twice-a-month magazine had run a Hammett story. But his gravy train ground to a halt. In April, a new editor, Phil Cody, started work and almost immediately rejected two of Hammett's stories. In the first half of the year, *The Black Mask* had run nine of his stories. In the second half of the year, it would run only two. The new editor demanded stories that were less frequent but of higher quality. Hammett's bread-and-butter publication was no longer a sure thing. He put more work into his stories for *The Black Mask,* but he looked for other outlets.

That May the U.S. House and Senate passed a bonus bill for World War veterans over President Coolidge's veto. The new bonus bill theoretically entitled Hammett to $1 per day for his service, a total of $340. He needed that money, but his bonus was more illusory than real. The odd terms of the bill did not provide veterans with the cash that many of them needed. Instead, it created a twenty-year endowment policy for each entitled veteran. Instead of receiving his full $340 bonus, Hammett could borrow from the government up to twenty-five percent of its full value.

The bonus was better than nothing, but it made many veterans disgusted, angry men.

For his June disability check, the Veterans Bureau paid Hammett $9 and then cut him off completely. He had fought with the Veterans Bureau longer than he had served in the war, and now he was back where he started.

In July the Democrats came out in favor of the League of Nations and denounced the lawlessness of the Ku Klux Klan. They nominated John W. Davis for president. The pro-Klan Republicans nominated Coolidge for re-election. He beat Davis almost two to one.

Hammett had been a fiction factory in the first half of 1924, but in the second half only four of his stories appeared. His steadiest customer was no longer certain. His disability checks had stopped. He had turned thirty that year, and still had no steady source of income for his family.

PART FIVE

1925,
Established
Writer Quits?

———————————

THE NEW YEAR STARTED with another Continental Op
story. It appeared in the January issue of *The Black Mask*.
Hammett was writing longer stories for *The Black Mask* now—a
good idea for a starving writer paid by the word—and that magazine was paying him a higher per-word rate, which helped make
up for the decrease in frequency of appearances. This year he
would average one story every other month in *The Black Mask*.

His next appearance was in the February issue of the humor
magazine *Experience*. It was a mystery parody, possibly inspired by
"The Detective Detector," one of O. Henry's well-known Sham-
rock Jolnes parodies of Sherlock Holmes. Again, Hammett shows

his knowledge of and disdain for the conventions of the mystery genre, especially the cliché that the most obvious suspect is *never* guilty. Note Hammett's low regard for the accuracy of newspaper crime stories.

Another Perfect Crime

Although convicted of Boardman Bowlby Bunce's murder, I did kill him. I forget why; I dare say there was something about the man I disliked. That is not important; but I feel that the attentiveness with which the public has read the interviews I did not give and looked at photographs of photographers' personal friends entitles that public to know why, here in the death cell, I have made a new will, giving my fortune to the fiction department of the Public Library. (Before starting that, however, I wish to state that while I do not object to having been born in any of the other houses pictured in various newspapers, I must, in justice to my parents, repudiate the ice-house shown in Wednesday's *Examiner*.)

To get on with my story: when I determined, for doubtless sufficient if not clearly remembered reasons, to kill Boardman Bowlby Bunce, I planned the murder with the most careful attention to every detail. A life-long reader of literature dealing with the gaudier illegalities, I flattered myself that I of all men was equipped to commit the perfect crime.

I went to his office in the middle of the afternoon, when I knew his employees would be all present. In the outer office I attracted their attention to my presence and to the exact time by arguing heatedly that the clock there was a minute fast. Then I went into Bunce's private office. He was alone. Out of my pockets I took the hammer and nails I had bought the day before from a hardware dealer who knew me, and, paying no attention to the astonished Bunce, nailed every window and door securely shut.

That done, I spit out the lozenge with which I had prepared my voice, and yelled loudly at him: "I hate you! You should be killed! I shall injure you!"

The surprise on his face became even more complete.

"Sit still," I ordered in a low voice, taking a revolver from my pocket—a silver-mounted revolver with my initials engraved in it in four places.

Walking around behind him, carefully keeping the weapon too far away to leave the powder-marks that might make the wound seem self-inflicted, I shot him in the back of the head. While the door was being broken in I busied myself with the ink-pad on his desk, putting the prints of my fingers neatly and clearly on the butt of the revolver, the handle of the hammer, Bunce's white collar, and some convenient sheets of paper; and hurriedly stuffed the dead man's fountain pen, watch and handkerchief into my pockets just as the door burst open.

After a while a detective came. I refused to answer his questions. Searching me, he found Bunce's fountain pen, watch and handkerchief. He examined the room—doors and windows nailed on the inside with my hammer, my monogrammed revolver beside the dead man, my finger-prints everywhere. He questioned Bunce's employees. They told of my entrance, my passing into the office where Bunce was alone, the sound of hammering, my voice shouting threats, and the shot.

And then—then the detective arrested me!

It came out later that this would-be sleuth whose salary the property holders were paying had never read a detective story in his life, and so had not even suspected that the evidence had been too solidly against me for me to be anything but innocent.

NEAR THE END of the previous year Hammett had written a story set in the Sulu Archipelago—a chain of islands in the southwest Philippines—shortly after the 1898 Spanish-American War. This story, "Ber-Bulu," is one of the rare stories Hammett set outside the United States, and the only story he set in a time period other than the present.

It ran in the March issue of *Sunset*, today a glossy magazine that runs no fiction. Then it was a slick-paper magazine more prestigious than the pulps, but paying low rates.

"Ber-Bulu" is one of my favorite Hammett stories.

Ber-Bulu

S AY IT HAPPENED on one of the Tawi Tawis. That would
make Jeffol a Moro. It doesn't really matter what he was. If
he had been a Maya or a Ghurka he would have laid Levison's
arm open with a machete or a kukri instead of a kris, but that
would have made no difference in the end. Dinihari's race matters as little. She was woman, complaisant woman, of the sort
whose no always becomes yes between throat and teeth. You
can find her in Nome, in Cape Town, and in Durham, and in
skin of any shade; but, since the Tawi Tawis are the lower end of
the Sulu Archipelago, she was brown this time.

She was a sleek brown woman with the knack of twisting a
sarong around her hips so that it became a part of her—a trick a
woman has with a potato sack or hasn't with Japanese brocade.
She was small and trimly fleshed, with proper pride in her flesh.
She wasn't exactly beautiful, but if you were alone with her you
kept looking at her, and you wished she didn't belong to a man
you were afraid of. That was when she was Levison's.

She was Jeffol's first. I don't know where he got her. Her
dialect wasn't that of the village, but you couldn't tell from
that. There are any number of dialects down there—jumbles
of Malay, Tagalog, Portuguese, and what not. Her sarong was

a gold-threaded *kain sungkit*, so no doubt he brought her over from Borneo. He was likely to return from a fishing trip with anything—except fish.

Jeffol was a good Moro—a good companion in a fight or across a table. Tall for a Moro, nearly as tall as I am, he had a deceptive slimness that left you unprepared for the power in his snake-smooth muscles. His face was cheerful, intelligent and almost handsome, and he carried himself with a swagger. His hands went easily to the knives at his waist, and against his hide—sleeping

She wasn't exactly beautiful, but if you were alone with her you kept looking at her, and you wished she didn't belong to a man you were afraid of. (Painting of Dinihari by Louis Rogers)

or waking—he wore a sleeveless fighting-jacket with verses from the Koran on it. The jacket was his most prized possession, next to his *anting-anting*.

His elder brother was datto, as their father had been, but this brother had inherited little of either his father's authority or his father's taste for deviltry. The first had been diluted by the military government, and Jeffol had got most of the second. He ran as wild and loose as his pirate ancestors, until Langworthy got hold of him.

Langworthy was on the island when I came there. He hadn't had much luck. Mohammedanism suited the Moros, especially in the loose form they practised. There was nothing of the solemn gangling horse-faced missionary about Langworthy. He was round-chested and meaty; he worked with dumb-bells and punching-bag before breakfast in the morning; and he strode round the island with a red face that broke into a grin on the least excuse. He had a way of sticking his chin in the air and grinning over it at you. I didn't like him.

He and I didn't hit if off very well from the first. I had reasons for not telling him where I had come from, and when he found I intended staying a while he got a notion that I wasn't going to do his people—he called them that in spite of the little attention they paid him—any good. Later, he used to send messages to Bangao, complaining that I was corrupting the natives and lowering the prestige of the white man.

That was after I taught them to play blackjack. They gambled whenever they had anything to gamble for, and it was just as well that they should play a game that didn't leave too much to luck. If I hadn't won their money the Chinese would have, and anyway, there wasn't enough of it to raise a howl over. As for the white man's prestige—maybe I didn't insist on being *tuaned* with every third word, but neither did I hesitate to knock the brown brothers round whenever they needed it; and that's all there is to this keeping up the white man's prestige at best.

A COUPLE OF YEARS EARLIER—in the late '90s—Langworthy would have had no difficulty in getting rid of me, but since then the government had eased up a bit. I don't know what sort of answers he got to his complaints, but the absence of official action made him all the more determined to chase me off.

"Peters," he would tell me, "You've got to get off the island. You're a bad influence and you've got to go."

"Sure, sure," I would agree, yawning. "But there's no hurry."

We didn't get along together at all, but it was through my blackjack game that he finally made a go of his mission, though he wouldn't be likely to admit it.

Jeffol went broke in the game one night—lost his fortune of forty dollars Mex—and discovered what to his simple mind was the certain cause of his bad luck. His *anting-anting* was gone, his precious luck-bringing collection of the-Lord-knows-what in a stinking little bag was gone from its string round his neck. I tried to buck him up, but he wouldn't listen to reason. His security against all the evils of this world—and whatever other worlds there might be—was gone. Anything could happen to him now—anything bad. He went round the village with his head sagging down until it was in danger of being hit by a knee. In this condition he was ripe fruit for Langworthy, and Langworthy plucked him.

I saw Jeffol converted, although I was too far away to hear the talk that went with it. I was sitting under a cottonwood fixing a pipe. Jeffol had been walking up and down the beach for half an hour or more, his chin on his chest, his feet dragging. The water beyond him was smooth and green under a sky that was getting ready to let down more water. From where I sat, his round turban moved against the green sea like a rolling billiard-ball.

Then Langworthy came up the beach, striding stiff-kneed, as a man strides to a fight he counts on winning. He caught up with Jeffol and said something to which the Moro paid no attention. Jeffol didn't raise his head, just went on walking, though he was polite enough ordinarily. Langworthy fell in step beside him and they made a turn up and down the beach, the white man talking away at a great rate. Jeffol, so far as I could see, made no reply at all.

Facing each other, they suddenly stopped. Langworthy's face was redder than ever and his jaw stuck out. Jeffol was scowling. He said something. Langworthy said something. Jeffol took a step back and his hand went to the ivory hilt of a kris in his belted sarong. He didn't get the kris out. The missionary stepped in and dropped him with a hard left to the belly.

I got up and went away, reminding myself to watch that left hand if Langworthy and I ever tangled. I didn't have to sit through the rest of the performance to know that he had made a convert. There are two things a Moro understands thoroughly and respects without stint—violence and a joke. Knock him round, or get a laugh on him, and you can do what you will with him—and he'll like it. The next time I saw Jeffol he was a Christian.

In spite of the protests of the datto, a few of the Moros followed Jeffol's example, and Langworthy's chest grew an inch. He was wise enough to know that he could make better progress by cracking their heads together than by arguing the finer theological points with them, and after two or three athletic gospel-meetings he had his flock well in hand—for a while.

He lost most of them when he brought up the question of wives. Women were not expensive to keep down there and, although the Moros on that particular island weren't rolling in wealth, nearly all of them could afford a couple of wives, and some were prosperous enough to take on a slave girl or two after they had the four wives their law allowed. Langworthy put his foot down on this. He told his converts they would have to get rid of all except the first wives. And of course all of his converts who had more than one wife promptly went back to Allah—except Jeffol.

He was in earnest, the only idea in his head being to repair the damage done by the loss of his *anting-anting*. He had four wives and two slaves, including Dinihari. He wanted to keep her and let the others go, but the missionary said no. Jeffol's number one wife was his only real wife—thus Langworthy. Jeffol almost bolted then, but the necessity of finding a substitute for his *anting-anting* was strong in him. They compromised. He was to give up his women, go to Bangao for a divorce from his first wife, and then Langworthy would marry him to Dinihari. Meanwhile the girl was turned over to the datto for safe keeping. The datto's wife was a dish-faced shrew who had thus far prevented his taking another wife, so his household was considered a safe harbor for the girl.

Three mornings after Jeffol's departure for Bangao we woke to find Levison among us. He had come in during the night, alone, in a power-yawl piled high with wooden cases.

Levison was a monster, in size and appearance. Six and a half feet high he stood and at a little distance you took him for a man of medium height. There were three hundreds pounds of him bulging his clothes if there was an ounce—not counting the hair, which was an item. He was black hair all over. It bushed out from above his low forehead to the nape of his neck, ran over his eyes in a straight thick bar, and sprouted from ears and great beaked nose. Below his half-hidden dark eyes, black hair bearded his face with a ten-inch tangle, furred his body like a bear's, padded his shoulders and arms and legs, and lay in thick patches on fingers and toes.

He hadn't many clothes on when I paddled out to the yawl to get acquainted, and what he had were too small for him. His shirt was split in a dozen places and the sleeves were gone. His pants-legs were torn off at the knees. He looked like a hair-mattress coming apart—only there was nothing limp or loose about the body inside of the hair. He was as agile as an acrobat. This was the first time I had seen him, although I recognized him on sight from what I had heard in Manila the year before. He bore a sweet reputation.

"Hello, Levison," I greeted him as I came alongside. "Welcome to our little paradise."

He scowled down at me, from hat to shoes and back, and then nodded his immense head.

"You are—"

"I'm not," I denied, climbing over the side. "I never heard of the fellow, and I'm innocent of whatever he did. My name is Peters and I'm not even distantly related to any other Peters."

He laughed and produced a bottle of gin.

THE VILLAGE was a double handful of thatched huts set upon piles where the water could wash under them when the tide was in, back in a little cove sheltered by a promontory that pointed towards Celebes. Levison built his house—a large one with three rooms—out near the tip of this point, beside the ruins of the old Spanish block-house. I spent a lot of time out there with him. He was a hard man to get along with, a thoroughly disagreeable companion, but he had gin—real gin and plenty of it—and I was tired of *nipa* and *samshu*. He thought I wasn't afraid of him, and that error made it easier for me to handle him.

There was something queer about this Levison. He was as strong as three men and a vicious brute all the way through, but not with the honest brutality of a strong man. He was like a mean kid who, after being tormented by larger boys, suddenly finds himself among smaller ones. It used to puzzle me. For instance, old Muda stumbled against him once on the path into the jungle. You or I would simply have pushed the clumsy old beggar out of the way, or perhaps, if we happened to be carrying a grouch at the time, have knocked him out of the way. Levison picked him up and did something to his legs. Muda had to be carried back to his hut, and he never succeeded in walking after that.

The Moros called Levison the Hairy One *(Ber-Bulu)*, and, because he was big and strong and tough, they were afraid of him and admired him tremendously.

It was less than a week after his arrival when he brought Dinihari home with him. I was in his house when they came in.

"Get out, Peters," he said. "This is my dam' honeymoon."

I looked at the girl. She was all dimples and crinkled nose—tickled silly.

"Go easy," I advised the hairy man. "She belongs to Jeffol, and he's a tough lad."

"I know," he sneered through his beard. "I've heard all about him. The hell with him!"

"You're the doctor. Give me a bottle of gin to drink to you with and I'll run along."

I got the gin.

I WAS WITH LEVISON and the girl when Jeffol came back from Bangao. I was sprawled on a divan. On the other side of the room the hairy man was tilted back in a chair, talking. Dinihari sat on the floor at his feet, twisted round to look up into his face with adoring eyes. She was a happy brown girl. Why not? Didn't she have the strongest man on the island—the strongest man in the whole archipelago? And in addition to his strength, wasn't he as hairy as a wanderoo, in a land where men hadn't much hair on face and body?

Then the door whipped open and Jeffol came in. His eyes were red over black. He wasn't at home in Christianity yet, so he cursed Levison with Mohammedan curses. They are good enough up to a certain point, but the climax—usually pig—falls a bit flat on western ears. Jeffol did well. But he would have done better if he had come in with his knives in his hands instead of in his twisted sarong.

The hairy man's chair came down square on its legs and he got across the room—sooner than you would think. Jeffol managed to loosen a kris and ripped one of Levison's arms from elbow to wrist. Then the Moro was through. Levison was too big, too strong, for him—swept him up, cuffed weapons out of hand and sarong, took him by arm and thigh and chucked him out of the door.

Dinihari? Her former lord's body hadn't thudded on the ground below—a nasty drop with the tide out—before she was bending over Levison's hairy arm, kissing the bleeding slit.

Jeffol was laid up for a week with a twisted shoulder and bruised back. I dropped in to see him once, but he wasn't very cordial. He seemed to think I should have done something. His mother—old toothless Ca'bi—chased me out as soon as she saw me, so my visit didn't last long. She was a proper old witch.

The village buzzed for a day or two, but nothing happened. If Jeffol hadn't gone Christian there might have been trouble; but most of the Moros held his desertion of the faith against him, and looked on the loss of Dinihari as just punishment. Those who were still Christians were too tame a lot to help Jeffol. His brother the datto washed his hands of the affair, which was just as well, since he couldn't have done anything anyway. He wasn't any too fond of Jeffol—had always been a bit envious of him—and he decided that in giving up the girl at the missionary's request, Jeffol had surrendered ownership, and that she could stay with Levison if she wished. Apparently she did so wish.

Langworthy went to see Levison. I heard of it a few minutes later and paddled like mad out to the house. If the missionary was going to be smeared up I wanted to see it. I didn't like the man. But I was too late. He came out just as I got there, and he limped a little. I never found out what happened. I asked Levison, but if he had done all the things he told me the missionary wouldn't have left standing up. The house wasn't upset, and Levison didn't have any marks that showed through his hair, so it couldn't have been much of a row.

Jeffol's faith in Christianity as a substitute for an *anting-anting* must have been weakened by this new misfortune, but Langworthy succeeded in holding him, though he had to work night and day to do it. They were together all of the time— Langworthy usually talking, Jeffol sulking.

"Jeffol's up and about," I told Levison one day. "Better watch your step. He's shifty, and he's got good pirate blood in him."

"Pirate blood be damned!" said Levison. "He's a nigger and I can handle a dozen of him."

I let it go at that.

T HOSE WERE GOOD DAYS in the house out on the point. The girl was a brown lump of happiness. She worshipped her big hair-matted beast of a man, made a god of him. She'd look at him for hour after hour with black eyes that had hallelujahs in them. If he was asleep when I went out there, she'd use the word *beradu* when she told me so—a word supposed to be sacred to the sleep of royalty.

Levison, swept up in this adoration that was larger than he, became almost mellow for days at a time; and even when he relapsed into normal viciousness now and then he was no crueler to her than a Moro would have been. And there were times when he became almost what she thought of him. I remember one night: We were all three fairly drunk—Levison and I on gin, the girl, drunker than either of us, on love. She had reached up and buried her brown fists in his beard, a trick she was fond of.

"Hold on!" he cried, kicking his chair away and standing up.

He reared up his head, lifting her from the floor, and spun round, whirling her through the air like a kid swinging on a May-pole. Silly, maybe. But in the yellow lamplight, his beaked nose and laughing red mouth above the black beard to which her fists clung, her smooth brown body slanting through the air in a ripple of gay waist and sarong, there was a wild magnificence to them. He was a real giant that moment.

The Colt in Jeffol's hand was too large and too steady for even a monster like Levison to jump at. (Painting by Louis Rogers)

But it's hard for me to remember him that way: my last picture of him is the one that sticks. I got it the night of Jeffol's second call.

He came in late, popping through the door with a brand-new service Colt in one hand and a kris in the other. At his heels trotted old Ca'bi, his mother, followed by broken-nosed Jokanain and a mean little runt named Unga. The old woman carried a bundle of something tied up in nipa leaves, Jokanain swung a heavy *barong*, and Unga held an ancient blunderbuss.

I started up from where I was sitting cross-legged on the floor. Unga centered the blunderbuss on me.

"*Diam dudok!*"

I sat still. Blunderbusses are wicked, and Unga had lost twelve dollars Mex to me three nights before.

Levison had jerked to his feet, and then he stopped. The Colt in Jeffol's hand was too large and too steady for even a monster like Levison to jump at. Dinihari was the only one of us who moved. She flung herself between Jeffol and Levison, but the Moro swept her out of the way with his left arm, swept her over into a corner without taking eyes or gun from the hairy man.

Old Ca'bi hobbled across the floor and peeped into each of the other rooms.

"*Mari,*" she croaked from the sleeping-room door.

Step by step Jeffol drove Levison across the room and through that door, Ca'bi going in with them. The door closed and Unga, holding me with the gun, put his back against it.

Dinihari sprang up and dashed toward him. Jokanain caught her from behind and flung her into her corner again. Beyond the door Levison roared out oaths. Ca'bi's voice cackled excitedly in answering oaths, and in orders to her son. Bind (*ikat*) and naked (*telanjang*) were the only words I could pick out of the din. Then Levison's voice choked off into silence, and no sound at all came from the sleeping-room.

In our room there was no motion. Dinihari sat still in her corner, staring at her feet. Unga and Jokanain were two ugly statues against two doors. The chatter of flying foxes busy among the cottonwoods and the rustling of thatch in a breeze heavy with the stink of drying *tripang* were the only things you could hear.

I had a dull, end-of-the-road feeling. A Moro is a simple son of nature. When he finds himself so placed that he can kill, he usually kills. Otherwise, it runs in his head, of what use is the power? It's a sort of instinct for economy. I suspected that Levison, gagged, was being cut, in the Moro fashion, into very small bits; and, while my death might be less elaborate, I didn't doubt that it too was in the cards. You don't last long among the Moros once you let them get the bulge on you. If not tonight, some young buck will cut you down tomorrow night, just because he knows he can do it.

Half an hour or more went by slower than you would think it could. My nerves began bothering me: fear taking the form of anger at the suspended activity of the trap I was in; impatience to see the end and get it over with.

I had a gun under my shirt. If I could snake it out and pot Unga, then I had a chance of shooting it out with Jeffol and Jokanain. If I wasn't fast enough, Unga would turn loose the blunderbuss and blow me and the wall behind me into the Celebes Sea, all mixed up so you couldn't say which was which. But even that was better than passing out without trying to take anybody with me.

H OWEVER, THERE WAS STILL gin in the bottle beside me, and it would make the going easier if I could get it in me. I experimented with a slowly reaching hand. Unga said nothing, so I picked up the bottle and took a long drink, leaving one more in it—a stirrup cup, you might say. As I took the bottle down from my mouth, feet pattered in the next room, and old Ca'bi came squeezing out of the door, her mouth spread from ear to ear in a she-devil's grin.

"Panggil orang-orang," she ordered Jokanain, and he went out.

I put the last of the gin down my throat. If I were going to move, it would have to be before the rest of the village got here. I set the empty bottle down and scratched my chin, which brought my right hand within striking distance of my gun.

Then Levison bellowed out like a bull gone mad—a bellow that rattled the floor-timbers in their rattan lashings. Jeffol, without his Colt, came tumbling backward through the door, upsetting Unga. The blunderbuss exploded, blowing the roof wide open. In the confusion I got my gun out—and almost dropped it.

Levison stood in the doorway—but my God!

He was as big as ever—they hadn't whittled any of him away—but he was naked, and without a hair on him anywhere. His skin, where it wasn't blue with ropemarks, was baby-pink and chafed. They had shaved him clean.

My gaze went up to his head, and I got another shock. Every hair had been scraped off or plucked out, even to his eyebrows, and his naked head sat upon his immense body like a pimple. There wasn't a quart of it. There was just enough to hold his big beaked nose and his ears, which stood out like palm leaves now that they weren't supported by hair. Below his loose mouth, his chin was nothing but a sloping down into his burly throat, and the damned thing trembled like a hurt baby's. His eyes, not shadowed now by shaggy brows, were weak and poppy. A gorilla with a mouse's head wouldn't have looked any funnier than Levison without his hair; and the anger that purpled him made him look sillier still. No wonder he had hidden himself behind whiskers!

Dinihari was the first to laugh—a rippling peal of pure amusement. Then I laughed, and Unga and Jeffol. But it wasn't our laughter that beat Levison. We could only have goaded him into killing us. Old Ca'bi turned the trick. The laughter of an old woman is a thing to say prayers against, and Ca'bi was very old.

She pointed a finger at Levison and screeched over it with a glee that was hellish. Her shriveled gums writhed in her open mouth, as if convulsed with mirth of their own, her scrawny throat swelled and she hopped up and down on her bony feet. Levison forgot the rest of us, turned toward her, and stopped. Her thin body shuddered in frenzies of derision, and her voice laughed as sane people don't. You could almost see it—metal lashes of laughter that coiled round his naked body, cut him into raw strips, paralyzed his muscles.

His big body became limp, and he pawed his face with a hand that jerked away as if the touch of the beardless face had burnt it. His knees wobbled, moisture came into his eyes, and his tiny chin quivered. Ca'bi swayed from side to side and hooted at him—a hag gone mad with derision. He backed away from her, cringing back from her laughter like a dog from a whip. She followed him up—laughed him through the sleeping-room door, laughed him back to the far side of the sleeping-room, laughed him through the thin wall. A noise of rippling as he went through the thatch, and a splash of water.

Dinihari stopped laughing and wiped her wet face with her sleeve. Her eyes were soft under Jeffol's cold gaze.

"Your slave (*patek*) rejoices," she cooed, "that her master has recovered his *anting-anting* and is strong again."

"Not so," Jeffol said, and he unbent a little, because she was a woman to want, and because a Moro loves a violent joke.

"But there is much in the book of the Christian (*neserani kitab*). There is a tale the missionary (*tuan padri*) told me of a hairy one named Sansão, who was strong against his enemies until shorn of his hair. Many other magics (*tangkal*) are in the book for all occasions."

S O THAT DAMNED LANGWORTHY was at the bottom of it! I never saw him again. That night I left the island in Levison's yawl with the pick of his goods. He was gone, I knew, even if not in one of the sharks that played round the point. His house would be looted before morning, and I had more right to his stuff than the Moros. Hadn't I been his friend?

———————

DETAILS HAVE BEEN LOST, but we know that when "Ber-Bulu" was published it impressed both readers and critics.

First, the editors of *Editor* magazine were enthusiastic enough about his story to ask Hammett to write an article telling how he wrote it. This invitation was an honor for a young, unknown writer. His article explains his story's origin in the Bible's account of hairy strongman Samson, combined with a remark by artist James Montgomery Flagg, who said the only two excuses for a man to wear a beard were to disguise a criminal past or to hide a weak chin. The tribes of Israel inspired the hairy character's name (Levi-son). Hammett "framed and wrote it in three days, an almost miraculous speed for me, who can seldom do anything in less than three weeks."

The second evidence we have of the positive reaction to "Ber-Bulu" is that *Sunset* bought another story from him right away, and its editors told Hammett that they wanted to run his bio and a photo of him with it.

Meanwhile, he continued to write Continental Op stories for *The Black Mask*.

That summer Hammett grew bored with his Continental Op character—he had written twenty Op stories in twenty-four months—and Phil Cody, editor of *The Black Mask* was giving him trouble, always asking for more action and violence. For variety, Hammett moved his Op out of San Francisco for a story in an Arizona cow town, allowing him to write a parody western, with so much action it is comical. He followed with two more San Francisco-area Op tales, good ones, but stuffed with wholesale murders.

Then Hammett tried to escape the Op. He wrote two stories about Robin Thin, a gentle poetry-writing detective, a new series poking fun at his own writing style and the now-common tough detective genre he and Carroll John Daly had fathered. Phil Cody bought one Robin Thin story. Hammett sold the other to another magazine, which never printed it.

Next he tried a new detective, Alexander Rush, the world's ugliest detective, an ex-cop who works out of a shabby office in Hammett's home town, Baltimore. The first Rush story was also the last.

In September, about the same time Hammett was writing the Rush story, he and Jose received the October issue of *Sunset* magazine. It included "Ruffian's Wife" (his story that the *Sunset* editors purchased earlier that year), plus, on the table of contents page, a photo taken by Jose on the roof of their Eddy Street apartment building on August 10, showing Hammett with their four-year-old daughter Mary Jane. This text appeared beneath the photograph:

DASHIELL HAMMETT is introduced, "in person," to *Sunset* readers this month. With him in the picture you'll observe his daughter and—for no reason at all—their elephant.

Some five months ago Mr. Hammett brought us "Ber-Bulu;" you remember the story? For this issue he has written "Ruffian's Wife."

How did he come to write fiction? Oh, well, he's been a railroad man, a stock broker, a detective, a soldier, and a husband and father. Some outlet for the piled-up experience which these various jobs must have meant was undoubtedly indicated. Moreover, as he says himself, he likes to write.

And, since we (and others) like to read what he writes—well "quod erat etcetera!"

Sunset lacked a "Letters to the Editor" feature, so we have no way of knowing what response the magazine received from readers about "Ber-Bulu." The parenthetical "(and others)" hints at a positive reaction. The Latin phrase is nonsense. It means "which was and the others" or "which was and so forth." In any case, when *Sunset* published this photo it was probably the first time Sam saw his picture in print. It was a moment of triumph. I wonder if he sent copies of that issue to his relatives back East.

He went back to the grind and cranked out another Continental Op yarn for *The Black Mask*. Called "The Creeping Siamese," it involved the Burmese gem-beds he mentioned in his first detective story, "The Road Home." Then Hammett had a spat with Phil Cody about $300 that Hammett claimed the magazine owed him. Cody said it didn't and refused to pay it. That was a lot of money for Hammett.

He took stock of his situation. He had been writing for three years. He was not famous. He was not rich. In fact, he was so poor that he could afford only the cheapest newsprint for final drafts of his stories. For first drafts, he could not even come up with money for cheap newsprint. He typed first drafts on the backs of carbons of old stories, on flyers, on junk mail, on any free paper he could get his hands on that was blank on one side. His writing income was not steady, and it did not look as though it would improve.

His wife was pregnant with their second child. They needed a stable income. He decided to get a fulltime job. His health seemed better; he thought he was strong enough to work.

Sometime in the fall of 1925, Hammett quit writing.

PART SIX

1926-1930,
Ad Man and Novelist

THE THREE STORIES HAMMETT sold to *The Black Mask* before he quit writing—the Robin Thin story, the Alexander Rush story, and "The Creeping Siamese"—ran in the January, February, and March 1926 issues of the magazine. Then there were no more.

In the meantime, Hammett talked his way into a job as advertising manager for Albert S. Samuels Jewelers. He earned about $350 a month—equal to more than $8,000 per month in 2005 dollars—more than his fiction sales and his disability check put together. For the first time, he was doing well. The Hammetts could afford to move up from their studio apartment to a one-bedroom apartment in the same building. Their daughter Josephine Rebecca Hammett was born on May 24, three days before her father's thirty-second birthday.

He was a success in his new job. He enjoyed his work and enjoyed his co-workers. As Richard Layman pointed out in *The Selected Letters of Dashiell Hammett*, "the social aspects of the job were very attractive to a man who had been a virtual shut-in for most of the past six years." It changed him. He grew a moustache. Instead of eating at home, he went to business lunches and dinners. With his new social life, he drank frequently.

Researchers have proved something that doctors did not know then: Drinking aggravates tuberculosis.

At work one day in July, Hammett coughed up a pool of blood, passed out, and was found by his co-workers lying unconscious in the red puddle.

The Public Health Service determined that he had hepatitis in addition to his TB, and ordered the family to separate to protect their two little girls from infection. Hoping to get well enough to return to work, Hammett moved closer to the Samuels offices, to a tiny apartment on Monroe Street (now renamed Dashiell Hammett Street). Jose and the girls left San Francisco to live in Montana with her aunt and uncle. Albert Samuels helped the family financially.

After the Hammetts moved their things out of their old apartment, the law required a health officer to nail a sign on its door: "Tuberculosis is a communicable disease. These apartments have been occupied by a consumptive and may be infected."

Hammett stayed alone in his small Monroe Street apartment, trying to get better. After two months he notified the Veterans

---

RIGHT

This Hammett advertisement ran in the San Francisco Examiner *for Sunday, June 12, 1927. The front page's banner headline:*
"500,000 FRENZIED ADMIRERS CHEER
WHEN COOLIDGE HONORS LINDBERGH."

COMFORTABLE
DIAMONDS

Because diamonds are always noticed,
they should be fine enough to feel at home
in any company. A Samuels diamond, no
matter how modest in size, can stand
any comparison, can smile right back
at the sternest critic. Whether you are
wearing it, or someone else is, you *know*
a Samuels diamond is fine.

These comfortable diamonds
$50 *to* $5000

MONTHLY PAYMENTS

Albert S. Samuels Co.
JEWELERS

110 Geary ⋅ SAN FRANCISCO ⋅ 895 Market
1520 Broadway [*Roos Building*]
OAKLAND

Bureau that his poor health had forced him to quit work and that he wanted his disability payments restarted.

By October he visited Samuels Jewelers again. He wrote to Jose that he wanted "to know whether anything is going to come of the advertising racket or not," and he accused Samuels of being "afraid that I'll die on his hands"—a reasonable fear after finding his employee near-dead in a pool of his own blood.

That month Hammett's life was shaped by two seemingly disconnected events. First, a new publishing sensation debuted, a mystery novel called *The Benson Murder Case*, written by an pseudonymous author using the pen name S. S. Van Dine. The book received favorable reviews and its sales were phenomenal. By the end of the year its formerly poverty-stricken author would be thousands of dollars richer. Its financial success made publishers pay more attention to mysteries, and enthusiastic early reviews led the top critics to pay serious attention for the first time to an American detective novel.

The second event in October was that the November issue of *The Black Mask* arrived in America's newsstands and mailboxes. Hammett's nemesis, Phil Cody, was no longer listed as editor. A new name appeared on the masthead: editor Joseph Thompson Shaw, who by October had been on the job long enough to discover the quality of Hammett's stories in back issues. Shaw was determined to persuade him to write for *The Black Mask* again.

Hammett had recovered his health enough to return to work part-time as advertising manager at Samuels Jewelers. Shaw contacted him and agreed to pay a higher rate of four cents per word and said *The Black Mask* would pay the $300 that Hammett and Cody had quarreled over. Shaw and Hammett discussed a plan to make Hammett more money: Hammett would write longer stories, connected novelettes which could be joined into potentially lucrative novels.

Hammett wrote to Jose, "Tomorrow morning I'm going to start in on the *Black Mask* junk, putting my mornings on that and my evenings on the novel." This was an ambitious schedule. It meant that in his afternoons he would continue working part-time for Samuels Jewelers, so if his disability checks continued he would have three sources of income.

Actually, four. Somehow *Saturday Review of Literature* hired him to write book reviews of new mysteries. Maybe Shaw set it up. Hammett's first reviews discussed the book everyone was talking about, *The Benson Murder Case* by S .S. Van Dine, and its fictional detective, Philo Vance:

> "This Philo Vance is in the Sherlock Holmes tradition and his conversational manner is that of a high-school girl who has been studying the foreign words and phrases in the back of her dictionary. He is a bore when he discusses art and philosophy, but when he switches to criminal psychology he is delightful. There is a theory that any one who talks enough on any subject must, if only by chance, finally say something not altogether incorrect. Vance disproves this theory: he manages always, and usually ridiculously, to be wrong. His exposition of the technique employed by a gentleman shooting another gentleman who sits six feet in front of him deserves a place in a *How to be a detective by mail* course."

Hammett was one of very few reviewers to point out that any attentive reader would know the murderer's identity right from the start. He was right, but few readers cared. *The Benson Murder Case* sold 50,000 copies by early 1927 and showed no signs of stopping.

Within a few weeks Hammett completed and sent Shaw "The Big Knock-Over," a novelette. For its beginning he reached back three years to resurrect his old character Itchy Maker. The novelette starts with the Continental Op delivering a message from Itchy, who is locked up in Folsom prison. Hammett packs his tale with colorful criminals, possibly more of them than in any other crime story by anyone. He brings back rogues from his own stories, uses at least one real thug from Pinkerton's past, and even names two crooks Holmes and Vance, after other writers' famous fictional sleuths.

"The Big Knock-Over" appeared in the February 1927 issue of *Black Mask* (editor Shaw having dropped the word *The* from the magazine's title). That same month, the short satire that follows appeared in the humor magazine *Judge*. Ad man Hammett probably had written it in the fall of the prior year. This is the first time the complete version of this satire has appeared in a book.

The Advertising Man Writes a Love Letter

Dᴇᴀʀ Mᴀɢɢɪᴇ:
I LOVE YOU!

What is love? It is all in all, said Rossetti; it is the salt of life, said Sheffield; it is more than riches, said Lucas; it is like the measles, said Jerome. *Send for leaflet telling what these and other great men of all times have said about love!* It is FREE!

WILL YOU MARRY ME?

Will you be the grandmother of my grandchildren? Or will you, as thousands of others have done, put it off until too late—until you are doomed to the penalty of a lonely old age? Do not delay. *Grandchildren are permanent investments in companionship!*

But simply to marry is not enough! You must ask yourself, to whom? Shall you marry a man just because you like his eyes, or his dancing? *Or will you insist on the best?* IT COSTS NO MORE!

A man who is educated, brilliant, witty, thoughtful, handsome, affectionate, honorable and generous—a man who is made of the best moral, mental and physical materials obtainable—a man in every way worthy, not only of being grandfather to your grandchildren, but great-great-grandfather to your great-great-grandchildren.

All this can be yours if you act NOW!

Read what others have said (full names and addresses on request):

"He was one swell guy." —*Flora B——*.

"In the four years we roomed together he never once left a ring in the bathtub." —*Paul G——*.

"I laughed more the months I knew him than at any other time in my life." —*Fanny S——*.

"He's one of those fellows who knows everything." —*Doris L——*.

All this can be yours! Can you afford to be without it?

Mail the coupon TODAY!

Yours for prompt action,

FRANK.

Tear, cut, or bite this coupon along dotted line

FRANK WHOOP,   B 132-F 10¾ h
    1243 Bunny Street

    Please send me FREE leaflet telling what great men of all times have said about love.
    I am interested in obtaining ETERNAL HAPPINESS without added cost.
    You may call to explain particulars on ....
at .... o'clock. It is understood that this does not obligate me in any way.

Name   ....

Address ....

THE COUPON IS THE punchline of Hammett's joke. The first time I read it, I laughed out loud. As an advertising man myself, I enjoy that the coupon's upper right corner includes a parody of a response tracking number—indicating that this love letter is a mass mailing sent to thousands of people! The coupon also adheres to the advertising principle of restating your offer's main benefits in the first line of your coupon. In fact, this entire piece follows and exaggerates established direct mail techniques. Hammett was showing off how he knew his stuff, from his use of testimonials to the plea at the end for immediate action.

Where Did Hammett's Love Citations Come From?

Hammett began "The Advertising Man Writes a Love Letter" with views of love from four writers. Who were those writers and where did those citations come from?

The citation from English poet Christina Rosetti (1830–1894) is from her poem "The Convent Threshold," which appears in her 1879 book *Goblin Market, The Prince's Progress and Other Poems*:

Knowledge is strong, but love is sweet;
Yea all the progress he had made
Was but to learn that all is small
Save love, for love is all in all.

English poet John Sheffield, earl of Mulgrave and duke of Buckingham and Normanby (1648-1721) writes "Love is the salt of life" in canto v. of his 1721 poem "Ode on Love." "Lucas" is probably English essayist, novelist, and publisher Edward Verrall Lucas (1868-1938), but I have not been able to find the source of Hammett's citation.

English humorist Jerome K. Jerome (1859–1927) was a friend of Arthur Conan Doyle, and, like Hammett, had been an ambulance driver in the World War. In his 1889 book *Idle*

Thoughts of an Idle Fellow, in chapter 2, "On Being in Love," he writes: "Love is like the measles; we all have to go through it. Also like the measles, we take it only once. One never need be afraid of catching it a second time."

JOSE AND THE GIRLS had moved back from Montana to the San Francisco area, but still needed to live separately from Hammett, both to avoid TB infection and because Hammett wanted his time alone. He needed solitude to write, and he was a man who valued having time to himself. Rents were expensive in San Francisco, much less in the surrounding countryside. Jose had grown up in the country and never enjoyed living in a city. She and the little girls moved to the rural town of Fairfax in woodsy Marin County north of the City. Hammett visited on Sundays, riding a ferry boat across the bay and catching a train.

By February, Hammett finished another novelette, "$106,000 Blood Money." Its plot continues from "The Big Knock-Over." The two novelettes together can be considered Hammett's first novel. "$106,000 Blood Money" ran in the May issue of *Black Mask.*

That same month, another magazine caused a national sensation with a different detective story. *Scribner's Magazine,* a stodgy literary journal, ran the first chapters of *The Canary Murder Case,* the second Philo Vance novel by S.S. Van Dine. Newsstands instantly sold out. Critic Arnold Palmer wrote in the *Illustrated London Sphere* that the novel was "a model of everything a detective story should be—a monument, a cathedral amongst detective stories." In *The Chicago Post,* Robert John Bayer said that it proved "the writing of such a novel can be raised to high art."

The biggest event in May 1927, however, was not literary. It was the arrival on May 21 of one man in France: twenty-five-year-old Charles A. Lindbergh, who made the first solo nonstop flight from New York to Paris. Communicated worldwide through the new medium of radio, the 33½-hour flight sent the country into a state of joy that is hard to imagine today.

On top of Lindbergh euphoria, Hammett had other reasons to feel good. In May Hammett celebrated his daughter Josephine's first birthday and his thirty-third, an age he once had believed he never would reach. His health was better. He had moved to a bigger apartment, a studio on Post Street. In a few months, he would be able to afford the higher San Francisco rents for a second apartment so he could move Jose and the girls to San Francisco and stop commuting by ferry to see them. The advertisements he created for Samuels Jewelers seemed to work well. With the higher per-word rate *Black Mask* paid him, he was making a reasonable income as a writer. And he was about to try his first full-length novel.

His title for the novel was *Poisonville*. His plan was to write four linked stories for *Black Mask* and then join them into a novel to send to a book publisher. The stories were based on his Pinkerton experience in Butte, Montana, and included local landmarks such as the M&M Cigar Store, the Columbia Gardens, and Park Street. He sent the first *Poisonville* story to Joe Shaw in July. Shaw promptly sent back a check, words of praise, and his wish for "quicker action" in the following three stories.

That month the hardcover edition of *The Canary Murder Case* by S. S. Van Dine was published. It sold 20,000 copies its first week, 60,000 its first month. By the end of the year it broke every sales record for a mystery. It was a literary phenomenon. The book and its popularity generated a great deal of news coverage, much of it speculating about the identity of the unknown author. One of the few details the publisher admitted was that the secretive author was American; all other mystery kings were Brits. Literary reporters and gossip columnists had a field day speculating who had really written the two novels by "S. S. Van Dine."

Hammett continued to write fiction and kept at his ad work for Albert Samuels. Advertising manager Hammett was interviewed in the October issue of *Western Advertising* about his strategy of using striking modern designs and short text for Samuels Jewelers advertisements, enabling the company to run smaller ads with greater frequency. Hammett bragged about his results: "In spite of materially increased competition, our stores have shown large gains since this advertising was instituted. Our Oakland store has shown an increase of 29 per cent; our two stores in San Francisco have gained 18 and 40 per cent respectively."

The November and December issues of *Black Mask* printed the first two *Poisonville* stories. The December issue of *Western Advertising* contained a long article by Hammett reviewing books about advertising from the past year, and this short news item:

HAMMETT RESIGNS FROM SAMUELS CO.

Dashiell Hammett, 891 Post Street, San Francisco, has resigned his position as advertising manager for the Albert S. Samuels Company, San Francisco and Oakland jewelry concern. Hammett has not announced his plans for the future.

The last two *Poisonville* stories ran in *Black Mask* in January and February. Hammett's higher per-word rate with *Black Mask* meant he had been paid more than $2,000 for the four stories—about $45,000 in 2004 money. Hammett retyped all four stories into one connected novel. In February he mailed his novel *Poisonville* to the publishing company Alfred A. Knopf in New York. It was addressed not to an individual, but to "Editorial Department," its destination the slush pile of unsolicited manuscripts that every publisher accumulates, graveyards where writers' broken dreams lie undisturbed for months.

Not Hammett's. Whether because Joe Shaw provided a kindly word to Knopf or because Hammett's cover letter name-dropped H. L. Mencken (whose *American Mercury* magazine was making good money for Knopf), someone at Knopf read the *Poisonville* manuscript quickly. In only twenty-nine days after Hammett had dropped *Poisonville* in the mail, Mrs. Blanche Knopf, who managed the publisher's line of mysteries, read his manuscript, determined what changes his novel needed, and wrote to him that if he made the changes, Knopf might be interested in publishing it. Oh, and she hated his title, *Poisonville* .

Hammett was eager. In less than a week he made most of the suggested changes and sent them to Mrs. Knopf, along with a list of alternative titles. He also mentioned he was working on a new novel, called *The Dain Curse*.

From Hammett's list of possible titles, Mrs. Knopf chose *Red Harvest*. She sent back a contract for three novels. Hammett signed the contract in April. He asked the publisher to add a dedication to *Red Harvest*: "To Joseph Thompson Shaw." In May he visited Los Angeles, trying to persuade a movie studio to buy a story from him. No sale.

He returned to San Francisco. He was finishing four connected stories for *Black Mask* about murders involving a family named Dain. For fun, he named characters after employees of Samuels Jewelers. He rewrote the four stories as a novel and sent a manuscript of *The Dain Curse* to Knopf in June. It was not accepted as quickly as *Red Harvest*. For five months, letters flew back and forth between San Francisco and New York as Hammett and his editor battled over what changes *The Dain Curse* needed to become publishable. In the middle of their haggling, in July, Hammett wrote that he was working on another novel, *The Maltese Falcon.* By then, he had already received more than $2,000 from Joe Shaw for selling the magazine rights to *The Dain Curse* to *Black Mask.* Finally, in late November, after the first two Dain stories had already run in *Black Mask,* the battle ebbed when Knopf accepted *The Dain Curse,* still arguing that Hammett should make more changes.

In the meantime, the September issue of *American Magazine* revealed the secret identity behind detective Philo Vance's creator, bestselling author S. S. Van Dine. He was really Willard Huntington Wright, literary and art critic, and the pre-Mencken editor of *The Smart Set.*

And a new U.S. president had been elected. The continuing wave of Roaring Twenties prosperity helped sweep Herbert Hoover, another Republican president, into office that November.

Hammett's editor at Knopf closed 1928 by setting a deadline for Hammett to submit the manuscript of *The Maltese Falcon*: April 1, 1929.

As he began the new year of 1929, Hammett must have been eager to get a copy of his first hardback novel, to hold it in his hands. *Red Harvest* was officially published February first, so he probably received his ten complimentary copies in January. Opening the carton from Knopf containing his first book must have been a proud, exciting moment.

Hammett had been working on *The Maltese Falcon* for more than half a year by the time *Red Harvest* was published. He wanted to see what reviewers would say about his first book. One of the first reviews appeared in a magazine Hammett had written for, *Western Advertising.* It called *Red Harvest* "an exciting and sanguinary mystery yarn" that gave "a disturbing sense of reality." Mystery novels were not normally covered by this trade magazine for advertisers, so the reviewer felt he had to explain why the book was mentioned: "because it is the first full-length work of Dashiell Hammett, former advertising manager of Albert S. Samuels Company, San Francisco."

Most reviews were favorable, some even enthusiastic. Some, however, hated it.

Hammett did not finish *The Maltese Falcon* by his publisher's April 1 deadline, but was a month and a half late. This time, instead of writing interconnected stories and linking them, he wrote—for the first time—one continuous novel-length narrative. And instead of featuring the Continental Op, the novel was about a new character, Sam Spade. Hammett sold *The Maltese Falcon* to Joe Shaw for magazine publication for more than $2,000. Shaw broke the novel into five parts and ran them in *Black Mask* as a serial.

In spite of the money he had received from *Black Mask*, by the time Hammett sent *The Maltese Falcon* to Knopf in mid-June, he wrote that he was broke and desperately needed money.

The next month, July, Knopf offered Hammett $1,000 as an advance against another three books. (Remember that at this time, $1,000 was enough money to support a family of four for a year.) Hammett started writing the first of the second contract's three books, *The Glass Key*. In July, Knopf published his second novel, *The Dain Curse*, which Hammett dedicated to his friend and former boss Albert S. Samuels. He autographed a copy for Samuels "for all the reasons in the world."

In August, Hammett saw his first royalty check. He found that *Red Harvest* had only mediocre sales. His royalty payment was probably between $100 and $300. He spent it.

Fortunately, his publisher sold the movie rights for *Red Harvest* to Paramount. In mid-September, Hammett received a check for his share, well over $1,000, "which," he wrote, "arrived at a time when I was considering hocking my typewriter [sic]." Again, he spent it all.

He decided to move to New York, the center of publishing. Hammett expected to write for books and magazines in New York and the movies in Hollywood, and to travel back and forth between the two coasts. He bought Jose a new trunk and put Jose and the girls on a train to Southern California. He and Jose had lived apart for three years. Their time together was over. They agreed that she would take care of the girls and he would take care of her financially. They would remain married, but he would live his own life.

Hammett was broke. The thousands of dollars he earned that year from *Black Mask*, Knopf, Paramount, and his book reviews for *Saturday Review of Literature* were gone. What he did with all his money is an unsolved mystery—perhaps he gambled it away. He needed $500 (about $15,000 in 2004 money) to pay debts and buy a train ticket. Albert Samuels loaned it to him. Hammett moved from San Francisco to New York by the middle of October 1929.

The New York Stock Exchange made headlines that month. On Monday, October 28, stock prices fell sharply. In one day, General Motors stock lost nearly $1 billion in value, equal to a $25 billion drop now. The next day was even worse, earning October 29 the bitter name Black Tuesday. Within a few weeks stocks on the New York exchange fell more than forty percent in value. Companies fought to survive the only ways they could: they cut salaries, fired workers, closed plants and offices.

Meanwhile, Hammett discovered he was a minor literary celebrity in New York. He met H. L. Mencken, who thought him a "strange Marylander." He met writer Nell Martin. Four of her novels had been published. She had sold more than a dozen scripts and stories to the movies. She introduced Hammett to people in show business. His expanded social life distracted him from writing. He quit writing book reviews for *Saturday Review of Literature* and lost momentum on his novel, *The Glass Key*.

He was working on it intermittently when he received his second royalty check in February 1930. It covered sales for both *Red Harvest* and *The Dain Curse*. His second book sold better than his first, but only a little.

On Valentine's Day, February 14, Knopf published *The Maltese Falcon*. It bore Hammett's dedication "To Jose." Hammett sought out reviews of the novel and saved them in a scrapbook. Most were extremely favorable.

The same month, Paramount premiered the movie based on *Red Harvest*. The studio had changed its title to *Roadhouse Nights,* and changed the plot so it was unrecognizable. Hammett's name was not even listed in the credits.

Also in February, the March issue of *Black Mask* hit the newsstands. It included the first quarter of *The Glass Key*—but Hammett had not yet finished writing the last quarter! Joseph Shaw must have been in a panic. He had only three months before the magazine with the missing conclusion was due in his subscribers' mailboxes.

Between bouts of drinking and socializing, Hammett managed to finish *The Glass Key*, but months past his deadline for *Black Mask*. He had allowed his disciplined work habits to deteriorate. Now he had to cram to make up for it. He later claimed he " ... finished the last third of *The Glass Key* in one continuous sitting of thirty hours." My guess is that Hammett misremembered or exaggerated the amount, but whether it was the last third or last quarter, Shaw took it, ran it through typesetting, printing, and mailing, and got the magazine issue out in time. Because Hammett finished *The Glass Key* months late, it put him behind schedule on delivering the next book his contract said he owed Knopf.

Black Mask paid Hammett about $3,000 for *The Glass Key*, so while writing his next novel he should have been in good financial shape—unlike many other people.

By spring 1930 more than four million Americans were out of work. For the first time in many years, breadlines appeared in cities—starving people, waiting in lines for a cup of coffee and a piece of bread.

By March, five months since the October crash, the number of families on relief in New York City had tripled. City shelters overflowed. The city allowed homeless men to sleep on a barge on the East River docks, whipped at night by freezing winds.

It was the same in other cities across America. A Detroit official of the American Federation of Labor said "the men are sitting in the parks all day long and all night long, hundreds and thousands of them, muttering to themselves, out of work, seeking work."

With his newly established reputation, Hammett found getting work no problem. To bring in extra cash, in April he started writing "The Crime Wave," a mystery book review column for *The New York Evening Post*.

April 30, 1930: 35,000 people gathered in a park fourteen blocks from Hammett's apartment to hear Communist speakers. When one speaker asked the peaceful crowd to march to City Hall, hundreds of policemen and plainclothes detectives went berserk. With nightsticks, clubs, and blackjacks, they smashed the skulls and faces of men and women. Thousands of people fled through the streets, pursued by out-of-control policemen. Could Hammett hear screams and sirens while he worked in his apartment? Did he see people with bloodied faces? He must have read newspaper headlines about the police riot, and talked about it with friends or neighbors.

Never before in America had Communists been able to attract a crowd of 35,000 people. Why were they able to now?

Because people were in a panic. The old ways weren't working. People were searching for answers. The Communists said they had answers. Maybe the Communists were onto something.

Men searching for work became grim, then despairing. As their searches continued, their clothes wore out and their shoes fell to pieces. Men slipped newspapers under worn shirts to keep out the cold, replaced inner shoe soles with cardboard, wrapped gunny sacks around disintegrated shoes to keep out the cold. Mothers tried to find work. Children tried to earn pennies after school. Families began to starve.

To deal with the crisis, President Hoover appointed an Emergency Committee for Unemployment. Then he told his committee that unemployment was strictly a local responsibility. He allowed his committee to do nothing.

Hammett continued writing his next novel, which he titled *The Thin Man*. Set in San Francisco, it featured John Guild, a dark-skinned detective who worked for the fictional Associated Detective Bureaus, Inc., with offices in a version of the same building in which both the fictional Continental Detective Agency and the real Pinkerton's National Detective Agency had their offices.

Hammett's column "The Crime Wave" for Saturday, May 24, carried his review of S. S. Van Dine's latest Philo Vance detective novel, *The Scarab Murder Case:* "The plot has several interesting twists, though its ending is not altogether convincing and its course is slowed up by the irrelevant profundities that Mr. Van Dine's public is supposed to expect of him." It was a kinder review than *The Scarab Murder Case* received from others, but Philo Vance was reviewer-proof. The public didn't care, and the book sold 80,000 copies by the end of summer, pushing the sales of the first five Philo Vance novels to more than one million hardcover copies.

In June, Hammett appeared in the offices of the Knopf company and signed a contract to sell motion picture rights to *The*

Maltese Falcon to Warner Brothers for $8,500. The next day, Warner Brothers countersigned the contract. Hammett's share was a check for $6,375, about $180,000 in 2004 dollars.

Hammett had written 65 pages—about a third—of *The Thin Man*. He later wrote, "By the time I had written these 65 pages my publisher and I agreed that it might be wise to postpone the publication of *The Glass Key*—scheduled for that fall—until the following spring. This meant that *The Thin Man* could not be published until the fall of 1931. So—having plenty of time—I put these 65 pages aside and went to Hollywood for a year."

Hammett was in Hollywood by mid-July, looking for more big money from the movies.

PART SEVEN

1930-1941, Rich and Famous

HOLLYWOOD WELCOMED HAMMETT with open arms and open checkbooks. David O. Selznick persuaded Paramount Pictures to hire Hammett for $300 per week (over $6,000 per week in 2005 money), plus a $5,000 bonus if Paramount accepted any original story he wrote. Hammett visited Jose and the girls, who were happy to see him after nearly a year apart.

In New York, Hammett's publisher was talking with Warner Brothers about selling motion picture rights to *The Glass Key*. From Hollywood, Hammett telegraphed Knopf that he thought they could get more money from his new employer, Paramount.

Hammett received his third check for royalties from his three novels. Thanks to the success of *The Maltese Falcon*, it was probably for $1,000 or more. His publisher Knopf found that to date Hammett had neglected *The Thin Man* in favor of writing for Paramount. Knopf was not amused.

With money rolling in, Hammett didn't need to write *The Thin Man*—or anything else, for that matter. In early October he quit writing his column "The Crime Wave." He concentrated on having a wild social life: parties, women, gambling, and outrageous drunken binges with movie writers, producers, directors, actors, actresses.

In November at a Hollywood party hosted by Darryl F. Zanuck, Hammett met screenwriter Arthur Kober's twenty-five-year-old wife, Lillian. Her maiden name was Hellman. She was eleven years younger than Hammett, not beautiful but well dressed, intelligent, lively, and bold. They began a passionate affair.

Paramount needed ideas for movies to star Gary Cooper. Hammett wrote six movie stories, hoping Paramount would buy one. One was "The Ungallant," about a man rescuing a Russian princess, like Hammett's short story "Laughing Masks." The studio preferred a story first titled "After School," then renamed "The Kiss-Off." Paramount bought it on November 26 and paid Hammett his $5,000 bonus. A family of four could live for five years on $5,000. Hammett went to the Clover Club and gambled it away.

It was the second winter of the Depression. With no money for rent, thousands of unemployed families moved to vacant lots and built shacks from old packing crates, dead car bodies, tarpaper, and sticks. These shack towns quickly found names: Hoovervilles. The lucky ones lived in Hoovervilles. Most unemployed slept in boxcars, cardboard boxes, doorways—anywhere they found shelter from the cold winter winds.

If you were hungry, you could go to soup kitchens. There you could wait for hours to get a tin cup of coffee and a bowl of mush, often with no milk or sugar. Other people waited in garbage dumps; when a garbage truck dumped its load, they dug in with hands and sticks, digging in garbage for food they could eat.

Hammett seemed insulated from economic worries. He left Paramount and signed a contract to write a story for Warner Brothers about a crooked detective. He was paid $5,000 as an advance, was promised another $5,000 when he finished his story, and a third $5,000 if Warner Brothers accepted it.

In February, Hammett's fourth royalty check from Knopf probably was almost $1,000, thanks again to brisk sales of *The Maltese Falcon*, which had sold more than his first two books combined.

The tide of money continued to flow in; Hammett's luck was running good. As he had predicted, Paramount bought movie rights for *The Glass Key* for a higher amount than Warner Brothers paid for *The Maltese Falcon*. Hammett's share was worth about $500,000 in 2005 money. He spent it as quickly as he could: drinking, gambling, extravagant gifts. He hired servants. He rented a limousine and hired a chauffeur.

His old boss Al Samuels was ill, so the chauffeur drove Hammett up to San Francisco to repay the $500 Samuels had loaned to Hammett for his move to New York. Then Hammett rented a suite at the Fairmont Hotel and partied hard. A week later he returned to Samuels, hat in hand. He'd burned through his money. To return to Hollywood, Hammett needed to borrow $800 to pay his San Francisco bills.

The Depression deepened. By March 1931, unemployment had doubled since March 1930.

After months of putting off *On the Make*, Hammett finally finished it. He had to. He needed money that April to pay income taxes. Amazingly, he had exhausted his big windfall, *The Glass Key* movie money. "I owe all Southern California money," he wrote, probably referring to gambling debts. "I've got to do something approaching the desperate." He turned in *On the*

Make to Warner Brothers, received his second $5,000 payment, and it was spent. He needed the third $5,000 installment. But that final payment was Hammett's only if Warner Brothers accepted his story. Instead, the studio rejected it. Hammett was left in the lurch.

An agent earned Hammett a few hundred dollars by getting him a deal to edit a collection of horror stories, but that wasn't enough. Hammett sent Alfred Knopf a telegram that he was "IN DESPERATE NEED OF ALL THE MONEY I CAN FIND" and asked Knopf to wire a thousand dollars into his bank account. Knopf did and Hammett was saved.

Knopf had an incentive for advancing so much cash. (Remember to multiply that $1,000 by 20 to 30 times to understand its value.) That month Knopf had published Hammett's novel *The Glass Key* in its U.S. edition—the first edition had been published in England back in January. Reviews were positive and sales were brisk. *The Glass Key* became Hammett's first best-selling novel. The U.S. edition sold 23,027 copies for Knopf—Hammett's best to date (but a tenth of the sales of S.S. Van Dine's books). Each of Hammett's novels sold more than the one before it, making Alfred Knopf eager to do whatever he could to get Hammett to finish his next book, even advancing such large sums.

Also in April, Paramount released the Gary Cooper movie based on Hammett's story "The Kiss-Off." Its title was now *City Streets*. For the first time, Hammett could see his name in movie credits. *City Streets* supposedly became gangster Al Capone's favorite movie.

In May, Warner Brothers released the second movie with Dashiell Hammett's name on it: *The Maltese Falcon*. It starred Ricardo Cortez as Sam Spade, with Bebe Daniels, Thelma Todd, and Dwight Frye. The movie earned good reviews and was considered a modest financial success by studio brass.

While Hammett lived in Hollywood, he sent the sixty-five-page beginning of *The Thin Man* to his agent, who, in turn, sent copies to magazine publishers, hoping to get quick money from an advance sale to one of the top magazines, now that Hammett was a best-selling author. On May 14, Hearst's *Cosmopolitan* agreed to pay $26,500 for magazine rights to the still-unfinished *The Thin Man*.

Publisher Knopf somehow quashed the *Cosmopolitan* sale. Hammett's hope of getting a fast buck from advance money disappeared.

Hammett was not the only person short on funds. In Europe, Austrian Credit-Anstalt failed, triggering investors to quickly withdraw foreign funds from Germany. Financial panic splashed across Europe.

By June nearly one-quarter of the state of New York's labor force was out of work, a staggering quantity. One social worker wrote, "Have you seen the uncontrollable trembling of parents who have gone half-starved for weeks so that the children may have food?" Researchers found that in many schools 85 to 99 percent of the children were underweight and lethargic from malnutrition.

Monetary ruin continued to sweep Europe. By mid-July, all German banks had closed.

Hammett's August royalty check wasn't enough. On August 6, he telegraphed Alfred Knopf that he was "IN TERRIFIC FINANCIAL DIFFICULTY" and asked Knopf to wire $2,500 more. The publisher did.

Due to his drunkenness, irresponsibility, and habit of missing deadlines, Hammett was unable to get more film work. In September he took a train back to New York. For quick money, his agent convinced him to write short stories again. Now that Hammett was a well-known author, instead of selling stories to pulps for a few hundred dollars, he could sell them to slick magazines for thousands. Hammett got to work, writing magazine short stories for the first time in more than a year.

While he wrote short stories, the European financial crisis hit Great Britain so hard that it pushed the Bank of England off the gold standard.

The diary of H. L. Mencken records that on November 27, 1931, he attended a party at the New York apartment of Alfred and Blanche Knopf with Willa Cather, Fanny Hurst, and George Gershwin, where Hammett, "the writer of detective stories, came in drunk and became something of a nuisance. After we left, so Blanche told me today, she had to get rid of him."

That fall, Hammett effectively disappeared. He stopped responding to letters from his publisher and from Jose. He kept up contact with his lover Hellman and with his agent—his only source of income except for his twice-a-year royalty checks from Knopf.

In the winter of 1931, government relief funds ran out. Private charities were depleted. In New York City entire families got relief averaging $2.39 per week. In Toledo, Ohio, meal funds were less than three cents per person per day. (Even with inflation, that's only ninety cents.) In many places no assistance was available at all.

As the new year of 1932 began, Japan completed its military takeover of South Manchuria in China. World leaders did nothing.

It was February before the first of Hammett's new batch of stories appeared in print. "On the Way" was the first new Hammett story to appear in sixteen months. It ran in the March issue of *Harper's Bazaar*, and is unlike anything he had written before. It is an autobiographical story about a declining older Hollywood scriptwriter who, like Hammett, detests the movie business, and whose lover Gladys' career is rising, with a contract to work on a movie called *Laughing Masks*. Hammett's story seems to predict his own decline and the rise of his lover Lillian Hellman. She wanted to be a writer, but her only published writings were a handful of book reviews.

Hammett used his short story money to hide out in the Biltmore, one of New York's most expensive hotels, where he could work undisturbed on *The Thin Man*. He had stopped writing the novel nearly two years earlier. Now he reviewed what he had written "and then I found it easier, or at least generally more satisfactory," he later wrote, "to keep only the basic idea of the plot and otherwise to start anew." Even though he had finished one-third of the San Francisco version of *The Thin Man*, he put it aside and started a new version, set where he lived now, in New York.

The discontent of a hungry nation was rising. In three years the average monthly wage had dropped sixty percent. The song "Brother, Can You Spare a Dime?" became a popular hit.

The Republican Party nominated President Hoover to run for office again. The Democrats nominated Franklin Delano Roosevelt on a platform of changes in farm policies, reform of the banking and financial system, and the repeal of Prohibition.

Hammett's August royalty check from Knopf would have been small or zero, since he had had no new novel published for more than a year and had taken so many advances. He moved from the Biltmore to another expensive New York hotel, the Hotel Pierre. He wrote and sold three Sam Spade short stories for between $1,000 and $2,500 each, but that couldn't keep up with his spending. He ran out of money, so at the end of September Hammett and Hellman snuck out of the Hotel Pierre to avoid paying his bill.

Knopf paid him yet another advance—a small one this time—so he could keep working on *The Thin Man*. Hammett and Hellman moved into a cheap residential hotel. Hammett interrupted *The Thin Man* long enough to write a novelette called "Woman in the Dark," which his agent sold to a slick magazine for a couple of thousand dollars.

That September a mob of starving unemployed men in Toledo, Ohio, attacked grocery stores and seized food.

Franklin Delano Roosevelt won the presidential election in November, and the Democrats won control of both branches of Congress. The economic breakdown continued to get worse. Farm income had dropped to one-third of what it had been three years earlier. Debts and farm taxes drove thousands of farms into foreclosure. The deepening global economic crisis pushed the United States closer to collapse than any new president had seen since Abraham Lincoln.

In Germany, the economy was improving. A new chancellor appointed in January 1933 took credit, even though the improvements were generated by events that happened before he was sworn in. The ambitious new chancellor's name was Adolf Hitler.

In March Roosevelt was sworn in as the new U.S. president. He gave a rousing inaugural address, proclaiming "the only thing we have to fear is fear itself." It would take more than words to fix America. By Roosevelt's inauguration day, U.S. banks had become so weakened that 5,504 banks had failed and nearly all others had been placed under state government restrictions. People had lost faith in banks and refused to deposit money in them. Roosevelt declared a four-day banking shutdown, with all U.S. banks closed until they were declared sound by federal examiners. About seventy-five percent of banks reopened. Hoarded currency was redeposited and the banking system was healthy again. Within two weeks stock prices rose fifteen percent.

One of the first moves of the new Democratic Congress was to pass an act legalizing wine and beer, the first step toward the repeal of Prohibition. Beer and wine were already so easy to buy that the new law may not have made much difference for alcoholics such as Hammett.

He was still plugging away on *The Thin Man* and low on cash. His agent sold the movie rights for the "Woman in the Dark" story to quickly bring in a $500 advance towards a $5,000 price payable at some later date.

Hammett completed *The Thin Man* in May and turned it over to his publisher Knopf, two years behind schedule. His agent immediately tried to sell the finished novel to magazines, but found little interest. Most publishers of major magazines considered this version of *The Thin Man* too daring.

The same month Hammett submitted *The Thin Man* he found a new plot idea in a collection of true crime stories called *Bad Companions* by William Roughead. The story told of two women who ran a girls' school in Edinburgh, Scotland, and how their lives were ruined when a schoolgirl accused them of being lesbians. He gave the plot to Hellman and a title, *The Children's Hour*. Under Hammett's guidance she began turning it into a play during summer 1933.

In July Hammett's agent finally sold *The Thin Man* to one of the leading magazines, *Redbook*. The *Redbook* editor cut out the novel's "objectionable" parts. The price was $5,000—less than one-fifth of Hammett's offer from *Cosmopolitan* magazine for his earlier incomplete version.

Hammett took the money and Hellman and went to Homestead, Florida, where they fished and worked on *The Children's Hour*.

By the late summer or early fall Hammett needed more money, so he wrote another batch of five short stories. He wrote one of the five stories due to a mistake. Somehow Hammett or his agent had promised the same story to two different magazines: to Arnold Gingrich for the first issue of his new magazine *Esquire,* and to Frederic Dannay (one-half of the writing duo who created the Ellery Queen mysteries) for the first issue of his new *Mystery League Magazine. Esquire* got the first story, and Hammett wriggled out of his predicament by writing another story for *Mystery League*. He called it "Night Shade."

It includes an example of a playful Hammettism, his habit of using names of people he knew in his stories. In this story his lover Hellman becomes a street.

Night Shade

 A SEDAN with no lights burning was standing beside
the road just above Piney Falls bridge and as I drove
past it a girl put her head out and said, "Please." Her
voice was urgent but there was not enough excitement in it to make it either harsh or shrill.

I put on my brakes, then backed up. By that time a man had
got out of the sedan. There was enough light to let me see he
was young and fairly big. He moved a hand in the direction I
had been going and said, "On your way, buddy."

The girl said again, "Will you drive me into town, please?"
She seemed to be trying to open the sedan door. Her hat had
been pushed forward over one eye.

I said, "Sure."

The man in the road took a step toward me, moved his
hand as before, and growled, "Scram, you."

I got out of my car. The man in the road had started toward
me when another man's voice came from the sedan, a harsh
warning voice. "Go easy, Tony. It's Jack Bye." The sedan door
swung open and the girl jumped out.

Tony said, "Oh!" and his feet shuffled uncertainly on the
road; but when he saw the girl making for my car he cried
indignantly at her, "Listen, you can't ride to town with—"

She was in my roadster by then. "Good night," she said.

He faced me, shook his head stubbornly, began, "I'll be damned if I'll let—"

I hit him. The knockdown was fair enough, because I hit him hard, but I think he could have got up again if he had wanted to. I gave him a little time, then asked the fellow in the sedan, "All right with you?" I still could not see him.

"He'll be all right," he replied quickly. "I'll take care of him all right."

"Thanks." I climbed into my car beside the girl. The rain I had been trying to get to town ahead of was beginning to fall. A coupé with a man and a woman in it passed us going into town. We followed the coupé across the bridge.

The girl said, "This is awfully kind of you. I wasn't in any danger back there, but it was—nasty."

"They wouldn't be dangerous," I said, "but they would be—nasty."

"You know them?"

"No."

"But they knew you. Tony Forrest and Fred Barnes." When I did not say anything, she added, "They were afraid of you."

"I'm a desperate character."

She laughed. "And pretty nice of you, too, tonight. I wouldn't've gone with either of them alone, but I thought with two of them . . . " She turned up the collar of her coat. "It's raining in on me."

I stopped the roadster again and hunted for the curtain that belonged on her side of the car. "So your name's Jack Bye," she said while I was snapping it on.

"And yours is Helen Warner."

"How'd you know?" She had straightened her hat.

"I've seen you around." I finished attaching the curtain and got back in.

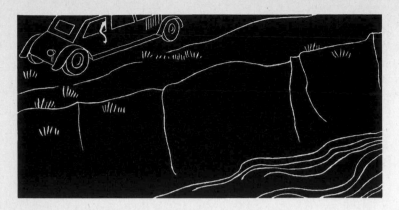

"Did you know who I was when I called to you?" she asked when we were moving again.

"Yes."

"It was silly of me to go out with them like that."

"You're shivering."

"It's chilly."

I said I was sorry my flask was empty.

We had turned into the western end of Hellman avenue. It was four minutes past ten by the clock in front of the jewelry store on the corner of Laurel Street. A policeman in a black rubber coat was leaning against the clock. I did not know enough about perfumes to know the name of hers.

She said, "I'm chilly. Can't we stop somewhere and get a drink?"

"Do you really want to?" My voice must have puzzled her: she turned her head quickly to peer at me in the dim light.

"I'd like to," she said, "unless you're in a hurry."

"No. We could go to Mack's. It's only three or four blocks from here, but—it's a nigger joint."

She laughed. "All I ask is that I don't get poisoned."

"You won't, but you're sure you want to go?"

"Certainly." She exaggerated her shivering. "I'm cold. It's early."

Toots Mack opened his door for us. I could tell by the politeness with which he bowed his round bald black head and said, "Good evening, sir; good evening, madam," that he wished we had gone some place else, but I was not especially interested in how he felt about it. I said, "Hello, Toots; how are you this evening?" too cheerfully.

There were only a few customers in the place. We went to the table in the corner farthest from the piano. Suddenly she was staring at me, her eyes, already very blue, becoming very round.

"I thought you could see in the car," I began.

"How'd you get that scar?" she asked, interrupting me. She sat down.

"That." I put a hand to my cheek. "Fight—couple of years ago. You ought to see the one on my chest."

"We'll have to go swimming some time," she said gayly. "Please sit down and don't keep me waiting for my drink."

"Are you sure you—"

She began to chant, keeping time with her fingers on the table, "I want a drink, I want a drink, I want a drink." Her mouth was small with full lips and it curved up without growing wider when she smiled.

We ordered drinks. We talked too fast. We made jokes and laughed too readily at them. We asked questions—about the name of the perfume she used was one—and paid too much or no attention to the answers. And Toots looked glumly at us from behind the bar when he thought we were not looking at him. It was all pretty bad.

We had another drink and I said, "Well, let's slide along."

She was nice about seeming neither too anxious to go nor to stay. The ends of her pale blond hair curled up over the edge of her hat in back.

At the door I said, "Listen, there's a taxi-stand around the corner. You won't mind if I don't take you home?"

She put a hand on my arm. "I do mind. Please—" The street was badly lighted. Her face was like a child's. She took her hand off my arm. "But if you'd rather . . . "

"I think I'd rather."

She said slowly, "I like you, Jack Bye, and I'm awfully grateful for—"

I said, "Aw, that's all right," and we shook hands and I went back into the speakeasy.

Toots was still behind the bar. He came up to where I stood. "You oughtn't to do that to me," he said, shaking his head mournfully.

"I know. I'm sorry."

"You oughtn't to do it to yourself," he went on just as sadly. "This ain't Harlem, boy, and if old Judge Warner finds out his daughter's running around with you and coming in here he can make it plenty tough for both of us. I like you, boy, but you got to remember it don't make no difference how light your skin is or how many colleges you went to, you're still a nigger."

I said, "Well, what do you suppose I want to be? A Chinaman?"

"NIGHT SHADE" was the beginning of a long working association between Hammett and Frederic Dannay, a relationship that would have a profound effect on Hammett's popularity and critical reputation during his later years and even after his death.

"Night Shade" on Trial

This story resurfaced in unusual circumstances twenty years after Hammett wrote it, when he was under attack for his political beliefs. On March 24, 1953, the U.S. Senate Permanent Subcommittee on Investigations met behind closed doors in a private session in the Senate Office Building in Washington, D.C. It was a fishing expedition. Hammett had never publicly admitted he was a Communist. In this private session, investigators wanted to get Hammett to say something that would associate him with Communism so they could get him to say the same thing in a public session and disgrace him. Failing that, they wanted to get Hammett to repeatedly invoke the Fifth Amendment, which would at least make him seem suspicious.

Chief counsel Roy Cohn was the point man for Senator Joe McCarthy. In the middle of his interrogation, Cohn asked Hammett, "Did you write a story which could be classed as other than a detective story?"

"Yes," Hammett replied.

"What?" asked Cohn.

"I have written quite a number of short stories that were not detective stories."

Cohn was instantly on the alert. Hoping to find a Hammett story with a Communist subject, he asked, "Any that deal with social problems?" The phrase *social problems* meant *Communist causes.*

"I don't think so," Hammett said. "Yes, I remember one, if you take it as a social problem. Some short stories have been in paperbound books that have been published in book form."

"Did any of those deal with social problems?" pressed Cohn.

"Yes," said Hammett. "As a matter of fact, roughly one that I remember, a short story called 'Night Shade.'"

"'Night Shade'?"

"'Night Shade,' which had to do with Negro-white relations," Hammett explained.

Cohn asked, "When you wrote this short story, 'Night Shade,' were you a member of the Communist Party?"

Hammett invoked the Fifth Amendment by responding, "I decline to answer on the ground the answer may tend to incriminate me."

Cohn hoped he had uncovered evidence that Hammett's writing promoted Communism. He asked, "Did that story in any way reflect the Communist line?"

"That is a difficult—on the word 'reflect' I would say no, it didn't reflect it," Hammett replied. "It was against racism."

Senator Karl E. Mundt was another investigator. He tried a different tack. "Would you say that it resembled—whether it reflected or not—the Communist line with respect to race problems?"

Hammett answered, "No, I couldn't pick out—I could answer that question if you just put it, 'Did it at all?' But did it reflect that more than, say, other political parties, I would have to say no. I think the truth would be that it didn't reflect it consciously or solely."

The subcommittee abandoned its attempt to paint "Night Shade" as a Communist plot—in both senses of the word—and moved on to other topics. Hammett was grilled in a public McCarthy hearing two days later, and "Night Shade" was not mentioned.

While the *Mystery League Magazine* containing "Night Shade" appeared, S. S. Van Dine's new Philo Vance mystery was published, *The Dragon Murder Case*. Reviewers were not kind. The days were past when critics saw S. S. Van Dine as a creative force revitalizing a stale literary genre. After a decade of Hammett and his followers, Van Dine's novels seemed artificial and old-fashioned.

In December *Redbook* magazine published its condensed, expurgated version of *The Thin Man*. The month was no doubt more memorable for Hammett because the Twenty-First Amendment to the U.S. Constitution was passed, which repealed Prohibition. Selling alcohol was legal again. And that month, William Randolph Hearst's syndicate, King Features, contacted Hammett with an idea: a detective comic strip.

In January 1934, King Features haggled with Hammett, and Knopf published *The Thin Man* in book form. It was dedicated "To Lillian." Hammett pored over its reviews and sales reports. "It got very fine reviews—as you can see from the enclosed clip-

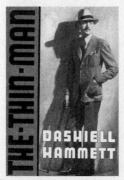

pings," he bragged to his wife, Jose, "and last week sold better than any other book in New York, Philadelphia, and San Francisco, besides being near the top of the list in most other cities."

Sales may have been helped by the book's dust jacket. Hammett complained to his publisher that his prior dust jackets, especially for *The Glass Key*, were ineffective advertisements, and asked to have a hand in creating the dust jacket for *The Thin Man*. Publisher Knopf invited Hammett to write the text, but Hammett got even more involved, posing for a photograph used on the front and spine of the dust jacket.

Sales of *The Thin Man* were also boosted by text that was shocking for its time, and by vivid, memorable characters in an entertaining story that to most readers appeared carefree and escapist. But some saw another level beneath its glossy surface. Author Donald Westlake: "When I was fourteen or fifteen I read Hammett's *The Thin Man* (the first Hammett I'd read) and it was a defining moment. It was a sad, lonely, lost book, that pretended to be cheerful and aware and full of good fellowship, and I hadn't known you could do that: seem to be telling this, but really telling that; three-dimensional writing, like three-dimensional chess. Nabokov was the other master of that."

The surface gloss of *The Thin Man* was enough for MGM. It bought movie rights in mid-January. Hammett's share was more than $15,000 (worth $300,000 or more today).

Yet another source of money arrived. Hammett wrote to his wife, "I'm writing a story for a cartoon strip for Hearst's syndicate, which will bring me a regular and, I hope, growing income perhaps forever. If it goes over well it can make me a lot of money."

The comic strip was *Secret Agent X-9*, about a government secret agent whose undercover identity was to act as a private detective. Hammett was lucky in whom he was teamed with as co-creator, a young artist named Alex Raymond, now famous as the creator of *Flash Gordon*. Hammett earned $500 per week for writing stories and dialog. For drawing the art, Hearst paid Raymond $20 per week.

To promote the strip, newspapers ran full-page advertisements proclaiming Hammett "America's most famous detective story writer," photos of him, articles calling him "a great detective himself, and recognized as the greatest detective story writer of the Twentieth Century." Newspapers urged boys and girls to join the Secret Agent X-9 Club to receive a membership card, "a real bright and shiny detective badge," and a secret message decoder.

The promotions—and Hammett's sources of money—did not stop there. At that time, newspapers included fiction. The Hearst syndicate paid Hammett for rights to revive his earlier stories and novels in newspapers. The syndicate created new illustrations for the stories, often repackaged them as weekly or daily serials, and sold them to papers. Hammett's old stories recirculated across America for the next eight years, making him well known to millions of readers who had never seen his work in *Black Mask*. Most readers did not know they were reading old stories. They thought Hammett was writing new ones.

At about this time, Hammett's agent received the $4,500 balance for movie rights to "Woman in the Dark." Hammett was doing so well financially that his February royalty check from Alfred Knopf was almost superfluous.

Seemingly at the crest of Hammett's wave of fame, the March 24, 1934 issue of *Collier's*, one of America's most popular magazines, published a Hammett short story called "This Little Pig." It was not about a detective. It was about a screenwriter who saw himself as Hammett did: smarter than those around him, but wasting his talent on trivial projects. "This Little Pig" was the last of the bunch of five short stories Hammett had written in 1933 when he needed quick cash. When it appeared, neither readers nor the publisher nor Hammett himself had any way of knowing that "This Little Pig" was the last story he would write for magazine publication.

In addition to the Hammettism "all right" (appearing eleven times in this single story), you can spot another Hammettism here: the double entendre *dingus*, which Hammett inserted into several stories and novels. The *Random House Historical Dictionary of American Slang* (1994) explains that in Hammett's day, *dingus* meant "thing," "penis," or "the rump."

Although this story is comic, knowing that it is Hammett's last makes reading it a bittersweet experience. This is the first time "This Little Pig" has been printed in a book.

This Little Pig

MAX RHINEWIEN'S TELEGRAM brought me back from Santa Barbara. He glared at me over his bicarbonate of soda and demanded, "And where've you been?"

"Where'd you wire me? I've been trying to finish a play."

"Is there a picture in it?"

"Why not? You bought *Soviet Law,* didn't you? And that's a bibliography."

"Never mind," he said, "it's a good title anyway. Listen, Bugs, I want you to hop over to Serrita and—"

"Nothing doing. I've still got nine days coming to me and I want to get the play finished."

"As a favor to me, Bugs. It won't take over a week, I promise you. Is a week going to hurt? You can take your nine days afterwards—take ten days—take two weeks if you want. I wouldn't ask you if I wasn't in a hole. My God, I'd be the last person in the world to interfere with your play. But maybe it'll be better for you this way. Maybe you'll come back to your play with a clear mind—you know—better perspective. You got some problems, haven't you, that you ain't been able to clear up yet? Well, you get away from it for a little while and give your self-conscious mind a chance to work and—"

I never had much luck arguing with Max. I said, "All right, I'll go."

"Thanks. That's fine. I knew I could count on you. Did you see the *Go West!* script?"

"No."

"Well, I said all along it needed something, but it wasn't till last night I could put my finger on it. It ain't a bad story at all—this Blaine's got something—but it needs just that one thing; and you know what it is? Sexing up."

"You mean you're going to put sex in a Western picture?" I asked.

"Yep!"

I shook my head.

He beamed on me. "Can't see it, huh? I guess a lot of people can't, but stick around and you will. And you'll see Westerns grossing in the first-run houses instead of just in the neighbs and the sticks. Listen, Bugs, is Sol Feldman a dope?"

"Not that I know of."

"Exactly. Not that anybody knows of. Well, I happened to hear only last night that they're sexing up this *The Dogie Trail* plenty."

"Why don't you let him? Why don't you wait and see how—"

He slapped a hand down flat on his desk. "You know that ain't my way," he said. "I got to be always first in the field. You know that. And we can beat 'em to release by a week or two easy."

"It's all right with me. It's not my baby. What do I do?"

"I want you to sex up *Go West!* Keep it clean, see, but cram it with that stuff. You're the boy to do it. You'll have to get over there right away—take a plane—and you'll have to work your stuff up as they go along, because they already been shooting a couple days, but you can do that all right. This fellow Lawrence

Blaine that wrote the script is out with them and you can either make him help you or send him back, whichever you want. And you won't have any trouble with Fred."

"That part's O. K.," I said, "but tell me one thing: how are you going to sex up Betty Lee Fenton?"

"Why not—so you keep it clean? She ain't crippled. She can throw herself around if somebody shows her how, can't she? Anyhow, you don't have to depend on her. There's other girls over there—Ann Meadows and Gracie King and—and if you want to take anybody else, go ahead. I'm sending Danny Finn along with you. I was thinking you might work him in something along the line that he's a drunk piano player that Gracie—say—is taking along to open a dance-hall in this mining town, and she's got some girls with her and—you know—you can work it up."

"Didn't Paramount try something like that with Gene Pallette in *Fighting Caravans* three or four years ago? I didn't see the picture, but I heard—"

"What of it?" Max asked. "Is the stuff you write going to be like anybody else's? That's what I'm counting on—the Parish touch—the angle you got that nobody else can come anywheres near."

"Go on," I said, "I bet you tell that to all the writers. Have you got a copy of the script?"

"Miss Shepherd'll give you one. I appreciate this a lot, Bugs." He shook a fist at me. "Like that, see, but clean."

I said, "Absolutely," and—with Danny Finn—flew over the mountains to Serrita.

I found Fred LePage in his tent—besides housing the company, the tents served as a U. S. cavalry encampment in the picture—rehearsing a small dark girl in a one-eyed fade-away. (A one-eyed fade-away is where a character that has been rebuffed glances sidewise—fearfully or reproachfully as a rule—into the camera or at whoever did the rebuffing, and slinks off.) Fred greeted me with open arms. "Hello! What are you doing here?"

"Didn't Max wire you?"

His grin went away. "Maybe. I stopped reading his wires. He's driving me nuts."

"A fine business," I said. "The director of a horse opera going temperamental."

He had the decency to seem embarrassed. "Well, if you were in my shoes—" He broke off. "Uh—you know Kitty Doran? This is Bugs Parish."

The small dark girl dimpled and held out her hand. "How do you do?"

Fred growled, "Come on, what's the bad news?"

When I told him he hit the top of the tent and spun there. I had expected him to yell his head off, of course, but he put on a really grand performance.

"You know how Max is," I said with soothing intent as soon as I could get a word in. "He hears Feldman's going in for sex in the open spaces—we've got to have sex in our open spaces. What the hell? He'll probably change his mind before—"

"That's just it," he howled. "He'll change his mind again and stick me with a week's retakes and I'm already three days behind. What was the idea of sending us way over here in the first place? And with nothing ready. I got to do every damned thing myself. What's he trying to do—make a bum out of me? Why don't he give me some of those crooner shorts if that's what he's trying to do?"

Fred was only a run-of-the-mine director, but his habit of getting pictures into the can a little ahead of his schedule and a little under his budget made him worth his wages, and he knew it.

I said, "I don't blame you for squawking. Let's see what you've shot and we'll save as much of it as we can."

He said, "I know it's not your fault, but, by God, Max is driving me nuts."

Betty Lee Fenton, our little gingham girl, came in and said: "Hello, Bugs. Say, is Max sticking this guy Finn in the picture? He knows I don't like to work with him."

"Danny's a good comic, whatever else you say about him."

She made a face. "The else is plenty."

"How are you on good clean sex?"

"What?"

"I don't mean tonight, or anything like that; I mean in the picture."

"What is this—a gag?"

I moved my head up and down. "And it's got Fred here rolling on the floor. The picture's new title is *Go West with Sex*."

Then it was her turn. "I might've known it," she shrieked. "Once I let Max talk me into a ride-ride-bang-bang, he thinks he can do anything to me. Well, he can't, and he might just as well find it out right now. If he's crazy, I'm not. Don't he think my public's got a right to the kind of a characterization they expect of me? Does Fox try things like that with Janet Gaynor? Of course not. Sheeban's got too much sense. Max is a fool."

Fred said to her, "Now for God's sake don't you start cutting up."

She turned on him: they were not very fond of each other. "Listen, Mr. Lubitsch, I've had—"

I said, "Come, come, my gal, you're yelling before you're hurt. Maybe—"

She turned on me. "You're damned right I am! And I'm yelling long distance to Max right now." And out she went.

Kitty Doran said primly, "I think she's unreasonable."

Fred said: "What? Oh! Uh—better scoot, Kitty. We got to work."

"All righty." She smiled brightly at him and came over to me. "I'm awfully, awfully glad to have met you, Mr. Parish, and I hope— Well, by-by, Freddy." She waved her hand at both of us and went out.

"Whaty is thaty?" I asked Fred.

"She's all right, just a kid that had a couple of bits in my last picture. I'm giving her a small part in this." He looked as if a thought had struck him. "We might build it up a little. She's pretty good."

"She must be—if she needs private coaching in one-eyed fade-aways."

"She's just a green kid, of course," he admitted, "but—you'll see. You don't think you got a chance of changing what La Fenton calls her characterization, do you?"

"No. I'm counting on Ann for the chief—"

"Sure," he said, "and we can build up Kitty's part, too. She's just a green kid, but she takes direction swell and—"

"What the hell is this?" I asked.

He scowled at me. "Are you going to start that too? Any other director can pick a girl out of the line because he knows talent when he sees it, but with me it's got to be because I've fallen for the dame and she's playing me for a sucker. You and Ann ought to incorporate."

"Ann doesn't think your Kitty's got talent?"

"Ann's just being disagreeable. What's the matter with women? Look here, Bugs: I'm not saying this kid's a Hepburn; I'm saying she's got something. What do you know about it? You've never seen her work. Wait till you do."

That seemed reasonable enough. I said: "O. K., Freddy. Get your author and let's start pushing his masterpiece around."

I sat beside Ann at dinner that night and we went for a walk down a canyon afterwards. "What's the matter with everybody?" I asked.

"I hadn't noticed," she said. "Location fever, I guess."

"Sure, but that oughtn't to come till you've been out a couple of weeks, and here you've all been out only since—what?—Sunday and you're already split up into tight little groups going around dog-eyeing each other."

"Well, Fred's been in a bad humor and I guess it's catching."

"What's the matter with him?" I asked.

She laughed, though not very happily. "It started with the Indians. It was somebody's bright idea to send us to hell and gone over here because these Indians had never been used in pictures before. You know what I mean? Simple, natural, unspoiled, that kind of junk. What a bright idea that was! Never having worked in pictures before, these little red brothers had no idea of what extras get. All they knew was what they read about Garbo and Gable and they started off putting anything from a hundred dollars a day up on their price tags. Then, when we got 'em over that, we found out they didn't have any horses and most of 'em didn't know how to ride, so we had to get horses and teach them. Then Fred tried shooting them without putting Indian make-up on 'em—some more of that natural stuff—and had to shoot 'em all over again. All that wasted time and money—and you know how Fred is about the schedule and budget." We took about ten steps in silence, then she said, "And then this cutie."

"The Doran girl?"

"Yes. You know her?"

"I met her before dinner."

"Sure. If you've seen Fred you've seen her."

"Why don't you write that guy off, Ann?" I said. "What do you want to waste your time on him for when you can have a fellow like me?"

"Probably because I'm a sap," she said, "but neither of us can help that. How big a part is Fred persuading you to give her in the new script?"

"It depends on what she can carry. Is she any good?"

"Terrible!" She took hold of my arm. "She really is. It's not just that I am jealous, though I am—awfully. Oh, Bugs, can I help it that I'm nuts about that guy?"

"Maybe not," I said, "but I can do without hearing too much of it."

She squeezed my arm and said, "I'm sorry," as if she were thinking of something else. Presently she asked, "Do you think she's pretty?"

"She is."

"Prettier than I am?"

"What the hell is this?" I asked.

"I'm sorry," she said again. "I've got to talk to somebody. You're the only one that knows how I really feel about Fred. I—I hoped maybe you could help me."

"You mean help you get him back?"

"Yes."

"That's a sweet job to give me. You're not just nuts about him—you're nuts. Anyway, how do you know he isn't really in love with the girl—and through with you?"

"Don't be silly," she said with complete certainty. "You know what a push-over he is for a new face and a new line—and how soon it blows over."

"Then the answer's easy. Just wait it out."

She caught her breath. "I'm afraid. I'm always afraid that this time he'll get himself so tangled up that he won't—maybe won't want to get out of it."

I thought, that would be swell. I said, "There's nothing I can do about it, but I'll see."

She squeezed my arm. "Thanks, Bugs. I knew you—"

"Better wait till you see whether you've got anything to thank me for. Let's go back. I've got a couple of hours' work to do."

The next day I discovered that Fred was right, Ann wrong, about Kitty Doran's ability. Her part in the scene I watched was pretty simple and she had to be told how to do everything, but, once told, she managed to do it with a sort of fake naturalness and an aliveness that were very effective.

When they had cut, Fred came over to me. "Well?" he asked, grinning.

"Not bad," I said. "How does she photograph?"

He laughed. "Wait till you see the rushes. Hey, Lew!" The camera man joined us. Fred said, "Bugs wants to know how Doran photographs."

Lew said, "Easy to handle. How about a little poker tonight, Bugs?"

"If I get through in time. Maybe we'll—"

Kitty Doran said, "Oh, hello, Mr. Parish."

I said, "Hello."

One of the boys handed me a telegram from Max Rhinewien:

AFTER CONSIDERATION THINK YOU RIGHT ABOUT
INADVISABILITY OF CHANGING FENTON CHARACTERIZA-
TION STOP DID YOU SEE QUOTE EAT EM ALIVE UNQUOTE
QUERY SUGGEST SHOTS OF BATTLE BETWEEN SNAKES
OR SPIDERS OR PERHAPS SNAKE SWALLOWING FROG AS
SYMBOL OF EVIL ATTACKING GOOD STOP SEVERAL HUN-
DRED FEET OF BISON BEING DRIVEN THROUGH SNOW
TO YELLOWSTONE WINTER QUARTERS AVAILABLE IF YOU
CAN WORK IT IN STOP BEST REGARDS

I passed it over to Fred. "Betty Lee F. made her squawk stick as usual, which is all to the good."

"That's all to the good," he agreed, and read the telegram. "A fine time we'd have trying to make that bum look like anything but Virtue-in-a-simple-frock! You ain't gonna put no varmints in this yere fillum, air yuh, pardner?"

"No, suh," I said. "I hates a snake like pison and I just ain't got no use fuh buffalo. You sure you want that swimming-hole sequence we were talking about?"

"Sure. It's a natural for Kitty."

"O.K. I'm going back and work a while. When you get through with Danny Finn, send him over. He remembers the old Ray Griffith gags better than I do and we need some of them."

Kitty Doran caught up to me when I was within twenty feet of my tent. "Oh, Mr. Parish, I'm so happy! Freddy says you're going to give me a real part in the picture."

"That depends," I said, "on whether you can handle it."

She looked at me wide-eyed. "But—but Freddy said I was doing fine. Was that just because—just because he likes me? Tell me what I do wrong, Mr. Parish. I'll stop doing it. Honest, I will. Honest, I want so much to— Am I awful bad?"

"No."

"But I'm not very good?"

"I don't know. What I've seen is all right, but I haven't seen enough yet."

"Oh, then I think—" She laughed. "I mean I hope you'll not be disappointed. I mean in Freddy's opinion." She went into the tent ahead of me. "Could you tell me what my part is?"

"It hasn't been worked out yet. You're probably the cut-up of the expedition. Tomorrow you sneak off to go swimming and are surrounded by Indians or cavalrymen or something and can't get to your clothes—that kind of junk."

"I think that's fine," she said.

I let that go at that.

"You're a friend of Ann Meadows, aren't you?" she asked. "I saw you with her last night."

"Yes."

"She hates me, doesn't she?"

"She's in love with Fred."

"I know, but it's not my fault that he likes me."

"She thinks it is. She thinks you're stringing him along for a break in the pictures."

"Well, what of it?" she demanded. "Didn't he give her her first break?"

"Maybe, but she happens to be in love with him."

"Well, I like him very much too."

"That's not the same thing."

She stood in front of me and her lower lip trembled. "I guess you think I'm a dirty little tramp, Mr. Parish, but, honest, I want so bad to make good in pictures that I guess I'd do anything to get a break."

"Could I count on that?"

"You're making fun of me," she said, "but yes."

"That's honest, anyhow. Now run along: I've got to work."

"But—"

"Scram. I've got to work."

She laughed and held out her hand. "I like you. Can I call you—your first name's Chauncey, isn't it?"

"Uh-huh, but you don't know me well enough to call me that. Make it Bugs."

"Bugs," she said, "and thanks."

I thought about her for a couple of minutes after she had gone and then settled down to the typewriter. A page and a half later Ann came in.

"Don't stop," she said. "I don't want to interrupt you." She sat down and lit a cigarette. Her face was red and angry.

"That's all right," I told her. "What's the matter?"

"Mr. LePage and I have just had a row. He accused me of sulking in front of the camera, so I told him what I thought of him and walked off the set."

"After all," I reminded her, "we are making a picture."

"I don't give a damn about the picture."

"That's not the spirit of Pagliacci. The show must go on

though our hearts—"

She dropped her cigarette on the floor and stamped on it. "Cut it out, Bugs. I don't feel like kidding. I'm sick. You know what she did?"

"Kitty?"

"Yes. She told him I was trying to persuade you not to fatten her part up any more than you had to."

"That's true in a way, isn't it?" I asked.

She looked at me suspiciously. "It is not. I never— You didn't tell her that?"

"No. You're being a chump, Ann."

"I suppose I am," she said gloomily, "but who cares? I ought to—" She broke off as Danny Finn came in, said, "Hello, Danny; be seeing you, Bugs," and went out.

Danny smacked his lips. "I could go for that dame. I got a swell Indian gag, Bugs. Listen to this."

I listened and said, "No, Groucho would be sore. He used that in *Duck Soup*."

"But there's no Indians in *Duck Soup*."

"The gag's the same. I want something for a swimming-hole sequence we're using Kitty Doran in."

"Doran, huh?" He smacked his lips. "I could go for that dame. How about this? Eddie Sutherland used it in one of the Oakie pictures." He described it to me.

"Yes, maybe we can kick that around, but cut out the double-wing-and-scram on the end. Now let's see what else we can dig up."

We had five more gags—two early Sennetts, a Chaplin, one from *As Thousands Cheer*, and one that practically everybody had used—by the time Fred came in from his day's work afield. Betty Lee Fenton and Kitty Doran were with him.

Betty Lee paused at the door only long enough to ask, "You heard from Max?"

"Sure," I said. "Your virginity's safe."

"I thought it would be," she said and went away.

Danny, looking after her, automatically smacked his lips and muttered, "I could go for . . . "

Fred asked, "What've you guys got?" and, when we told him our six gags, said, "I guess they'll do."

Danny went away.

Fred yawned and spread himself on my cot. "Ann tell you about the blow-up?"

"Yes."

"I can't do anything with her," he complained. "She's just laying down on me."

Kitty said, "It was disgraceful." Neither of us paid any attention to her.

"The part can be whittled down," I said. "She doesn't have to be the one that Wiley seems to be falling for."

"We've got to do something," he growled. "She's wooden. Why the hell does she have to take her spite out on the picture?"

Kitty clapped her hands. "Oh, Freddy, couldn't I have that love scene with Wiley? I know I could do it. Please."

"It could be written that way," I said.

He scowled at her and at me. "Max wouldn't stand for it. It'd have to be too big a part—we'd need a name."

"Max wants sex," I said. "Here it is."

"Please, Freddy!" she cooed. "Please, darling! Just try me."

He shook his head. "Max'd raise hell."

"Well, I've got to do something," I said. "What?"

Kitty said, "Please, sweetheart!"

He looked at me.

I said, "I'll front for you to Max."

He jumped up from the cot. "All right, damn it! Go ahead!" Kitty laughed happily and put her arms around his neck. I said, "Clear out, youse mugs, this means a solid night's work for me."

Kitty came back alone at a few minutes before midnight. "I just had to come in to thank you," she said, "because I owe this wonderful chance all to you and I'm so excited I know I won't be able to sleep a wink tonight. Could I see what you've written for me? Just a tiny peep, Bugsy?"

"Stop talking like that," I said. "One more Bugsy puts you back among the people who call me Mr. Parish."

"I'm sorry, Bugs, but I'm so happy I don't know what I'm doing." She began to dance around the tent. "Freddy likes me to call him Freddy."

"Would he like your being here?"

She laughed. "Then maybe I'd better stay till late—till we're sure he'll be asleep and won't see me leaving. Can't I see what you've written?"

"Help yourself."

She read the new pages of script carefully and said: "I like that. I think it's fine. But look, I've got an idea. I know an awfully cute little dance. I'll show it to you—and see if you don't think it could be worked in in that campfire scene. You know, I could dance around the fire."

"Sure," I agreed. "We could have thirty or forty Nubian slaves bring you on in a silver chariot and while you were dancing around the fire we could release a flock of swans."

She pouted. "You're making fun of me again, but let me show you. It's a cute dance."

She showed me and it was a cute dance.

I said, "It's a cute dance."

"And you'll let me do it?"

"No."

"You're a meany. I guess you think I'm an awful pig, but there's something else I want to ask you—another favor. Freddy's been awfully nice to me, but he's mostly a Western picture director, isn't he?"

"Most of his pictures have been outdoor he-man stuff, yes."

"That's what I thought. Well, will you help me with the love scenes? I'm so awfully anxious to make good and they're the kind of things you write and you'd know more about it. Will you?"

"Sure, but it's not going to do you any good at this stage of the game to let Fred get the idea that you're slighting him. He—"

"I know, but we can be tactful about it, can't we? I wouldn't want to hurt his feelings for worlds."

"Your sentiments do you credit," I said. "Now you'd better—"

"Oh, no, I can't leave till we're sure Freddy's gone to bed. He might see me. I'm going to curl right up in this corner and I won't bother you one teeny-weeny bit."

So I wrote her a love scene with Ted Wiley, the male lead, and we shot it against the campfire almost in silhouette, and I directed it, and if I do say it myself it was every bit as good as when Murnau first did it against a sky in *Sunrise*. And everybody except Ann agreed that we had a find in Kitty.

Ann took me aside to say, "I've seen a lot of hammy performances, but . . . "

I said: "I'm very sorry to hear you say that, Miss Meadows. I thought we were all great artists working together in a great art form."

She wrinkled up her forehead. "Listen, Bugs, what are you up to? On the level."

"I'm fixing things—for everybody."

She looked at me suspiciously. "I wonder."

I crossed my heart.

"How?

I told her. "By simply doing what everybody wants. It's a beautiful plan. You want Fred back. You get him. Fred and Kitty want her to get a chance in pictures. She gets it. Betty Lee wants to keep her virginal characterization. She keeps it. I don't want anything. As usual, I get it."

"But how does that bring Fred back?"

"Wouldn't he break with his own mother if she sent him over his schedule and budget? Well, with Kitty carrying the sex burden, she steals the picture completely from Fenton. Whether your jealousy will let you see it or not, she's not bad, and when Fenton sees the finished film she realizes it and squawks her head off in her usual refined manner. Max has got too much dough tied up in her to let her be buried by an unknown, and Kitty's part is written so that if the big scenes come out the rest will have to come out and something else will have to be put in its place—and that means more money and time. And who does Fred blame for that but me and Kitty? He can't do anything to me: he can bounce her out of his affections and his picture. On the other hand, you have only a small part in the dingus now and he probably still loves you and—"

"Maybe," she said slowly, "but I don't like it. You're being malicious and you could've—"

"Sure, I'm being malicious, but I've got to have some fun. Besides, a lot of people get good lessons out of it. Max learns he oughtn't to try to sex up westerns; Fred, that if his gods are Budget and Schedule that he should stick to them; Kitty, that little pigs who go to market shouldn't carry too big baskets; and maybe all of you that I'm not just an amiable boob."

She shook her head. "There's more to it than you're telling me, and I don't like it."

There was more to it.

Ten days later I finished my work on the script and went back to Hollywood, but, of course, not immediately on to Santa Barbara and the play. Max Rhinewien had bought a Hungarian comedy which he said needed more epigrams and he talked me into doing the adaptation. That took about four weeks and I finally escaped by simply ducking out on him.

I had been in Santa Barbara eight days when Ann tele-phoned me. She said, "Bugs? I think you ought to know that your plan worked so well that Kitty Doran is dying in St. Martin's Hospital," and hung up.

Kitty wasn't dying. Her mouth and throat were burned, but they had pumped the stuff out of her before it got a chance to work. She raised her head a little and smiled painfully at me when I came into the hospital room.

"What the hell is this?" I asked. "Never mind. Don't try to talk."

"I can talk," she said. "Bugs, they took all my stuff out of the picture and when I asked Freddy about it he was awful nasty and he said Ann Meadows told him you meant them to."

"Forget it. We'll fix you up."

"But it was my chance to make good and now—" She began to cry.

"Stop it. You'll get another one as soon as you're up. I've got an original with a part in it for you that won't be cut and—"

She sat up in bed. "Honest?"

"Uh-huh," I said, making it up as I went along, but not working too hard at it, "it's about a boy and a girl and another girl and maybe another boy."

She smiled at me as if I were handing her *Romeo and Juliet*. "You're a darling, Bugsy! How soon do you think my mouth will be all right?"

"It'll never be all right till you stop that Bugsy stuff. Look at me. Did you really try to kill yourself, or was it just another act?"

She hung her head. "I—I—now don't get mad—I don't really know, Bugsy—Bugs, I mean. I thought I meant it, but I guess I did kind of spit it out. Maybe—at first I meant it, all right, but maybe after I started I thought it might be just as good if I didn't actually—you know—die, if I— Listen, B-Bugs, now you tell me something. When you played that dirty trick—it was an awful dirty trick—on me, wasn't it a little because you thought I liked Freddy and you liked me and you thought you could—"

"Don't be a dope," I said. "You were only a very small cog in the wheel. I was up to something that had nothing to do with you, then you got into this mess and I—God knows why—thought I ought to do something about it. I'm willing to give you a boost up, but get this straight: I'm not tangled up with you now, I've never been, and I'm never going to be."

"You don't have to be so nasty about it," she said.

"I'm not being nasty, I'm being definite."

"Will—will you kiss me?"

"What for? Sure, if you want."

"Oh," she said, "then that'll be all right."

"This Little Pig": The Revised Ending

"This Little Pig" is one of two stories in this book for which Hammett's original typescript survives. When I examined the typescript to restore the story to its original form, I was delighted to discover that Hammett had written two different endings. His original ending is the one you just read. This one, marked "revised," is the one used by *Collier's* when it printed "This Little Pig" in 1934.

I had been in Santa Barbara eight days when Ann telephoned me. She said, "Oh, Bugs, you've got to come down. Kitty Doran is dying in St. Martin's Hospital."

"What?""

"She committed suicide. Hurry, Bugs."

I had a car that could do plenty and a chauffeur who could get plenty out of it, but that ride to Los Angeles seemed the longest I had ever made.

Kitty wasn't dying. Her mouth was burned and her face was white and thin, but she raised her head a little and smiled painfully at me when I came into the hospital room.

"What the hell is this?" I asked. "Never mind. Don't try to talk."

"I can talk," she said. "Bugs, they took all my stuff out of the picture and when I asked Freddy about it he was awfully nasty to me and he said Ann Meadows told him you meant them to."

"Forget it. We'll fix you up."

"But did you?"

"I'm sorry. I'll do my best to square it. Get well and I'll see that you have another chance. I can make Max—"

"Will you? You're a darling, Bugsy! I'll—"

Ann came in.

Kitty sat up straight in bed and cried, "Make her go away. I told them not to let her in."

Ann said, "I only came in to thank you."

"Make her go away," Kitty screamed. "Make her go away!"

I said "All right" and took Ann out into the corridor. "Now what?" I asked.

She leaned against the wall and laughed. "But I ought to thank her," she said through her laughter. "I might've gone on and on being so silly."

"This makes a lot of sense to me," I growled.

"Don't you see? When I phoned you—when I thought she had really tried to kill herself—it was you I was worried about—about your having it on your conscience that your trick had driven her to it, and I knew then that—"

"Didn't she really try?"

"No. The doctor said she could've taken gallons of the stuff she took, and they found out she'd done the same thing twice before and knew it wouldn't kill her. But I didn't know that then and I found out it was you I— Honest, Bugs, I knew it even before Fred put the finishing touch to it."

"What's he up to?"

She laughed. "Not up—down. If he kept on in the same direction and at the same speed he's in Panama by now. He lit out for Mexico as soon as he heard what she'd done."

"And you're sure you're not just—"

She held her face up to me. "Aw, Bugs, don't be as stupid as I was."

I had my arms around her when the first slipper whizzed past our heads. The second one grazed my shoulder as we escaped around the nearest corner, leaving Kitty standing in her doorway screaming un-nice things about us.

"See how sick she is," Ann said, "just like Tarzan, but just the same don't let's ever think up any more smart schemes."

"I don't know," I said. "This one got out of hand for a while, but the result seems to be O. K."

BY THE TIME that story was on newsstands, Hammett and Hell-man were back in Homestead, Florida. "The place is a fishing camp on Key Largo," Hammett wrote to his wife Jose, "an island about forty miles southeast of Miami and there is absolutely noth-ing to do here but fish and swim and eat." And drink, of course, and work with Hellman on the play *The Children's Hour.*

The play's script opens with schoolgirls reading from Shake-speare's play *The Merchant of Venice.* Shakespeare's characters include Antonio, who is traditionally played as a homosexual, and three women who disguise themselves as men. An appropriate choice for a play involving homosexuality, *The Merchant of Venice* is the same play homosexual Joel Cairo attends in *The Maltese Falcon.*

It is an interesting coincidence that characters in *The Chil-dren's Hour* include two compulsive liars named Lily and Mary. Hammett's lover Lily and daughter Mary were both compulsive liars.

May 1934 was Hammett's fortieth birthday. He was on top of the world. He was rich, famous, handsome, and relatively healthy. He had many friends and lovers. His affair with Hellman was still passionate. He had two daughters he loved, and a wife he respected taking care of them.

It was quite a change from his thirtieth birthday ten years earlier, poor and ill in a small apartment in San Francisco, barely getting by on irregular disability checks and struggling with the rejection of his stories by *The Black Mask* editor Phil Cody.

At the end of June, the movie *The Thin Man* opened, star-ring William Powell and Myrna Loy as Hammett's Nick and Nora Charles. The movie opened to rave reviews and smash hit business. It saved Myrna Loy's career and made her a major star overnight. Because Hammett was so famous, his name was used to promote the movie, and the book cover with his photo on it was used in advertisements, on posters, and behind the opening credits of the film. Seldom has an author's photo been used so extensively to promote a movie.

Summer in Florida grew hot. Hammett and Hellman went back to New York. He wrote to his wife that he was "comfortably settled and hard at work on a moving picture and a play, both of which I hope to have finished by the middle of September."

In September the finished play of The Children's Hour was read by Broadway producer-director Herman Shumlin. He immediately wanted to produce it. The author's name was listed as Lillian Hellman.

Hammett's contributions to The Children's Hour went far beyond those of a typical editor. It was Hammett who thought of the play's story and its title. He shaped its structure, its characters, its dialog. Hellman later told Ralph Ingersoll that Hammett had almost written the play himself, pushing her through it one line at a time, but Hellman preferred to embroider life, so her testimony might or might not have been the truth. If Writers Guild rules to determine authorship were applied to The Children's Hour, would Hammett be named co-author? We cannot be certain. But given Hammett's dominance in his relationship with Hellman at the time, and the commercial strength of his name, he could have listed himself as co-author of The Children's Hour if he had wanted to.

Why did Hammett not want to put his name on the play? He loved Hellman; maybe he hid his name for love. Maybe he was more interested in building her career than his own. Maybe he wanted to prove something to her. Maybe he was tired of the annoyances of celebrity. Maybe he hated show business. Maybe he didn't want his wife, Jose, to claim the fifty percent of his income from the play that she would be entitled to by California's community property laws. Maybe he felt that Hellman's contribution was more important than his own. Maybe he didn't give a damn. We do not know.

Hammett certainly did not need whatever profits, if any, a risky venture like *The Children's Hour* might make. He was still making money from the daily *Secret Agent X-9* comic strip, from two *Secret Agent X-9* books of his comic strips, from newspaper syndication of his old stories, from *The Thin Man* royalties, and from movie work.

Now that the motion picture version of *The Thin Man* was a huge hit, studios wanted anything with Hammett's name on it. On September 27 he sold Universal Pictures his old story *On the Make*, the one that Warner Brothers had rejected. Then he haggled with MGM over how much the company would pay him to write a sequel to *The Thin Man*.

At the end of October, MGM agreed to pay Hammett $2,000 a week for ten weeks. He took a train to Hollywood and left Hellman in New York with *The Children's Hour*—which was now in rehearsals—giving her a chance to have the spotlight of authorship to herself. He rented a $2,000 per month six-bedroom penthouse hotel suite in Beverly Hills complete with servants. He reported to work at MGM and was lionized by its publicity department. Among other stories the PR flacks generated, one in *The Hollywood Reporter* claimed that Hammett was going to act in the sequel. He quickly fell back into his bad habits, getting so drunk he was ashamed of himself, missing work for days at a time.

In early November the movie based on Hammett's *Woman in the Dark* opened. On November 20, *The Children's Hour* opened on Broadway to rave reviews. At the age of twenty-nine, Hellman was credited with a huge hit. She was famous—more accurately, notorious, because the play mentioned homosexuality, a subject that decent people did not discuss. The play would run for more than a year-and-a-half, earning Hellman $125,000 (over $3 million in 2005 dollars), more than any piece of Hammett's had earned.

Instantly, Hellman was in demand to write movies. She arrived in Hollywood on December 18 and moved into Hammett's hotel penthouse. She paid half the extravagant rent. She could afford it. On top of her money from *The Children's Hour* on Broadway, legendary producer Samuel Goldwyn had hired her for $2,500 a week—more than MGM was paying Hammett.

He began the new year of 1935 by giving MGM the first version of his new story for *After The Thin Man*. It wasn't finished. He had not decided who the killer was.

He missed so many deadlines for the *Secret Agent X-9* comic strip that he was fired. He had contributed four stories to it. His material ran until April. Afterward, the strip continued to run, but without Hammett's name. Rights to the X-9 character were owned by the Hearst syndicate, so after he was fired Hammett received no more money from the strip, which continued to run until 1996.

Hammett moved out of the hotel, first to a big house near the ocean, then to another big house in the posh Bel Air district. Oscar nominations were announced. *The Thin Man* had been nominated for best picture, best actor, best director, and best screenplay. It lost in all four categories to Frank Capra's *It Happened One Night*, starring Clark Gable.

While Hammett partied and intermittently worked on *After the Thin Man*, Samuel Goldwyn paid Hellman $50,000 for movie rights to *The Children's Hour*. Goldwyn was warned against buying the notorious play because censors would never let him make a movie about lesbians. "That's all right," he supposedly said. "We'll make them Americans."

The play *The Children's Hour* was so infamous that movie censors would not let Goldwyn even use its title. He hired Hellman to write a new script, deleted all mentions of lesbianism, tacked on an improbable happy ending, and changed the title to *These Three*.

Hammett's story *On The Make* was changed as well. Universal Pictures had it rewritten as a cliché detective story, changed the main character's name to T.N. Thompson (TNT—get it?), and renamed it *Mister Dynamite*. Little was left of Hammett's story, but the movie's advertisements exploited his famous name. It opened on May 25, two days before his forty-first birthday, and generated good reviews.

The next month Paramount released the movie version of Hammett's novel *The Glass Key*. It starred George Raft. Ads for *The Glass Key* called Raft's character "The Thin Man's Hard-Boiled Brother" and mentioned Hammett's name prominently.

Hammett's writing contract with MGM expired. The company signed him to another, paying $1,000 a week for him to act as assistant to the producer of *The Thin Man*, Hunt Stromberg, plus an extra $750 a week if Hammett wrote anything. Over the next few months he made small contributions to MGM films produced by Stromberg, worked sporadically on *After the Thin Man*, got drunk, and partied.

He celebrated the Fourth of July by visiting San Francisco with author S. J. Perelman's wife, Laura. Lillian Hellman found out and erupted in fury. Hammett's sexual adventures with prostitutes and actresses were bad enough, but this affair was with a friend of hers. Hellman stayed in New York and fumed. Hammett stayed in Hollywood and continued to drink, party, and gamble.

In September he turned in the final version of *After the Thin Man*. No matter how much money Hammett was paid, he could spend it even faster. He was broke again. On September 24 he telegraphed Alfred Knopf, pleading for $1,000. Knopf wired him $500. On October 28 he asked for another $500, which Knopf sent.

In January 1936 Hammett collapsed. He had a mental and physical breakdown, alcoholic depression combined with the venereal disease gonorrhea. He flew to New York and stayed at the Plaza Hotel instead of living with the still-angry Hellman. He couldn't pay his bill, so the Plaza kicked him out. His old friend Nell Martin took him in. He went to a hospital for a couple of weeks, then checked into the snobby Madison Hotel. Eventually he got together again with Hellman on a nonexclusive basis. She had affairs with other men. He had affairs with other women.

In March, *These Three*, the movie based on the play *The Children's Hour*, opened to rave reviews. *The New York Times* named it one of the year's ten best. In July, the second version of *The Maltese Falcon* opened, receiving terrible reviews. Titled *Satan Met a Lady*, it starred Bette Davis, who later called it the worst turkey she ever appeared in.

In Europe that same month, Hitler's German army reoccupied the Rhineland territory it had agreed to demilitarize when it lost the World War. France and Britain protested but did nothing in response.

In the summer of 1936, the motion picture studios squashed the fledging Screen Writers Guild. About this time, Hammett became active politically. He may have been influenced by Hellman. Years before she met Hammett, Hellman had joined the John Reed Club, a Marxist group controlled by the Communist Party.

Now that historians have had access to Soviet archives, we know there was a large-scale, well-organized Communist plan to infiltrate and subvert movies, radio, and publishing in many countries to convert media and news into propaganda outlets for Communist causes. The Communist Party organized a clandestine program to recruit celebrities, especially authors, and to use them as secret soldiers for Stalin, endorsing Communist agendas but never publicly admitting their Communist memberships. Hammett and Hellman were steered to promote Communist causes by Communist recruiter Otto Katz, "one of the most complex secret agents of his era," according to Stephen Koch in his 1994 book *Double Lives: Spies and Writers in the Secret Soviet War of Ideas Against the West.*

Both Hammett and Hellman became prominent Communists. To be more precise, they became Stalinists, unquestioningly supporting whatever point of view Stalin's organization proclaimed to be correct, switching positions whenever Stalin switched positions.

One of Hammett's first propaganda activities was to join Hellman, Archibald MacLeish, Dorothy Parker, Ernest Hemingway, and John Dos Passos in a group named Contemporary Historians, formed to produce a documentary film on the civil war then raging in Spain. Hammett backed the movie with a $500 contribution.

It was August before doctors were able to clear up Hammett's gonorrhea, through a painful and life-endangering treatment. The doctors barely interrupted his frequent drunkenness, with Hellman as his companion or without.

Hellman's new play, *Days to Come,* opened on Broadway on December 15. It was reviled by reviewers and closed in six days, a flop in every way. Hellman was devastated. Hammett didn't seem to care. The movie *After the Thin Man* opened four days after *Days to Come* closed. It was a big hit.

Hammett always needed money. In February 1937 he agreed to sell his rights in the characters Nick, Nora, and Asta (except radio rights) to MGM for $40,000 (equal to more than $800,000 now). MGM had a secret agenda. The company wanted to withhold paying the $40,000 until he agreed to write the third *Thin Man* movie story for a cheap price. Hammett resisted.

The documentary on the Spanish Civil War that Hammett supported, titled *The Spanish Earth,* was first shown privately in early April.

By mid-April Hammett had come to an agreement with MGM about the third *Thin Man* movie. On the previous movie

MGM had paid him weekly, and Hammett had goofed off on a grand scale. This time there was no weekly pay. Hammett would be paid $35,000, but only when he delivered work: $5,000 for a story synopsis, another $10,000 if MGM accepted his synopsis, and a final payment of $20,000 when he finished the story.

Hammett and Hellman lived together in Hollywood from April to August. Hammett was back at work at MGM. San Francisco's Golden Gate Bridge, an engineering marvel, was dedicated and opened on Hammett's forty-third birthday in May.

The next month, the Hollywood cell of the Communist Party was formed under the direction of Otto Katz.

In July *The Spanish Earth* was shown first in the White House to President and Mrs. Roosevelt. Then it received a Hollywood premiere.

Hellman got pregnant and wanted Hammett to marry her. In late August he convinced his wife, Jose, to sign for a Mexican divorce. He appeared not to know that it was not valid in the United States. Instead of marrying Hammett, however, Hellman grew upset over his unchanged philandering, left him to go to Europe, got an abortion, and visited Moscow.

While Hammett and Hellman battled each other, war between Japan and China broke out in earnest with waves of terror bombing of Chinese cities by Japan's air force. World powers did nothing to stop the Japanese onslaught.

In September Hammett was still living in style, back in the six-bedroom penthouse of the Beverly Wilshire Hotel. He was supposed to be writing the story for the third *Thin Man* movie, but he and Hellman had been elected to the board of directors of the Screen Writers Guild, and he took his role seriously. He spent his days recruiting new members. He represented the guild at a hearing before the federal government's National Labor Relations Board and argued for the legitimacy of the writers' union, which the studios were still determined to kill off. The Screen Writers Guild won its case before the board.

In December Hammett was elected chairman of the Motion Picture Artists Committee for 1938. The committee's purpose was to raise money for the Stalin-supported antifascist fighters in Spain and China. It was too late for much of China. On December 12 the key city of Nanking fell. This was the beginning of the horrific Rape of Nanking, in which Japanese soldiers tortured and killed thousands of Chinese civilians.

Hammett apparently rang in New Year's Day of 1938 sober. In January he bragged—or complained—that he had not been drunk for ten months. He kept busy by working for Communist-backed and anti-Nazi organizations and going to rallies.

In March, Hitler took over Austria by simply marching in his German troops. There was no resistance. In fact, Austrian crowds cheered the Nazi soldiers as they marched in. England and France protested verbally, but otherwise did nothing.

As the year went on, Hammett felt tired and lost weight. For him, this was always a sign of underlying health problems. He remained active with the Screen Writers Guild, making a speech against the mob-run International Association of Theatrical Stage Employees (IATSE) union's attempt to take over the guild. IATSE was defeated. Hammett signed public letters and advertisements supporting Communist causes, including Stalin's notorious purge trials.

He was recruiting members for the Hollywood branch of the Communist Party in May. Lillian Hellman was on the East Coast, struggling to write a new play, The Little Foxes. On May 13 Hammett finally turned in his finished story for Another Thin Man. MGM had forced him to make changes to his story. He was not happy about them.

The next day he had bottles of scotch sent up to his hotel suite and for the first time in more than a year he got completely soused. Drunk and alone in his luxurious Beverly Hills rooms, he sat down to write a letter to Hellman. Like his novel *The Thin Man*, his letter is sad, lonely, lost writing. It pretend to be playful while stating "but I know as well as you do that just about now what little imagination I've got is used up."

He went on a drunken binge that ended quickly in an emotional and physical breakdown. A few days later Frances Goodrich and Albert Hackett, married writers who were friends of his, found Hammett lying in bed in his hotel room. The husband at first thought he was dead. He was so weak he couldn't talk. He was frighteningly thin—he had lost twenty-five pounds and weighed less than 125. His unpaid hotel bills added up to about $200,000 in 2005 money, so friends snuck his belongings out a little at a time in briefcases and small boxes to avoid alerting hotel managers. Then they half-carried a staggering Hammett out of the hotel and put him and his secretary on a plane to New York and Hellman.

She checked him into a New York hospital. Doctors said he "felt weak, frightened, and panicky" and was afraid of going insane. They said his heart was smaller than normal. He was diagnosed with neurosis, pituitary hypofunction, and infected gums from neglecting his teeth. He stayed in the hospital for three weeks and gained ten pounds.

He left the hospital and moved into Hellman's house in Tavern Island, Connecticut, to recuperate. She was writing her next play and she was scared. Her first play, *The Dear Queen,* had been so bad that it was never produced. Her third play, *Days to Come,* had been a total flop. She was afraid that *The Children's Hour* had been a fluke, that she was a one-hit wonder, that she would never have another success. She turned to Hammett. He was thinking about working on *My Brother Felix*, a novel he had started and interrupted some time ago. Instead, he went to work on Hellman's current project, *The Little Foxes.*

In July, MGM offered to pay Hammett $15,000 for the right of first refusal to make movies of any of his past writings and anything new he would write throughout the coming year. Hammett did not sign the MGM agreement until the end of August, after the federal government had supervised an election in which movie writers overwhelmingly voted for the Screen Writers Guild to be their union. Now the government recognized the Guild. Studio brass, however, still refused to deal with it.

Hammett was as concerned as Hellman that *The Little Foxes* would not repeat the *Days to Come* disaster. He worked with her on the new play through September, intensely involved with every scene, every character, every line. As with *The Children's Hour*, examination of the surviving drafts of *The Little Foxes* makes it plain that Hammett's participation went beyond that of a typical editor.

Near the end of September he moved to The Plaza in New York City, where he wrote long letters to his daughter Mary explaining the Communist point of view. He was in The Plaza on September 30 when Great Britain, France, and Italy signed a pact to give Germany most of the country of Czechoslovakia in return for Germany's promise to avoid future expansion plans. Hitler had conquered Czechoslovakia without firing a shot.

From his swanky hotel room, Hammett wrote and gave speeches for fundraising events, and promised to write a paper "comparing the modern utopian socialists like Upton Sinclair, Townsend, etc. with the earlier ones like Owen, Fourier, and Saint-Simon." Such abstruse theoretical pursuits were shoved into the background November 9. That night was Kristallnacht in Germany, the Night of Broken Glass. Morning news revealed the violence to New Yorkers. Hammett was appalled by the organized large-scale Nazi attacks on Jews: more than seven thousand Jewish businesses and homes looted, nearly one thousand synagogues set on fire, up to thirty thousand Jews arrested and sent to concentration camps, about one hundred Jews killed.

This man near death only six months earlier now launched into a whirlwind of anti-Nazi activity. Eleven days after he first heard about Kristallnacht, he spoke to an audience of twenty-two thousand in Madison Square Garden—with thousands more outside listening on loudspeakers—at a rally held by the American Sponsoring Committee Against Nazi Outrages. He wrote speeches for other anti-Nazi and pro-Communist causes as well. Drawing on his detective-story fame, he titled one speech "The Case of the Mysterious Disappearance of the Free Ballot." One week he gave four speeches: a fundraising event for antifascists in Spain, a dinner for the League for Peace and Democracy, an anti-Nazi mass meeting, and a radio address supporting Jewish refugees. He joined the editorial board of a magazine called *Jewish Survey* and the advisory board of an organization called Films for Democracy. He headed a Communist-backed organization called Professionals Conference Against Nazi Persecutions.

On top of all this, he still worked with the National Labor Relations Board to persuade the movie studios to bargain with the Screen Writers Guild, he still worked with Hellman on editing and rewriting *The Little Foxes*, and MGM expected another *Thin Man* story from him. He had been paid $80,000 (think $2+ million in 2005 dollars) by MGM in 1938, making him one of the highest-paid writers in the world. On December 7 he gave MGM an eight-page outline for a fourth *Thin Man* movie story. Some MGM executive working on Christmas Day rejected it and, on December 25, Hammett's contract with MGM was suspended.

In January of 1939 *The Little Foxes* was in rehearsal. Hammett visited Baltimore in February for the play's tryout run, where he saw his father for the first time in eight years. In Baltimore, Hammett was busy working on *The Little Foxes* rewrites "with my long nose to the grindstone night and day, with hardly a chance to go to the toilet." The play opened on Broadway on February 15, and was a huge moneymaker.

In March Hammett got involved in the creation of a new daily newspaper for New York, a Stalinist evening paper named *P.M.* Hammett was excited by it. The new paper would be an American version of the Stalinist *Ce Soir* newspaper of Paris, and was guided by the founder of *Ce Soir*, secret agent Otto Katz.

But Hammett was soon back on the MGM payroll, writing an adaptation of one of his best Continental Op stories, "Fly Paper." His movie story was given the more exploitable title *Girl Hunt*.

Hellman started a new anti-Nazi play, *Watch on the Rhine*. Hammett may have given her the idea for it. Apparently, its plot was from his unfinished novel *My Brother Felix*.

By May another Hammett project bore fruit. With Hellman, Bennett Cerf, Moss Hart, Dorothy Parker, Donald Ogden Stewart, and others, Hammett founded Equality Publishers to produce books and periodicals furthering tolerance. The new company's first publication was a magazine with the bulky title *Equality: A Monthly Journal to Defend Democratic Rights and Combat Anti-Semitism and Racism*. Hammett's name was listed on the magazine's masthead as part of its editorial council.

With the money from *The Little Foxes*, Hellman bought a 130-acre farm in Pleasantville, New York. Hellman and Hammett considered Hardscrabble Farm to belong to both of them, but only her name was on the deed as owner.

Most other people were not as prosperous. The Great Depression continued. Despite Roosevelt's New Deal, ten million people were still unemployed.

Flush with money from MGM, Hammett lived well, alternating between the rural peacefulness of Hardscrabble Farm and the high life of New York. Gossip columnists reported him as a regular at the Stork Club, 21, Negro nightclubs in Harlem—the Big Apple's in-crowd hangouts. He continued to fund political causes and write speeches for them. In June he took the stage at Carnegie Hall to speak on "Tempo in Fiction" at the Third American Writers Congress, sponsored by the Stalinist-backed League of American Writers. Two drafts of his speech survive. Out of the hundreds of speeches Hammett wrote, it is apparently the only one that exists today.

On August 12 MGM rejected Hammett's *Girl Hunt* story. MGM had paid him highly, but his work habits were unreliable and his political beliefs were questionable, especially his support of the Screen Writers Guild. *Girl Hunt* was his last work for MGM.

As before, Hammett remained a spokesman for Stalin. He worked hard on anti-Nazi fundraising, rallies, and political efforts. Now there were rumors of secret negotiations between Nazi Germany and the Soviet Union. Hammett and others issued large newspaper advertisements proclaiming the impossibility of a Hitler-Stalin pact. Bad timing. Nine days later the Soviet Union and Germany signed a treaty pledging not to attack each other. Overnight, Hammett stopped his attacks against Nazi outrages. He reversed course with the Communist Party line, and now spouted propaganda to persuade Americans not to go to war against the Hitler-Stalin team.

His goal became increasingly difficult, thanks to the behavior of German and Soviet armies. In September they invaded Poland. The Poles fought furiously, but their country was conquered by the end of the month. Germany and the Soviet Union split Poland between them. In turn, Great Britain and France declared war on Germany. Belgium tried to save itself by proclaiming it was neutral.

In November, Finland was invaded by the Soviet Union. Hammett, normally a rooter for the little guy, signed an open letter to President Roosevelt urging the United States to declare war against Finland. While Finland crumbled, the movie *Another Thin Man* opened to favorable reviews and box office success.

With Finland conquered, Hammett turned to anti-war activities. In January 1940 he was active in the Keep America Out of War Committee of the League of American Writers. When the league switched to supporting Nazism many members quit in disgust, but in public Hammett kept as busy scolding Finland, Britain, and France as he had been attacking the Nazis. The first half of the year Hammett shuttled back and forth between New York and Hollywood. He backed Communist causes on both coasts, tried to get the studios to deal with the Screen Writers Guild, and, when in New York, worked on the newspaper *P.M.* He wrote for its prototype issue, hired writers (screening them for Stalinist political correctness), and acted as an editor.

It was a good time to launch a newspaper. The world was in turmoil, and people wanted news. In April, Germany invaded Denmark and Norway. It conquered them in about a month. Belgium's CYA proclamation of neutrality did the country no good. German armies invaded it, Luxembourg, and the Netherlands in May and took all three countries in about two weeks. The day after the Germans attacked, Winston Churchill became the British prime minister. At last Hitler, Mussolini, and Stalin faced one European leader with enough resources, backbone, and brains to stand and fight.

In June Germany and Italy conquered France in less than a month; the Soviet Union conquered Lithuania, Latvia, and Estonia; and the first issue of New York's new daily newspaper, *P.M.*, hit the streets. Hammett worked in its newsroom as an editor. He helped publisher Ralph Ingersoll write his first editorials. The next month, New York newspapers printed stories about Communists who worked at *P.M.*, with Hammett's name prominent. Ingersoll refused to repudiate the stories, so he and Hammett argued and Hammett left the paper.

A more serious struggle began on August 8. Hitler's air force had never been defeated, not even seriously resisted. His attack strategy was to bomb a country into helplessness, then rush ground troops in before the shocked country had time to mount any resistance. He sent his largest air fleet ever to bomb Britain into submission. Given the overwhelming numbers and overpowering firepower of Hitler's Luftwaffe, experts predicted the Battle of Britain would end in a few days. The last major European country unconquered, fighting by itself, would surely fall.

Britain ignored the predictors. It battled the Luftwaffe through September, when Japan, Germany, and Italy signed the Axis pact to fight together in war. In October, Germany occupied Rumania and Italy invaded Greece. The British sent sixty thousand soldiers to help Greece. In its own country, the outnumbered and dwindling British Air Force desperately fought back wave after wave of German air attacks. At the end of October the Nazis gave up and stopped their air war over Britain. British fliers had held Hitler off.

Hammett ended October 1940 by sending telegrams to the heads of New York labor unions, urging them to support the Communist Party candidate in the November presidential elections. Roosevelt was reelected anyhow.

Hammett had not worked since he left *P.M.* in July. Once again, he was broke. In February 1941 he wrote to Jose that money would be hard to come by in the near future.

The news was nothing but war, raging on in Europe, Africa, and Asia; on land, in the air, on the sea. The United States remained officially neutral while providing *sub rosa* assistance to China and Britain, which both continued to suffer heavy losses.

In April the Germans invaded Yugoslavia. The country fell in less than two weeks. German forces joined the Italians in attacking Greece. Aided by the British, Greece resisted for about three weeks. Then it, too, collapsed, and the British troops fell back.

On April first, Lillian Hellman's new play, *Watch on the Rhine,* opened on Broadway. Communists did not know what to make of it. It was written by a party loyalist who actively worked for Communist causes, so they wanted it to succeed. On the other hand, the subject of the play is an anti-Nazi activist who flees from Germany to the United States and wakes up a placid American family to the dangers of Nazism. The Nazis were Stalin's allies. It was not politically correct to bad-mouth Hitler, so American Communist reviewers were in a quandary. Fortunately for Hellman, the American public had no such dilemma. The play was another big hit.

In June the movie studios finally came to an agreement with the Screen Writers Guild. Hammett must have savored the union's victory. It had been a five-year struggle, and he had played a key role.

On June 9 an article appeared in *The New York Times* headlined "Hammett Elected by Writers League: Resolutions by Group Generally Follow Communist Line." The story reports that the Fourth Congress of the League of American Writers had unanimously elected Hammett as its president. The theme of this year's conference? "Keep America Out of War."

On June 22, Hitler's armies launched a massive surprise attack along a two-thousand-mile front against its friend the Soviet Union. Funny thing: when Hitler attacked Stalin, suddenly American Communists dropped their support of Hitler. And Communist reviewers fell all over themselves to praise *Watch on the Rhine*.

By the end of June Hammett's finances had improved enough for him to send a check to Jose. The money may have come from a new source: radio. On July 2 *The Adventures of the Thin Man* radio series began on NBC. Hammett had wisely retained radio rights when he sold *The Thin Man* and its characters to *MGM*, and now he would receive $500 a week while the series was broadcast. Hammett's contract specified that he was not to write a word for the series nor act as a consultant, just receive money and have his name featured prominently in the show's credits. *The Adventures of the Thin Man* was a big success, and it promoted Hammett's name to millions of listeners each week. Many thought he wrote every episode.

But Hammett was more interested in political causes. Once again he reversed course when Stalin did. He flip-flopped and worked *against* the Nazis. He brought refugee writers—those sympathetic to Stalin, of course, or at least antifascist—to America. He was also one of the founders—with Alain Locke, Henrietta Buckmaster, Rockwell Kent, Theodore Dreiser, and others—of a new publishing company called the Negro Publication Society, publishing neglected books and new scholarship of interest to African-Americans, by authors such as Langston Hughes.

The movie version of Lillian Hellman's play *The Little Foxes* starred Bette Davis. It opened in August and was one of the biggest successes of the year. Screenplay credit was given to Hellman. Years later, Hammett took his daughter Jo to the movies to see *The Little Foxes* and told her that he had scripted its prologue.

Frederic Dannay/Ellery Queen returned to Hammett. His *Mystery League Magazine* had folded, but Dannay planned a new one with a more commercial title: *Ellery Queen's Mystery Magazine.* Hammett did not write a new story for the magazine, but he did agree to let Dannay use one of his old stories. The first issue of *Ellery Queen's Mystery Magazine* reprinted a Sam Spade short story, the first of many Hammett stories the magazine would recycle. With Hammett's stories and those from other authors, Dannay became known for condensing stories to fit in his little magazine and for giving them new titles.

In October yet another movie version of *The Maltese Falcon*— the third—opened. The low-budget movie was a big unexpected hit and made Humphrey Bogart a star. Hammett saw it and wrote to his wife: "They made a pretty good picture of it this time, for a change." First-time director John Huston decided to stick closely to Hammett's original novel, lifting Hammett's dialog word for word, and the cast was unforgettable, especially Bogart as Sam Spade, Sidney Greenstreet as fat man Casper Gutman, and Peter Lorre as villain Joel Cairo.

The fourth movie in *The Thin Man* series, *Shadow of the Thin Man*, opened the month after *The Maltese Falcon*. Since MGM had purchased the rights to *The Thin Man* characters, the studio did not need Hammett to contribute to the script. The first film in the series that was not based on a story by Hammett, it was nonetheless successful critically and financially.

With *The Thin Man* in the movies and on the radio, in December a Thin Man story appeared in a magazine. The magazine, *Click*, presented the story "The Thin Man and the Flack" as being written by Dashiell Hammett. In spite of including a couple of Hammettisms—a Russian character and the phrase "all right"—there is only a scant chance that Hammett wrote this story. It was probably written by a writer for the radio series *The Adventures of the Thin Man*. Actors from the radio show posed for photos to illustrate the tale, a gimmick *Click* named "Cameradio."

When this story appeared, readers had gone almost eight years without a new short story by Dashiell Hammett.

The Thin Man
and the Flack

CAMERADIO is a brand new word. Briefly, Cameradio Dramas are special and original scenarios written and produced exclusively for *Click* by the authors and producers of America's leading radio dramas. Drawing on all of the talents used on the radio performances and adding to them the efforts of crack photographers, Cameradio Dramas will contribute to your enjoyment of your favorite radio plays.

First of *Click's* Cameradio Dramas is *The Thin Man and the Flack*. Every Wednesday evening over the NBC Red Network *The Thin Man* radio series reaches a greater audience than ever saw any of *The Thin Man* movies. When Dashiell Hammett originally presented Detective Nick Charles and his wife, Nora, in his 1933 novel, *The Thin Man*, the thin man of the title was a corpse that never appeared. Somehow—perhaps it was because William Powell became the movie Nick Charles—people forgot about the corpse, and started to think of *The Thin Man* as the nickname for the detective. Finally, Hammett gave up. Even he believes it now.

Cast of Characters

 NORA CHARLES is the wife and constant heckler of the retired private detective known as *The Thin Man*. She is played by Claudia Morgan, the youthful daughter of Frank Morgan. She has already appeared in 32 plays, is now in *The Man Who Came to Dinner*.

 NICK CHARLES, the Thin Man who's always there with a drink and a solution to any dastardly deed, is played by Lester Damon—one of America's outstanding radio actors. He started to act after graduating from Brown in 1933, has played in London and N.Y.

 AL THORNTON, the Flack, is played by a natural. Flack is Broadwayese for Press Agent. Ex-actor, ex-surrealist poet, ex-architect, ex-newspaperman, Ivan Black—our Cameradio Flack—is a leading Broadway press agent. In fact, he publicizes this very program.

 SONIA BELLKOFF, the rapturous Russian movie star of our Cameradio Drama, is created for *Click* by June Wilkins. Hollywood's gift to radio, she has acted in plays and pictures, is rapidly rising to the front ranks of the radio acting profession in New York City.

 BILL BRADY, Sonia's husband, is not exactly typecasted. He is created by William N. Robson, Director of Radio for the Lennen & Mitchell Advertising Agency, which presents the Thin Man series for Woodbury's cosmetic products. He's an ace radio director.

 HELEN ROBERTS, Sonia's English teacher, proved to be a role cut to order for the versatile talents of Kay Brinker. A veteran of stage and radio, she has acted in theaters from coast to coast. She is a native of Seattle, Washington, where she did her first acting.

Exclusive Click *photos by Eric Schaal*

1. I was minding my own business, my own wife, and my own drink at Barney's. Al Thornton was sitting at the next table with Sonia Bellkoff (the Russian lollypop Monarch Pictures signed up) and another couple. Al was Sonia's flack. I was still minding my own drink when Nora got sore.

"Why don't you whistle?" she said.

"You know that's the wrong approach," I said, "but I'll bet the Hays Office never okayed that gown."

Nora looked puzzled. "Hays Office?" she asked.

"Don't tell me you can't recognize my admirer?" I said.

Nora finished her drink. "The body," she said, "is familiar. I just can't place the face."

I shook my head. "It's Sonia Bellkoff," I said.

I was going to make a crack, but Al left his table to join us. I saw he had do-me-a-favor-pal written all over his face. After he got through telling me that Helen Roberts, the other girl at the table, was Sonia's English teacher, and that the guy was Sonia's husband, Bill Brady, he said, "Sonia's in a hell of a jam, Nick. You've got to help her out."

2. Then he shoved me out to the terrace to see Sonia. Sonia started to talk as soon as she saw we were alone.

"First letters, then telephone calls," she said. "They say they kill me."

I handed her a fresh handkerchief. Hers was in shreds. "Maybe it's just your imagination," I said.

Sonia went to work on my handkerchief. "Then comes candy to my house," she said. "I give one to Tovarish, my dog. He die. I have great fear. I . . . "

3. A barking pistol cut her short. She fell like a plummet at my feet. I was bending over to help her when I saw that we now had company. Brady, Helen Roberts, Al and Nora were leaning over my shoulder. The bullet had missed Sonia.

"Get me some brandy," I told Nora.

I held Sonia's head on my arm, tried to force the brandy through her lips. It brought her to.

4. Brady said he could look after his own wife.

"No . . . no," Sonia sobbed. "I do not want to go home. Do not let them take me."

Brady started to haul her up. "She wasn't hit, was she?" he said.

"You sound disappointed," I said.

Sonia bit her lip. "He is," she cried. "He wants me dead so he can marry Helen."

Al helped me pick her up. "We'd better get her home," he said. "She's upset."

Al helped Helen and Brady take Sonia home. I went with them as far as Barney's bar. Then I headed for the terrace. Nora was still there.

"Darling," she said. "Your slip is showing."

I gagged. "My what?"

She took a sip from my glass. "Never mind," she said. "I found the shell." She handed it to me with a straight face.

5. I knew that face of Nora's. It was the same one she put on the time that I was nearly taken in by that con man at San Francisco.

"It's a blank," she said. "See?"

I wanted to crawl into a hole and die. "We've been took," I said. "The whole brawl is one of Al Thornton's publicity gags."

Nora snorted. "And you fell for it, Nick."

We had another drink and went home. Nora was still kidding me when we got into bed.

Then Al phoned. "Nick," he said. "It's a matter of life and death. You've got to come out here."

Nora heard every word. "Here we go again," she said. I pushed her face into the pillow.

"O.K., Al," I said. "We'll be there in an hour."

Nora kept singing "Otchi Chornya" until we reached Sonia's house.

6. Al was helping her out of her wrap when the second shot of the evening rang out.

"Ten will get you one it's a blank," Nora said.

Al started to go to pieces. "Nick, that shot came from Sonia's room!" he shouted.

I tried the door. It was locked. Al tried to force it.

"Sonia," he yelled. "Open up. It's Al."

"Yo Ho Ho Ho," caroled Nora. "Where do you suppose they keep the brandy? Or is it a different routine this time, Al?"

I forced the lock and made my way to the bed.

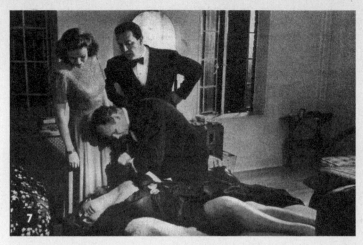

7. "Never mind the brandy," I said. "Come on in here."

Nora grew pale. "Nick . . . Nick, you don't mean . . . "

I dropped Sonia's limp white hand. "I'm afraid I do, Nora," I said. "This time she's dead."

Nora shuddered. "The killer," she said. "He shot her through the bedroom window while we were at the door."

8. I poured myself a drink. "You're so wonderful," I said. "Now all we have to find out is who he is and why he did it." I turned to Al. "Was that fairy tale Sonia poured into my ear your brain-child?" I asked him.

"What if it was?" he said.

"Then you fired the blank," I said.

Al nodded. "For publicity," he said. "But why don't you find out who fired the shot that killed her?"

"All right," I said. "All I want is a simple yes or no. Was Bill Brady's behavior towards his wife tonight a fair sample of what usually went on?"

Al looked away. "Why ask me?" he said. "Why don't you ask Helen Roberts?"

Someone walked through the front door. It turned out to be Brady and Helen. "You wanted to see me?" she said.

9. Brady stepped in front of her. "Who gave you a license to annoy people?" he asked.

"Now I'll ask one," I said. "Suppose you tell me why you had your face lifted?" His hand jumped to his face. I pointed to the little scars near his ears. Quickly I said, "A guy with a face lift should better be annoyed by me than by coppers. How did you and your wife get along, Brady?"

My question caught him off guard. "Sonia never brought me anything but trouble," he said. "She's a low-down, double-crossing . . . "

Helen stopped him this time. "Button your lip, Bill," she said.

I laughed. "So you're an English coach," I said.

"Don't make me laugh," she said. "Sonia and me—we're from the Brooklyn burleycue."

10. She started to demonstrate her strip routine.

"She's Sonia's sister!" Nora said.

Helen patted Nora's head. "Yeah," she said. "We're sisters all right. Brady caught our act in Brooklyn two years ago and called Al in to do the Russky ballyhoo dressing."

She started to get hysterical. Brady took her out of the house. Al said he felt dizzy. He took some aspirin and went to sleep on the couch. I never saw a man go to sleep so fast. It was a case of the nerves being completely fagged, I thought. I shook him, and when he kept on snoring, I gave him up for the night.

"Let's look around," I said to Nora. "I'll take the clues closet."

11. Nora started to go through the drawers in Sonia's room.

In Al's jacket pocket I found a California intention-to-wed certificate. It was three years old. A year older than Sonia's marriage.

Nora found something, too. "Sonia had a secret vice," she said. "She liked to chew toast in bed. I found this toaster under her bed. It was connected and piping hot, Nick. Nearly burned my . . ."

12. I cut her short. "Look what I found," I said.

She read the certificate. "But Sonia was already married," she said.

"Not when that was filed," I said. "Nora, I'm a blundering, stupid idiot. Boy, would I like to speak to Al right now!"

Nora pointed to the living room. "That's easy," she said. "He's still in there."

I put the certificate in my pocket. "Yeah," I said, "and I have a hunch he is also in trouble."

Al was in trouble all right. Brady had returned and was backing him up against a chair with a gun.

"Nick," Al pleaded, "don't let him kill me. He killed Sonia and . . . "

Brady took a step closer to the flack. "You're a trouble-maker, Al," he said. "You've had a slug coming to you for a long time." He never took his eyes off Al. That was all I had to see. I jumped him.

13. After I took his gun away, I poured myself a nice stiff drink. Al poured a big one for himself.

"He was going to kill me, Nick," he said.

"That's funny," I said. "I thought so, too, Al."

Brady started to come to. He rubbed his jaw where I clipped him.

14. "This is still my house, Charles," he said. "Now get out."

I helped him up. "Sure," I said. "But first my good wife is going to phone for the police."

Nora picked up the phone. "Nick," she said, "shall I reserve one in the west wing for Mr. Brady?"

I made sure the gun was loaded before I answered her. "No," I said. "I think you'd better make that reservation in Al's name."

Al jumped up. "Have you gone crazy, too?"

I showed him the gun. "I'm not crazy," I said.

We went home after the police took Al away. Nora didn't want to sleep.

15. "How about a drink?" I said.

"No. Explain things to me, Nick. What was Al's motive?"

I kicked off my shoes. "After marrying Brady, Sonia promised to divorce him and marry Al. Then she double-crossed Al for the second time."

Nora nodded. "But when did he kill her, Nick?"

I looked for the whiskey. "Just before he phoned us, Nora. When he heard us coming, he placed a blank cartridge on that toaster. The toaster's heat exploded the blank. Satisfied?"

Nora had more questions. I stopped her. "How about a drink?" I said.

CLICK MAGAZINE'S INNOVATION of Cameradio, introduced by that Thin Man story in its December 1941 issue, did not cause the excitement its publishers hoped. Instead, that month its readers were surprised by a big distraction. Hammett found out about the distraction one Sunday while adjusting his radio. He heard that the American fleet at Pearl Harbor had been bombed by Japanese planes.

Now America joined World War II. American lives would be broken apart like so many puzzle pieces, then put back together—but never the same way.

PART EIGHT

The Long Sunset

HAMMETT HAD STOPPED WRITING stories for magazines, but he had not stopped writing. Warner Brothers paid him $30,000 to write a screenplay of *Watch on the Rhine*. He finished it in April 1942. Where his earlier writing had been taut and controlled, this screenplay was loose and sloppy. Hellman cleaned it up.

Hammett wanted to join the Army to fight in the war. He tried to enlist but was rejected for his age, his thinness, and the tuberculosis scars on his lung x-rays. But in September he talked or bribed his way in. Twenty-five years after he enlisted for the first World War, he was a soldier again.

A Writer Goes to War

The Army sent Private Samuel Hammett to Fort Monmouth, New Jersey, where he was put to work teaching courses and rewriting training materials on "Army Organization." Corporal L.T. Shackelford, Jr., showed him his cartoons of Army life. Hammett liked them and encouraged him to turn them into a book, *As I See It... Story Drawings of Life in the Army,* published the next year by Hammett's publisher Knopf. Meanwhile, Paramount Pictures released the second movie version of *The Glass Key,* starring Alan Ladd and Veronica Lake.

As 1943 began, *The Adventures of the Thin Man* radio series moved to CBS, where it continued to generate a weekly radio royalty check for Hammett. The Army shifted his work to rewriting basic training guides. In June he wrote the script for a training film.

While he wrote for the Army, his two connected novelettes "The Big Knock-Over" and "$106,000 Blood Money"—which he had written sixteen years ago, and which together formed his first longer work—were finally published as a novel. They appeared in a cheap paperback digest under the title *$106,000 Blood Money.* (A hardcover edition was published that October as *Blood Money.*)

In July Hammett was transferred to Fort Lewis in the state of Washington. He visited his old haunts in Seattle for the first time in twenty-two years. At the end of the month the Army shipped him north to Fort Randall, Alaska, where he talked to the staff at the post radio station about doing "some broadcasting" for them, marched over mountains and tundra, practiced stabbing with bayonets and firing machine guns.

In September he was shipped to Adak, a remote Alaskan island that had been taken by the Japanese and retaken by the Americans. Fear of a Japanese counterattack was high; the last Japanese-held island in the chain had been retaken by the Americans only the month before Hammett arrived.

Adak was treeless, freezing, foggy, swept by never-ceasing, roaring winds of up to 110 miles per hour, constantly covered with clouds. It was sunless, isolated, bleak, and depressing. Men were miserable. The suicide rate for soldiers was the highest of any place in the war. Hammett loved it. In Adak's bleakness he found beauty and he thrived.

The soldiers called him "Sam" and "Pops," and regarded him as a celebrity. Army radio carried his *Thin Man* series, his movie *Watch on the Rhine* had just opened in the States to enthusiastic reviews, and the U.S. Maritime Commission had launched a C-2 cargo ship named the SS Maltese Falcon. The military news magazine *Yank* ran a story on Hammett in Alaska with his photo. He sent it to Hellman. She wrote back saying the photo made him "look like an aging tulip tree."

Local Army brass struggled with the problem of troop morale so low that soldiers committed suicide, and they used Hammett's fame and his writing talent to help.  They put him to work conducting a weekly radio show and writing a history to explain the Aleutian Islands war to the troops. He finished writing *The Battle of the Aleutians* by Thanksgiving of 1943, and it was quickly printed and distributed.

His next assignment: start and run a daily newspaper for the men isolated on Adak. He gathered a racially-integrated staff—rare at that time—and worked thirteen-hour days to launch the paper. He published the first trial issue of *The Adakian* on January 19, 1944. In it he wrote: "We want to give the Adak soldier—every morning—a paper that he will like to read and that will keep him as up-to-date as possible on what's going on in the world."

Hammett guided *The Adakian's* artists and edited its writers' stories. He wrote articles himself, came up with ideas for cartoons, and wrote cartoon captions. He solved supply difficulties and distribution problems for the paper, and turned his men into a smoothly-running team. He felt good about his work, and being part of an outfit gave him "a feeling of belonging, and that's one of the nicer Army feelings."

In March actress Olivia de Havilland toured the Aleutians to boost morale. Hammett wrote in letters that he was surprised by his own reactions to meeting her. She was the first woman he had talked to in nearly nine months. He had forgotten how refreshing a woman's spirit and softness can be to a man.

Meanwhile, back in the States Hammett was nominated for an Academy Award for best screenplay for *Watch on the Rhine*, and a paperback digest was published: *The Adventures of Sam Spade and Other Stories*. It collected all three Sam Spade short  stories plus four non-Spade tales. Frederic Dannay, writing as Ellery Queen, edited the book and wrote its introduction, and Lillian Hellman apparently revised Hammett's stories and Dannay's introduction. The book sold well. Over the next seventeen years, Dannay followed it with eight more volumes of Hammett stories, reprinting the chopped-down, often-retitled versions from *Ellery Queen's Mystery Magazine*. For more than forty years, unfortunately, books and magazines reprinted only those condensations, not the originals, so the unrevised stories became lost except to collectors of rare magazines. The "edited by Ellery Queen" books kept many of Hammett's stories in print for years and sold hundreds of thousands of copies, introducing Hammett to thousands of readers worldwide. The books reinforced his prominence in the mystery field even while he no longer wrote mysteries.

Hammett was still editing *The Adakian* on May 27, his fiftieth birthday. His staff surprised him by publishing a humorous parody issue devoted to him, his career, and his activities in Alaska. In July he wrote "Editing an Army newspaper in such a theater as this is often like walking an invisible tight-rope between two moving towers while juggling hot stove-lids and trying to eat a sandwich."

Even so, he grew bored with the predictable problems of *The Adakian* and finagled a transfer to Fort Richardson, near the town of Anchorage. From there the Army flew him to military bases across the Aleutian chain, where he conducted orientations and was promoted as a celebrity to new soldiers.

Near the end of 1944 he met a pretty thirty-year-old writer named Jean Potter. They struck up a romance, and he edited her book about Alaskan pilots, *The Flying North*, while he was creating a new monthly magazine called *Army Up North*. Its first issue was printed in January, 1945, and Hammett returned to Adak.

That March Hammett was denounced by the *Chicago Tribune* as being a Communist propagandist in the Army. He returned to Fort Richardson, where in April he wrote he was "nursing along a round-table weekly affair for enlisted men on the Post radio station, editing a magazine for Information-Education personnel, and writing another pamphlet about Alaska."

He also worked with the cartoonists of *The Adakian* to put together a book of cartoons from the paper. They wanted to call it *All Wet and Dripping*, but a general did not approve, so it was titled *Wind Blown and Dripping*. Hammett wrote

an introduction and looked for a publisher without success. He finally paid for its publication himself.

That month the Congressional Committee on Un-American Activities produced a pamphlet describing suspected Communist activities of U.S. armed forces members. It listed more than forty Communist-related organizations in which Hammett was a member.

On May 8, Germany formally surrendered. It was VE Day, Victory in Europe, and everybody celebrated. The war was not over, however, in the Pacific. Japan still fought furiously. Soldiers in the Aleutian Islands remained alert. Hammett continued to work on Army writing and editing projects. In May he wrote: "I'm now in the midst of an attempt to render the Bretton Woods proposals into a language that Army personnel can be expected to understand: it's kind of fun."

On July 20, the front page of *The Stars and Stripes,* the official daily newspaper of the U.S. armed forces, ran a story headlined: "Author of 'The Thin Man' listed Among 16 Army Reds." It announced that a House Military Subcommittee had made public the names of sixteen Army personnel whose backgrounds "reflect Communism in some form." Hammett was the most prominent.

President Truman announced on August 14 that Japan had surrendered. Hammett applied for a discharge from the Army, and received it in early September.

Radio, Reds, and Booze

Hammett returned to New York City. Hellman had another lover, so he rented an apartment of his own.

He quickly moved back into political action, joining a staggering number of political and civil rights organizations, most of them Communist-sponsored. He was just a member of dozens, such as the American Labor Party, or the Committee of 102 Writers and Artists, which protested the arrest of Communist poet Pablo Neruda. For other organizations, he was a chairman or officer. He supported dozens more financially, such as the American Peace Crusade, which protested the Korean War, and Consumers Union, famous for publishing *Consumer Reports*. And, as he did before the war, Hammett wrote and delivered speeches.

And he got very drunk, very often.

ABC radio premiered a new detective series in January 1946, *The Fat Man*. The show's name was a chapter title in *The Maltese Falcon*. Hammett allowed the producers to feature his name in the show's credits and publicity. For that, he received a healthy weekly payment. Many people assumed he wrote or at least edited the scripts, but the only writing Hammett did for the show was signing his name on paychecks. He had become his own best advertising client; he had built his name into a brand more recognizable than any product or store he had advertised back in his ad man days. Millions of listeners tuned in to the new Hammett radio show, and *The Fat Man* was a success.

A new political organization was formed, the Civil Rights Congress of New York. It supported Communists who came under attack for their political beliefs. Hammett was named its president. He was no figurehead. He wrote speeches, he organized, he led protests, he built the CRC into a successful organization.

The May 1946 issue of *Ellery Queen's Mystery Magazine* contained an announcement from its editor: "We have just completed negotiations with Mr. Hammett which permit us to continue reprinting adventures of the Continental Op. This is an *EQMM* exclusive: *EQMM* has first choice of all the unreprinted Continental Op stories your Editor can rediscover. No other detective-story magazine can reprint a Continental Op yarn unless it has first appeared in *EQMM*. To date, not including the present issue, we have brought you six exploits of the Continental Op, and during the rest of 1946 and throughout 1947 we plan to bring you at least nine more operations of the Op."

Even though Hammett was no longer writing stories, his old ones continued to appear in print, winning new readers and influencing other writers. And his old characters appeared in new

forms.

A new mystery radio show premiered in July: *The Adventures of Sam Spade*. Each week, the show's opening said it was from "Dashiell Hammett, America's leading detective fiction writer and creator of Sam Spade, the hard-boiled private eye," but other people wrote the scripts. The series became the top-rated mystery series, and earned producer William Spier an Edgar Award.

Hammett was paid $400 a week for the use of his name and his characters for the radio series, and also for a series of *Adventures of Sam Spade* comic strips. The radio shows were sponsored by Wildroot hair care products for men, and it ran the color strips as advertisements in comic books and Sunday newspapers to promote the radio shows and its Wildroot products.

Hammett's three radio series earned him more than $500,000 a year in 2005 money. He did not need to work. He was free to concentrate on political activities and getting drunk.

He decided to write a play on his own, without Hellman. Near the end of 1946, Hammett wrote a plot outline for *The Good Meal* and pitched it to Broadway producer Kermit Bloomgarden, who liked it and wanted to produce it. Its title came from the saying, "A good meal is worth hanging for." Bloomgarden hired top designer Jo Mielziner to create sets for "A murder mystery, to take place in present-day wheat country, east of Rockies. Takes place in prosperous farmer's house in autumn." Mielziner created a floor plan for the farmer's house set, but it was never used. Hammett worked sporadically on *The Good Meal* the next few months, but like the novels and stories he started, he never finished the play.

He did continue his political activities throughout 1947, though, such as joining the editorial board of the magazine *Soviet Russia Today* and becoming a member of the United Negro and Allied Veterans of America.

Hammett's father died in March 1948. Hammett paid for the funeral but did not attend it. Later he wished that he had.

In May 1948, one day after Hammett's fifty-fifth birthday, Warner Brothers sued the broadcaster, director, writers, producer, sponsor, and advertising agency of *The Adventures of Sam Spade* for copyright infringement and unfair competition. Warner Brothers complained that its movie contract for *The Maltese Falcon* gave it exclusive broadcast rights to the characters from the novel and their names, and the radio series had used material from *The Maltese Falcon* that belonged only to Warner Brothers. Hammett filed an affidavit citing Sir Arthur Conan Doyle's Sherlock Holmes, S. S. Van Dine's Philo Vance, and other famous fictional detectives to prove that it was normal for mystery writers to create different stories with new adventures of the same detectives. The lawsuit dragged on for years.

Hammett got more drunk more often until December 1948, when he suffered an alcoholism-induced physical collapse. A hospital doctor told him he could either stop drinking right then and there or die. Remarkably, Hammett stopped drinking, although with difficulty. After leaving the hospital, he moved in with Hellman again at Hardscrabble Farm.

He worked a little in 1949 as a script doctor for producer Bloomgarden on the play *The Man* by Sidney Kingsley. It flopped.

Movie director William Wyler, a friend of Hammett's, got him a several-thousand-dollar advance for a job writing a screenplay based on the play *Detective Story*. Hammett went to Los Angeles in January 1950 to work on the script. While there, he may have also worked briefly on the script for Wyler's movie *Carrie*. After three months working on *Detective Story* Hammett grew disgusted with Hollywood and the movie business. He quit, paid back the advance, and returned to New York.

Hellman was glad to have him back. They worked together on her new play, *The Autumn Garden*. Sometimes Hammett spoke of the play as Lillian's play, sometimes as a joint project. She wanted him to direct it. He refused.

Blacklisted and Jailed

Hammett wrote an introduction to the second edition of George Marion's 1950 book *The Communist Trial: An American Crossroads*. It was his last original writing for book publication.

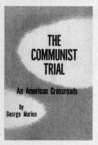

Hammett's introduction was only one of many contributions he made to aid the Soviet Union's plans to influence American political values. In June his pro-Communist past collided with the rise of anti-Communist forces. He was listed in *Red Channels: The Report of Communist Influence in Radio and Television* as a pro-Communist. *Red Channels* listed Communist-related activities by 151 writers, directors, and performers before World War II. It was the foundation of the Hollywood blacklist. Anyone suspected of being pro-Communist lost the ability to work in radio, television, or the movies.

All three of Hammett's radio series were cancelled because of his politics. Due to the high ratings of *The Adventures of Sam Spade*, NBC brought the series back two months later, with no mention of Hammett's name in the credits, and without actor Howard Duff as Sam Spade. Duff also had been listed in *Red Channels,* so he was replaced by Steve Dunne.

On May 24, 1950, three days before Hammett's fifty-sixth birthday, and on his daughter Jo's twenty-fourth, she gave birth to his first grandchild. Jo and Loyd Marshall named the baby girl Ann, after Hammett's beloved mother Annie. Hammett was thrilled. He flew to Los Angeles to love and spoil his granddaughter, then returned to New York.

The Autumn Garden was finished in January 1951. Hellman gave Hammett a fifteen percent royalty, something she had not done with the earlier plays. The play opened on Broadway in March, and received mixed-to-good reviews. It played a respectable length of time but lost money.

That spring, Hammett again flew to Los Angeles to visit the Marshalls. When he returned, he brought granddaughter Ann with him to Hardscrabble Farm, where he and Hellman adored the baby. New mother Jo followed ten days later for a happy, relaxing visit in the country before bringing her baby back home.

The Fat Man, a movie based on the now-cancelled radio series, opened in May. In April 1951, mounting anti-Communist pressure finally shut down the Sam Spade radio series and comic strip advertisements.[1]

Now Hammett's politics generated more publicity than his fictional detectives. Typical of the exaggerations was the July 13 issue of *Hollywood Life:* "Hammett is without any question one of the red masterminds of the nation, with main headquarters in

---

1. Advertiser Wildroot started a new radio series and comic strip called *Charlie Wild, Private Detective.* It was *Sam Spade* moved from San Francisco to New York under a new alias. The first *Charlie Wild* episode was even introduced by Howard Duff, and the series kept Hammett's character Effie Perine as Sam's—er, Charlie's—secretary. When *Charlie Wild* became a TV series, Hammett's Effie remained. She was played by future Academy Award winner Cloris Leachman.

Hollywood and a suboffice in New York."

In addition to being president of the Civil Rights Congress of New York, Hammett was chairman of the organization's bail fund committee. It posted bail for Communists arrested on political grounds. The fund bailed out four men who fled and became fugitives. Almost thirty years before, Hammett had written a story about a detective chasing a fugitive on a sailboat cruising down a crocodile-infested river. The reality of dealing with these fugitives was quite different.

In July, 1951, the officers of the bail fund committee, including its chairman Hammett, were ordered by a United States District Court to appear and testify. They were asked the whereabouts of the four fugitives and told to produce records identifying contributors to the bail fund. By the time Hammett's turn came to testify, one of his fellow defendants had invoked the Fifth Amendment and had been sentenced to prison for contempt of court. Hammett knew he could expect exactly the same treatment if he, too, refused to name contributors. That did not deter him. He invoked the Fifth Amendment and was sentenced to six months behind bars.

Hellman abandoned him and fled to Europe. The IRS attacked, claiming Hammett owed more than $100,000 in back taxes. He was so broke he could not send money to his wife, Jose. He had promised to take care of Jose financially as long as she took care of their girls, but now he could not. She was forced to go back to work as a nurse for the first time in thirty years. He served his jail sentence without complaining and earned four weeks off for good behavior. He was released from prison on December 9, 1951, a fifty-seven-year-old man whose already frail health had been permanently broken. His finances were ruined, radio shows cancelled, books out of print. Hellman met him after his release from prison. He found that without telling him she had sold the Hardscrabble Farm he loved.

The blacklist cut off Hollywood money for both Hammett and Hellman, but blacklisted writers could still make money on Broadway. Hellman persuaded Kermit Bloomgarden to produce a revival of The Children's Hour and to let Hellman be its director. Tony Award winner Patricia Neal and recent Academy Award winner Kim Hunter were cast as the leads.

For this 1952 production of The Children's Hour, somebody revised the play. Somebody added two new speaking parts. Somebody replaced the opening quotations from The Merchant of Venice with quotations from the suicide scene in Shakespeare's Antony and Cleopatra. In the original Children's Hour, the character Evelyn spoke with a lisp. Hellman wanted that lisp so strongly that when the director of the original production tried to remove it, she fought heatedly with him and kept Evelyn lisping. In the new version, somebody de-lisped Evelyn. Somebody made many changes to dialog throughout the play. Somebody expanded the original seven-sentence description of the schoolroom set to a superspecific thirty-one-sentence description unlike any set description in any of Hellman's other plays. Somebody changed characters' actions throughout the play by adding detailed stage directions unlike those in any of Hellman's other plays.

Whoever was responsible, the new version of The Children's Hour opened on Broadway in December 1952 and was a success. During the play's run Hammett tried again to write a novel. He called his new novel Tulip. Its title seemed to come from the letter Hellman had written to him during World War II, claiming one

photo of him as a soldier made him look "like an aging tulip tree."
He set the novel after the war and wrote about an old writer-
soldier just like himself.

Senator Joseph McCarthy's House Un-American Activities
Committee called Hammett to Washington, D.C., for a hearing in
March, 1953. McCarthy did not make any criminal charges against
Hammett. He seems to have dragged the ailing, thin man in front
of the news cameras simply because he was a famous author and
his politics were notorious.

One Last Victory

In June Hammett wrote to his daughter Jo that he had not
worked on *Tulip* for months: "Not working on it is partly a sort of
stage fright, I think—putting the finishing touches on a book can
be kind of frightening."

After playing for more than half a year, the money-making
Broadway production of *The Children's Hour* closed. It was prof-
itable enough to generate a touring version. Hellman was in
Europe, so Hammett took charge of the road company. He cast
the actors and hired the staff. Because Hellman had directed the
Broadway version, Hammett needed someone else to direct the
touring production. Instead of hiring an experienced director, he
chose Del Hughes, who had been the stage manager of Hellman's
Broadway production. The road company opened in September
in Wilmington, Delaware, and toured the country profitably for
several months.

Warner Brothers' lawsuit against the key people involved with
the radio series *The Adventures of Sam Spade* was finally settled by
the U.S. Court of Appeals in 1954, more than six years after the
suit had been filed. Hammett won. He was awarded no damages,
but was reimbursed for lawyers' fees and other court costs. The

radio series had been off the air for three years, so Hammett's financial gain from his long legal struggle was nothing.

Hammett's case was still important, however, because it set legal precedents that influenced the entire entertainment industry. It established that writers own the right to compose sequels to their own stories. Without Hammett's victory, for example, George Lucas would not have been able to make *The Empire Strikes Back* and his other sequels to *Star Wars*.

Hammett's case also helped establish that when an author sells a story, the author retains the right to re-use characters from that story. The clearly-defined legal right to license characters gave root to a steadily growing industry that manufactures products featuring popular characters. If you are a parent, whenever you buy your child a toy or doll based on a character from a book, movie, or television program, you can bless or curse Hammett.

Finally, legal historians cite Hammett's case as the most important self-plagiarism case in United States legal history. In essence, Warner Brothers accused Hammett of copying his own writing. The court decided that it is normal for two works by the same author to share similarities, so similarities by themselves do not violate copyright if the similarities come from the same author. Hammett's precedent has been used to defend many legal cases.

But all that would happen years in the future. For now, Hammett had won a legal and moral victory without any financial benefit.

The next year, in 1955, he was hauled before yet another legislative investigation of the Civil Rights Congress, this time from the New York state legislature. Legislators questioned Hammett and got their names in the paper, but nothing else happened as a result. About half a year later Hammett had a heart attack. His health steadily grew worse, as did his finances. By the end of 1956, interest charges and penalties swelled his IRS debt to more than $140,000. The state of New York added more for state taxes.

In 1957 a new television series premiered: *The Thin Man* starred Peter Lawford and Phyllis Kirk as Nick and Nora Charles. The series ran on NBC TV for two years, but Hammett had sold his movie and television rights for *The Thin Man* to MGM twenty years earlier, so the series was not a financial windfall for him.

His health deteriorated. He moved in with Hellman, and she took care of him.

His daughter Jo, her husband Loyd, and Hammett's three grandchildren (Ann, now ten years old; Evan, eight; and three-year-old Julie) flew from Los Angeles in 1960 to visit Hammett and Hellman at Hellman's home in Martha's Vineyard. He enjoyed the visit, but Jo could tell he was slowly dying. It was the last time she saw him.

In the end, his lungs killed him. Not from the tuberculosis he had feared, but from a souvenir of smoking: lung cancer. He died on January 10, 1961, in New York City. As a soldier in both World Wars, he chose to be buried in Arlington National Cemetery.

We All Hear Hammett's Voice

The man is gone. His works remain.

Not all writers' works do. In his day, S. S. Van Dine's mystery novels far outsold Hammett's. Nobody reads Van Dine today. While Hammett wrote for *Black Mask,* enthusiastic readers voted Carroll John Daly's hardboiled stories more popular than Hammett's. Only a closetful of buffs read Daly anymore.

But Hammett's readership has grown with time. Some say the growth thrives because his terse, unsentimental style seems fresh today. Others say it's because his attitudes fit our time: tough, smart-assed, sharp. He gets credit—depending on whom you talk to—as the father of the modern mystery, the American mystery, the working-class mystery, private eye fiction, hard-boiled fiction,

modern popular fiction. Some people say this historical significance makes Hammett's readership grow. Maybe a little, but hell is
packed with writers who are historic, dull, and unread.

Hammett's writing is anything but dull. Some people say that's
why his readership grows: he is enjoyable to read. I agree. Readers
appreciate Hammett's skill at building tension, his plot surprises,
his blink-and-you'll-miss-it humor, his love of colorful characters,
his unclichéd wordplay—here a tickle, there a rusty razorblade.
We get involved in his storylines. He makes us feel emotions. We
care about his characters, and we remember them: Sam Spade,
Nick and Nora Charles, a hairy giant on a Pacific island, a small-
time crook panicked over too much money, a bandit who wants
to be debonair.

All that is a start. I see an additional reason why Hammett's
readership grows, one that goes beyond amusement, one—much
to my surprise—rarely mentioned by reviewers: Hammett's writing *transforms people.*

I know people who changed their careers to law enforcement, becoming detectives or policemen after reading Hammett.
I know other people who have read Hammett and changed
careers to become writers. Some people who encounter Hammett and already are writers change the way they write, such as
novelist Leonie Stevens, who said, "I pretty much burned everything I'd written after reading Hammett." Other people change
their moral outlook after finding Hammett.

Then we have the copycats. Hammett's writings have been
copied by thousands of writers around the globe, and subsequent
writers have copied his imitators, and his imitators' imitators—
not just for mystery stories, but across all genres and in all media.
These Hammett mimics don't interest me as much as the Hammett readers who experience personal transformation.

Their metamorphoses are evidence that Hammett affects
readers—some readers, at least—on a deeper, more powerful

level than all but a few writers. What makes his writings inspirational? Why are readers affected strongly? What does he say that some people find important? I've read bookshelves of writing about Hammett. Critics show little awareness and no agreement about the effects his works have on people. Nobody yet has put a finger on what force in Hammett's writing has redirected people's lives. That type of investigation is beyond my scope here. I hope someone will research it elsewhere.

Oddly, Hammett's stature as a significant writer—and his popularity—are larger *outside* the United States. This means that in one form or another we all hear Hammett's voice, everywhere around the world. It is pervasive. Some of us listen to the original voice in Hammett's own stories. All of us hear the echoes from his unavoidable followers. As we do, his influence—direct and indirect—expands.

Hammett's readership expands as well. Successive waves of new readers continue to find pleasure—and sometimes something deeper than pleasure—in reading Hammett's stories. That is his accomplishment. That's the way it was while he wrote.

And that's the way it has been ever since.